EMILIE

A N O V E L

ARLETTE COUSTURE
Translated by Käthe Roth

Stoddart

English language edition copyright © 1992
Stoddart Publishing Co. Limited

French language edition: © Éditions Québec/Amérique 1985

First published in 1992 by
Stoddart Publishing Co. Limited
34 Lesmill Road
Toronto, Ontario
M3B 2T6

French language edition first published in 1985 by
Éditions Québec/Amérique

Canadian Cataloguing in Publication Data

Cousture, Arlette.
  [Filles de Caleb. English]
  Emilie

Translation of: Les filles de Caleb.

ISBN 0-7737-5551-9

I. Title. II. Title: Filles de Caleb.

PS8555.O88F513 1992   C843'.54   C92-094958-4
PQ3919.2.C68F513 1992

Typesetting: Tony Gordon Ltd.

Printed and bound in Canada

*Stoddart Publishing gratefully acknowledges the support of
the Canada Council, Ontario Ministry of Culture and
Communications, Ontario Arts Council and Ontario
Publishing Centre in the development of writing and
publishing in Canada.*

Contents

Prologue

Saint-Stanislas,

Champlain County

Spring, 1892

$\mathcal{C}$ALEB CAME IN from the barn. The cow had finally dropped her calf, but he'd had to spend many hours helping her. A heifer usually calved quickly, but Grazillia had decided to take her time. Caleb, impatient, had begun to feel the dampness gnawing at his bones, in spite of the heat in the building.

He closed the door of the summer kitchen so that the wind wouldn't sweep in, took off his rubber overshoes and unlaced his felt inner boots. He sighed with relief. Without a word, he went to the pump in the main kitchen, let water splash into the metal basin and washed his hands. Célina gave him an anxious look, ready to do his bidding as soon as he acknowledged her presence. Her husband seemed preoccupied. Her heart always sank a little when he looked like this, for it usually meant a bad mood, a disappointment or trouble of some kind. She didn't see how Grazillia's calving could have put him in such a state.

Caleb wiped his hands methodically — as he always did before a meal — by passing the towel between each finger and rubbing the palms and backs of his hands each twice. Emilie, the oldest of the children, signalled to her brothers and sisters that they'd better keep quiet. She had a feeling it was one of those times when they should melt into the woodwork.

Célina started to twist her fingers in her apron. She didn't like the feeling that was creeping into the house. Instinctively, she started toward the door to make sure that it was latched. But almost before she'd begun to move, Caleb curtly reported that he had shut it well. Like a child caught in the act, Célina retreated, forcing a smile to reassure the children. Caleb threw his towel onto its hook and went to the table.

"What's for supper?"

Célina nervously listed the menu: soup, fried bacon, beets, eggs, yellow potatoes and —

"Again?"

At a glance, Emilie saw that her mother had no idea how to answer this rude question. Even she, a thirteen-year-old, knew very well that her mother had to stretch her imagination to put food on the table, especially now, at the end of March, when provisions were getting so low.

Since Célina was taking so long to collect her thoughts, Emilie came to her rescue. "If you like, Papa, I could heat you up some meat loaf."

Caleb grunted a response, which neither mother nor daughter understood. Emilie, a little fed up with her father's mood, gathered her courage and asked him if he meant "yes" or "no." Caleb shot her a furious look and said he had meant "whatever you like."

Célina gestured for the children to move the rocking chair so that she could open the trap door to the basement, but Emilie, with a fiercely decided air, promptly sat down in it. Astonished, Célina asked what she was doing. Emilie answered that her father had left it up to her, and as far as she was concerned, she'd rather *not* reheat the meat loaf. Since supper was already on the table, she didn't see why the family should have to wait half an hour before eating.

Célina, her eyes wide, opened her mouth to speak, but not one of the many words crowding her thoughts found a voice. She had always been unable to bear confrontation, even the children's quarrels. Without thinking, she went to Emilie, yanked her by the arm and ordered her to stand up.

Caleb watched all of this, half amused, half irritated. He had never seen Célina lose her temper, nor seen one of his children oppose her. He figured he'd better intervene.

"Let her go, Célina. Emilie is big enough to stand up all by herself." He gave Emilie a hard look, certain that she would obey both his words and his icy stare. Instead, she began to rock, gently at first but then more and more rapidly, until all of the chair's joints began to squeak. The younger ones, sensing trouble brewing, took refuge at their mother's side. Célina frantically stirred a wooden spoon around in an empty soup pot, to keep herself occupied but mostly to avoid having to witness the gathering storm.

Caleb drummed his fingers on the table, from little finger to thumb, in time to Emilie's rocking. As soon as she noticed this, she changed her rhythm. This annoyed Caleb even more.

"If you keep at this rocking game long enough, supper'll be cold."

Quick as a flash, Emilie retorted that there'd be nothing unusual about that.

Caleb winced. "Are you trying to say I'm not a good provider for my family?"

Emilie swallowed before answering, feeling a twinge of guilt. She had long wanted to have this discussion with her father, but she knew this wasn't the right time. She had wanted to speak to him in private; what she had to say should not be heard by the younger ones. Once again, her impulsiveness had got her into a mess, but her pride was pushing her to finish what she had started.

"I'm trying to say that we girls have to do a lot more work than our brothers." She stopped, waiting for her father's reply, but Caleb just raised his eyebrows.

"In the morning, we get up the same time as you. We help out with the animals, we gather the eggs, we clean the henhouse. Then we have to hurry and make breakfast, serve it, sweep up and make the beds. While we're doing all this, the boys are taking their time eating and washing. When they finish breakfast, we have to help Mama clean up. Then we run and wash up so we don't smell like cows at school. Most of the time, the boys are halfway there by the time we catch up to them, running so we're not late. Sometimes we still have a slice of bread in our hands."

The more she talked, the more impassioned she became; she could hear her own voice rising. Caleb had stopped drumming his fingers and was glaring angrily at her.

She decided not to let him intimidate her. "What I mean is . . ."

"You mean that's not all?"

She paused for a few seconds. "What I mean is, you ask more of us. You don't even check to see if we have too much to do. We spend our Saturdays cleaning house and doing laundry, and on weeknights we help Mama with the food while you and the boys play checkers or cards. Sometimes I'm so tired I have trouble staying awake to do my homework and my lessons. My grades aren't as good as I'd like —"

"Ha! So that's what this is all about!"

Emilie knew that she had said too much. She looked at her mother, begging for help. All Célina did was wipe the nose of her second-youngest, who had had a lingering cold all winter long.

Emilie felt terribly alone. She softened her tone. "What I mean to say, Papa, is that I think it's not fair."

Now she had struck a chord. She knew that her father considered himself a fair man, doing what every man did — raising his family as his father had before him. And now she was saying that he wasn't fair.

"There are two places here, my girl," he said. "A place for men and a place for women. The men work by the sweat of their brow for the blessing of our daily bread. The women's place is to make sure the men have everything they need. You're just thirteen years old, and at your age you have no business telling me how to run this family." With those words, Caleb's pent-up anger exploded. He stood up.

Emilie stopped rocking. Before she knew what was happening, she found herself halfway up the stairs, firmly in her father's grip, her feet barely brushing the treads. She heard him shouting, but she couldn't make out a word. She started yelling, too.

"Let me go! I can walk by myself."

Her father didn't react, so she went on, overcome with rage and tears. "I want to eat at the same time as you and I want to go to school rested."

"If you're tired, my girl, all you have to do is stop going to school. Your mother could use you at home. Besides, you're already smart enough for a girl."

The supreme threat! Emilie choked back her tears. She couldn't let him know that he had hurt her.

"No one's smart enough," she said.

Caleb opened the door to the girls' room and pushed Emilie toward one of the beds. She didn't resist.

"You won't be eating anything tonight," Caleb shouted. "You will say an act of contrition for fooling with God's Fourth Commandment."

"There should be one like it for the children," she muttered, but Caleb overheard her.

"All right, that's it! You want to change the whole household! You want to tell me how to raise my family! And if that's not enough, you tell God He doesn't know how to write His commandments! That's blasphemy! You'll go to confession for it. I won't have my children committing sacrilege!"

He turned on his heel and slammed the door behind him. Then he reopened it just long enough to tell his daughter to go down and clean up after supper.

"No!" Emilie yelled. "No supper, no housework!"

Caleb slammed the door so hard that one of the hinges gave. Then he pushed back in through the crooked door, went over to his daughter and slapped her with the back of his hand. Emilie took the blow without flinching, looked her father straight in the face, then calmly turned the other cheek. Caleb did not hit her a second time. He had never hit a child. He was shaken by a spasm; whether it was a sob or a wave of nausea he didn't know. As he left the room, Emilie turned her back and crossed to the frost-covered window.

$\mathcal{C}$aleb descended the stairs slowly. Célina watched him, ready for anything. She had never seen her husband so upset. She and the other children had heard every word of the fight through the grille in the ceiling, and they'd stayed frozen where they were standing.

Caleb looked at the anxious little group, his forehead wrinkled with distress. He signalled his sons to sit down. Célina and the girls hurried to serve them. Everything was cold. Caleb started to eat, grimaced, but didn't say anything. The girls worked extra hard, fearing that the slightest slip might cause another explosion.

When Caleb had eaten as much as he could stomach — usually he cleared his plate and wiped it clean with a slice of bread — he rose and went to his rocking chair. His sons followed him. He watched his daughters as they cleared the dirty dishes off the table and timidly sat down with their mother to eat what the men had left behind.

This evening, there was more food than usual in the dishes; since the meal was cold, the men hadn't eaten much. Caleb was stunned to see that, unlike his sons, the girls served themselves generous portions, apparently not caring that the food was almost inedible. They began to talk of their usual girlish, insignificant things, whispering at first, then daring to let a few peals of laughter escape. Caleb had the sharp feeling that he had just lost a little authority. He left the kitchen, put on his fur overcoat, laced his felt inner boots and slipped into his rubber overshoes. All he wanted was to get some air.

The minute he closed the door, a feeling of relief washed through the kitchen. Only Célina didn't relax; tears were still burning her eyes. She took her second-youngest by the nape of the neck, undressed him and suddenly decided to give him a bath, even though it wasn't Saturday. The child began to struggle, but when he saw the hot water being poured into the tub he knew there was no use trying to fight it.

"You girls, for once you could do the dishes without waiting to be asked. Boys, your homework. And in silence. I don't want to hear a single complaint, not a single word. Not one! Is that clear?"

The children were troubled. It was unlike their mother to raise her voice. As soon as the girls had wiped the wooden table, the boys sat down and silently opened their books.

Célina scrubbed her son's ears with more vigour than usual, and he began to snivel. She cuffed the back of his head, but when she realized what she had done, she burst into tears. The child, stunned, forgot to cry. The older ones looked up but didn't say a word. Overwhelmed by the sight of their mother in tears, and aware that they could do nothing to comfort her, they didn't budge. Célina dried her eyes with a corner of her apron and tried half-heartedly to reassure her children by telling them that she had got some soap in her eye. No one was fooled.

*F*or the first time in her life, Emilie was scared. Scared for herself, scared for her father and especially scared that she might have to quit school. To stop learning. To face the horrible prospect of seeing her brothers and sisters go off each day without her.

She stayed at the window, not wanting to lie down. She had long known that tears come more easily when you're lying down. From the window, she saw her father leave the house, pace back and forth, look up at the moon and then storm into the barn. She felt certain that she and her father were going through the same anguish. She rubbed her cheek, more to calm the pain of her humiliation than the sting of her father's slap. She still hadn't told him what she was feeling.

In spite of this defeat, she was convinced that she could find a way to improve things in the house without starting a war. She reflected, surprised, that she felt no rancour toward her father. She knew that he was fair. Stubborn, but fair. She was mortified that she had taken him to task in front of the whole family. If only she had chosen her moment better. She vainly tried to soothe her remorse by telling herself that it was her father who had provoked her, with his foul mood.

*C*aleb watched Grazillia lick her calf with great swipes of her smooth, pink tongue. Not even two hours old, the calf was standing steadily and nursing contentedly.

"Damn, Grazillia! What do you think I'm going to do with a little steer? It's heifers I need. A steer means almost a year lost. While he's nursing you can't give milk, and after that I have to slaughter him if I don't want him to eat me out of house and home. *Damn, Grazillia!*"

Suddenly, he remembered the day Emilie was born. When he had held his first-born in his arms, he hadn't dared to voice his disappointment at not having a son. It seemed so normal to want sons for a farm: sons to ensure succession, to do the work. He smiled, aware that, as a farmer, he had contradictory ideas. When a woman had children, one wanted her to have males — as many males as possible. On the other hand, with a cow, all one wanted was females.

His heart skipped a beat. Hadn't Emilie tried to show him that he, Caleb, didn't treat all of his children the same? He had thought she was exaggerating until the moment he sat down at the table. The cold supper was revolting. Seeing his girls eat so eagerly, he realized that perhaps Emilie was right. Caleb didn't like questioning things that had always been taken for granted, and he liked questioning himself even less. How was it that none of her sisters had ever complained? Emilie read too much. She was getting too smart, getting too many ideas from those books. But her spirit wasn't old enough to understand all the subtleties of life.

There was only one thing to do: pull Emilie out of school. Make her learn to be a good housewife, a woman happy to satisfy her family. She had to learn to be like her mother. Anyway, who would teach her all of this when, in five or six years, she got married and set up her own home? No book would teach her the language of the land.

A belch brought up the taste of supper — as detestable to him as his own behaviour. But a father was a father. All he had done was act like a father who wanted to raise his children right. He would have to talk to Célina.

*W*ithout being told, the children decided that it was time for bed. Sleep would be preferable to the tension that had taken over the house. Célina wondered if she should take something to Emilie. She hated feeling torn like this. On the one hand, she felt that Emilie's punishment was entirely justified. On the other hand, she didn't think a growing child should go without food. She convinced herself, nevertheless, that she should stand behind her husband. His authority had been put to the test, and Célina had no intention of opposing him.

She nursed the baby, holding him close for a long time before she put him down. Since she didn't hear any more noise from upstairs, she decided to distract herself by knitting. But her hands were shaking too much; she dropped one stitch, then another. Finally, she threw the work back into her knitting bag and went to the window to look for Caleb. The moon was full and brighter than usual — the night would be frigid. Through the frost on the window pane, she searched the darkness, but saw nothing.

As soon as she heard her brothers and sisters coming upstairs, Emilie hurried into her nightgown and got into bed. She didn't want to answer their questions.

By the time she finally fell alseep, though, she knew what she had to do. She knew she could endure her father's stubbornness for a few days, maybe even a few weeks. On the other hand, she had to keep him from making good his threat to pull her out of school. She would do everything: she would get up earlier; she would do double her usual chores; she would study at night, by lamplight if necessary. But she would never accept leaving school. Never!

Unable to calm her anxiety, Célina finally decided to go to bed. She was sure she wouldn't be able to sleep without her husband, but she would rather close her eyes than have to face him.

She undressed slowly. The house was cold. She realized that she had forgotten to stoke the wood stove for the night and wearily returned to do so. Once in bed, she tossed and turned a little, then felt under her pillow for her rosary. She prayed for two things: first, for God to forget that Caleb had, for the first time in his life, not said the blessing and grace, and second, for her own peace.

Caleb came in long after Célina had gone to bed. He knew from the puffiness around her eyes that she had cried herself to sleep. He took the rosary from her hands and tucked it back under the pillow. Then he quietly got undressed, genuflected and made the sign of the cross, blew out the lamp and slid between the sheets warmed by his wife's sorrow.

In the morning, Emilie was at her post. She cleaned the table with nerve-wracking meticulousness, put on her coat and left for school without eating a thing. Célina was worried and called after her to come back for at least a piece of bread dipped in molasses. Emilie thanked her but said that she had to hurry not to miss a test. Her mother closed the door, wondering if Emilie had got up during the night for a snack.

Caleb told her not to worry. Taking advantage of these few moments alone with her, he told her that he was thinking of pulling Emilie out of school. Every argument he had come up with during the long, sleepless night was put to his wife. But, to his great surprise, Célina replied that it was out of the question, that Emilie needed school like he, Caleb, needed to see the sun and listen to the rain. Caleb tried to make her see that there was a world of difference between the land and books, but Célina was adamant. Emilie must continue to go to school. As he knew, she wanted to be a teacher.

"A little girl's dreams!" he said, disdainfully.

"It's no dream. In two or three years, if she's ready to take the government exam, she could have a school of her own. I think if she wants to be a schoolmistress, she should be a schoolmistress."

Caleb reminded her that her own health wasn't good, and that Emilie could help her when she was ill or indisposed. Célina retorted that Emilie had never complained when she asked her to stay home from school to help out.

Finally, Caleb admitted that Emilie was, in spite of her slightly quick temper, an obliging girl. Then, after much hesitation, he asked Célina if she had any idea what the previous evening's fracas had really been about. She responded, blushing, that Emilie's moods probably meant that she would have to use rags soon. Caleb just grunted; he didn't like to hear about women's matters.

Finally, cranking up his courage, he tried to sound out whether she thought he was raising the children unfairly. Célina told him that he was a good husband and father — no worse than other fathers. Life was hard, and everyone had to put a shoulder to the wheel.

"Do you think the girls' wheel is heavier than the boys'?" he asked softly, hoping for a negative answer.

"The girls' wheel is the girls' wheel."

Caleb knew her well. When she was afraid to speak her mind, she responded with a ready-made phrase. Caleb stood up and put on his jacket and boots.

"I'm going to see if the tools need greasing before spring."

Célina nodded, though she knew very well that he had oiled them long ago.

Just before he reached the door, Caleb turned. "Is the food you eat always as cold as what we ate yesterday?"

Célina hesitated a moment. "Was it cold?"

Caleb shook his head and slipped out the door.

*W*hen she came home from school, Emilie seemed to be in a better mood. She helped her mother prepare supper and made a point of seeing that the men of the house had everything they needed. Caleb smiled at her several times — a timid attempt to indicate that the battle was over — and Emilie smiled back. The men left the table and the women, after setting the table a second time, sat down to eat. Caleb had discreetly tried to get his sons to eat faster so that the food wouldn't get cold. He was proud of himself for thinking of it. Célina understood, and as she sat down she threw him a quiet look of appreciation.

"Aren't you sitting down, Emilie?" she asked.

"No, thank you. I prefer to eat standing up."

"What do you mean, you *want* to eat standing up?"

Caleb's smile disappeared. She was showing him up. She was showing him up, the stubborn mule! Emilie ate as quickly as her father had, and then, all by herself, washed every dish she could get her hands on.

Her sisters watched her, perplexed. "Wait for us," they called to her.

"Oh, no, it's faster this way. Enjoy it — I won't always be this obliging."

A snake in the grass, thought Caleb. But he didn't say a word.

The next morning, Emilie got up earlier than usual and had already milked several cows by the time her father got to the barn.

"What are you doing here?"

"The milking. Then I'll sweep."

"It's not your turn to sweep."

"If you say so. I'll go sweep in the house, then."

Caleb watched her leave, suspicious.

*C*aleb had no idea what to do. Emilie hadn't sat down to eat in a month. But would it be fair to scold her? She always did her chores, and more. She did her work in record time. At Easter, the teacher had told him and Célina that Emilie was first in her class yet again, and added that if she kept it up, she would soon be teaching the teacher! She even admitted that Emilie's French was better than her own. Even though he didn't approve of Emilie continuing her studies — especially if she was planning to be a teacher — Caleb was proud of his eldest child. This pride, however, was overshadowed by her daily stubbornness.

Célina adroitly avoided all discussion of the subject. She knew that Emilie's behaviour got on her father's nerves, but she also knew that Emilie was opposing him so politely that it was hard to figure out exactly what she was after. When her husband, one evening at the end of April, sighed and asked her if she knew what Emilie wanted from him, Célina knew the time had come to say something. Apparently, Caleb's pride was melting with the snow.

"I'm not sure, Caleb, but it seems to me it might have something to do with the meals."

Surprised, Caleb raised an eyebrow. "What about the meals? I belch all the time from eating too fast so the food doesn't get cold."

Célina, smiling sympathetically, didn't bother to respond. Caleb thought about her remark for several days.

The following Sunday, while the older children were out attending a piano recital in the convent hall, Caleb asked Célina to set the table with a place for each member of the family. Célina, seeing that he had finally understood, did what he asked without comment.

The children came home, and the girls put on their aprons to set the table. Célina simply told them that it had already been done. Emilie was the first of the girls to notice that there were more places set than usual. Cautiously, she said that by the look of the table you'd think it was Christmastime.

The entire family sat down together. The boys, feeling put out, complained that they were too crowded. Caleb told them that they could always eat standing up. Emilie burst out laughing. Caleb cleared his throat and spoke to his curious children.

"It always seemed to me this table wasn't big enough for all of us. Today, your mother and I tried, and we found it could be done. There's enough room. Anyway, I'm going to make another table, a little bigger . . . We also thought that the girls, Emilie, Année and Eda, could take turns serving. We men, we'll do what they do in the lumber camps. We'll take our plates and cutlery to the dishpan. That way, your mother won't have to walk so much. We all know her legs hurt . . . Now, everyone stand up, and I'll say the blessing."

Everyone stood, Emilie first. She also was the first to sit back down, and the first to dig in with her fork when the plates were served.

"Potatoes taste better when they're hot, don't they, Mama?"

Part One

1895–1897

One

"EVA, IT'S YOUR TURN to wash the blackboard this evening. Give it a good wipe, I want it to shine like a new penny. You, the bigger boys, you'll split the wood and bring it in. I don't want to see a single log roll away. The middle ones, this week it's your turn to sweep up. And I don't want to hear any arguments about whose turn it is to sweep and whose turn to hold the dustpan. Little ones, you'll line up the desks. I'm sure you know the secret to making sure they're very straight." Emilie winked at them. "I want beautiful straight lines."

The twenty-seven children stood up. The big ones shrugged, just to show that they could easily refuse to obey, but then they hurried out to fetch the wood. Sitting at her desk, Emilie put her work in order. She filed her papers in the large right-hand drawer, then thought twice, took them out and put them with the pile of things to take with her. Then she changed her mind again and put them back in the drawer, shaking her head. She went over to little Charlotte's desk and tapped her on the shoulder.

"It's time, Charlotte."

Charlotte understood. She immediately stopped working and

went to the back door of the classroom, where a board with nails sticking out of it served as a coatrack. She looked for her coat. She thought she'd hung it on the nail nearest the door, but she didn't see it. She looked at the second and the third nails. She began to worry. Where had she put her coat? She absolutely had to find it. She went back to the nail near the door and looked under the coat that was hanging there, but she couldn't find hers. She turned back to the classroom and tried to get Emilie's attention, but Emilie was talking to Eva and didn't see her. Charlotte was too shy to call out.

Where was her coat? Her mother had forbidden her to go out without it. She decided to look once more before asking for help. But now she couldn't see anything very well, for she was blinking back tears and her chin was trembling with the effort to keep from crying. It's time, she said to herself, it's time. But for how long had it been time? She had absolutely no idea what to do. She looked back into the classroom and saw that big Joachim Crête was watching her, with a strange look on his face.

Joachim elbowed Paul, who kicked Lazare, who poked Emile, who coughed to get Ovila's attention. Ovila glanced at Emilie, frowned, hunched his shoulders and went back to work. He put down a log which, to his embarrassment, rolled on the floor.

Emilie turned around. "Ovila Pronovost! Would you please watch what you're doing!"

"Excuse me, Miss. It just got away from me. Look, I've piled them all up."

"Fine, but be more careful."

Emilie began to feel that something was not quite right, something she couldn't put her finger on. Her eyes swept across the classroom. Everything seemed normal. The children were talking softly, as they had permission to do, and they were all in their proper places. But something was not right. She asked Eva what was going on, but Eva didn't know what she meant. Emilie turned again to the other students, but they all looked busy. Then she noticed a funny sort of squeaking sound, like a cross between the shriek of the winter wind and the whining of a puppy.

"What is that noise?" she asked.

Joachim looked at her innocently. "Could it possibly be Charlotte, Miss?"

Emilie hitched up her skirt and went to the back of the classroom. There was a sorry sight. Charlotte was standing beside the coats, her eyes riveted to the floor. Urine was trickling down her legs.

"Charlotte! What happened?"

Charlotte burst into tears. At the same time, big Joachim and his friends burst into laughter.

Emilie knelt down to comfort Charlotte, then turned to the class and ordered them to sit down.

"Charlotte pissed on the floor," Joachim yelled in his cracking, adolescent voice.

Emilie shot him a look and warned him that she didn't want to hear another word, then she turned back to Charlotte, who was inconsolable. Emilie tried to elicit the cause of the accident, but Charlotte was now hiccuping too much to explain.

"Eva, bring me the washcloth and the bucket."

Eva brought them as quickly as she could. She handed the cloth to Emilie and stayed to watch. Emilie started by wiping Charlotte's legs, then her boots, then the floor. She was furious, Charlotte was miserable, and Eva was too curious.

"Thank you, Eva. You can sit down now."

Eva returned to her seat but whispered as she went that it was true, Charlotte had peed on the floor. Big Joachim retorted, loud enough for everyone to hear, that they could see it, and smell it, too. "And it stinks like anything," he added.

His neighbour snorted with laughter — too loudly, unfortunately, to escape the attention of the teacher. Emilie marched right up to him, pulling Charlotte by the hand. She rapped violently on the desk. The laughing boy jumped, blushed and then blanched.

"That's enough!" Emilie growled. She took Charlotte up to the second floor to get her away from the others.

From the top stair, she clearly heard Joachim asking his friends if he didn't look like he was about to burst into tears, too. Emilie wanted no more of this. She told Charlotte to sit and wait, then she dashed back downstairs. The students froze.

"All right, children! Can someone tell me . . ." She stopped. Big

Joachim's shoulders were shaking with laughter. She walked over to his desk, fixed him with a stare and planted her fists on his desk.

"You big fool . . ."

Joachim stopped, a look of mock fright on his face. "Hey, little girl, don't get on your high horse. You don't scare me."

He stood up, towering over her by a head, put his hands on his hips, puffed out his chest and returned her stare. Emilie could no longer control herself. She went around the desk and grabbed his left ear in her left hand, his belt in her right hand, gave him a knee in the rear end to set him in motion and sent him to the back of the classroom.

The children froze. They had never seen Emilie Bordeleau lose her temper. The girls were impressed, the boys even more so. Joachim had no idea what was going to happen. Before he'd figured out that the schoolmistress was handling him like a pig taken to slaughter, he found himself on his knees beside the bucket, his head plunged into the water soiled with chalk powder and urine. Emilie grabbed a handful of hair and pulled his head out, grabbed the rag with her other hand and threw it at his face.

"Here, dry yourself with that. Now you stink, too."

She left him to his shock and rage and went back to the head of the class, exhorting herself to calm down. Seeing the terrified eyes of the children, she got a hold of herself.

"It's been two months since the school year began. Now I want something to be clear once and for all. The only person who gives orders here is me. Not Joachim Crête, even if he is fourteen and you know that I'm only sixteen. Age is not important. What is important is respect. Charlotte is Charlotte. I know you understand what I mean. Do you understand?"

"Yes, Miss Bordeleau," the children answered in unison.

"I said that there would be no homework or lessons for All Saints' Day. But because of what has happened today, I am obliged to ask the fourth-, fifth-, sixth- and seventh-grade children to write a composition at least twenty lines long on 'respect.' This means you too, Joachim Crête. Now, each class will put on their boots and coats and leave. And not a sound out of you! I'll see you Wednesday morning."

The class emptied in record time and in absolute silence. Contrary to her habit, she did not see the children to the door. Instead, she hurried up to Charlotte, whose sobs could now be heard in the classroom.

"It's all over now, Charlotte. You can stop crying. Take off your wet clothes. I'll rinse them out and hang them over the stove to dry. If they aren't dry by the time my father arrives, I'll find you something to wear, and we'll drive you home."

She took a handkerchief out of her pocket, wiped the little girl's face and pointed to a corner where she could undress. She forced herself not to look, to save the child from further humiliation. Charlotte brought her soiled clothes and handed them to Emilie without lifting her eyes.

"You know, Charlotte," Emilie began as they went downstairs, "this reminds me of when I was little. I dreamed that I had gotten up to go make peepee. In my dream I had gone to the outhouse. Can you guess where I was when I woke up?"

"No," said Charlotte uneasily.

"You promise you won't tell anyone?"

Charlotte nodded.

"I was making peepee in the drawer of my dresser."

Emilie burst out laughing. A moment later, Charlotte joined in. Emilie kept talking as she washed the little girl's clothes. She told Charlotte that she had never been so embarrassed in her life, that she had thought no one would ever forget that incident, and that she hadn't been six years old but all of ten when it had happened. Charlotte, absorbed in the story, had stopped crying. Then she dashed to the back of the classroom. Emilie followed her. Charlotte bent over and picked up what Emilie guessed was her coat. Then she began to cry again.

"My coat is ruined."

Emilie leaned down and took the coat. It had been rolled up and hidden under the overshoes. She recognized the prank — it had Joachim Crête's fingerprints all over it.

"I guess your coat fell down."

Charlotte, despondent at the sight of her rumpled, mud-covered coat, didn't answer. Emilie stood up and went back to the front of the class, motioning Charlotte to follow her.

"Give me five minutes. I'll make it good as new." She brushed it vigorously, put an iron on the stove, checked the drying clothes as she passed, then pressed the coat.

Charlotte sat down, pulling her dress down to hide her bare legs. "My mother's going to be mad. She'll think I was fooling around."

"Don't worry, I'll talk to her."

Emilie managed to clean the coat, to Charlotte's great relief. She asked the child to wait downstairs while she went up and closed her suitcases, but Charlotte followed her like a puppy. Emilie was amused. The little girl was shy. I guess I would be too, she thought.

Charlotte didn't so much as open her mouth, but Emilie noticed that she often glanced anxiously toward the window, and understood why.

"I think my father will be here in about fifteen minutes," Emilie said.

"Will my underpants be dry in fifteen minutes?"

Emilie felt them. "Yes, they will be."

That won a smile from the little girl.

Two

CALEB SIGHED WITH a mixture of fatigue and satisfaction. He had just driven his buggy across the new wooden bridge over Rivière des Envies. He liked the sound of wooden bridges: with each step, the hooves of his mare made a ringing sound, as if they were echoing through a valley. He shook his head as he thought of all the metal bridges the engineers were building these days. Since they had started construction on that awful bridge at Montreal, and especially since they had feasted their eyes on the plans for that monster of a tower going up in the old country, these engineers swore up and down that nothing was better than metal. Caleb tried to convince himself that they were wrong, but deep down he knew that what they were saying was probably true.

After the bridge, he turned right and urged his mare along the last two miles to Emilie's school. They were entering the Bourdais concession. Caleb didn't force the animal; he let her mosey along at a leisurely trot while he looked at the gently rolling land around him. The farmers of Saint-Tite worked just as hard as those of his own village. Everywhere, the land was demanding, he thought.

Caleb's thoughts turned to Emilie, whom he hadn't seen since the school year had begun. Caleb was a little annoyed with her, and he hadn't tried to hide it. Since she had left home, though, she had written almost every week. Célina read the letters out loud, and everyone, big and small, listened eagerly. The house had lost a little of its gaiety when Emilie left.

Caleb felt that his daughter was too young to go and live in a faraway village. When he'd finally let her accept the offer in Saint-Tite, he thought she'd be teaching in a two-room school. When she then announced that it was in fact a one-room schoolhouse — where she'd be alone with her pupils during the day, and all by herself at night — he found it hard to believe that she hadn't known this all along.

Until the first letter arrived, Caleb was anxious. What if Emilie had problems? Or found the nights too long? Or some troublemaker tried to bother her? A two-room school would have been better. Emilie would have had a companion to share the work and the chores, and someone to talk to. But Emilie never seemed to worry about what was ahead. Caleb was surprised. She was prepared to change her way of life from one day to the next — to leave her family, leave her village. To become an adult. She had written that she was responsible for twenty-seven pupils.

Caleb looked across the river at the farms dotting the north shore. In each of those houses there must be one or more of Emilie's pupils. In front of him was the school, nestled between two hills. It was a pretty little schoolhouse, though he was sure it wasn't well enough caulked to keep out the cold north winds. Another quarter of a mile and he'd be there.

Caleb urged his mare on. He pulled his watch from an inside pocket. He had told his daughter that he would arrive around four o'clock on the last Friday of October. It was ten after four when he stopped his buggy. He jumped down and covered the mare with a wool blanket.

Emilie saw him coming and helped Charlotte into her clothes. The little girl was relieved that they were almost dry. Emilie went out to greet her father.

Caleb nodded hello as he started to unload bricks. "I hope your stove is still warm."

Emilie assured him that it was, then asked him if she could borrow the buggy to drive home one of her pupils who'd had a little accident. Caleb asked if the child was hurt, and she told him no. Caleb looked at his sweating mare and made her promise that the trip wouldn't take more than fifteen minutes. He took off the blanket and stowed it in the back of the buggy.

"I'll heat the bricks while you're gone," he said.

Emilie hurried to get Charlotte, whom she introduced to her father. Charlotte gave a little curtsey.

Caleb lifted her onto the seat, then bent over to get the last bricks. "Don't push the mare too hard, Emilie. She already has fifteen miles behind her."

Emilie told him not to worry and to make himself at home. "I've put a kettle on. Make yourself some tea. That'll put the colour back in your cheeks."

Caleb waved his thanks and went into the schoolhouse. What he saw surprised him. Emilie had wasted no time in making the school her own. She had completely rearranged things, moving her desk to a different spot. The pupils' desks were lined up like soldiers on parade. Looking down, he saw that the floor was covered with little pencil marks. That was Emilie, always inventing ways to make things easier. On the blackboard she had drawn flowers and written all the letters of the alphabet: on the top line were the lower-case letters; below were the capitals. There wasn't a speck of dust on the windowsills, and the panes were as clean as could be.

He went to the stove to put down his first load of bricks. Emilie must have spent endless hours scouring and blacking it; it looked good as new. He went back for the rest of the bricks, which he had left near the door, and put them down beside the first ones. Emilie had left him a cup with tea leaves; all he had to do was pour in the hot water and wait for the tea to steep. Settling comfortably in Emilie's chair, he looked around the classroom and tried to imagine what his daughter felt when there was a pair of eyes watching her from each of the desks. Suddenly he felt like playing schoolmaster.

"Take out your readers, please."

When he heard his own voice, he felt ridiculous. He decided to go upstairs to Emilie's living quarters. The staircase was steep, almost a ladder. He had trouble keeping his balance and had to take care not to upset his tea.

If the changes in the classroom had surprised him, here he was stunned to find that, with almost nothing, she had managed to create a pleasant room. She had made white cotton curtains, embroidered with white thread, which she had hung in the window on a long rod. On the small metal bed was a comforter decorated with a matching pattern. An old butter box, covered with a piece of fabric, had been transformed into a night table. On it, an oil lamp sat beside a dictionary. Caleb smiled. Emilie had not lost her habit of reading the dictionary before going to sleep. Near the icebox were a table and some shelves on which she had put her provisions, dishes and cooking utensils.

There were only two chairs in the room. The first, which was missing a plank out of the back, had a cushion on the seat. This must be the chair she sat in when she ate. The second, a rocking chair, was placed near one of the windows. Here was where she sewed or read a book, he thought. A chipped vase held dried flowers. He didn't like this; dried flowers seemed to carry the smell of death. Finally, she had made a sort of screen to hide the washstand. The walls weren't painted, but Caleb was relieved to see that there were two layers of planks everywhere. The north wind would have a hard time finding a chink to blow through.

Caleb put down his empty cup, then decided to take Emilie's suitcase downstairs. They would leave right away, without resting the mare long. Emilie came in as he was depositing the suitcase at the door.

"I put the blanket back on the mare. Should I give her her oats right away?"

"No, let her cool off. Then she can have her oats. And we'll let her digest a little before we go."

They sat down together on the little porch. The day was cool; the bright sun was playing leapfrog with the clouds. Emilie liked this kind of autumn day. Father and daughter sat quietly, watching the mare.

Suddenly, they heard neighing coming from behind the school. The mare heard it, too. She raised her head and her nostrils quivered.

The neighing grew louder. Caleb and Emilie got up and went to see who was serenading their mare. In the farm pasture next to the school, they saw a handsome brown stallion proudly sporting an uncommonly thick, golden mane, which looked even more burnished in the glorious beams of the setting sun. Caleb whistled. He had never seen such a beautiful stallion.

"If we had a stallion like that nearby, I would have asked his owner to service my mare long ago. Who does he belong to?"

Emilie told him that this was the first time she had seen the magnificent animal; had she known about him, she surely would have mentioned it in her letters. Caleb went and hung a bag of oats around his mare's muzzle. She blew into the bag twice, blinked from the dust, then started to eat.

Knowing that he hated to start a trip on an empty stomach, Emilie invited her father in to have a bowl of soup. They ate sitting face to face, Caleb in the straight chair, Emilie in the rocking chair, which she had brought to the table and immobilized by sticking two blocks of wood under the rockers — a clever trick, Caleb thought. They didn't talk much as they ate, though they smiled when they heard the stallion neighing, each whinny more desperate than the last.

"If things were different, he wouldn't have to beg to service her. It's a good thing she's already in foal because, I'm telling you, I would have her covered right away. Maybe next year we could do something about it. Anyway, he must know what he's saying because even though she's in foal, the mare looks pretty interested."

Emilie smiled; she knew her father's obsession with horses. She washed the dishes and put them away on a shelf. Caleb got up, looked at the time and decided that they'd better get going if they wanted to reach the main road before nightfall. Emilie agreed. They went downstairs, and Emilie carefully closed the trap door that led to her living quarters.

The fire in the stove was almost out. Even so, as a simple precaution, she completely closed the damper then turned it back a quarter of a turn, so that there would be no smoke if the flames rekindled. She glanced around the room. Everything seemed to be in order.

Her father was already outside putting the warmed bricks on the floor of the buggy. He knew that it wasn't really cold enough to need them, but he liked to keep his feet warm when he had a long way to go. He took his seat and called for Emilie to hurry up. She rushed out, closed the door, then asked him to wait. She went back inside and looked through the papers she had put on her desk. Again she changed her mind, for she knew that these papers were her sole links to and the only proof of her new life — she had to take them with her to be sure that she would return. She firmly closed the door, bumped it with her hip to make sure that the latch had caught and turned the key to lock it.

The stallion let loose a cry of despair when he saw them rolling away. The mare raised her head, but Caleb quickly urged her on. "She might not be pretty," he said, "but at least she's obedient."

Emilie smiled and covered her legs with the blankets Caleb had brought. The mare settled into a steady trot.

In amiable silence, father and daughter watched the sun sinking toward the horizon. Emilie breathed in deeply. She liked the smell of autumn and the sight of the autumn sun winking at her through bare branches. She turned for a last look at her little schoolhouse, with all its shimmering windows, nestled between the two hills as if it depended on their slopes to protect it from the wind. Caleb glanced at his daughter as she discreetly, almost lovingly, blew a kiss to the scene she was leaving behind.

Caleb had secretly hoped that Emilie would regret her decision. He had been waiting to hear her say that she was coming home to stay, that she was bored. But from the tone of her letters, and now the fond glance she had thrown back at the little school, he knew that she was not about to change her mind. How could he have thought she would be bored? She never had enough time to do all the things she wanted to.

Caleb remembered the story his grandfather had told him about their ancestor Antoine Bordeleau, a soldier in Carignan's regiment who had married a *fille du Roi*, one of the women sent from the old country to be a bride in the new colony. After bearing him two children, she went back to France. Bordeleau waited for her for thirty-six years. She never contacted him or asked for news of her children. Caleb knew that Emilie wasn't like this Pérette Hallier; unlike the French girl, she would never return to the old country.

For the first time since Emilie had left, two months ago, he had a sharp feeling of loss. The first time a child leaves home was like a secret that nature whispered in your ear, telling you that your own youth was over. Time stole away your youth when those you had fathered left you. Caleb sniffed. If he had remembered what it was like, he would have known that he was weeping — dry sobs, without tears.

"Light a lantern, Emilie. It'll be dark soon."

She did as he asked, but this time, when she sat back down, she drew the blanket up around her shoulders as a shawl. She looked at the streaks of clouds, coloured by the last rays of the sun, from deep red to pale blue, with every shade of pink in between.

"It's going to be clear and cold tonight," she said.

"Yup, there'll be a frost. We already had one last week. I don't like it when the ground frosts too long before the snow falls. It looks like it suffers from the cold. It gets wrinkled like an old lady. I'm always worried it'll die before spring, and they'll say the earth died in its sleep."

Emilie looked at him, a little startled. He always liked to talk about the land, but this evening he was letting his feelings show much more than usual.

The dark night pushed the last glow of sun beyond the horizon, and Emilie lit the second lantern. The silence was broken only by the clip-clop of the mare's hooves and the squeaking of the right front wheel.

They were about an hour away from the school when they saw the lights of Saint-Séverin twinkling in the distance, fifteen minutes away. Caleb told Emilie that they would stop at the house of his niece, her cousin, Lucie. "I told her on my way up we'd stop for a bite. She's expecting us."

Lucie's house was on the border between the parish and the Saint-Séverin countryside. Caleb stopped the buggy, pulled the blanket over the mare and started to carry the bricks to the door, while Lucie and Emilie greeted each other and went inside. Phonse,

Lucie's husband, brought in the last bricks and put them on the stove.

"Are the kids in bed?" Emilie asked her cousin.

"Oh, no. I usually put them to bed at seven-th-thirty. That way, Phonse and I have time to play with them. They're outside in back. I'll g-go and get them."

Lucie came back right away with her two children. The older boy, just three years old, had a beautiful head of black hair. The younger one, a cheerful eighteen-month-old, toddled about happily.

"Do you recognize your cousin Em-Emilie, Jos?"

The black-haired boy nodded yes. He went over to Emilie, and the younger one followed him.

"They're not at all wild," Emilie said.

"Don't t-talk to me about wild children. I've already h-had them inside me for nine m-months. I don't want them under m-my skirts for nine years!"

After they put the bricks in the kitchen, Phonse and Caleb went out to see the livestock. The women fed and washed the children and dressed them for bed. Lucie decided to put the younger one to bed, "in case he's sleepy," and sat the older one in a corner of the kitchen with a deck of cards.

"I don't know why, but Jos s-spends hours looking at them. The game he plays is m-my favourite card g-game. I call it 'the g-game to give the m-mistress of the house some peace.'"

In no time at all, the two cousins had set the table and laid out the food. Lucie called the men and they all sat down. The baby, to his mother's great relief, had indeed gone to sleep.

"So, Uncle C-Caleb, what's new with you these days? You came through so quickly before, the dust b-barely had time to settle before you were on your way again."

Caleb smiled and told her that nothing was really new. Célina was still not feeling well after the pneumonia she'd had back in mid-September.

"Poor Aunt Célina. I guess you'd have to say that she's never been too strong."

"I guess you would," Caleb agreed, shaking his head. He chewed his food carefully.

"But I guess you'd all have to admit that my wife sets a good table," Phonse bragged. "All you have to do is look at me to see that I've been well fed for the last four years."

In fact, Phonse had been skinny as a rail when he and Lucie had wed. In the first year of their marriage, he had put on some weight. In the second year, people remarked that he was getting portly. In the third, he was indubitably stout. Now, only the word "fat" could describe him. Lucie looked at him, her head tilted and a mocking smile playing at the corners of her mouth.

"Imagine what they would say if I c-cooked like I speak. They would say that I p-put three or four times the ingredients in m-my recipes."

They all laughed, Phonse the loudest. The child looked up to see what had provoked the hilarity. Not seeing anything, he went back to his cards.

"Listen," Lucie continued, "have you heard that there have been robberies in the c-concession?"

"Robberies?" Caleb said, eyebrows raised in surprise.

"Yessir. And not just stealing a goose or two. Real robberies, with a robber abroad at night with a sack on his b-back, picking up whatever he likes. Especially chickens. But he's crafty like a fox — he only takes one per coop. He thinks no one will n-notice. Except that he always takes the b-best layer."

"It's true," Emilie said. "He knows the neighbourhood."

"Like the back of his hand. The worst thing is, everyone knows who it is."

"So how come you don't say something to him?" Caleb asked.

"Because we've never seen him do it. I told you, he's crafty like a fox. But that didn't keep me from g-giving him a piece of my mind."

"You didn't tell me that," Phonse said, surprised.

"What do you want, it takes me so long to g-get things out, I d-don't always have the time to t-tell you."

"What did you say to the old man?"

"Well, I was taking some biscuits to old Mrs. Rocheleau. Since the l-little one was sleeping, I t-took Jos with me. I was hurrying home, b-because I didn't want the b-baby to wake up before I got b-back. The old man was digging in his garden. He s-said hello as nice as you please, then he t-told me that I was walking too fast for Jos. So I l-looked at him, and I said, 'At least my boy walks f-fast during the day, not at night.'"

Phonse burst out laughing. Lucie never ceased to amaze him. He asked her what the old fox had said.

"He didn't say anything. His eyes got b-big and he said, 'Uuuhh,' and that's all."

*E*milie knew that they were near water. The air was heavy with the smell of moist earth, no more than a hill away. Then she heard it. The Batiscan. Her river. She had spent many hours dreaming by its banks, and its burbling waters had swallowed up all her secrets. Now she forgot the sharp sadness that sounded in her heart, which only Lucie, for a moment, had been able to silence.

"It's a good thing we have blankets. It's cold tonight."

Absorbed in her thoughts, Emilie hadn't really heard him. "What did you say, Papa?"

He repeated himself, and she agreed.

"You're very quiet. Usually, you're full of stories." He paused a moment, then spoke again, his tone as gentle as if he were talking to a baby. "You're thinking about your school, eh?"

"Yes." Emilie told her father about the trick Joachim Crête had played on Charlotte, about how furious she'd been, and about how she had completely lost her temper. Caleb listened carefully, realizing that she was asking his approval for the punishment she had inflicted on the Crête boy. When she finished, he reflected for a few minutes, then he told his daughter that, in her place, he would surely have done worse.

"Your Crête boy, he reminds me of Hervé Caouette."

"Hervé Caouette is an angel compared to Joachim."

"Well . . . it seems to me that you may have gotten through to him. With people like that, you don't wear kid gloves."

"I'm just scared that he's going to make more trouble. I tell you,

Papa, except for him I've had absolutely no problems since the term began."

"Maybe you've taken care of him."

He waited another minute before daring to ask the question that had been burning in his mind since they had left Saint-Tite.

"So, Emilie, is being a schoolteacher the life you dreamed of?"

Emilie thought for a long time before telling him that it was very close to what she had dreamed of — Joachim Crête excepted, of course.

"Do you know what I like the most, Papa? It's that every Friday I'm sure that the children know more than they did at the beginning of the week. You see, Papa? Me, all alone, Emilie Bordeleau, I teach them new things. Do you think any of them will remember me when they're all grown up?"

Three

DECEMBER HAD RELEGATED AUTUMN to the attic of memories. Cold had gripped the land, the trees, bodies and spirits. Emilie watched the snow fall, suddenly aware of how alone she was. Although there were houses near the school, the uniform whiteness of the snow, blanketing the fences and roads, had erased the familiar scenery. She had just realized that she was alone for the holidays. She would have been happy to see her pupils seven days a week.

She was putting on her overshoes when she heard the jingling of sleigh bells. Leaning out the window, she saw that it was Ovila Pronovost, and she wondered if he had forgotten something in his desk. She saw him grab the rails of the school porch and hurried to open the door for him. He took off his hat before speaking. She suppressed a smile; this was a sign of courtesy that she had attempted to ingrain in her pupils.

"Good day, Miss. I didn't see you go by, so I thought maybe you'd like to go to church by sleigh. It's not exactly a warm day to walk four miles."

"That's nice of you, Ovila. I was just getting ready to go."

"If it's all right with you, we'll pick up my family as we go."

"That would be fine."

"Oh, good!"

There was something in Ovila's "Oh, good!" that caught her off guard. She tilted her head and glanced at her student through narrowed eyes before hurrying out the door.

She climbed into the sleigh and, to her great astonishment, Ovila placed a large bearskin over her legs. What surprised her was not so much that he had thought to bring the fur, but the delicate gesture with which he had placed it. She thanked him. He murmured a shy "It's nothing."

When Ovila stopped the team at the top of the hill, Mr. Pronovost came out to greet Emilie.

"It's much too cold to walk today, Miss. That's why I thought my boy had a good idea to go and get you."

"It's very nice of you. I was just about to set out."

She got up to yield her place to Mrs. Pronovost, who was holding her youngest child in her arms, but Mr. Pronovost told her to stay where she was. Instead, he helped his wife up to sit beside her and told the children to climb in back. When they were all aboard, he joined them. Emilie was a little surprised. She had thought that Mr. Pronovost would take the reins, but he didn't. Ovila stayed where he was, puffed with pride in the confidence his father had shown in him. His older brothers were in back with their father.

Emilie had already met the entire family. In fact, Lazare, Ovila, Rosée, Emile and Eva were her pupils. She had only spoken to Ovide and Edmond, the eldest, in passing, and knew that the following year Oscar would be coming to school. As for little Télesphore, who had just fallen asleep on his mother's knee, he couldn't be more than two or three years old.

Emilie was intimidated. Never, since the beginning of the year, had she gone anywhere with the Pronovosts. She avoided looking behind her, instead complimenting Ovila on his handling of the horses and chatting a little with Mrs. Pronovost about her children, especially the youngest, of whom she was very fond. Although Mrs. Pronovost was just a bit of a thing, she was very impressive. She was quite different from Emilie's mother: she talked, laughed heartily and even joked about her husband. She told Emilie that, in her opinion, Dosithée had a lot more fun in the back of the sleigh than he did when he had to drive the team.

"He's really just a little boy, even if he *is* forty-five years old. And you, Miss Bordeleau, how old are you?"

Emilie cleared her throat before answering that she was sixteen, embarrassed by the fact that she was not much older than several of the children in the sleigh. She hastened to add that she would soon be seventeen. Mrs. Pronovost just shook her head and said that it was a nice age, about the same age as her eldest, Ovide. Emilie smiled. Ovila noticed and asked if she had smiled at the mention of Ovide or at the thought that seventeen was a nice age. He shot a furtive glance toward his brother, who was sitting directly behind Emilie. Ovide caught his young brother's eye and teased him by pretending to pat Emilie's back. Ovila turned back around, furious.

Ovide had a way of making everything ridiculous. When Ovila had suggested that he go get his teacher, Ovide had begun to tease him on the subject of the lovely Miss Bordeleau. The more Ovila tried to defend himself, the more his brother pointed out to everyone how he blushed every time Emilie's name was mentioned. With all the pride of his fourteen years, Ovila asked him to be quiet. Mr. Pronovost winked at Mrs. Pronovost. No one was fooled.

Dosithée smiled to himself. At least his son had the good taste to choose a fine strapping girl for his first crush. The new teacher had set tongues to wagging. No one dared to doubt her competence, the proof being the story of big Joachim Crête, who never wanted to set foot in the school again. On the other hand, everyone thought that, with her good looks and her pride, Emilie wouldn't stay long at a little concession schoolhouse. Already, some young men of marrying age had set their caps for her. But Emilie seemed to discourage suitors before they could even make their first move. Despite her youth, there was something about her that inspired respect. She seemed to keep young people at a distance, which was a good thing in her position — there had been stories about teachers who kept company with young men in their schoolhouse! Even his Ovide, who had quite an eye for the ladies, had known better than to try to invite sweet Miss Bordeleau to any parties.

That morning, when Ovila had left the house, slamming the door, Ovide was chanting, "Emilie in your suit of grey, when I see you I blush all day."

"Hush now, Ovide," his father had growled. "You can see Ovila is upset."

But Ovide kept chanting, tapping his foot in rhythm. His siblings didn't appreciate his attitude. They liked their teacher and found it unseemly that she was the subject of a rhyme in such poor taste.

"Are you jealous?" Rosée asked.

"Jealous of what?" Ovide said.

"Well, that we get to see her every day, and you almost never see her."

"Are you kidding? What do you think I'd do with a school-mistress?"

"The same thing you want to do with the other girls!"

"That's enough, you two," Félicité scolded. She hated such innuendo. "Hurry up and get ready. Ovila will be here soon with Miss Bordeleau."

The children obeyed. Félicité looked at her Ovide. Yes, he was very handsome. And the girls liked him. Ha! That was for sure! There were many who would love to have him for a husband. Strong and tall, and almost of marrying age . . . already . . .

Ovila slowed the horse to let the other sleighs going to church pass by. People were in a good mood. The white-and-blue morning promised a beautiful Christmas. Ovila thought about the pageant he and the other students were feverishly preparing for. Miss Emilie — his private name for her — had put so much time and energy into it, and he wanted to help more. He would ask his father for permission to go to school in the evening — with Rosée, of course — to help Emilie get everything ready for the performance on December 21, just three weeks away.

Never in living memory had there been a pageant in a village schoolhouse. At the convent, yes, but never in the schoolhouse. Even though he hated his part, Ovila couldn't wait: Miss Emilie had asked him so nicely to do it that he couldn't refuse. He was to play the Negro Wise Man. He would have to blacken his face with charcoal. He had tried to dissuade her, but she had insisted, saying, "We can't change history. If the Holy Writ says that one of the Wise Men was a Negro, then the pageant needs a Negro Wise Man."

Emilie was discreet. She didn't want to sit in the Pronovost family pew. It would be better to sit alone and join them at the end of the mass. As was her habit, she sat near the front of the second half of the nave: neither too far forward nor too far back. If she sat too far forward, people might think she was showing off; too far back, they would think she wasn't very pious. In the middle was her place. She liked Father Grenier very much; fortunately, his sermons were interesting. In any case, she would never stay away from mass without a very good reason.

During the offertory, she allowed her mind to wander as she looked at the Pronovost boys. At the consecration, she forgot to bow her head. Returning from communion, she sat in the wrong pew. Finally, she kneeled at the *Ite missa est* instead of standing.

The Pronovosts invited her to join them for Sunday dinner. She happily accepted, eager to enjoy a meal with a family — her last had been the All Saints holiday — and enchanted with the idea of eating food she hadn't prepared herself. She was treated as a special guest by her young students, who waited on her eagerly. Only Ovide and Edmond seemed indifferent to her presence. Ovide talked to his father about the harvest and about money. Emilie had the disagreeable feeling that he was deliberately avoiding her. She could only wonder what she had done to this boy for him to hold her in such contempt.

Finally he turned to her, giving her a full-toothed smile. "Is it true what the kids are saying? That you put big Crête in his place?"

Her jaw dropped. Since the end of October, not a week had passed without someone reminding her of Joachim.

"It seems that you pulled him by the hair . . ."

"By the belt . . ."

". . . then you stuck his head in the trash . . ."

"In the water bucket . . ."

". . . and wiped him off with a rag!"

"The rag part is true. But I didn't wipe him off. Joachim did that all by himself, like a big boy."

Ever since he had heard the reasons for the altercation between

Emilie and Joachim, Ovide had nursed a secret but growing admiration for the fearless little teacher. However, he never let his feelings be known; instead, like all his friends, he made fun of both Joachim and Emilie.

"You must have brothers, Miss, or else you'd never have taken on an icebox like Joachim."

"My brothers are smaller than me."

Dosithée, who had followed his son's line of thought, started to laugh. "Come on, Ovide! Do you think that a schoolmistress like Miss Bordeleau wouldn't know how to defend herself?"

"That's not what I meant to say, Father."

"But that's what you said."

Dosithée smiled at Emilie, and changed the topic of conversation. Ovide found nothing better to do than retreat to a corner of the kitchen, furious with his father for having put him in his place. He started to tap out a rhythm with his foot that everyone in his family recognized. He hummed the tune of his little rhyme for Ovila. The children watched him, holding their breath, afraid that he might be rude enough to put words to the ditty.

Four

EMILIE HADN'T EXPECTED anyone but the parents of her students to attend the Christmas pageant, so she was surprised that a number of families from the village had also come, and that Father Grenier himself was in attendance. The children were very nervous. Even big Ovila showed a few signs of stage fright.

Ever since Emilie had been to the Pronovosts' for dinner, he and his sister Rosée had come in the evenings to help her put the finishing touches on the show. Emilie and Rosée sewed costumes for all of the students, recycling clothes that mothers had consigned to the rag-bag into magnificent angels' robes. Emilie designed the patterns and did the main sewing, while Rosée matched the colours and did the finishing work. As for Ovila, he undertook construction of the sets. In the front left corner of the classroom, there was now a crèche, almost life-sized. Ovila had impressed Emilie with his talent in designing and building the sets; he explained that he liked working with wood.

They had spent at least an hour every evening working. Since the beginning of Advent, two hours during each school day had been used for rehearsal. The students had memorized their parts and practised their songs and speeches. Every morning, they arrived with gunny sacks stuffed with straw for the crèche, so that Emilie didn't have to ask the parents to bring it themselves.

The big night had finally arrived. The parents had been invited for seven o'clock, leaving them enough time to have supper and finish milking the cows. The school was quickly filled with smiling faces and sounds of laughter. Emilie and three of her students, the ushers, seated everyone as comfortably as possible; with such a crowd, the youngest had to sit on the floor. Her students were all hidden. One group was behind the bedspreads doubling as stage curtains, another group was in her quarters on the second floor. They had been told to keep silent, but Emilie heard incessant whispering.

"Hey! Father Grenier is here."

"That's not true! Liar!"

"It is so true! Take a look yourself if you don't believe me!"

From time to time, Emilie went backstage or poked her head up through the trap door to ask them to keep it down. During one of her pleas for quiet, she heard a wave of silence passing from the back of the classroom to the front. She frowned and peeked through the curtain. In a moment she understood: big Joachim Crête had made his entrance, flanked by his parents. Emilie rushed in front of the curtain, praying to heaven that Joachim wouldn't make a shambles of the whole event. She held her breath, composed herself and aimed a friendly smile at him to make it clear that she was in control.

To distract herself, she counted the audience: seventy-seven people. She glanced out the window to see if there were any more sleighs or cutters in sight. Not seeing any, she took all the lamps in the room and and brought them to the front of the curtain. Again, there was silence. She went upstairs to remind the children to be quiet until it was their turn. Little Charlotte was trembling from head to foot. She whispered in Emilie's ear that she had gone to the bathroom, but she thought she had to go again. Emilie reassured her, telling her it was just nerves. She wished good luck to everyone and went back to open the curtain.

The set was met with a great "Ooh!" followed by a burst of

applause. Hearing the response, the children elbowed each other. At Emilie's signal, the members of the chorus, dressed as shepherds, began to sing, placing themselves to the right of the crèche. They lit into "*Venez divin Messie*" with such enthusiasm that they forced their voices off-key. She stopped them immediately, gave them their note, and they started again without any mistakes. Emilie smiled her satisfaction. When they finished the song, the children withdrew like true shepherds, leaning on their staffs and following an invisible herd of sheep. The audience applauded, stopping only when they saw Joseph and Mary make their entrance.

"Aaah! I can go no farther Joseph. I believe it is time for my child to come. We must find shelter since the cold and the night are coming quickly."

"Rest here Mary while I go to the inn to ask for shelter."

Joseph sat Mary down on a bale of hay and left the stage. It was so quiet you could almost hear the fluttering of eyelashes. Emilie signalled Joseph that he could enter.

"Alas . . . alas! There is not a single room for us. We must go to the valley."

Father Grenier pretended to cough to cover his laughter, then took out a handkerchief and wiped his eyes.

"Oh my poor child will be born without a roof over his head."

"Don't worry Mary we . . . uh . . . we . . ."

Joseph, desperate, turned toward Emilie. "We what?" he pleaded.

"We have God . . ." Emilie prompted.

"Oh, yeah . . . We have God in our hearts and our faith will lead us to the place He has chosen for the birth of His son."

Joseph helped Mary up, and together they walked to the centre of the crèche.

"I believe we shall lie down here my husband since the child wants to be born."

Mary turned her back to the audience, pulled out the cushion that had swollen her belly, dropped it in the straw and picked up the swaddled doll hidden in the manger. She cradled it in her arms and turned back to the audience.

"It's a boy, Joseph. We shall call him Emmanuel."

Father Grenier wiped his eyes again. Mary moved behind the manger and put down her baby while Joseph knelt down.

"He's so small Mary."

"Yes but one day he will be big."

The shepherds returned to the front of the crèche, singing "*Il est né le Divin Enfant.*" This time, they got the right note. As they sang, a star, dangling by a ring, slid slowly along a string stretched from the back of the class to a corner of the roof of the crèche. The Wise Men (none other than the ushers) entered from the rear of the room and made their way through the audience to the crèche. They never took their eyes off the star, but excused themselves each time they had to move someone or stepped on a hand or a foot. Father Grenier dabbed at his eyes yet again. The shepherds exited and the Wise Men fell to their knees before the manger.

"Oh, my King," the first said, "I have brought you incense."

The second Wise Man looked at him, stunned. *He* was supposed to offer the incense. "Oh, my King," he continued, "I have brought you *gold.*" He shot a look at the first Wise Man, trying to make it clear that he had gotten him out of a mess.

"Oh, my King," the third Wise Man finished, "I have brought you myrrh."

The audience, already impressed by the arrival of the Wise Men and the appearance of the star, were even more so when they saw the angels descend from the second floor performing "Silent Night" in soprano and alto parts — singing almost as beautifully as the parish choir. Spontaneously, the parents lifted their voices to accompany the children. Even Father Grenier put away his handkerchief and joined in enthusiastically. The last notes were buried under clapping and whistles. The children bowed, red-cheeked and smiling. The applause doubled. They bowed even lower.

Emilie pulled the bedspreads closed and calmed those who wanted to continue their curtain calls, reminding them that they had to get ready for the speeches. Carried away by their success, the children had completely forgotten about the second half of the show. They panicked, sure that they had forgotten every word. Emilie told them to do their best. She pulled back the curtain and introduced the first student, who came forward and began his speech about St. Nicholas and Christmas presents. The second child followed, speaking of the poor who were hungry and cold but rejoiced in their faith.

When the speeches were over, Emilie, bursting with pride, invited all of her students to take another bow. They didn't have to be asked twice, and they were even shoving each other a little to get to the front. Father Grenier stood up. He congratulated then blessed all the children — except Charlotte, who had quietly left — thanking them in the name of the Son of God for the magnificent work they had accomplished. When he sat down, one of the commissioners stood up in his turn, went to the front of the room — which Father Grenier had not done — and asked Emilie to join him.

"When one is a commissioner, one is given certain pieces of information. In this particular case, I told what I know to my boy so that he could pass it on to the students. If you'll permit me now, Miss Bordeleau, I will let them have the floor."

Emilie was stunned to see the children gather in front of Eva. In unison they proclaimed "Happy Birthday!" Charlotte gave her a bouquet of artificial flowers that the children had made with paper, wire and dried seeds. Emilie took them, gave the children a warm look and turned toward the parents. Obviously, she was the only one who hadn't known the secret. Both children and adults erupted in gales of laughter. Emilie thanked them all, then burst into tears. She wiped her eyes, furious with herself, blamed her lack of self-control on exhaustion and emotion and invited everyone to enjoy the cakes that the children had made themselves on the schoolhouse stove.

The evening finished in euphoria. Emilie had but one regret: no one from her family had been there.

*E*milie had great difficulty getting to sleep. She went over the evening's events, mentally correcting each of the small mistakes. She smiled, hummed, happily punched her pillow and tried to get comfortable, smoothing her sheets twenty times. She was jubilant. And the most satisfying part was this feeling of belonging to the community of Saint-Tite, which had come so easily.

Even when Joachim had arrived, it was her reaction that people had looked to, not his.

Finally, sleep evened out her breathing and smoothed her brow. Unresisting, she let herself be taken by the master of dreams to where she bowed and smiled before a delirious crowd and had a long discussion with one of the Wise Men over the colour of his skin, while Charlotte glowed with joy and told her that she hadn't missed the flowers. Then Emilie was plunged into a nightmare. The straw of the crèche caught fire, and the Infant Jesus knocked with all His strength against the sides of the manger for someone to come and rescue him. He knocked . . . and knocked . . . and was still knocking when Emilie, realizing that she couldn't save him, with her limbs paralyzed and her voice silenced, woke up with a start. The crash of a fallen icicle confused her for a few seconds; it sounded like a crackling fire.

The illusion vanished when she became aware that someone was knocking at the door of the schoolhouse. She looked at the time. It was only six o'clock. Nerves jangled, she buttoned her housecoat crooked and forgot to put on her slippers. She went downstairs more anxious than distressed, noticing as her feet hit the floor of the classroom that it was icy cold, and ran hopping to the door, afraid of freezing her feet.

"Yes?"

"It's Fred Gélinas, Miss. I have a message for you."

She opened the door wide enough for Mr. Gélinas to enter, then quickly closed it against the wind, which billowed under her nightshirt.

"What is it?"

"Well, my brother-in-law's just come from Saint-Séverin. Your father had a little accident last night, and he spent the night in the snow with his mare. My brother-in-law found him this morning at the edge of the village and took him to your cousin's to get some colour back in his nose and his cheeks. Your father is fine, but he asked me to tell you that one of the blades on his cutter is broken. He'll come and get you as soon as he can."

"What was my father doing in Saint-Séverin last night?"

"Well, it seems he wanted to surprise you by coming to your

show." Gélinas stepped toward the door and put his toque back on. "Anyway, I won't disturb you any longer."

Emilie thanked him and slowly went back upstairs, sad to think that the previous evening she had felt sorry that no one from her family had thought to come to her show. She was concerned about her father's health, and hoped that the frostbite wasn't serious.

She couldn't get back to sleep, so she decided to make herself a nice cup of tea, but before going back downstairs, she put on a big pair of thick wool socks. When she saw the state of the classroom, she was momentarily discouraged. Hay on the floor stuck to her socks, the crèche had to be taken apart, there were dirty plates to wash, desks to put back in place — all in all, a day of cleaning up ahead.

Normally, she would have left Saint-Tite around two o'clock. Now she didn't know when she would leave, and for the first time since September she had a sharp sense of impotence. If only she had a horse and sleigh, she wouldn't be at the mercy of the fates. She looked at the four walls around her and had the unpleasant feeling that they were closing in on her. She chased the sensation from her mind.

After chewing on a heel of bread, she got dressed, put on an apron and covered her head with a kerchief to keep the dust from getting in her hair. She contemplated all the work ahead of her, sighed, then got down to business.

She'd worked for five hours when she realized that she had only enough provisions to last two days. There was lots of jam and pickles, but not a speck of flour or sugar — nothing with which to make a loaf of bread. She abandoned her cleaning, took off her apron and kerchief, put on her warmest overclothes and set out for the village to buy some food. Four miles to walk in air so cold it burned the lungs.

Her step was determined. She had underestimated the wind; in spite of her efforts to protect her neck, it crept down her collar, sending torturous shivers right down to her backside. By the time she finally reached the bridge, she didn't have the energy to take another step. Gathering her courage, she knocked at the door of the Rouleau home.

The women of the house hurried to make her a hot drink. The fire in the stove and the cheery welcome warmed Emilie up in no time at all. The Rouleaus offered her the provisions she needed so that she wouldn't have to go all the way to the village and, in a surfeit of kindness, hitched up their horse to drive her back to the schoolhouse. She didn't know how to thank them for such generosity.

"Don't thank us. It's we who should thank you for the lovely crèche last night. We don't have time to warm the bricks, but for just two miles a good fur should be enough."

The horse headed along the road to the top of the slope and climbed the hill without too much fuss. They were almost at the school when, from out of nowhere, one of the Pronovosts' dogs leapt out and attacked the back legs of the horse, managing to get a good bite of its hock. Dieudonné Rouleau couldn't calm the terrified beast. It went completely out of control and swerved, overturning the cutter in the ditch. Emilie was stuck under one of the blades. She teetered between laughter and tears but, thinking of her father, let laughter win. It was the best laugh she'd had in weeks.

"It's a good thing you're not hurt," said Mr. Rouleau as he got up. "I'll go ask Dosithée for help. Hold on, we'll straighten things out in a minute."

Flat on her belly, nose in the snow, she didn't see them coming. She was still laughing at her misfortune when she heard Mr. Pronovost asking Ovide to hitch up a horse to pull out the cutter. She called out that she wasn't hurt, but she couldn't wait to be rescued from her prone position, if for no other reason than to wipe away the icy water that was running down her back. In a few minutes, she was freed, thanks to the handsome stallion she had not seen since the previous October, when he had serenaded her father's mare.

"Does that beautiful horse belong to you, Mr. Pronovost?"

"Yes and no. In fact, I bought him for Ovide and Edmond."

"Oh . . . anyway, I've never seen such a handsome animal."

"Which one? Ovide or Edmond?"

Taken aback, Emilie didn't know what to say. Dosithée laughed to himself. As he talked about the horse, he drove her to the house.

Emilie was embarrassed as she once again recounted the day's misadventures. Mr. Rouleau said that if he had known she was born under a bad star, he would never have offered her a ride. Emilie hesitated before laughing at this jibe, unable to tell if he was serious or not.

After a good hot cup of tea, she thanked the Pronovosts and asked them all to excuse her, since she had to go back and finish the work awaiting her at the schoolhouse. Mr. Pronovost asked Emilie's pupils if they would mind using one day of their holiday to help her. They didn't need to be persuaded; together they finished the big clean-up she had started.

The classroom was sparkling in record time, and Emilie's good mood returned. She watched the children, who were down on all fours engaged in the "pieces of straw contest." In fact, even after the place was swept three times, bits of straw were still stuck between the floorboards. Armed with hatpins from Emilie's "fineries box," the children dislodged them one by one, as happy each time they succeeded as if they had caught the first catfish of spring.

"Miss," Rosée joked, "don't you think this is all backwards?"

"What do you mean?"

"Well, usually you look for a needle in a haystack, but we're looking for hay with a needle!"

Emilie burst out laughing. She loved word games. She was still smiling when Mr. Pronovost showed up at the schoolhouse. Suddenly aware of the time, Emilie was full of excuses the moment he walked in the door.

"We were having so much fun, I completely forgot that it's chore time."

"There's no problem, my dear lady" — the children blushed at this familiarity — "but that's not why I'm here."

Without waiting to be invited, he took off his hat, unbuttoned his coat and sat at one of the desks. Emilie offered him a cup of tea, but he politely refused.

"Do you think that your father will fix his sleigh in time to come and get you?"

"Oh, yes! A little thing like that would never stop him. I imagine he'll be here by dinnertime. We should be home before midnight, for sure. But why do you ask?"

"My wife and I thought you might want to visit with us while you wait."

"Thank you, but I'd rather stay here."

The children also tried to convince Emilie to accept their father's offer, but she wouldn't budge. Once it was clear that the discussion was over, Dosithée asked his children to get ready to go. They obeyed, even though they would have preferred to stay at the school a while longer. Emilie saw them to the door, thanked them for their kindness and wished them a merry Christmas, adding that they'd better rest up before the second term began.

When they left, she went upstairs, wiping a tear from her eye, and went to the window. In spite of the dark night, she could distinguish their silhouettes. She parted the curtains a little and watched them playing around in the snow. Now her cheeks were wet. What she would have given to be out having fun with them . . .

Emilie knew that, since September, she had been wearing the mantle of adulthood on her person and on her soul. That mantle was weighing heavy right now; her youth and her need for carefree times were knocking at the door of her heart. But here in Saint-Tite, her heart had no one to open up to. Here in Saint-Tite, she had to be serious, adult, a lady. She wiped her eyes and nose on the back of her hand. Like a child.

She couldn't eat a single bite, so preoccupied was she with the imminent arrival of her father. At seven o'clock, she still couldn't see anything on the road. At eight o'clock, she decided to interrupt her vigil and read a page of the dictionary. By chance, she fell upon the word "desolation." She wept inconsolably. At nine o'clock, she resigned herself to opening her suitcase and taking out a nightgown. She sniffed it and grimaced — she had neglected to separate it from the dirty laundry. She couldn't bring herself to put it on, and so she decided to sleep in her underclothes. When she went to bed, she put three handkerchiefs under her pillow.

*D*ecember 23 sneaked into Emilie's life whispering winter from every window of the schoolhouse. When she opened her eyes, although they were still clouded with sleep, she saw that it was blowing snow outside. She sighed as she got up and washed, furious with herself. What with the misery that had overtaken her the previous evening, she had neglected to feed the stove. She shivered as she washed up, then hurried to pull on her petticoat and dress, covering her shoulders with a heavy wool shawl she had crocheted.

Sitting in front of her mirror, she started to roll her long, rebellious auburn hair into a bun, the way she had been wearing it since she started teaching. But then her thoughts of the evening before resurfaced, and she pulled it down almost angrily and started to make braids — simple "Indian braids," as her father would have said. She was amused. To emphasize this youthful look, she made two enormous bows with white ribbon at the end of each plait. Cheered up, she went down to the classroom and stuffed the stove full of wood, although she soon regretted this rash move. If her father was to arrive, they wouldn't be able to leave until the logs were reduced to coals, which would take a few hours with the amount she had crammed in. Her father would never forgive her such a delay.

The stove roared. She opened the damper to accelerate the burning. The fire raged, and the stovepipe was choked with smoke. Frightened, she closed the damper. Now the stove settled down and purred. She put water to boil for tea while she tried to calm down. Then she went back up to her room to eat what little she could find — she had not, the previous evening, made bread as she had intended — and fume because she didn't yet have a stove on the second floor. It wasn't fair that she had to run up and down the stairs whenever she wanted to eat. And she used much more wood this way, because she had to heat both the classroom and her own quarters. With a second stove, she would heat the upstairs and cook there as well, using the first stove just to keep the dampness out of the classroom. She promised herself to write yet again to the commissioners asking when they planned to install one, as they had agreed. It bothered her to have to do this; she didn't want to give the impression that she was a complainer.

The sun had long ago finished its climb to its winter summit, and it stopped to catch its breath before beginning its descent. Emilie was glued to her rocking chair, her nose practically stuck to the window. Every five minutes, she scratched away the newly crystallized frost and looked down the village road. There was nothing on the horizon, which was obscured by blowing snow. She sat down again, sighing. From time to time, she reluctantly got up and put another log in the stove, each time telling herself that this was the last.

At two in the afternoon, there was a knock on the door. She knew that it wasn't her father, but she was surprised to see Edmond Pronovost standing on the porch.

"I'm supposed to come and heat the place while you're away. Except we thought you'd gone this morning. Hasn't your father come yet?"

She invited him in. He declined, waved and promised to come and feed the stove morning and evening.

❁

"Good God, Edmond," Dosithée said, "you did that fast." "Miss Emilie was there. Her father hasn't come yet," Edmond replied.

Dosithée frowned. He thought he had seen her leave early that morning with her father. The blowing snow had kept him from making out the passengers in the sleigh, which he had assumed belonged to Mr. Bordeleau.

He looked at the time and clucked his tongue. If he were Mr. Bordeleau, it certainly would worry him to know that his daughter was alone in a little schoolhouse lost on a windswept country road. He looked at Félicité and raised his eyebrows, pursing his lips. Catching her eye, he shrugged and nodded toward the school. Félicité, peeling potatoes, made a sign with her hand indicating that she didn't know what to do. Then he looked at Ovide, who was busy repairing a bridle, and smiled.

"Ovide, get out the warming bricks. Your mother wants us to go to Saint-Stanislas to see her cousin."

Félicité smiled at the lame excuse her husband had invented. As for Ovide, he continued to work and asked, without looking up, why his father wanted to go to Saint-Stanislas. Ovila, who had figured it out, offered to accompany his father if Ovide didn't want to. Dosithée replied that two men were needed to make the trip. Ovila was mortified and took refuge in silence, but he couldn't escape Ovide's mocking look and his comment that he should wait a few more years and grow himself a nice moustache like his before claiming to be a man.

"A pitiful moustache, sure," Ovila grumbled.

Dosithée decided to put an end to the argument between his sons before it turned into a fight.

"Get moving, Ovide. Either you come, or I'll take Edmond."

Ovide sighed, got up and agreed with very poor grace to accompany his father, reproaching him in front of the entire family for always being flat on his belly before the schoolmistress, and even asking him if he did it so his children would get better marks.

Dosithée raised his voice. "If you're just going to make stupid remarks, I'd rather not take you along."

Knowing the threat was serious, Ovide put on his coat and went to harness the stallion to the little cutter. He thought that it would be better not to take the sleigh, which was too heavy to steer in the powdery snow. Ovila got out the warming bricks, and Félicité asked the girls to prepare a "just in case" food basket. In no more than half an hour, father and son were ready to go.

Félicité took her husband aside and reminded him to be careful. It wasn't his decision to drive the little schoolmistress to Saint-Stanislas in such bad weather that she was thinking of, and Dosithée guessed what she didn't dare say.

"If it was our Rosée who was stuck, wouldn't you like it if someone brought her home?" he asked.

Félicité smiled at him. Yes, she understood. Her only fear, the one she would never admit, was the gossip. People would surely notice the eagerness with which the Pronovosts had come to Emilie's aid. She didn't like that. She worried that wagging tongues would start to say Dosithée was trying to marry off his oldest son — and that was indeed what he was trying to do, she was certain. In fact, she did not disapprove. She liked the young teacher, with her pleasant, joyful character, and she liked how she led her classes, and how her nimble fingers could transform the humblest rag into an angel's robe. She liked her looks: she was tall, taller than most of the girls in Saint-Tite, and she carried her head, with its crown of long, thick hair, proudly.

Ovila ran out of the house carrying a pile of covers just as his father and brother were urging the stallion on. His mother, he said, was worried that the biting cold would get even worse by nightfall. Dosithée took the covers and thanked him, even while he scolded him for leaving the house without his coat. Ovila raced back inside. Ovide, upper lip curled and nostrils pinched, gave his father a sceptical look.

Dosithée laughed. "What did you want Ovila to say? He couldn't very well say that he was worried about the health of his beloved schoolmistress."

$\mathscr{E}$milie hated the position she was in. She was sitting between father and son, embarrassed and uncomfortable to be taking charity once again — though happy to be going home at last. The sky was overcast, and the wind had died the moment the sun set, as it often did. The weather had turned mild, so they took off one of the three covers that protected them. Dosithée and Ovide discussed all the details of a wood-cutting contract they were hoping to win after the holidays. Out of politeness, Emilie felt that she should follow the conversation.

They stopped at Saint-Séverin to ask whether Mr. Bordeleau had passed and learned that he had gone back home to get a new harness, and no one had seen him since. They hadn't left the village far behind, though, when they saw a sleigh lantern.

Emilie sat forward on her seat, her back straight, trying to see where the sleigh was going. "That's my father! My father and my uncle!"

Dosithée stopped his cutter and Ovide got up to let Emilie down. She jumped to the ground, suddenly full of energy. She went to the centre of the road, waving her arms and yelling. Caleb stopped.

"Can you tell me, Emilie, what you are doing here in the middle of the road barking like a dog on a leash?" he yelled back.

Before she had time to respond, Ovide was behind her carrying her luggage, followed by Dosithée. Emilie hurriedly made introductions. The two fathers clumsily shook hands, though it was too cold to take off their thick mittens.

Caleb thanked the Pronovost men profusely and said how happy he was that his daughter had such good neighbours. He asked if she had got his message, then invited the Pronovosts to come and get a good night's sleep at Saint-Stanislas. Dosithée declined; he preferred to go back to Saint-Tite right away so that his wife wouldn't worry unnecessarily. Ovide wanted to accept the invitation, but his father was having none of it. The entire conversation lasted only a couple of minutes, and soon Dosithée had turned his rig around, following Caleb's directions.

Once the cutter was facing toward home, Caleb supervised his brother's driving. The road was narrow, and he was worried that the sleigh would end up in the ditch. As a precaution, Dosithée waited until Caleb's sleigh was well placed on the road before waving and wishing them a merry Christmas.

Emilie turned only once to wave. She was concentrating on the road in front of her. If she had been unusually quiet since Saint-Tite, she made up for it now, first finding out about the accident, then telling her father and uncle about everything that had happened since the beginning of November. Caleb was entertained by her stories and happy to hear that she had solved the problem of big Joachim Crête. Emilie said she still had great difficulty accepting his behaviour toward her, and added that she would never forgive herself for having treated the boy so violently.

"Life is full of surprises," Caleb said, slowly. "Some are nicer than others. One of the worst is finding out that you don't know yourself as well as you thought."

Caleb asked his daughter if she recalled the scene they had had about sitting the girls at the table. She remembered it only too well. Then, in a confidential tone even his brother couldn't hear, Caleb told Emilie that he had seen himself in a new light that evening, and he hadn't liked what he saw. She took his arm and held it very tightly. He said that now that she was seventeen, she could understand. Emilie hugged him, laughing.

"I thought you'd forgotten my birthday."

He patted her cheek. "Did you really think that a father could forget his first child's birthday?"

"No, but sometimes you're so absent-minded . . ."

"You may be right. Anyway, your mother will think so when she sees the sleigh. She'll think I forgot to go get you."

The two of them laughed at this family joke. Caleb was indeed absent-minded from time to time. His greatest blunder, the one that he still paid for at family get-togethers, was the time he'd forgotten Célina in the village. He had left her at the general store, and while she was shopping he had gone to the church to light a candle in memory of his mother. After talking to the priest, he went home, completely forgetting his wife. He unhitched the mare, put the buggy away in the barn and went inside. Not seeing Célina, he asked where she was. The children looked at him, incredulous, then reminded him that she had gone with him. Caleb leapt up, ran to hitch up the mare and hurried off to the village. The merchant at the general store sighed with relief when Caleb came in.

"Where were you? Your wife's been waiting for you for more than an hour! We thought we saw you going by the store a while ago. We thought you were going all the way to the coast!"

Caleb went to get his wife. Célina, sitting in the back room, was clutching her purchases on her knee and fuming. She stared daggers at him, sprang to her feet, left the store with her head in the air, climbed into the buggy and sat without putting down her bags. She dryly refused all his attempts to help. They started out.

"Caleb Bordeleau, you fool," she said at last, "can you tell me what took you such a long time? I suppose you were off gossiping. Did you think it'd take me two hours to buy flour, sugar and soap?"

Caleb tried to hold back his spasms of laughter by closing his eyes, but his shoulders were shaking with hilarity.

"Ha! And you find it funny to keep me waiting like a turkey! You have no respect, as God is my witness!"

She didn't open her mouth again until they got home, when the children met them with gales of laughter.

"My good Lord, Caleb, it looks like the children are laughing at me!"

Caleb finally let his own laughter explode as the children rushed to tell their mother what had happened. At first Célina didn't believe them. But knowing that they couldn't be lying, she brightened up and laughed as well.

"That's the silliest thing I've ever heard! The absolute end! To forget your wife because you're thinking too hard. Caleb Bordeleau, I will remember this. And believe me, you haven't heard the end of it!"

That night, they were still laughing at bedtime: Caleb, at the scope of his absent-mindedness; Célina, at seeing him have such a good laugh.

Five

JANUARY GAVE EMILIE NO RESPITE: the bitter cold obliged her to get up each night to heat the schoolhouse, which was buffeted incessantly by the wind. She would have been able to bear it more easily had she not been afflicted with a terrible cold, which made her feverish and impatient. The children, not used to seeing her so irritable, became nervous, which made her even harder on them. Finally, at the beginning of February, she was able to iron and put away her handkerchiefs. She regained her health just as winter called a truce.

February was dressed in sunshine. The earth, believing spring had come, shed its thick layer of snow. The farmers feared a bad year for maple sugar, but they optimistically predicted that March would bring back the cold weather.

March was coming tomorrow. Emilie explained to the children that 1896 was a leap year, because it had a twenty-ninth of February. The children asked if the extra day meant that Christmas would come on December 24. Emilie was just about to relate the history of the calendar when Lazare Pronovost cried out, clutched his desk, went as stiff as an iron bar and toppled backwards, his chair under him and his desk above. Emilie thought it was a joke until she saw the Pronovost children move into action. Ovila and Eva righted the desk, Emile the chair. Rosée took a book and tried to force it into Lazare's mouth.

Lazare was arched like a bridge, his face was contorted, and he was groaning horribly. Some of the children began shrieking. The first-graders ran to hide behind Emilie, and she had to force them to let go of her as she moved closer to Lazare.

His body had begun to leap in place, moved by a force such as she had never seen. His lips contorted, and he began to foam at the mouth. Drool ran down his chin. Rosée took a handkerchief and tried to wipe up his saliva. Ovila told the children to move away, which they did readily enough. Some of the small ones started to cry. Charlotte ran to the back of the classroom, grabbed her coat and left the schoolhouse.

One of the seventh-graders began to exhort the children to ward off the devil that had taken over Lazare's body. Emilie vaguely heard "Hail Mary" and "Get thee from me, Satan," but she didn't intervene. She was mesmerized by the sight of Lazare, and had absolutely no idea what to do. Emile, the youngest Pronovost, started to shout at the other students that his brother was not a devil. He shook his fist and gave a violent kick at fat Marie, who was calling on all the saints in heaven to protect her.

Emilie finally got hold of herself. She went to stop Emile and told the children to be quiet. In a nervous but authoritative tone, she asked them all to go upstairs. Then, when the last child had disappeared through the trap door, she turned back to the Pronovost children.

To her great surprise, Lazare was now sitting up. His face was ashen and he seemed exhausted. Emilie was afraid to approach him, fearing that the scene would start again. Ovila was rubbing his brother's neck, and Rosée was wiping his face. Except for Lazare, all of the Pronovost children were looking at Emilie, waiting for her to say something.

Emilie asked Ovila to take his brother upstairs. The moment she said this, however, she realized the absurdity of it: all the other children were upstairs. She went to the foot of the stairs and asked them to come down, without jostling. Meanwhile, Lazare, hanging onto Ovila's neck, was trying to stand up. Once he was on his feet, he let himself be led to the stairs.

Two little first-grade pupils had not had time to descend by the time Lazare began to climb the stairs. They turned, let out cries of mortal fear and ran to hide. It was a ridiculous scene: Emilie urged the terrified children to come down, and in response they screamed themselves hoarse. Lazare paled visibly. She grabbed the two children and took them downstairs, one under each arm, depositing them on the classroom floor. The Pronovost children had meanwhile begun to climb the stairs, wounded by the disdainful, horrified and disgusted looks of their classmates. Rubbing her right shin, fat Marie kept her eyes closed and again implored the saints to deliver her from evil.

Disorder reigned in the classroom. Eva and Rosée, quietly weeping, began to tidy things up. Emilie looked at the time and dismissed anyone who wanted to go home. Only the Pronovosts and Charlotte remained. The latter, her jacket on, stayed sitting on the bottom stair, gazing up toward the second floor.

"Why are you still here, Charlotte?" Emilie asked quietly.

"I want to see Lazare — to make sure he's still alive."

"Come with me, we'll go see him," Emilie said, taking her hand.

Lazare was lying on the bed, still flushed, and Ovila silently indicated that he was sleeping. Emilie nodded and took Charlotte back down to the classroom.

"Are you sure he's asleep, Miss?" Charlotte asked.

"Yes, Charlotte, absolutely."

Charlotte went out again, but a few minutes later she returned, looking more cheerful. She told Emilie that Lazare must have died, but like his namesake, Lazarus, risen to life again.

Emilie was surprised at this remark, but she told Charlotte she must be right.

Charlotte left, for good this time, light-hearted.

The Pronovost children had cleaned up the classroom. Rosée went upstairs and asked her brothers and Eva to go for help. They left the school, shaken and upset. Emilie took a long breath before going back upstairs.

Rosée smiled at her. "I know it's scary, Miss, but it's not serious. It's the *grand mal*."

"That's what I thought, but I'd never seen it so I wasn't sure. I didn't know that Lazare suffers from *grand mal*."

"My parents didn't tell you?" Emilie shook her head. "I guess because he hasn't had a fit for three years. We thought he was cured."

The two sat beside the bed. Emilie felt like they were holding a wake. She made sure that Lazare was breathing, then her thoughts overwhelmed her and she saw again the horrible scene she had just witnessed. Trying to stay calm, she got up quickly, took down her hand bowl from the hall and ran downstairs. She just had time to reach the bottom step before she vomited up all the fear she had in her stomach.

She was rinsing her bowl by the time Ovila arrived with his father and Ovide to take Lazare home. Dosithée understood Emilie's discomfort. She tried to cover her embarrassment as she escorted Mr. Pronovost and his two sons to Lazare's bedside. Rosée was still sitting near her brother, who had just woken up. She explained to him that he was still at school and everything was all right. As she told the others, Lazare got upset when he came to in a strange place.

"Well now, my boy! Seems you gave everyone a good scare!" Mr. Pronovost was talking a little too loudly. Lazare tried to smile, but his face twisted and he began to cry.

"Come on now, don't cry," Mr. Pronovost said. "Everything was fine for three years. You should be fine for another three years now. Calm down. Ovide and me, we'll make a chair and carry you home."

"I can walk by myself!"

"But I think it would be better if you let us carry you like a king. Tomorrow you'll walk and run as much as you like. Today, we're taking care of you."

He backed up his words with a discreet signal to Ovide to lift the child, and a gesture to Rosée to cover him with one of the blankets they had brought. Dosithée and Ovide took him downstairs, while Ovila picked up his coat and boots. Emilie walked beside them, feeling useless. It didn't even occur to her to open the door. She could think of nothing to say or do. When Lazare said goodbye to her, she didn't react. Ovide wouldn't look at her. Dosithée murmured some words of thanks.

When she closed the door behind them, Emilie ran to vomit a second time. Then she rinsed her mouth, dipped her handkerchief in the icy water and went upstairs to lie down. But the minute she saw the bed, she couldn't go near it, so she sat in her rocking chair. She put a cushion behind her head, placed the handkerchief on her brow and closed her eyes. She breathed very deeply, trying to suppress a new wave of nausea.

Sunlight was no longer washing in through the windows by the time she began to feel revived. She decided to drink some warm broth, but her stomach rebelled. When it settled a little, she lit a lamp and tried, in vain, to clear her mind by reading her dictionary. She tried to find an explanation for Lazare's problem under "*grand*" and then under "*mal*," but she didn't find anything. She got up, looked out the window and saw a light in the Pronovosts' barn. Then she went down to the classroom, arranged some papers, opened and closed some drawers without knowing what she was looking for and went back to the window.

Now the barn was dark. Emilie looked at the time: six-thirty. The Pronovosts must be eating supper. Convincing herself that she was hungry, she chewed on a crust of bread and managed to keep it down. Pacing back and forth, she wondered what she could do to fill this evening. She didn't want to read. She didn't want to think. She didn't want to be alone. She went to the coatrack, put on her overshoes, wrapped herself in her coat and shawl and went outside.

The cold was less harsh now, it seemed. She looked down the road to the left and the right and decided to walk to the left, avoiding the Pronovost house. The snow squeaked under her boots and she could hear that she was walking slowly and dragging her feet, so she picked up her pace. It was fifteen minutes before she realized that this was the first time since September that she had gone out like this, for no particular reason — without errands to run, without a mass to attend. She looked around, took a breath of fresh air and turned back.

Arriving back at the school, she saw that there were lights on at the Pronovosts' and headed over. She knocked softly, almost hoping no one would hear. But someone did.

"Good evening, Miss. Come in."

"Good evening, Ovide. I just wanted to find out how Lazare is."

"Come in anyway. We can't stand here with the door open."

She entered but didn't take off her coat. Rosée waved and smiled at her. Emile was busy with his homework. Ovila was whittling a bit of wood. Everything seemed normal, and yet Emilie saw a sad look in the parents' eyes that she had never noticed before.

Félicité came over. "I don't think Lazare will be at school tomorrow."

"That's not why I came. I just wanted to tell you to let me know if you need any help." She felt a little ridiculous, knowing that she didn't have much to offer — she hadn't even been able to open the door when they had left the school. "Well, I'd better get going if I'm going to be in any shape to teach tomorrow."

"Thank you, Miss," Dosithée said, not getting up to see her out.

Emilie was hurt. Ovila dropped his bit of wood and hurried to render the courtesy his father had neglected. Emilie thanked him, waved once more to everyone and left. The minute the door closed behind her, she burst into tears. Why were they angry at her?

Back in her schoolhouse, she blew her nose, wiped her eyes and decided to go to bed, although she didn't feel the least bit sleepy. Only hours of tossing and turning could possibly await her.

*E*milie threw back her covers and leapt out of bed. She had tried in vain to sleep there, but she kept smelling Lazare's odour, the odour of sickness. She wrapped herself in her housecoat and began, for the hundredth time, to relive the events of the day. Wearily, desperately, she searched for sleep, but each time she was about to sink into its depths she jumped, and her wide-awake mind fought off the drowsiness. She got up again and again, each time putting yet another useless log in the stove. The Pronovost house was lost in the night shadows.

To her despair, she saw the sky lightening with dawn. Already! A sleepless night, completely sleepless. The first one ever filled with thoughts and not with rejoicing, like at Christmas. She felt weak. How would she teach today? She started washing, trying to wipe away the traces of insomnia and worry. She was happy to find that her appetite had returned, so she could gather some strength. She inspected the classroom to make sure that no trace of the previous day's events would frighten the children. Everything was impeccable by the time she heard the children's laughs and cries announcing the new day, the new month.

At morning prayers, she asked the children to say a special word for Lazare so that he would soon return to school. Charlotte closed her eyes. At recess, Emilie heard fat Marie say that she had refused to pray for Lazare to return — she was scared that the demons would return with him. Emilie took her aside and asked her to go into the schoolhouse to reflect on what she had just said. Marie said that she knew she wasn't the only one who had kept her eyes open — she had counted several during prayers. Emilie insisted that she go inside but she refused, threatening to tell her parents that Emilie was invoking the devil . . . Emilie lost patience and pulled her by the ear. Marie cried like a stuck pig and, instead of going into the schoolhouse, ran off toward home. Emilie refused to follow her, or to implore her to come back.

To brighten the darkness that had fallen over her class, Emilie announced that the entire afternoon would be for drawing. The children left the classroom for lunch, squabbling as usual.

Emilie was relieved that only four pupils were staying at school to eat lunch. She had noticed soon after she started teaching that these children were playing in the fields instead of going home to eat. When she asked the priest about this, he told her that if they didn't go home, it was because there was usually nothing to eat there. Without asking the commissioners' permission, Emilie had begun to make thick soups, full of big chunks of marrow and vegetables, to serve to the children. They had promised not to say anything about this new custom, and it seemed that they had kept their word, since she had never had a complaint.

She was serving the usual portions of soup when Marie and her parents came into the classroom.

"Mr. and Mrs. Lebrun, can I help you with something?"

"You little hellion," Mrs. Lebrun cried. "What right do you have to punish my child?"

Emilie motioned for the four children to leave the schoolhouse. "I asked Marie to reflect on charity, that's all."

"That's not true," Marie said, crying. "You said nothing to keep the devil from entering the classroom. You hit me right on the face because I told you I didn't want the devil to come back."

"Marie, I prayed for Lazare to get better. I asked you to do the same thing."

"The *grand mal*, little girl," said Mrs. Lebrun in an unpleasant tone, "is the devil's work!"

"You are a strange schoolmistress," Mr. Lebrun added. "You hit my daughter to make her think of charity?"

"That is not at all what happened — " Emilie began, when Mr. Lebrun flushed red and slapped her.

She was astounded. She had never been slapped since her memorable set-to with her father. Though she was enraged, she didn't react.

"So? Are you thinking about charity now?"

Mr. Lebrun's icy cynicism made her fume. She tried to control herself, though she saw Marie smile through her tears. She rubbed her cheek, trying to find a response to such a flat challenge.

"Marie lacked charity toward Lazare. Lazare is not responsible. Marie scared everyone with her stories about the devil."

"They are not stories!" Mrs. Lebrun cried. "It's not the first time that we've had people like Lazare Pronovost in the parish. Usually, when we see a *grand mal* fit, we bring holy water, then we give the person a good shaking, and I promise you, his spirits come back quick."

"It's surprising indeed that a schoolmistress doesn't have holy water in her classroom, especially when she knows that one of her students is visited by the devil from time to time," Mr. Lebrun added.

"Well . . . I didn't know until yesterday," Emilie pleaded, immediately furious with herself for having fallen into such an obvious trap.

Mrs. Lebrun gave Marie a handkerchief. The girl was still crying, saying that she never wanted to come back to this demon-filled school. Mr. Lebrun patted his daughter's cheek, telling her he would take care of it.

He turned back to Emilie. "You, little girl, you would do well to begin thinking of finding a new school, because I'm going to see to things. A seventeen-year-old schoolmistress who shows off, who fights with big boys like Joachim Crête, who insults the priest and the convent nuns by making a Christmas crèche almost bigger than the parish's, who feeds children when they are supposed to eat at home — we've just seen you do it — who walks all alone at night — we saw you yesterday — to meet who knows who. We don't need schoolmistresses like that. In fact, I'm going to see the commissioners right now to discuss your case. Good day."

He put his hat on and pushed his wife and daughter to the door. Marie was now weeping copiously, suddenly aware that Emilie did not deserve all the accusations Mr. Lebrun had heaped on her. She had always liked Emilie . . . until Lazare's fit, until she had pulled her ear.

Mr. Lebrun slammed the door. Emilie felt the vibrations all the way to her shaky stomach. The four children came in to finish their soup, but she put them outside, telling them that she'd like to be alone, pleading a sudden, violent headache.

The children went outside and sat on the freezing, hard planks of the school porch.

"Miss Bordeleau was crying," said the first.

"If Mr. Lebrun yelled at her, I can believe it. I know he yells loud, 'cause he lives next door to us," added the second.

"It's fat Marie's fault. My mother told me about kids like her, who don't have brothers or sisters — they're always making trouble for everyone."

They talked until the other children came back. Then the discussion took on new dimensions. Everyone, it seemed, knew what had happened, but no one wanted to believe that Emilie had been crying. They said it was inconceivable that a grown-up would cry over such a small thing.

Emilie rang the bell. The children entered in silence, aware of their teacher's fragile mood. They sat down and got out their drawing paper, then began their masterpieces. Emilie felt that she had things back in hand. She frowned only a few times, when she saw children trying to portray Lazare's fit or drawing horrible red devils with flaming pitchforks.

Absorbed by the colours and shapes, she didn't see the commissioners arrive. The door opened and they filed into the classroom. The children fell silent.

"Miss Bordeleau, we have come to watch the children work," Mr. Trudel said.

"Please make yourselves at home," Emilie answered, knowing that their sudden curiosity had nothing to do with the children. She noticed that Mr. Pronovost was not among them. Mr. Lebrun, on the other hand, was in the group. Her hands were shaking, her knees trembling. Even if her conscience was clear, their simple presence made her feel that she must be guilty of something she wasn't even aware of. Secretly, she aimed bad thoughts at Mr. Lebrun, who never took his eyes off her. He was obviously satisfied with the commotion he was causing.

The children had completely stopped working. Ovila Pronovost raised his hand, and Emilie let him speak.

"How come my father isn't here?" he asked.

Mr. Trudel turned toward Mr. Lebrun. "You told me that all the commissioners would be here . . ."

"Well, I didn't have time to stop in at Dosithée's," Mr. Lebrun said.

"Go and get your father, my boy," Mr. Trudel said. "We'll wait for him."

Ovila didn't have to be told twice. As he passed, he tried to reassure Emilie by smiling at her, then dropped his smile and gave Mr. Lebrun a hard stare. He was swaying back and forth, turning his toque in his hands.

Emilie told the children to put their things away, then asked the commissioners if they minded if the children went home. The commissioners looked at each other, and Mr. Trudel nodded toward Emilie. Emilie had the children say their prayers, told them there would be no homework or lessons "in honour of the commissioners' visit" and accompanied them to the door. One of the four children who had had lunch at the school quietly asked her if they were going to scold her. Emilie tried to reassure him, saying that they had probably come to tell her she was finally getting a stove for the second floor. The boy wiped away the tear that was running down his cheek.

The commissioners sat down at the larger children's desks. Without thinking, Emilie went and sat at hers, though she felt ridiculous. However, she realized that Mr. Lebrun had not convinced all of them that she had acted badly.

Mr. Pronovost rushed in, wondering what the commissioners were doing there. Mr. Trudel explained that Emilie had slapped Marie Lebrun. Given the chance to explain herself, Emilie specified that she had not slapped Marie, she had pulled her ear. Mr. Lebrun interrupted her constantly, trying to make her admit to the facts as reported by his daughter. It took Mr. Pronovost only a few minutes to figure out that the argument had begun over Lazare. Torn between humiliation at having a son who suffered from *grand mal* and his sense of justice, he rose to Emilie's defence.

For twenty minutes, Mr. Lebrun tried to blacken Emilie's image, accusing her of feeding four children and of asking students to bring in the wood — unpardonable actions for a teacher who abided by the rules. The weight of Dosithée's words, however, tilted the balance back toward Emilie. Furious, Mr. Lebrun put on his toque and left the school. Mr. Trudel asked him to come back, but Mr. Lebrun said that the whole thing was a waste of time.

"To hear you talk, you'd think you're schoolchildren trying to please the teacher, simply because she is a nice person. And what happens to my daughter?"

The commissioners lowered their eyes. Dosithée, however, was not giving up. He marched out after Mr. Lebrun. Emilie and the commissioners who had stayed inside heard their conversation clearly.

"Your damned daughter can go jump in the lake. If you keep treating her like she's a saint, you'll have a real little brown-haired devil."

"You're the one with a devil under your roof, Dosithée Pronovost. You act like Lazare is normal, when you know that it's almost a sin to take him to church on Sunday. In fact, it's almost a sin to let him into the classroom. The stories scare everyone! My Marie had nightmares all night!"

"And do you think Lazare slept well? And Félicité, do you think she slept well? And little Miss Bordeleau, how about her? *Grand mal* is just that, a sickness! It doesn't hurt just the person who has it. It hurts everyone around him, especially his parents. Which means that you, you lout, you better tell your daughter to shut her big trap — "

Lebrun had had enough. He punched Pronovost in the jaw. Dosithée was stunned for a second, but quickly came to his senses and hit Lebrun back. Emilie and the commissioners ran outside, vainly trying to separate them. Mr. Trudel, placing himself between the two furious fathers, received a punch for his troubles.

"Hey, damn it, now! Calm down, you two idiots!" he yelled. He jumped on Lebrun's back and pulled his hair. Lebrun, enraged, spun around, forcing Trudel to let go.

The other commissioners started to yell louder and louder. Some egged them on, while others tried to stop them. In a few minutes, all of the men were in the mêlée. Emilie ran into the school and came back out with the bell. She rang and rang until everyone stopped. The commissioners looked at each other, dazed. Then Pronovost, Trudel and Gélinas burst into laughter.

"It's been a long time since we've done something like this," Trudel said, slapping Gélinas' back.

"Put us in a school and we act like children," Gélinas said.

Lebrun and the other commissioners hesitated for a moment, then joined the general hilarity. They went back inside, Lebrun's arm around Pronovost's shoulders, the two reminiscing about their childhood days.

Emilie filled her wash bowl with cold water and distributed wet rags to all of the injured so that they could wipe their noses or knees. She served them tea, then Trudel took the floor and solved the problem in a way that allowed everyone to save face. He decided that Emilie, because she fed the children and asked her pupils to bring in the wood, would not have a stove in her quarters until the beginning of the next school year. (It had already been agreed that she wouldn't have a stove upstairs before September, since the commissioners had voted a sum of money for additional wood for the next season.) Emilie smiled at Mr. Trudel and whispered a thank-you in Mr. Pronovost's ear.

The men all went home laughing as if they were rolling home from a party. Emilie sighed; she had feared that Mr. Lebrun would succeed in carrying out his threat. But she gave herself a slap on the hip to remind herself that she had to learn to be more patient and, especially, to avoid pulling fat Marie's ears.

Six

LAZARE HAD MORE AND MORE SEIZURES, so Dosithée and Félicité decided that he should stay home until Easter. Lazare didn't complain. He never wanted to go back to school, where the other children might poke fun at him.

Every evening, his brothers and sisters brought home their lessons and homework and tried to explain to him what they had learned in class. Rosée and Ovila did their best, but Lazare spent long hours struggling with problems for which he hadn't received the proper preparation. Ovila proposed to his parents that Emilie be invited over once or twice a week to help Lazare, but they refused.

Emilie offered to stay with Lazare while the family went to Sunday mass. After much discussion, she convinced the Pronovosts that she could catch Lazare up in his studies — and at the same time earn indulgences for herself, making up for her not attending any masses during Lent. She was happy to do it, for it meant she could share Sunday dinner with the family. Ovide, who no longer teased Ovila, walked Emilie back to the schoolhouse after the meals.

Contrary to forecasts, March brought only two snowstorms. The farmers bled the maples dry of sap and said that the good Lord punished them this way about once every ten years for having broken the rules of Lent by stuffing themselves at sugaring-off.

Ovide invited Emilie to spend the last Sunday before Easter at the family's "sugar shack," where the maple sap was collected and boiled down to make syrup. When they finished Sunday dinner, the entire family, even Lazare, piled into the sleigh to go to the hillside. The snow had melted so fast that they had to get down several times to lighten the sleigh, so that the horses could pull it through the mud.

Dosithée decided it was time to close up the cabin. Emilie's task was to wash all the buckets and put them in the shed. Ovila kept asking if she needed help, but she always responded that she was "doing fine, thank you." On the other hand, when Ovide came to help and began to stack the freshly washed buckets, Emilie didn't object. Ovila was offended. When Emilie realized that she had hurt his feelings, she patted his cheek. Ovila put his hand over hers, held it there a couple of seconds, then let it go, telling her that he hated being treated like a child. Emilie blushed and wiped her hand on a wet rag.

Seeing this exchange, Ovide told Ovila to apologize, but Emilie said that Ovila was right, she had made a mistake. She asked both brothers to leave her alone, since they were falling behind in their own chores. They departed, throwing each other furious looks.

Emilie sighed, smiled, shrugged and went back to her work. A strand of hair kept falling on her forehead when she leaned forward over the basins, and she pushed it back with increasing impatience.

When night fell, everyone headed down toward Bourdais. Only Lazare and his parents rode in the sleigh; the others preferred to walk. Emilie, flanked by Ovide and Ovila, insisted on talking to Rosée, who was walking ahead of them. Little Emile was staring at her, and Emilie realized that he was trying not to laugh.

"Why are you laughing at me, little guy?"

"Because your hair is sticking straight up!" Emile chuckled.

Emilie lifted her hand to her forehead and felt that the rebel strand was indeed sticking up, stiffened by the sugary water into which she'd been dipping her hands all day. Embarrassed, she tried to pat it down, but it wouldn't stay put. Emile was laughing harder and harder. The other children, who had pretended not to notice, were now too exhausted to smother their hilarity; even Ovide and Ovila stopped biting their lips. But Emilie didn't crack a smile; she just walked all the more quickly. Soon, only Ovila and Ovide could keep up with her, but she didn't talk to them. She politely declined when they invited her in, saying that she preferred to go right back to the school; nor did she allow them the privilege of accompanying her.

She slammed the door, ran upstairs, looked in her mirror and raged. "I look like a true madwoman! I'm sure they're still laughing at me. Now I'll have to wash my hair."

She hated to wash her hair in the evenings. It was so thick that it took hours before it was almost dry and Emilie could, at last, go to bed.

*C*lasses ended on a Wednesday. Emilie's father came to take her home for Easter. She told him about various events of significance and recounted the entire story of Lazare, even though she had already written about it in a letter. She didn't mention the commissioners' visit or the "sugar hair-do."

The Easter holiday seemed to last forever. Emilie was eager to go "home," to open her texts and notebooks, to put wood in her stove for the night. Winter had vacated the countryside so that spring could take up tenancy. Emilie asked her father to take her to Saint-Tite two days earlier than planned.

"Are you so bored in your very own home, my dear?" he asked, a little taken aback.

"It's not that, Papa. It's that I have to get back to wash the windows, air out the schoolhouse, clean my clothes, prepare my classes for May, make sure the children are ready when the inspector comes . . ."

The more she went on, and the more she described all the work awaiting her, the more impatient she became.

"Fine, fine, you don't need to paint me a picture. If it makes you happy and if the weather's fair tomorrow, we'll hitch up the horse. Lucky for you the roads are passable. But it better not rain tonight."

Emilie hugged her father and went upstairs to close her trunks, which she had discreetly begun to pack with clothes suitable for the new season. Caleb looked at the ceiling, listening closely, trying to imagine what she was doing.

"Emilie's changed a lot," Célina said.

"You think so?" Caleb asked.

"First, she's grown like a weed. She must be five-five, even five-six now. She may even still be growing. And she doesn't talk the same way. She always finds a complicated word to say a simple thing. No, Emilie's changed a lot. I've never seen her spend so much time fussing over her looks in the morning."

"It must be a habit from school. After all, she has to give a good example of cleanliness."

Célina thought for a moment. "What I think is that our daughter has a suitor."

"What makes you think that? Where do you think such a suitor would come from?"

"Well, Caleb, you know the Pronovosts have several sons."

"They're Emilie's students."

"Except for Ovide and Edmond."

"That's true . . . but you know as well as I that she doesn't go out at night. And no one goes to the school at night either."

"No, but Emilie visits the Pronovosts . . . to see Lazare, of course."

Célina did not like the idea of a love affair between their daughter and the oldest Pronovost boy. A teacher shouldn't have a steady beau. She didn't want Emilie's affairs to be a bone for the gossips to chew on; she wanted even less for her to lose her job. Caleb tried to reassure her, but in his heart he feared the same things.

Emilie came down to join her parents and was surprised at their silence, their looks and their sighs. She had an uneasy feeling that they'd been talking about her. Finally, she asked what was bothering them. Caleb gave her a somewhat gentler version of the conversation he and Célina had had. Emilie burst out laughing.

"Ovide Pronovost! That's silly! He's a big freewheeler who thinks that all the girls want to rope him in. No, Ovide Pronovost is not the boy for me."

Caleb and Célina suspected that she was protesting too much.

Seven

THE CHILDREN WERE APPREHENSIVE. The commissioners had advised Emilie that the inspector would be visiting on June 3, and the fateful day had arrived. Emilie had written a note to the parents asking them to dress their children in their Sunday best. The inspector made only one visit a year; Emilie was finishing her first year of teaching, and had to demonstrate her talents as a teacher if she wished to be rehired the following year. The competition was stiff, and she knew that there was more than one young woman in Saint-Tite who would not turn down a teaching position at the Bourdais school.

The children had spent the entire previous evening scrubbing the place. So as not to lose time, Emilie had quizzed them on catechism, grammar, religious history and arithmetic as they dusted and swept.

By the time the inspector arrived, two hours before the end of the day, the students' clothes were a little wilted, their faces a little less shiny, their hands a little dirtier. He asked Emilie for her attendance book. Then, without even looking at the children, he read through all the notes and remarks she had inscribed in her neatest hand.

The children sat up straight. Emilie excused herself to the inspector, stepped down from her dais and went to remind Charlotte that it was time for a trip to the outhouse. When Charlotte returned to the classroom, the inspector still hadn't finished reading. The children began to wriggle on their chairs. Emilie tried to calm them by flashing a small, nervous smile. The inspector's visit usually made the children tremble, especially the highest achievers, who were questioned more often than the others in order to show off the teacher's great talent — also, no doubt, to avoid uselessly humiliating the others.

At last, the inspector closed the big book and raised his eyes. It was the first time this inspector had come to Saint-Tite, the old one having taken early retirement for health reasons. As soon as he looked at the students, they realized that there were problems ahead: he was badly cross-eyed. He reminded the students that his job consisted of making sure that the school programs had been well respected, and he assured them that he would only make them write on the blackboard, since he didn't have time to make corrections. The children forced a smile when they realized that he was trying to make a joke. He told Emilie that he would start off with a little catechism.

"Who can recite the Ten Commandments?" he asked.

Every pupil raised a hand, eager to answer such an easy question. The inspector glanced around the room and pointed. "You!"

Three students stood up at the same time. Emilie blushed. The three students, nonplussed, sat down again. The inspector frowned and looked severe. "You," he repeated. Now five students thought he was pointing at them. Not wanting to repeat their blunder — standing up and sitting down again — they asked, in unison, "Me?" The inspector closed his eyes, sighed, turned to Emilie and asked her to name a student. At her cue, Marie stood up and answered correctly. The inspector grunted his satisfaction.

The minutes went by slowly, each one longer than the last, and the confusion became unbearable. Finally, the inspector asked Emilie to name each child as he went along, reminding her that a good teacher always made a classroom plan indicating the name of each of her students. Emilie bit her lip; she had forgotten this detail.

After catechism, the inspector went on to religious history. The children again responded correctly. Emilie smiled at them. She avoided calling on Lazare, who had been absent for almost two months. The arithmetic questions were easy, and the grammar questions didn't pose any problems. When they got to spelling, Emilie began to breathe easier, knowing that her students had no problem in that department. But the inspector put down the books and pulled from his briefcase a list of words he had prepared himself.

"*Imbecility*. Who can spell the word *imbecility*?"

Three students lifted a hand. Emilie named the first.

"I-m-b-e-c-i-l-l-i-t-y."

"No," the inspector barked. "*Imbecility*?"

The student sat down, not knowing what his mistake had been. The inspector asked again for an answer to his question. No one dared to raise a hand.

Emilie wiped her hand on her forehead.

"Miss Bordeleau, who is your best student in spelling?"

"Rosée Pronovost," Emilie said.

"Rosée Pronovost, can you spell *imbecility* for me?" he asked, looking to his right.

Rosée stood up. She was to his left. The inspector took several moments to locate her.

"Mr. Inspector, I would have spelled it as it was spelled."

"You're the best? And you are incapable of spelling *imbecility*. I will tell you how to spell this word . . . unless Miss Bordeleau wants to do so instead," he added in a sugary tone.

Emilie swallowed. She too would have spelled it "i-m-b-e-c-i-l-l-i-t-y," but she couldn't reveal her ignorance. She took a guess, telling the inspector that there was just one "l." The inspector smiled. She let her breath out.

"Now, I would like someone to spell the word *February*, the month."

Rosée raised her hand. The inspector ignored her, specifying that he wanted a young pupil to answer the question. He asked them all to stand up. None of them managed to spell the word correctly; they all left out the first "r."

Emilie began to despair. The children's already shaky nerves were exacerbated by the unusually intense heat for early June. As much as they wanted to do their school and their teacher proud, they seemed incapable of spelling a single word correctly. The inspector appeared to be inordinately amused. Finally, seeing that the end of class was approaching, he proposed a last word.

"I want the singular form of the word *series*."

"S-e-r-i-e," said Rosée, relieved at having rescued her reputation.

"No!" the inspector bellowed. "*Series* doesn't have a singular form! Can you remember that? *Series* doesn't have a singular form! Think about it. I'll give you a trick so that you don't forget: a series is always more than one thing. Repeat after me: '*Series* does not have a singular form.'"

The students repeated the sentence, putting all the energy they had left into it. The inspector relaxed. He smiled at them and let them out of school, telling them they had no homework that evening. The students didn't say their prayers: they put away their things and left in almost total silence. Emilie accompanied them to the door and told them they had done well. Rosée was in tears, and Emilie tried to comfort her by telling her that it was only the spelling part of the examination that had caused a few problems.

Emilie returned to the inspector, who was staring at her. Ill at ease, she wondered which of his eyes was the good one. She cleared her throat before offering him a cup of tea. He refused in an exasperated tone, complaining of the heat, so she brought him a glass of water.

"I've heard about you," he said when he'd drained the glass. "It seems that you are very determined and well informed. You must pass on some of your knowledge to your students." He looked at her with one eyebrow raised and the other lowered, which exaggerated his cross-eyes even more. "I can't say that they are strong spellers."

Emilie didn't know what to say, torn between anger and disappointment. "I'll try to do better next year," she finally replied.

The inspector burst out laughing.

"What's so funny?" she asked.

He asked her for another glass of water and choked as he swallowed, he was laughing so hard.

"I have to chuckle, Miss. You see, I'm an old joker. When the students get all the right answers, I find it terribly boring. To break the monotony, I've made a list of difficult questions, just to scare them a little. Them and the teacher," he added, with a teasing look. "I don't bring out my list of words often, just when the teacher has done her job well. I try to have some fun, you see."

Emilie began to see, although she was not amused. "Does that mean that you'll keep me on next year?"

"Of course! You are wonderful! Saint-Tite should be proud to have such a good little concession school. Speaking of Saint-Tite, that reminds me, I was in Saint-Stanislas yesterday. There will be a school free there next year. Would you like me to recommend you?"

Emilie had never thought of teaching in Saint-Stanislas, and the question took her by surprise. "I'll consider it. If I decide I'd like to go there next year, I'll let you know. I would appreciate a good word from you."

"Think about it. Your family would be happy to have you at home . . ."

"I'll discuss it with them."

"Do that. Well, I have to get going. I have to be at a school in Sainte-Thècle tomorrow, so I want to travel this evening. My congratulations, Miss. You have done a good job."

The inspector left the school still laughing, apparently very pleased with his afternoon's work. Emilie made herself stand on the porch waving until he was out of sight. The minute the cloud of dust settled, she went back into the school, exhausted.

Eight

$\mathcal{E}$MILIE DIDN'T RECEIVE a teaching bonus that year, even though, as she had learned, the inspector had highly recommended her. On Saint-Jean-Baptiste Day, she finished packing her trunks. The big end-of-year school clean-up had been done by the children who were allowed off the farm — the little ones, most of them girls, since the boys were occupied clearing stones and weeds from the fields. All of the desks were washed, waxed with bee's-wax and pushed to a corner of the classroom. The floor was scoured with a stiff brush and also well waxed, even though the elbow grease Emilie put into it didn't quite yield the desired results. She blacked her stove, although she knew that this work would just have to be done again in September. The windows gleamed in the hot end-of-June sunshine. Emilie thanked her students, kissed them on the cheek and promised that she would be back in September. She had decided to return.

Caleb was to come and get her "between Saint-Jean-Baptiste Day and June 30, depending on how work on the farm is going." On June 25, she gave her room a good cleaning, even hauling her mattress outside for an airing. She hung all her blankets on the clothesline and beat them vigorously, promising herself to wash them when she arrived in Saint-Stanislas rather than doing it now in Saint-Tite. If it rained, they'd never dry before her father arrived. Finally, she moved all the furniture around in her room to free up enough space for the new wood stove.

She waited for four days, during which she was often invited for meals at the Pronovosts', and also with Charlotte's parents.

On the eve of her departure, Lazare Pronovost came to tell Emilie that he had decided not to continue with his studies. This saddened her, but she knew that he wouldn't get very far in school and would be happier working on the farm with his father and brothers. She smiled when he told her that she would still have the same number of Pronovost students, since Oscar would be coming to school in the autumn.

Ovide came to get his brother at the schoolhouse, anxious to hear what Lazare was saying about him, he claimed . . . Emilie offered both of them a cup of tea and agreed to play a few hands of cards. Since entertaining at the school was forbidden, they moved the game to the Pronovosts', where they found some more players.

Mr. Pronovost confirmed that Lazare was quitting school. He also told her that Ovila wanted to return for another year. "That one likes farm work much less than his brothers do."

True to form, Ovila was sitting in a corner of the kitchen whittling a piece of wood. Emilie gave him a smile and admitted to his parents that she wasn't crazy about farm work either, which was why she'd decided to become a teacher. The Pronovosts remarked that she would have difficulty making a good match in a village like theirs if she didn't want to be a farmer's wife. Grinning, Emilie replied that she wasn't in a hurry to get married; she liked teaching very much and, with a little luck, she'd find herself a teacher to marry . . . or maybe an inspector! At that, the children burst into laughter, and Emilie joined them.

No one had forgotten the new inspector's visit. He had even made a point of stopping at the school to say hello to Emilie when he passed back through Saint-Tite. She was quite amused and made use of the occasion to tell him that she had decided to remain in Saint-Tite. The inspector agreed and praised her good sense. Then, instead of moving on, he babbled away about nothing at all. This balding, grey-haired, thirty-year-old man, with his dusty frock coat, was clumsily courting her. The only promise he managed to wring from her, though, was that she would read all the books he was lending her. As he drove away, he turned around three times; each time, Emilie quickly put a smile on her lips and gave a little wave, in a reluctant attempt at coquetry.

Emilie left the Pronovosts' at eight o'clock. She knew that they didn't stay up late except on special occasions. Dosithée asked Ovide to walk her back. He was flanked by Edmond and by Ovila, who had dropped his knife and piece of wood, hastily run his hand through his unruly hair and buttoned his collar. Before she left, Emilie looked at each member of the family and said a kind word to her pupils. Then, overcome by an emotion she couldn't hide, she even dared to hug Dosithée and Félicité, thanking them for having made her feel so welcome.

*C*aleb arrived just as the lamps in the barns were extinguished and gave way to the dawn. He had driven at night in order not to lose a whole day to travelling. He would have liked to have fetched his daughter in his "piano-box," the elegant buggy he had brought her in the previous autumn, but he knew that it didn't have enough room to carry all the accumulations of the past ten months of her life. He knew her well enough to know that though she had arrived in Saint-Tite with only the bare essentials, she would go home with boxes and boxes of "absolutely necessary" mementoes.

He had to knock at the door of the schoolhouse for a good five minutes before Emilie came to open it. One glance told him that she probably had several wet handkerchiefs in her handbag. She was happy to see him and gave him a big hug. Caleb was quite surprised by so much enthusiasm, but he rapidly regained his composure, tapped her on the rear end and urged her to hurry. She tried to rush, but she burned her slice of toast, overturned her creamer, broke a plate, ripped the hem of her dress bringing a box down from upstairs and dropped a second box, the contents of which spilled onto the freshly waxed floor. Finally, she sat down at her desk and burst out crying. Caleb, who was always disarmed by tears, offered her a dry handkerchief and stepped outside to feed and water his mare. He then spent much more time than he would have liked loading and reloading his daughter's things in the buggy.

Emilie blew her nose, went upstairs to make sure everything was in order, paced back and forth in her classroom and finally resigned herself to joining her father, now sitting on the runningboard of the buggy, his hat firmly pulled down on his head.

"Here I come, Papa. Just two seconds."

She locked the door, looked around one more time at her own special domain, then climbed into the buggy. They had to stop at the Pronovosts' to leave off the key to the schoolhouse. Caleb, worried that long goodbyes would hold them up even more, took the key in. He returned almost immediately and urged the mare on. As he did so, Emilie turned around and saw, quick as a flash, the curtain move and then drop back into place.

Caleb wasted no time telling her that he had accepted a position for her that summer to tutor Saint-Stanislas children who were behind in their schoolwork. She was pleased, even when Caleb told her that he had insisted on one condition — that she be free to help with the harvest. She hated harvesting, but she accepted the compromise with good grace.

*T*he summer of 1896 seemed just like all the other summers Emilie had known. One week after her return, the sounds, habits, smells and routine of the family home were as familiar as ever. She took up residence in her corner of the girls' room, but she had difficulty sleeping the first few nights, as she was no longer used to hearing other breathing echoing her own.

She also reacquainted herself with her old friends, whom she told all about the past year, omitting just a few details. Only Berthe, her best friend, heard absolutely everything. And Emilie was the first to learn that Berthe was hoping to enter a convent. Although she was surprised at first, she realized that her seventeen-year-old friend, the eldest of thirteen brothers and sisters, was probably seeking the peace she never seemed to find at home, since her mother was always either in bed having children or being run ragged by them.

The days of summer lengthened and then shortened, and the colours in the fields turned more and more toward yellow. Emilie was coming alive while the earth seemed to be moving toward death. Finally the time came to pack her trunks, brimming with the new clothes she had sewn in her free moments.

Nine

HERE WAS THE SCHOOL, still nestled at the intersection of Bourdais and Montée des Pointes. Emilie dusted away its two months of idleness before beginning her second year of teaching, which was marked by the arrival of several new students. She had to rethink how to organize her time, since there were now as many small children as bigger ones. She visited the Pronovosts a little less often than she had the previous year, aware that certain people thought ill of the fact that a commissioner, the father of many boys of whom at least one was of marrying age, should spend so much time with the teacher. She did allow herself to go with Ovide to the wedding of one of his friends, but she refused to sing in the parish choir, preferring the calm and solitude that she had come particularly to appreciate after her trying days. When she attended the opening of a business school in Saint-Tite, she was pleased to discover that some of her graduates were going to further their education there, in the hope of finding a good position.

She returned to Saint-Stanislas for the same holidays as the previous year, but shortened her stay at Christmas in order to celebrate Epiphany at the Pronovosts'. Her father wasn't happy with this decision, but Emilie insisted. A number of families from the concession and the village had been invited. For the second time since she had arrived in Saint-Tite, Emilie danced and stayed up half the night. The guests had a good laugh when she was crowned queen. The men had to serve themselves a second piece of cake before Ovila wolfed it all down. He was crowned king, but he abdicated. Ovide then mounted the throne and kissed Queen Emilie on cheeks that were reddened by warmth, pleasure and shyness.

This winter wasn't as hard as the previous year's. Now that Emilie's room was furnished with a stove, she found it very comfortable, and began to split her wood herself. She wrote to the commissioners to thank them — even though the stove promised for September had arrived only in mid-December — and took the opportunity to request that a work party be organized to build an addition to the schoolhouse for a bathroom. Charlotte's ill health had given her the courage to make this request. In fact, Charlotte had had to stay home from school, sick in bed, a number of times. The frequency of her visits to the bathroom had increased. Now that she was seven years old and had more control of her weak kidneys, however, her parents had given her a pocket watch, which she put in plain view on her desk. Emilie's appeal to the commissioners was heard, and she was promised that the work party would be organized as soon as springtime softened the ground.

March was a mild month. By the time April came, the ground was free of snow. But April yielded, in spite of a few sunny days, to cold and snow, and the work party was put off to the following month.

The men arrived on the first Saturday of May, and Emilie hurried out to meet them. It was decided that part of the porch would be sacrificed and a new wall would be erected. The work took all day, and the schoolhouse shook from the incessant hammering. Emilie was surprised how quickly hands and feet were organized so as not to waste time: everyone had his job. The men even installed a window; she found the idea charming and began to choose from among her ends of fabric one that was suitable for a curtain. The work party returned the following day, even though it was Sunday, to hang the door on its hinges and whitewash everything. Emilie thanked them warmly and spent the rest of her day sewing a white curtain, on which she embroidered the letters of the alphabet.

The next morning, the surprise for Charlotte fell flat, for she was absent once again; she stayed away two weeks. When she finally came back, she was pale, drawn and worried that she had lost almost too much time to make up. Emilie invited her to stay after class and refused her parents' offer of compensation for the extra lessons. The two developed an unusual relationship, with Emilie as big sister and Charlotte as protégée.

In her seven years, Charlotte had acquired an uncommon maturity. Since Lazare's epileptic seizure, she had been transformed into an angel, constantly tending to anyone who wasn't feeling well. She confided in Emilie that she found Lazare nice and that, if he found her just as nice, she would marry him when they grew up. In spite of her serious nature, Charlotte had a gay laugh that was music to Emilie's ears. Between periods of intense study, they took the time to relax, telling each other little jokes.

June brought "inspector fever" back to the classroom and also signalled Emilie's departure for the summer. Charlotte did well on her exams and couldn't wait for September.

Emilie left her students, both sad to be going and happy to be getting some rest. Her mother had written her that she again had "summer students" in Saint-Stanislas. Emilie didn't complain, for the work gave her the feeling that she was useful twelve months of the year.

Her father came to get her the very evening of the first day of vacation. Again, she left her school knowing she would be back, for a third year. But now she was leaving more than the school; she was leaving a village where she felt she was starting truly to belong. Saint-Stanislas seemed farther away with every turn of the wheel that took her toward it.

Part Two

1897–1901

Ten

*O*VIDE WAS DRIVING his buggy home from the village. The cold March wind buffeted him constantly; even though he was bundled up, he was shivering. Taking care not to go too fast, he decided to take the summer road as far as Montée des Pointes. With a little luck, the children would be playing outside and he would see Emilie. But by the time he caught a glimpse of the school, the wind had died down and he could see that she had decided not to let the children out for recess. He sighed, coughed, spat and headed for home.

Ovide went into the kitchen and slowly took off his coat, too exhausted to object when his mother came to help him, and Edmond hurried to unhitch the horse. He went up to his room and collapsed on the bed, his body wracked by fits of coughing. Wiping her hands on her apron, smoothing over a belly already slightly swollen by a new child, Félicité followed him. Gently, she told her son to sit up and gave him a glass of water. He drank as much as he could and coughed twice, then spat up his last mouthful.

Félicité wiped his forehead with the corner of a towel. "I don't like this, Ovide. You're spitting too much. It's not good to spit like that. I'm going to send Edmond for the doctor."

Ovide waved a hand as if brushing away a fly. His lungs whistled as he took a breath. "The doctor doesn't have to come. I've just seen him."

"And?"

Ovide cleared his throat hoarsely. "Well, it looks like it's what I thought."

Félicité looked at her big, handsome son. Her eldest. He turned so she wouldn't see the tears that he'd been holding back since he got home. Even so, he couldn't hide the hiccups that shook his body, overcome now by fits of coughing, now by sobs.

"Get out of my room, Mama. I want to be alone." Félicité obeyed, reluctantly.

Down in the kitchen, she 3just shook her head when Edmond asked if Ovide was feeling better. Edmond got up, paced back and forth, then suddenly punched the wall. Félicité jumped, but at the same time she envied her son the power to express his rage.

"Is it serious?" he asked.

"I don't know. He didn't give me any details."

Edmond put on his coat. "I'm going to get the doctor."

"He's just been there."

"I'm going anyway. If Ovide won't tell us anything, we'll get the story from him."

Edmond hitched up the stallion and left for the village, and Félicité went back upstairs to see if Ovide had calmed down. He was lying on his back, an arm covering his eyes.

"Ovide, do you want anything?"

Ovide shook his head and turned on his side. Félicité told him that she was going to make him a mustard poultice and left the room before he could stop her. A few minutes later, she was back to put the poultice on his chest. Ovide nodded his thanks.

The children came home from school. Télesphore, the youngest, was with them, because Rosée was away for the day. She hadn't been back to school since October, as her mother's pregnancy, coming so late in life, required her daily presence at home.

When Edmond returned, Félicité wrapped herself in a big shawl and went out to the barn, where she found him putting away the bridle and harness.

"So?"

Edmond turned and looked at his mother. She looked so fragile in her pregnant state that he asked her to sit down.

"So . . . it's . . . it's tuberculosis," he managed to say.

A shiver shook Félicité from head to toe, pausing at her heart. She dropped her head. Edmond sat down beside her and put his hand, a bit awkwardly, on her shoulder. "You can count on me, Mama. I'll do everything I can to help the family while Ovide is sick."

*D*osithée was working at Lac Pierre-Paul with his brothers, Joseph-Denis and Claïre. They had finally won the cutting contract for the railway beds — one they'd been after for two years. Dosithée saw Edmond coming toward them through the woods.

"Edmond? What are you doing here?" he shouted, dropping his axe. "It's not your mother . . . ?"

Edmond approached slowly, trying to put off the moment when he'd have to tell his father the news.

"Say something, damn it! Is it your mother?"

Claïre and Joseph-Denis signalled to the other men on the site to stop working. The echoes of their axe blows faded away through the woods.

"It's not Mama. It's Ovide."

"Ovide? What's wrong with Ovide?"

"Well, you know . . . his cold that's been hanging on since winter . . . The doctor says it's not an ordinary cold. It seems that . . . well, we thought it might be pneumonia . . . but the doctor says it seems to be more serious . . ."

Dosithée was hanging on his son's every word. Each time Edmond trailed off, he nodded his head as if trying to guess what was coming next.

Edmond stopped. He hadn't realized that it would be so difficult to tell his father the news. He cleared his throat to find room for the words he had to say.

"The doctor . . . the doctor said that it's . . . it's tuberculosis."

Dosithée mouthed the diagnosis two or three times, then he turned to tell his brothers that he was packing his bag and going back to Saint-Tite. Joseph-Denis and Claïre accompanied him back to the camp, where he threw everything into the flour sack that served as his suitcase.

"Claïre, here's my axe. Make sure it doesn't rust, and bring it back to me in the spring. So long, everyone. I'm off."

Dosithée and Edmond travelled in silence. Although it wasn't a long trip, it was exhausting, since there was barely anything you might call a road. If it hadn't been for the tracks Edmond had made coming to the camp, they would have spent even more time getting out of the dense, suffocating woods. Dosithée kept his eyes fixed on the horizon.

They arrived in Bourdais as night fell. Dosithée jumped down from the sleigh, leaving his son to see to the horse and harness. He ran into the house, where he found his wife and kissed her cheek.

"Where's Ovide?"

"In the girls' room. He's been getting worse since morning. The doctor came, and he said that he has some bronchitis, too. We don't know what will happen."

Félicité tried to sound reassuring, but she had few reserves of calm left to draw upon. She knew it would be a long night. Dosithée took off his coat, hat and boots and tiptoed up the stairs. He sat at his son's bedside. Ovide was losing ground against a raging fever.

"Hello, son. How're you doing?"

Ovide opened his eyes and began to shiver. He told his father to stay away from him, and Dosithée retreated. Then, almost overcome by the fever, Ovide began to thrash around. When Dosithée put a cold, damp towel on his forehead, he threw it off. Helpless, Dosithée backed out of the room and went down to the kitchen.

"Do you think we should ask the priest to come?" he asked Félicité, trying to keep his voice from trembling.

"The doctor doesn't think so. If his fever breaks, everything'll be fine."

Dosithée went to his bedroom. He took down the crucifix that hung at the head of the bed, pressed it to his chest, then hung it back on the wall. When he returned to the kitchen, he noticed that all the children were sitting around the table. He looked at them, a little surprised that he hadn't noticed them before. They all looked anxious. Forcing a smile, he asked if they wanted to say a prayer.

"We've just finished a Hail Mary," Télesphore said sleepily.

Rosée shot him a look and suggested that they recite a rosary. Suddenly aware of how late it was, Dosithée said that it would probably be better if they all went to bed. With the exception of Rosée, Edmond and Ovila, the children all went upstairs. Eva went to the living room, where Félicité had put the girls to free up their room for Ovide.

"How's Lazare been since Christmas?" Dosithée asked.

"Just two fits," Rosée told him.

Dosithée turned to Ovila. "Ovila, your brother Ovide is too sick to do anything. You know that Lazare can't work steady any more. That means it's your turn to quit school and help out around here."

Without a word, Ovila put on his coat and went out for some air. Something inside him had just snapped. He knew that he didn't want to spend his life on a farm. In a few days, he would be seventeen. He didn't have a burning desire to stay in school, but at least it kept him from being a slave to the turning of the seasons.

He walked to the schoolhouse. A light was burning on the second floor. He wondered if he should tell Emilie himself that he wouldn't be back, or if he should wait and leave it to his father. Still debating the point, he knocked on the door.

Emilie, wrapped in her housecoat, her hair loose, came to see who it was.

Ovila was a bit intimidated. "Am I disturbing you?" he asked.

"Well, yes. But you might as well come in, just for a minute or two," Emilie said.

Ovila automatically went to sit at his desk. "My brother Ovide is sick."

"Yes, I know." Emilie sat down at the desk beside him. "I wondered all week why you haven't talked to me about it."

Ovila shrugged. Until he knew exactly how sick his brother was, he hadn't wanted to admit to her what he was thinking. His heart was torn. Part of him was actually glad that Ovide was sick, if only because Emilie hadn't been to visit him. That meant that his parents were right. She really wasn't interested in him; she saw him as a neighbour, nothing more. Ovila looked at Emilie and smiled sadly. If only he were Edmond's age, or even Lazare's, perhaps she would pay some attention to him. Perhaps she would realize that his crush, born three years ago, had never died. For three years, he had stubbornly continued going to school, partly for the pleasure of seeing her every day. He was now the oldest student in the class. He envied Rosée for having become friends with her. Since she had stopped going to school, Rosée could visit Emilie whenever she wanted to.

"Ovila, did you come to tell me about Ovide?"

The sound of Emilie's voice brought Ovila back to reality. He gave her the diagnosis of tuberculosis. She grimaced.

"I suppose you can guess the rest?" he said.

"The rest?"

"Now I'm going to have to stay home to take over from Ovide. Lazare can't work steady."

Emilie had never given a thought to Ovila's future. She was so used to seeing him in class that she hadn't really noticed that he had become a man. He had shot up to the height of six feet. His voice had changed. She had noticed, the first day of each school year, how his muscles had filled out.

"I'll miss you," she said at last.

"You'll get used to it. I won't be far. I'll keep visiting you and taking you to mass. And I'll chop the wood in secret. Even if you . . ."

He stopped. He couldn't say that she was only a couple of years older than he was, that she had just turned nineteen and he would be seventeen at the end of March.

"Even if?" she prompted.

"Even if you're still the schoolmistress. I mean, I'm not exactly, uh . . . not exactly like . . . well, what I mean is that I won't be your student any more. The commissioners won't be able to complain if I split your wood. It won't be against the rules."

Emilie forced herself to hide the wave of tenderness that washed over her. "If you like, Ovila, when the two of us are all alone you can call me Emilie. Rosée does. And if my memory serves me well, there's less of an age difference between the two of us than between Rosée and me."

Ovila looked at her, fascinated that her eyes were the same colour as her hair. She had said "the two of us." The silence in which their eyes held each other lasted minutes. She had said "the two of us." To save face, he started to gather his school books and pile them on the floor.

"I'll do these like I do the logs. I'll make good, straight piles."

He lifted his eyes to see her reaction. She hadn't caught on that he was making a joke. She was staring at him, lost in thought. Was she thinking about "the two of us"? He stood up, told her that he had to go, and added that his father was back from the lumber camp. Then he knelt again to gather up his things.

On her knees beside him, Emilie helped, trying desperately not to look at him. "If you give me two minutes, I'll get dressed and help you carry these home."

Ovila decided to risk everything. "I think I'd like to come back tomorrow for the rest." To his own ears, he sounded brash, so he hastened to add that he'd have more news about his brother.

Emilie shrugged with a smile to let him know that she no longer had any authority over him. She walked him to the door and opened it for him. "I really will miss you . . ."

"All six feet of me?"

Emilie let out a sharp little laugh. "Well now, Ovila, you're obliging me to do what I always do when a pupil leaves my class."

She stretched to give him a kiss on the lips, though her departing pupils usually merited only a peck on the cheek. He stood still for a moment, then he put down his things and went to her, kicking the door closed. Taking her face in his hands, he kissed her gently. He felt her arms slipping around his shoulders as his soul flew heavenward.

Eleven

*I*N THE WEEKS that followed, Emilie, embarrassed, did what she could to ignore Ovila's presence. He tried constantly to catch her eye, but she always averted her gaze. She had completed her fourth year of teaching with flagging spirits, and Ovila's departure had cast something of a shadow over her spring.

She had made the mistake of letting him know how she felt about him. Now she was quick to hide once again behind the role of "schoolmistress," burying deep inside her the woman who had revealed herself that winter night. She had repressed the joy that had taken hold of her following her brief loss of self-control. Although she was able, at first, to convince herself that she'd done nothing wrong, she was soon overcome by a great uneasiness, which gave way, finally, to the certainty of her guilt. She had no faith in Ovila; she even had nightmares about him telling everyone that she'd literally thrown herself into his arms. And so she decided never to refer to what had happened, nor to speak to him at all if she could avoid it.

Even so, Ovila kept his promises. He accompanied her to mass and brought the last cord of wood into the class and up to her room. But it was useless to try to talk to her.

Emilie greeted the arrival of June with barely concealed relief. Another few weeks and she'd be able to hide once again in the bosom of her family. Another few weeks and she could erase from memory the last few inglorious months.

She went to see the Pronovosts, to thank them again for their kindness. Since Easter, their spirits had risen; Ovide was now out of danger.

When she got back to the schoolhouse, her brother was just arriving. She was surprised not to see her father, but her brother said that he was now old enough to take his place. She smiled, suddenly realizing that he, too, was growing up. So they made the journey together, stopping on the way to see Lucie. Then Emilie took over the reins and drove furiously.

"My gosh, you'd think you were on fire!"

"I'm not on fire," she replied acidly, "I'm just in a hurry to get home."

Emilie swiftly unpacked her bags, trying to lend a sympathetic ear as Célina enumerated all the misfortunes of the past months. A few minutes later, she told her mother that she was going to visit Berthe as soon as the supper dishes were done, since she was too impatient to wait the eternity until tomorrow. Célina sighed at her daughter's lack of feeling, but made no comment.

Briskly, Emilie walked the mile that separated her house from her friend's; Berthe was lucky enough to live near the banks of the Batiscan. Since Emilie had left Saint-Stanislas, she'd kept up a regular correspondence with her best friend, but confined herself to daily events and innocent gossip. She was shy about expressing her innermost feelings, not knowing if they would find an echo in Berthe's sensitive soul.

The two friends slipped away together and sat on the trunk of a long-dead tree, whose branches dipped into the Batiscan.

"What is it, Emilie?" Berthe asked. "You seem so upset."

Emilie considered for a few moments, then decided to reveal her shameful secret.

"Your handsome Ovila, did he say anything after the night you kissed him?" Berthe asked, her eyes bright with curiosity.

"He tried, but I wouldn't talk to him."

After some deft questioning, Berthe got to the root of Emilie's trouble. That her friend was in love, she had no doubt. That her friend had gone a bit too far, she understood. But that her friend refused to admit that she was entitled to her feelings — this she could not accept. She didn't blame Emilie. She even congratulated her, in a teasing way, for holding out so long. Emilie was still puzzled. She asked her friend if she ought to see him again. Berthe answered that she had only to listen to her heart.

"But Berthe, don't you see? Not only was he my pupil, he's two years younger than I am!"

"How awful! When you're eighty years old, he'll only be seventy-eight. Imagine! Everyone will say you're an old fool running after young boys."

They burst out laughing.

"You'll make a funny kind of nun, Berthe, encouraging schoolmistresses to go out with their pupils."

"I do nothing of the sort! Let me point out that Ovila is no longer your pupil. And even if you'd let anything show beforehand, I could only have said that you were setting a bad example. But now, as far as I can see, the way is clear. Of course people will talk, so I . . ."

She stopped, trying to think what she would have done in Emilie's place. She knew that the commissioners were very strict about the teachers' conduct; in some districts, teachers couldn't even go skating in winter without risking their jobs. She also knew that it would be almost impossible for people to accept Emilie's keeping company with the brother of some of her pupils. How could she be impartial? Of course, Emilie wouldn't be able to see him at the schoolhouse . . .

Emilie, seeming to read her thoughts, picked up the thread. "So you'd have done the same. You'd have said nothing to Ovila, you'd have let him think nothing had happened, you'd have avoided looking at him, and every time you saw him looking sad your heart would have ached."

The two friends were silent a long moment. Darkness had crept up the banks of the Batiscan, and neither had found a solution to Emilie's dilemma. Slowly, they made their way back to Berthe's house, listening to the crickets chirping and the steady breathing of the animals sleeping just beyond the wood fences. Somewhere, a cock began to crow.

"There's someone else who's confused," Berthe remarked.

Emilie began to giggle, then gales of laughter overtook her. Caught up in the hilarity, Berthe elbowed her in the ribs, trying to get her to stop, but neither of them could. They ended up rolling around in the hay, wriggling like a pair of fish out of water, tangled in their skirts, their hair strewn with straw. When the cock crowed a second time, their laughter turned delirious.

"If that cock crows once more," Emilie gasped, "I'll know I have troubles ahead."

"You're a silly goose, Emilie Bordeleau!"

The cock crowed a third time. The two friends suddenly fell silent. Emilie sat up and pulled the straw from her hair.

"I don't mean to be superstitious, Berthe, but isn't that a bad omen?"

"Don't be silly," Berthe replied, standing and vigorously shaking out her skirt. "You're not going to get in a state over a little joke." But Berthe herself was not entirely at ease.

They parted a few minutes later, having agreed to spend their summer evenings making a quilt.

"You can keep it when it's done, Emilie. I wouldn't know what to do with it. You see, I'm entering the novitiate at the end of August." Berthe felt awkward making such an important announcement at a moment that had suddenly grown sombre.

Emilie didn't know what to say. She simply embraced her friend, patting her on the back as though to convince her that all would be well.

She went home, walking now forward, now backward. Her gait mirrored her thoughts. Forward: Berthe is going into the convent.

Now it's real. How happy Berthe will be. Then backward: But who will fill the gap that Berthe leaves? Once she's a nun, we'll never be able to do what we did this evening — frolic in the grass like a couple of kittens. Then forward: Ovila's just a fantasy. No woman can say that she fell in love with her husband when he was only fourteen years old. Ovila is still too young to know what I know. Then backward: Why didn't he say anything? Why was he so aloof? Why didn't he insist? Then forward: I'm going to tell him how I feel. He won't laugh at me. He loves me. I'm sure of it. Then backward: Does he love me? I want him to love me. Why did the cock crow three times?

Twelve

ERTHE AND EMILIE worked on their quilt together at the Bordeleau home. They decided that it would be too complicated to be always carrying their materials back and forth, and Berthe preferred to get away from her house. Emilie's house was almost as full of children as her own, but she found it calmer. And besides, the walk gave her a chance to gather her thoughts.

Their evenings passed happily. Emilie never dared broach the subject of Berthe's vocation, fearing that her judgment might be skewed by her self-interest. She would miss Berthe terribly. Berthe was also silent on the subject, unable to say that, for her, entering a convent was a form of escape. Emilie had never been able to understand why Berthe wanted to distance herself from her mother, brothers and sisters, for whom she had become more and more responsible. And so they chatted about this and that as they worked their needles into the kaleidoscopic quilt.

The month of July was threaded through the eye of time, and August arrived under a brilliant sun. Their work went quickly; the two friends combined monastic patience with remarkably quick execution. They sewed outside when the weather was good. Darkness caught up with them earlier now, but they put out lamps so that they could work a few hours longer under the stars.

One night, Caleb sat with them, marvelling both at their impressive work and at the beauty of the night sky, and hoping to catch sight of the northern lights. Suddenly, he piped up, "Who do you think that is coming up the hill?"

Berthe and Emilie raised their eyes from their work and looked toward the road. They saw the gleam of a lantern, then heard the sound of hooves.

"God help us," Berthe said in a choked voice, "I hope it's not my father coming to get me because my mother is ill."

The girls put down their needles, removed their thimbles from their middle fingers and laid the quilt aside. The horse and buggy stopped in front of Caleb's house. Emilie's father told the girls to stay where they were, picked up his lantern and made his way toward the road. Berthe and Emilie couldn't make out the conversation that followed.

"It can't be for me, because your father would have called me by now."

Emilie didn't reply. She thought the opposite: perhaps Caleb was buying time so that he could find the words to announce some bad news.

"Emilie! Come here," Caleb called. "I need you."

While Emilie went to see what Caleb wanted, Berthe sat on the edge of her chair, ready to jump as soon as she was called. She swallowed painfully. An accident. A disaster. The end of her dream of entering the convent.

"Berthe! Come here, Berthe." Emilie's cry resonated in Berthe's ears like an echo out of the fog. In an instant, she'd covered the ground to the road, then skidded to a stop. Emilie was laughing out loud, and Caleb was chatting amiably with a stranger.

"Berthe, may I introduce Ovila Pronovost!"

Berthe's jaw dropped. Ovila Pronovost. She had spent so many hours listening to Emilie describe him that she felt as if she knew his face already. Her eyes lit up.

"Well, well," she managed to say. "Company all the way from Saint-Tite." Discreetly, she nudged Emilie's right foot.

Caleb invited Ovila to rest his horse, delighted to see that the buggy was hitched to the beautiful stallion with the blond mane. He was even so courteous as to offer to lead the horse to the trough himself.

Ovila, tongue-tied but happy at the reception he had been given, followed the girls. Berthe flashed winks and meaningful glances at Emilie, who was struggling, unsuccessfully, to retreat to the cool façade she'd adopted since that memorable night in March.

Ovila brushed off his clothes before he sat down. Once Caleb had fetched Célina and introduced her, he invited everyone to the house for something to drink. Inside, Ovila's impressive stature quickly became an object of curiosity.

When Ovila explained that he was on his way to Shawinigan and Trois-Rivières to look for work, Emilie feigned a lively interest, although the thought of his being so far away chilled her soul. Oblivious, Ovila went on about where he'd like to find work that winter: "A lumber camp or a lumber yard, it doesn't matter."

Emilie decided to change the subject, and asked him if he had any family in Saint-Stanislas. In fact, she knew the answer, but she also knew that her parents had a passion for knowing all the family connections in Mauricie County. They were fascinated to learn that Ovila was related, through his mother, to Isidore Bédard.

"Is Isidore expecting you tonight?" Célina asked.

Ovila blushed a little and admitted that he wasn't expected, but that his mother had assured him he would be welcome.

Caleb stole a quick glance at Emilie. His daughter seemed utterly enthralled with Ovila, so he decided to force the issue a little.

"I don't see why you should turn up at Isidore's at such an hour, like a stray cat," he said cheerfully. "We've got room for guests here."

Célina, astonished, shot him a look. Emilie didn't say a word. She avoided even looking at Berthe, who had got up to fill the water jug.

"Well, now that we've settled that," Caleb continued, "I'll go unhitch that handsome beast of yours."

He was almost out the door, very pleased with himself, when Emilie announced that she and Ovila would drive Berthe home.

Emilie knew her father well; she knew that this delay would be unbearable for him, and she enjoyed the idea of torturing him, just a little.

"That's just like you, Emilie, to tire out an animal after a long trot," he said, disappointed. "But enjoy yourselves. We'll be waiting."

Not knowing how she could have made such a mistake, Berthe found herself seated between Emilie and Ovila. She spent the entire ride turning her head to the left, then to the right, feigning an intense interest in a conversation thick with innuendo. She spoke only once, to confirm what Emilie had said about their "wonderful summer." She made no comment when Emilie talked about all the parties they'd been to, knowing that in fact she'd gone to only one, the party her family had thrown when François-Xavier Bordeleau left for the Klondike.

When they arrived at Berthe's house, Ovila got down and extended his hand to each of the girls. Emilie walked Berthe to her door. They whispered together.

"Everything you said about him, he's all that and more," Berthe gushed.

"He is, isn't he?" Emilie replied, prouder than she'd ever been in her life.

Berthe quickly listed all of Ovila's qualities, and Emilie agreed with each one. Berthe promised to do all she could to get out of the house the next day to visit again.

Emilie got back in the buggy. Ovila, already seated, simply offered his hand, and she grasped it happily.

They drove back up Côte Saint-Paul at a walk, the stallion grateful for the restful pace. Ovila was silent. Now that he was alone with Emilie, he didn't know how to explain his presence. Emilie came to his rescue, asking if he really wanted to work in the camps. He said that he did, adding that several companies in Trois-Rivières and Shawinigan were hiring. Then, taking his courage in both hands, he told her that he wanted to get out of Saint-Tite.

"I can't bear to see you, and not be able to be with you," he said. "You can laugh at me if you want, but I had to come and tell you that I love you."

Emilie didn't laugh. She didn't speak. Ovila was at his wits' end. Steeling himself, he asked, "Will you write to me while I'm gone?"

"Yes, of course I will," she replied.

Finally, Ovila asked if there was any hope that she harboured feelings for him that were anything like his for her. There was no reply.

Ovila stopped the buggy. Emilie still didn't say a word. He turned to look at her. Her eyes were shining, and he realized that she was crying — tears of joy. Quickly, he took her in his arms to comfort her. She burst into unrestrained laughter. She agreed that she would wait for him. Ovila sprang to his feet, slapped his thigh and whooped for joy. Then he sat back down and urged the horse on, holding the reins in his left hand and Emilie's hand in his right.

Caleb was waiting for them on the porch. He said nothing of the fact that it had taken them almost half an hour to cover a distance that ordinarily took only ten minutes. Unhitching the horse, he began to brush its mane. Emilie and Ovila went to sit with Célina, who in their absence had sent the children upstairs, put away Emilie's sewing things and prepared a bed for Ovila in the living room.

"At least you'll be better off than a stray cat. You won't have to sleep behind the stove," Emilie said, to excuse the improvised nature of the arrangements.

Ovila apologized once again for having arrived without notice. Emilie knew perfectly well that he'd never have dared tell them in advance, for fear she'd say she preferred not to see him. She yawned. Ovila rose and suggested that it was time to turn in, and he was off to join Caleb in the barn, to make sure his animal was settled for the night.

On his way into the barn, Ovila hit his head on a beam. He bit his lip and held back the curse he was about to let fly.

Caleb noticed and guffawed. "This place is made for short people."

"Everything's made for short people," Ovila replied, rubbing his forehead.

Caleb was still brushing the horse's mane. "He must be eight years old by now. The first time I saw him was in the fall of '96. He's a damned handsome beast!"

Ovila agreed. The horse was nine years old, but still as frisky as a colt. Caleb told him how impressed he had been with its fine hooves and blond mane. After rattling on for a while about the stallion's merits, he finally got to what was on his mind. An acquaintance had offered him a filly, "ready and willing to be serviced," but he'd refused to buy her. He had no need for another horse. His old mare, though less spirited, still served him well. He had three workhorses — big, strong animals. But if Ovila was willing to give him a few hours, he'd buy the filly the next day and put her in the paddock with his stallion.

Ovila hesitated briefly, pretending that he was expected in Shawinigan, then agreed to stay on in Saint-Stanislas. Caleb was delighted.

*I*mmediately after milking the cows the next morning, Caleb went to see Elzéar Veillette. He hated Veillette. First of all, because the man always had to be right — which, according to Célina, was impossible, since it was Caleb who was never wrong. And second, because Veillette bred horses. On a small scale, to be sure, but still, he had some lovely animals. Caleb knew that Pronovost's stallion would make Veillette green with envy.

Veillette was surprised to see him. Caleb got right to the point.

"I hear you've got a decent filly for sale, Veillette," he began.

"I did, Caleb, a beauty, but you're a bit late. I sold her yesterday to some family of our priest's, visiting from Grand-Mère. They're probably hitching her up right now for the trip home."

"So, I'll find them at the rectory?" Caleb asked.

"If they haven't already left . . ."

Caleb thanked him and clucked at his horse.

"Hold on, there, Bordeleau. I thought you didn't want any more horses."

"Wasn't it you, 'Zéar, told me only fools never change their minds?"

Caleb arrived at the rectory just as the priest was seeing his visitors off. As politely as possible, Caleb interrupted the farewells. He asked the priest if he might "discuss some business" with his charming guests and was taken aback to discover that the visitors were three of the priest's nieces.

He explained — a little white lie — that there'd been a mistake. He'd promised Mr. Veillette that he would buy the filly they had just hitched up.

"Veillette said nothing to us about another buyer," said one of the nieces.

"Well, my friend Veillette can be a bit forgetful. Isn't that right, Father?"

The priest dared not contradict him, but he knew perfectly well that it was Caleb, not Veillette, who was known for his lapses of memory.

Caleb offered to buy the mare from the women, but they refused categorically. Smiling tightly, Caleb attached a price to his offer. The women didn't budge. He upped the ante, and finally the women softened. He added a few dollars more, and they accepted, but on condition that he go with them to Veillette's. If he didn't have another good animal to sell them, the deal was off.

Caleb took the priest aside and asked if he could advance him some money, as he didn't have the necessary funds with him. The priest went red in the face. Caleb tried to mollify him by promising to pay him back promptly, and . . . to make a generous donation at church every Sunday for a month. Still annoyed, the priest nevertheless agreed and lent him the money — on the condition that he could go along to Veillette's to see what all this wheeling and dealing was all about.

Veillette wasn't surprised to see Caleb return. He was surprised, however, to learn that the ladies wanted another animal. He had no other mare to offer them, only stallions. The women hesitated, then accepted an almost black animal strongly recommended by Caleb.

While the ladies said their goodbyes to their uncle, Veillette approached Caleb, who was tying the filly to the back of his buggy.

"What do you want with my mare?"

"Nothing at all. I just want a lovely filly to rest my old, tired eyes on."

"Don't play games with me, Bordeleau. You know as well as I do this is the most beautiful filly in the township."

"The township . . . the whole township," repeated Caleb, sceptically. "Sure, she's lovely . . . but what good is she if you don't have a stallion to service her?"

"I've got stallions! And damned handsome ones, too."

"You haven't got one as handsome as this filly."

Both of them paused to wave to the priest's nieces, who were leaving Veillette's drive.

"My stallions are handsome, Caleb Bordeleau! You know that as well as I do!"

"Now don't get on your high horse, 'Zéar! Of course your stallions are handsome."

"I know you, Caleb Bordeleau. It wouldn't surprise me a scrap if you were up to something."

"Now, now, 'Zéar! You know I've just got three old work-horses." He cast a glance at the priest. "You'll have to excuse me, 'Zéar. I don't want to keep the father waiting."

Caleb turned on his heel and climbed into his buggy; the priest sat down beside him. Caleb punctuated the journey back to the village with expressions of gratitude, each more heartfelt than the last. Though the priest had been suspicious of Caleb's behaviour at first, everything now seemed perfectly normal — until Caleb asked him to keep the transaction secret, along with the price he had paid for the filly. The priest glared at him, but gave his word.

When Caleb returned home, he was greeted by Ovila and Emilie, who were coming out of the henhouse with two baskets full of large, brown eggs.

"You certainly took your time!" exclaimed Emilie.

"Not that long, Emilie. Just time enough to go fetch my filly from Veillette."

Emilie gave her father a surprised look. His nose always perspired when he was lying. It was shiny now, she could see, even though he discreetly tried to wipe it dry.

"So, my boy," he said to Ovila, "shall we put our two fine creatures in the paddock?"

Caleb patted his filly, unable to contain his joy at the thought that she was ready to be bred. Ovila went into the barn, ducking carefully to avoid hitting his head, and came out leading the stallion by the bridle. When the stallion saw the filly, he shuddered. Ovila unbridled him.

Emilie stood off to one side, preferring to watch from a distance. She had often watched the coupling of a stallion and a mare, but this one had a very different significance. The Pronovost stallion and the Bordeleau filly . . .

"Whose filly is that?" Célina had come out to see what was going on.

Emilie replied that it was her father's most recent acquisition. Célina frowned, but she couldn't help commenting on the proud bearing of the animal. "Is she one of 'Zéar Veillette's?"

Emilie told her it was. Célina burst out laughing. As far as she knew, she said, Caleb and Elzéar hadn't spoken since Easter Sunday. "As usual, it took a female to get those two talking."

Célina had once kept company with Veillette, before her heart had turned toward Caleb. Veillette had never forgiven Caleb, even after he married a healthy woman who had borne him eighteen children, all living, while Célina's life had been plagued by one illness after another.

The horses sniffed at each other. Caleb perched on the fence, determined not to miss the show, and Célina joined him. Ovila sat with Emilie, each shy in the other's presence.

"You can't imagine, Ovila. My father's been waiting all his life to have such beautiful animals. He's like a little child who's finally got his favourite toy."

Ovila just smiled. Then, to fill the silence, he remarked that he'd never seen a farmer take the time to watch a coupling.

Berthe joined Emilie and Ovila just as the filly took off at a gallop, the stallion at her heels. All of the Bordeleau children had come out to watch.

"Is that filly ours, Emilie?" Napoléon asked.

The children gathered around their parents. The filly stopped in her tracks and spun off in a new direction; the stallion followed suit. Their race was magnificent.

"Did you see that?" Caleb cried. "You'd think they were wild horses."

The filly whirled around and reared, hammering the stallion with her hooves. The stallion warded her off. Then she calmed down, and the stallion, snorting, positioned himself behind her. The filly stamped her feet. Finally, the stallion heaved himself onto her back and bit her neck. Emilie trembled as she felt Ovila's hand touch the nape of her neck ever so lightly. She turned her head just lo.g enough to see that he was looking at her intensely. Then she concentrated fiercely on the animals. Ovila did the same. She felt Berthe's eyes upon her.

The coupling lasted an hour. Caleb sat still the whole time. Finally, the exhausted animals found a shady corner to recover their strength. The stallion's impressive erection had disappeared.

The spectators drifted away. Ovila went into the paddock to try to catch his horse, but the animal was having none of it. Even with Caleb's help, Ovila couldn't get near him, so he had to resign himself to staying for lunch. Emilie feigned concern at the thought that he would be late getting to Shawinigan, but she had long since guessed that he had no appointment and that he probably hoped to reach town on Monday, which left him still a day and a half of leisure.

The mating began again in earnest after lunch. Ovila didn't dare try to separate the animals; Caleb wouldn't have liked it, he was sure.

Berthe, who had stayed only a few minutes that morning, returned in mid-afternoon, with her mother's permission. Emilie and Ovila were delighted: as a chaperone, they preferred Berthe over Emilie's parents or her young brothers and sisters.

The three decided to take a stroll. Packing some biscuits for a snack, they made their way toward Caleb's woods. They had gone as far as they wanted — far enough to be hidden from the house — when Berthe tripped and sprained her ankle. Ovila lifted her up and sat her on a big rock.

Emilie asked to see the injured ankle, but Berthe refused. "Go on ahead," she said, grimacing. "I'll just wait here. Pick me up on your way back."

Emilie and Ovila went further into the dense woods, Ovila leading the way and making sure that the branches didn't spring back to hit Emilie in the face. She smiled at the ease with which he cleared the way along paths thick with branches and foliage. Ovila really is a woodsman, she thought. It was as though he himself were a moving tree, so well did he blend in with the forest. She found him irresistible, with his shoulders straight as fence posts, his big, powerful hands, his high cheekbones and his aquiline nose, which, despite the blue of his eyes, betrayed a mysterious trace of Indian blood.

They walked like this for an hour, in almost total silence. Emilie savoured every moment of this pleasure that, only a day earlier, she had been determined to forbid herself. For his part, Ovila was absorbed in his thoughts. When he heard Emilie growing short of breath, he slowed his pace imperceptibly. He didn't want the distance between them to grow; he wanted to keep hearing her breathe, though he knew what he was feeling was a crazy dream, knew such emotions couldn't really exist. Pretending to scratch his leg, he gave himself a hard pinch. No, he wasn't dreaming. Emilie, beautiful Emilie, the Emilie of his dreams, was there behind him. They were alone, under the arch of greenery.

When they retraced their steps, they found Berthe asleep, curled up like a snake on the warm stone. Emilie nudged her shoulder, and Berthe leapt to her feet.

"Your ankle seems to have healed," Emilie teased.

Berthe, her ruse uncovered, merely marvelled at the miracles that could be wrought by a simple prayer wrapped up in sunshine. They wolfed down their snack and set off for home.

The stallion and the filly were still in the paddock; it seemed that Caleb had made no great effort to bring them back to the barn. As she left for home, Berthe asked Emilie if she wanted to do some work on the quilt that evening. Emilie said yes, and Berthe promised to return as soon as she'd finished bathing the children.

Ovila rejoined Caleb, who was milking the cows.

"I decided to get it done a bit on the early side," Caleb explained.

"I hope the cows won't be shocked or confused. I figured, since we've got company, why not hurry things up a little so we'll have time for cards — a nice game of hearts. You like playing hearts?"

This was a well-disguised question concerning Ovila's motive for visiting Emilie and, as Ovila understood it, his intentions for her.

"Has a cat named Emilie got your tongue?"

Obviously, Caleb wasn't going to give up easily. Ovila took a deep breath, realizing that it was to his advantage to be frank. He replied that he'd been in love with Emilie since he was fourteen years old, and that the real purpose of his visit had been to find out what her feelings were. He pointed out that she'd always been independent. He'd always hoped Emilie would become "his girl," but he'd never known what she thought of him.

Caleb listened attentively. The young man had guts, he decided. He could imagine the extent to which his daughter, the stubborn mule, would have kept her pupil at a distance — a distance that he could guess had melted away the night before.

"You don't have to say another word. I know my daughter. As of now, you have my confidence. I already trust her. But there's one thing, young fellow: her reputation. I'm sure you care about that. For you to come here to court her, that's fine. But don't go sighing under her window at the school. That's just not done. Fact is, I hope you'll find yourself a job in Shawinigan or Trois-Rivières. That would be best."

Ovila smiled, and he couldn't help leaning over to wrest Caleb's hand from the cow's teats so that he could shake it vigorously.

"I don't know you, my boy. But I can tell you that my daughter's got a sense of things. She feels the way people are. I just hope you never make me regret my faith in you."

A few rays of sun still clung to the fence rails. The Bordeleaus insisted that Ovila put off his departure to the next day. Ovila hesitated before accepting. Emilie kept out of the discussion. Her young brothers were making her argument for her, by throwing themselves at Ovila's shoulders as though he were a sturdy tree waiting to be climbed. When Berthe arrived, at the stroke of seven, she was hardly surprised to see Ovila still there.

Caleb and Ovila immersed themselves in a game of cards, while the two girls unfolded their handiwork.

"Think of it," Berthe whispered. "This will probably be the first thing ready for your hope chest!"

Emilie shrugged and pretended to find the remark inappropriate while Berthe gave her a teasing smile. Célina made up Ovila's bed, then excused herself to go up to sleep.

*R*ain pattered on the roof. Opening her eyes, Emilie made a face at the sullen weather. She heard Caleb rousing the family and looked at the time. Half past six! She jumped out of bed. They'd have to hurry if they wanted to get the milking done and be ready for nine o'clock mass. She went down to the kitchen and looked round for Ovila. Caleb said that he was in the barn, and Emilie realized that he must already have harnessed his stallion. She went up to her room, dressed quickly and went out into the heavy downpour. Opening the door of the outbuilding, she saw that the stallion was still in his stall.

"Ovila?"

"Over here!"

Ovila was milking the cows. Emilie burst out laughing. She'd been sure he was about to leave, and here he was busy with the daily chores! He explained that since he had risen early and seen that the bad weather would delay his departure, he thought he might as well lend a hand. Emilie thanked him.

"Will you come to mass with us, as well?"

"If this rain keeps up," he said, "I'll be happy to."

Two buggies drove from Caleb's to the church. The first, driven by Caleb, carried the family, as usual. The second, with Ovila at the reins, carried Emilie and Berthe. No parishioners were lingering outside the church, the rain having somewhat rushed them to their devotions.

Caleb led his family to their two pews; Ovila brought up the rear, following Berthe and Emilie. They were not unaware of the murmurings occasioned by their arrival, and the two girls stifled their giggles. Caleb stopped a moment beside Elzéar Veillette and greeted him with a nod. Veillette turned to look at Ovila. Emilie had no need to make out the whispering to know what was being said. People were wondering at Ovila's presence, asking each other who he was. The young girls surely found him tall and handsome. But what Emilie hoped to hear was that the two of them made an attractive couple.

The high mass was sung with more heart than voice. Emilie whispered in Ovila's ear that the choirmaster was Isidore Bédard, his mother's cousin. Ovila hunched his head down into his shoulders, looking almost apologetic. She smiled. In the three years she'd been going to Sunday mass with Ovila, never before had she sat with him in the same pew.

A ray of sunlight over the altar illuminated the church's single stained-glass window, but Emilie and Ovila weren't there to enjoy the sight; they had been among the first to emerge from the church. Ovila waited on the steps for his mother's cousin to come down from the loft. He asked Emilie to point him out, sure he wouldn't recognize the man. Ovila approached him, tapped his shoulder and introduced himself. Isidore Bédard warmly shook his hand, then introduced him all round — a gesture that Caleb didn't appreciate, as he would have preferred to do it himself.

Caleb had other things on his mind. He kept Elzéar Veillette in view, anticipating the moment when he would catch sight of Ovila's stallion. Because of the rain, all the horses had been led to shelter. Caleb, who usually lingered on the church steps to talk to his neighbours, seemed anxious to leave. In fact, he was the first to go and fetch his team, suggesting that Ovila follow him, "so you won't lose any time now that the sun's out."

Ovila went along, not suspecting that he would soon be at the centre of a lively scene. He followed Caleb, who was driving his mare — the old one — right to the foot of the church steps. Veillette had his back turned. Caleb stopped his buggy and asked his family to climb in, while Ovila got down from his buggy and helped Berthe and Emilie up. Just then, Veillette turned around. When he saw the stallion, his mouth fell open and his pipe fell from between his teeth, breaking neatly in two on the steps.

"Well, I'll be damned!" he whispered, to avoid being heard by the priest, who had just joined them. He approached the animal. He circled it. Ovila and Emilie watched without taking offence; this horse always made a big impression. Caleb was laughing up his sleeve and keeping his eyes fixed on Veillette.

When Veillette had completed his inspection, he marched over to Caleb. He was furious.

"So that's your workhorse, is it, Bordeleau?"

"No, it's my visitor's horse. And let me tell you, 'Zéar, he didn't need any coaxing to service that beautiful filly you sold me. If you like, 'Zéar, you can come and see me in a few years. We'll negotiate a good price so the stallion that filly's going to give me can service your mares."

"She'll drop a mare, Caleb. She comes from a long line of mares." He took another look at the stallion, then turned back to Caleb. "Caleb Bordeleau, you're a damned two-faced chiseler!" Veillette gathered up his brood and was gone in a flash.

After church, Ovila had a bite to eat, accepted a snack for the road and left the house with Emilie. They walked slowly, he holding the horse's bridle, she strolling by his side.

"I'll come and see you at the school," he promised.

"No, promise me you won't," Emilie replied. "I'll see you when I call on your family."

They agreed to talk to no one about their new understanding, hoping it would take some time for the rumour to travel the fifteen miles separating their respective villages.

As they parted, their hearts were torn by contradictions. Emilie remained by the roadside, watching until he disappeared from sight.

Thirteen

HOT TEARS ROLLED down Emilie's and Berthe's cheeks. They gazed at each other and hugged. Fresh sobs welled up from the depths of their shared childhood. Respecting their need for privacy, Berthe's parents stood to the side with the priest, who had also come to the train station to see Berthe off. Emilie wouldn't let go of Berthe. She told her that she understood her vocation, but she didn't know why she hadn't told her that she was to be cloistered. Emilie had always thought Berthe would be a teacher; she had always taken it for granted that in her vocation she would be continuing to care for children, as she had at home. She was angry at herself for never asking her friend which community she was planning to join. Berthe, a Carmelite! Berthe, in a veil! Berthe, whom she would never see again. Berthe, who, today, was leaving the world.

Berthe tried in vain to console Emilie. For her, this departure was more than sad. She knew that her parents were proud of her, but she also knew that they saw her leaving as nothing less than abandonment. She should have devoted two entire days to good-byes, but fear of her own emotions had caused her to put her farewells off to the last minute.

A long whistle, followed by the clanging of a bell, made everyone jump. Emilie buried her face in Berthe's shoulder. Berthe hugged her one last time. Even the priest wiped away a tear. Berthe's entire family knelt for his blessing; Emilie stayed standing but made the sign of the cross. At last, Berthe climbed the first step of one of the train cars, holding a single small suitcase. Emilie blew her a kiss, then turned her back and walked away before the train started rolling. She heard two more whistles and the locomotive spewing steam. Then she heard the wheels clicking on the rails that ran through the grass. The sounds grew fainter. She guessed at the force of the train's driving wheels, and at the ever-increasing speed with which it was carrying her friend away.

Emilie ran to the buggy her father had lent her, resolutely climbed up and blindly drove to the riverbank where she and Berthe had passed so many hours of their childhood and adolescence. Her irreplaceable Berthe. Of course, she had somewhat neglected her while she was living in Saint-Tite, but Berthe had never had reason to doubt her friendship.

Emilie lay down on their special fallen tree trunk and looked up at the cloudless sky. All she had known of Berthe was what Berthe had allowed her to know. Berthe, a Carmelite! Emilie began crying all over again. Berthe, flat on her belly before the entire community if she did something wrong. Berthe, who had decided not to have a boyfriend but who had sympathized with all of Emilie's recent romantic tribulations. And now, a Carmelite! Not able to leave her room. Not even able to wander around Montreal, where she was to live. A cloistered nun. A woman who would never again show her charming dimpled smile. A bear who had decided to hibernate for the rest of her days.

Emilie mourned her loss for three long hours before finally heading home. She didn't eat supper, isolating herself in her room; her need for privacy was respected. She quickly packed her suitcases, first laying in the quilt that they had finished just two days earlier. She looked for the drop of blood Berthe had stained the quilt with when she had pricked her thumb. She couldn't find it.

Fourteen

HE SCHOOL YEAR started smoothly. Emilie slipped into
her little schoolhouse as she would change into a comfortable dress. She tried to put off her habitual visit to the
Pronovosts' to the next day, but she couldn't resist; impatience
gnawed her bones to the marrow. She and Ovila were discreet. It
surprised her how easily they could say everything they needed to
with their eyes. Félicité was now in the full bloom of pregnancy and
due any day. Never had she carried so heavy and cumbersome a
baby, and she blamed her advanced age for making the task so
difficult.

As she did every year, Emilie eagerly welcomed her new students,
convinced that the first day of school was of prime importance. The
fact that Charlotte was back made Emilie's day complete. Emilie
noticed, though, that the girl's face was tired and drawn.

September was at last unfurling its splendour, and Emilie let her
students out of school early because of the magnificent weather. She
was busy correcting their work when Ovila arrived, out of breath.
He blew into the schoolhouse like a whirlwind and glanced around
the classroom to make sure Emilie was alone. Then he went to her

without a word, took her hand and led her to the stairs. Emilie frowned. She didn't like this. If one person, just one, were to decide to pay her a visit at this moment, she would be sent packing in short order. Taking the lead, she ran up the stairs and turned around only once she had reached the top, ready to scold him. She stopped when she saw how upset he was.

"What's the matter?" she whispered.

"It's my mother, Emilie. My father has asked Edmond to go for the doctor because the midwife can't get the baby out. My mother is so weak they're scared her heart will quit." He stopped, afraid that tears might drown his words.

Emilie froze. Then she got hold of herself and went to each window, to make sure that there was no one in sight. Only then would she go back to Ovila. She sat him down beside her on the bed, gently took his head and cradled it on her breast.

Ovila stayed only long enough to ease his heartache. Emilie calmed him down, reassuring him as much as she could. His mother was giving birth to her thirteenth child; her body was used to it; he shouldn't worry. Ovila went home with a lighter heart. He knew that Emilie had the same effect on him as the doctor's medicine for quieting coughs had on Ovide.

*D*osithée had heard that his wife was pregnant while he was at Lac Pierre-Paul. The news of this unexpected child, and of Ovide's illness, which came less than two months later, strengthened his resolve to fulfil a promise he'd once made to himself — to surprise his wife by building a larger house. When he came home from the lumber camp and saw his girls sleeping cheek by jowl in the living room, he went quickly, without Félicité's knowledge, to discuss with old man Mercure the purchase of part of his land. Mr. Mercure drove a hard bargain, knowing that what he made from this sale would enable him to live out his days in the village, in the home of one of his daughters. Since his wife had not borne him any sons, he had found himself alone when she died. He had already sold a few acres to Dosithée, but he had clung to the utopian hope that his grandsons would grow up faster than he was growing old.

He had now reached the age when a man leaves his property to his successors, but the eldest of his grandsons was only ten years old. Resigned, he gave up the land to Dosithée. He was comforted by the knowledge that his land would be well maintained by the Pronovost boys.

The deed of sale was duly notarized. Mr. Mercure conceded his "upper land" to Dosithée and his "lower land" to another purchaser, who wanted his house and outbuildings. Dosithée took Edmond with him as a witness, making him promise never to mention the transaction to his mother. On the sly, he had materials brought to the spot where he intended to build the house. He let his sons in on the secret, and they helped him raise the frame when the weather wasn't good enough to work in the fields.

Félicité, from whom it was usually impossible to hide even the smallest matter, didn't suspect a thing, what with her difficult pregnancy, Ovide's illness and the fact that two of the four acres were quite heavily wooded. Since she didn't leave the house any more, not even to attend mass, she had never seen the site. Dosithée, convinced that this child would be their last — as he had been when Télesphore was born — had decided to provide his wife with the house she had always wanted but never dared ask for: a house with a big kitchen, a living room and two bedrooms on the ground floor, and four bedrooms and a huge cedar closet upstairs. In their current home, she had sacrificed the closet to make room for Ovide so that the girls could return to their room. If Dosithée needed proof that the family was too crowded, he had it now. The new house wouldn't be ready until the following summer, which would give Félicité time to pack up for the move.

Félicité still had no idea about the new house when, in the middle of the night, she began to feel the first labour pains. She waited until morning before sending for the midwife. Félicité's pains were sharper than she had felt since the first three births. She had lost three children before Ovide had been born, and the stillborn babies had made her seriously doubt her future as a mother. Dosithée had comforted her, blaming all the problems on her small size. The arrival of Ovide had reconciled her with life, and thereafter she had given birth to a child almost every year.

"I have to be frank with you, Mrs. Pronovost," the midwife said after her examination. "Unless I'm mistaken, something is not right here. The baby seems to be too high, but the passage seems ready. We'll have to wait a while and see."

Félicité bore her pain patiently. The midwife examined her again, and knit her brow. Dosithée was concerned that his wife was taking so long to give birth, and the midwife explained that the baby was coming feet first. He asked her to do what she could.

Returning to Félicité's bedside, the midwife told her to lie on her stomach, shoulders deep in the pillow, head turned to the side, and to hold herself on her knees with her rear end up in the air. Knowing how experienced the midwife was, Félicité obeyed, though she had never given birth in this position. She had heard, the midwife explained, that if the baby didn't want to turn around, the mother had to turn instead. Félicité, at the limits of her endurance, stayed in this uncomfortable position until she felt the baby start to slide. She told the midwife, who sighed and helped her turn over onto her back.

"Now I think the little one will come out head first."

But nothing happened. Félicité was perspiring heavily and breathing hard, and she asked for some water. Anxious, Dosithée knocked on the door again and asked quietly if the doctor should be sent for. The midwife said yes, and Dosithée sent Edmond to get him. Ovila went to find Emilie, his ears full of the gasps and groans that the closed door had not been able to muffle.

$\mathscr{T}$he doctor was helping another woman when Edmond found him. As soon as he could, he rushed to the Pronovosts'. He discreetly questioned the midwife, with whom he worked often.

"It's the cord, Doctor. At least three turns. I've been able to undo just one."

The doctor examined Félicité and told her to be patient a little longer.

"Do I have a choice?" she replied weakly.

When she asked the time, the doctor took out his watch and told her that it was eight o'clock. Felicité calculated the length of her labour: twenty-one hours. She knew that a baby wasn't that patient.

The doctor took off his jacket and rolled up the sleeves of his white shirt, the cuffs of which were already stained with the blood of his last patient. He looked at the midwife, shaking his head. She indicated the door with a tilt of her head, and he nodded his agreement. He got up, patted Félicité's cheek for encouragement and told her that he was going out for a couple of seconds, just to get a glass of water. He left her room and went to see Dosithée.

"Mr. Pronovost, can I talk to you?"

Dosithée had been kneeling, head bowed in prayer. Startled, he rose to his feet and invited the doctor into the living room.

"Mr. Pronovost," the doctor said, "your wife is suffering. Her pulse is very weak, and I'm having a hard time finding the baby's heartbeat. I'm afraid I'm going to have to use the forceps."

Dosithée didn't know what forceps were. The doctor explained the procedure to him, adding that he had never performed it before, but today it seemed that he had no choice.

Clearing his throat, the doctor asked, "If I have to make a choice, and I pray it won't come to this, should I try to save the mother, or the baby?"

Dosithée blanched. He had heard stories where a man acted as God and decided a person's fate. He knew that the Church required that the child be saved. He wept, his back turned. "Save my wife, Doctor."

The doctor didn't react. He had expected a different response, but he understood Dosithée. Too many children in this family still needed their mother. He put his hand on Dosithée's shoulder. Dosithée collapsed into one of the living-room chairs and asked Edmond to go for the priest. Edmond left right away.

Returning to his patient's bedside, the doctor asked the midwife to hold Félicité's head and give her a little alcohol. He was hoping to keep her from seeing the forceps that he was taking out of his bag. Félicité was vaguely aware that she was drinking something; all she wanted was for the ordeal to end. Then the doctor asked the midwife to help him move Félicité down to the foot of the bed. Félicité offered no resistance. She didn't even feel that she had two pillows under her kidneys and that her legs were swinging off the foot of the bed. The doctor brought over a chair and a lamp. He made the sign of the cross before holding up the forceps. The midwife also made the sign of the cross, frightened by the medical "ice tongs." Félicité howled in pain, revived by the fire in her belly. Feeling he should be by his wife's side, Dosithée came into the room. In the kitchen, the children were in tears.

Dosithée knelt beside the bed and took Félicité's frail hand in his. The doctor, nervous, withdrew the forceps and decided to give the now almost unconscious mother a shot of morphine. He didn't really like using this drug — he was convinced that a woman must give birth in pain, as was written in the Scriptures — but he had now reached the limit of his beliefs. He waited for the medication to take effect, then reinserted the forceps, watching their slow progression into flesh whitened from stretching. He located the baby's head and held it gently but firmly. He prayed, for he was scared of puncturing an eye or perforating the fontanelle.

When he felt that he had a good enough grip, he began carefully to pull out the baby. He asked the midwife to press on the stomach every thirty seconds to help push, for Félicité was no longer having contractions. When the midwife applied pressure, the doctor pulled the baby toward him. It took twenty minutes to bring the infant out of its prison. The doctor tried to untangle the cord right away. To his great astonishment, the baby moved and made a little sound. Félicité opened one eye, then closed it.

Dosithée now watched the doctor very closely, also astonished that the baby could have lived after being pulled out with the pincers. The doctor finished untangling the baby, quickly cut the cord and immediately slapped the newborn. It was obvious that the infant wasn't breathing. The doctor pinched her heels, tapped her buttocks and back, but still she didn't breathe. Fortunately, Félicité was beyond noticing what was happening.

When the priest arrived, he knocked at the door of the bedroom and entered without waiting for a response. He took in the scene in an instant, put on his stole without taking the time to kiss it and approached the bed. While the doctor was still trying to breathe life into the baby, the priest sprinkled the tiny, bluish, motionless creature with holy water. In his nervousness, he used much too much water, and the infant stirred in reaction to this cold shower. The doctor rushed to put her down on a commode. She groaned softly, then cried out. The doctor thought his heart would leap from his chest, he was so excited at the possibility of saving both mother and infant. But then the baby seemed to lose consciousness. The doctor pinched her heels again, and she murmured but didn't cry.

Meanwhile, the priest administered the last rites to the mother, whose waxy complexion led him to fear the worst. The doctor hadn't had time to look after her, since he had been occupied with the newborn. He now turned the infant over to the midwife and returned to Félicité. The priest moved away to allow him room around the bed. Dosithée prayed silently, his eyes wide open, fearing that death was about to still his wife's heart. He heard vague gurgles but didn't turn to look at the baby. He would have plenty of time to look at her later.

Félicité had not regained consciousness, nor had she expelled the placenta; the doctor made a rapid examination and saw that it was stuck. As the priest left the room to pray with the children, the doctor looked at Dosithée and sighed. He would try everything to save her, but he had rarely seen a woman survive so many complications. Dosithée urged him on. When he tried a first time to extract the placenta, nothing came out. He took the mother's pulse and decided to let her rest a few minutes while he tended to the baby. With a shake of her head, the midwife let him know that there was no longer a baby to tend to. He returned to Félicité, followed by the midwife, who had covered the little lifeless body.

"You'll push like before," the doctor instructed. "With any luck, it will come out."

Between them, they succeeded, trembling from exhaustion and tension. Dosithée, more dead than alive, had no strength left for fear.

Fifteen

$\mathcal{E}$MILIE SAT AT HER WINDOW, wondering and anxious. She had seen the doctor come running. Then she had seen Edmond leave. Her chest had tightened when she saw him come back with the priest.

Nightfall obscured the details of the unfolding drama at the Pronovosts'. She could distinguish silhouettes leaving the house. She thought she recognized the midwife, then the priest, along with Dosithée. For how long had she been sitting there trying to understand a story that no one could tell her? She looked at the time. Midnight. Still, she remained riveted to the window for a few more hours. So what if she was tired tomorrow, all she needed was to keep the children busy. Anyway, Friday was never a long day.

At three o'clock, she decided to abandon her observation post and sleep a little. She hadn't seen the doctor leave, probably because he had decided to spend the night at Félicité's bedside. Perhaps he also wanted to keep an eye on the baby. Emilie was scared; the priest's visit had sent chills down her spine. What was the trouble? *Who* was in trouble? Mother? Child? Both? She couldn't believe that such a terrible thing could happen. Mrs. Pronovost was small, but she was strong. Healthy. Nothing bad could happen to Mrs. Pronovost. If Mrs. Pronovost couldn't have a problem-free birth, no woman could.

Emilie wept as she undressed. She slipped under the covers like a sleepwalker and rubbed her feet together, as she always did when she was unhappy. Tonight her body hurt, crying to her that she too was a woman, she too would have to live through nights when her insides were ripped apart. Her heart, tender with love, was beating with the same anguish she suspected was in Ovila's heart. Like a little girl, she was scared of what she might learn in the morning. She thought of Berthe . . . Her feet moved frenetically for some time before falling still, and her sobs slowly gave way to irregular breathing as she fell into the few hours of sleep she had allowed herself.

At dawn, she woke with a start and ran to the window. The doctor's carriage was gone. The house seemed calm. Too calm, she thought — the calm of death, which she refused to think about. She turned, stretched and took the time to pray as she hadn't done in a long time, calling on Berthe to help her. Half asleep, the words of her prayers became confused with those of her dreams. Finally, she roused herself. Her eyes were swollen with tears and sleep. She sprinkled her face with icy water, dressed and went down to heat water for her tea. She decided to correct the final pieces of home-work that she had put aside the previous evening when Ovila had arrived.

She didn't manage to correct a single child's work — her nose was glued to the window. Finally, she saw Ovila leave his house, trudging toward the school with a world of pain on his shoulders. She left the schoolhouse and went slowly to meet him. He saw her but didn't speed up. They walked at the same pace, their shoulders rising and falling together. Emilie had the feeling that they would never reach each other, they were walking so slowly. She would have liked to run, but Ovila's eyes and the shaking of his head seemed to exhort her to stay calm. When they met, halfway between the school and the Pronovost house, they stood still, prisoners of a long, unbearable confrontation. Finally, Emilie found the strength to speak.

"Do you want to have some tea at the school?"

"No, I'd rather walk up the hill."

Emilie hesitated, then reminded herself that she had got up early enough; she had a few minutes to spare. They walked side by side to the top of the hill, where the road turned and hid them from the view of the school and the neighbouring houses. Ovila stopped short and took Emilie's arm, making her stop, too. He pulled her to him. Enclosing her in his suddenly weak arms, he burst into tears. Emilie trembled. She refrained from questioning him, afraid of the answers she might hear. She would know the reason for his sorrow soon enough. He remained leaning on her shoulders for an interminable minute, then he stepped back, blew his nose violently and told her that his mother had received the last rites and the baby had been baptized just before it died.

"Marie-Anne, Emilie. A girl who lived a little less than ten minutes. Quite a life, eh?"

He fell silent, for there was nothing more to say. Emilie finally ventured to ask how his mother was doing.

"The doctor left early this morning. If Mama lives through the day, she'll probably be all right."

He stopped himself. Emilie understood. A long day ahead. She squeezed his hand and told him that she was sorry to have to rush him, but she had to get back to school. Ovila whirled around, furious.

"My mother is in agony and you have nothing to say except you have to go to work? Good Lord, is your heart made of stone? Can't you stay with me, when I need you to stay?"

Her heart torn, Emilie turned on her heel and fled down the hill. Ovila wasn't fast enough to stop her. She heard him calling for her to wait, but she didn't stop.

"You aren't a woman, Emilie. You have a mind but no heart!"

*T*he day was long and trying. None of the Pronovost children came to school, and Emilie let her pupils go home early. She couldn't stand up straight, drained by anguish and lack of sleep. She neatened her classroom meticulously, hoping that busy hands would keep her mind from wandering. She waited for Ovila, sure that he had seen the children leave the schoolhouse. But he didn't come. His absence made her fear the worst.

She waited until sundown; then, unable to sit still any longer, she left the school and walked resolutely toward the Pronovost home. But then she stopped. What if she arrived just as Mrs. Pronovost was drawing her last breath? She decided to knock at the home of Mr. Pronovost's brother, Joseph-Denis. They would surely know the news.

Joseph-Denis's wife, Virginie, opened the door, a blue apron fastened over her white apron. Under other circumstances, Emilie would have smiled at the obsession that made her protect a clean apron with a dirty one. Virginie invited her in. Emilie accepted, glancing around the kitchen. She had never been here before, but she had heard that it was kept spotless. She was so impressed by the place that for a moment she forgot the reason for her visit. Not a speck of dust. Not a drop of mud at the kitchen door. The floor was waxed to a shine fit for a living room. The table was covered with an ironed and starched tablecloth.

Emilie's musings were interrupted when Virginie asked if she had heard the news.

"Nothing since this morning," Emilie answered. Then she paused for a couple of seconds to see if she had raised any suspicions by mentioning that she had already heard something. "Are there any new developments?"

Virginie smiled. "All things considered, Félicité is doing well. She sat up for her lunch and supper. Once again, praise God, the extreme unction has brought forth a miracle."

Emilie closed her eyes and heaved a long sigh of relief. She got up, her heart light, her spirits revived; she thanked everyone, complimented them on their lovely house and walked back up the road to the school.

For a long time, she sat in her rocking chair, waiting for Ovila to come. He was probably held up by chores. She started to worry when the sun had been down long enough for the animals to have been stabled. She lit the lamps and waited. She waited until all the lights went out at the Pronovosts', except those in an outbuilding.

*C*louds veiled the sun, throwing a shadow on the already grey faces of Dosithée and his children. Quite a crowd attended the funeral, watching as the small, white coffin Ovila had made, working Friday through the day and night, was laid in the ground. Since Félicité was still confined to her bed, the priest had proposed that neighbours come for the viewing only Saturday morning, and the baby be buried that afternoon. Emilie was not notified, so she didn't attend the burial, thinking that it would take place on Monday.

She was in the village shopping when she saw the hearse returning from the cemetery. The Pronovost family, on their way back to Bourdais, followed. She watched from the window of the general store, at first stunned when she realized what had happened, then angry that Ovila hadn't needed her with him, no matter how discreetly.

Sixteen

A COLD NOVEMBER FOLLOWED an Indian summer so glorious that one could almost believe the warm weather would last forever. Félicité had recovered from her terrible labour, to the secret surprise of the doctor and the midwife. She accompanied her husband to the cemetery to visit the child she had never seen. Marie-Anne slept peacefully beside her three brothers. Félicité squeezed Dosithée's arm and told him how much she regretted that they had had to bury the first three and the last of their children. Dosithée answered that he had never understood God's will, but he thanked Him for having permitted Félicité to stay among the living. He had never told her all the details of the birth, simply explaining that the doctor had tried to get the baby out using pincers, and that if he had succeeded, the baby would have survived without problems. The doctor had told him that the baby had died without ever drawing a breath; it wasn't the forceps that had killed her.

Dosithée wanted to wipe from his memory the dilemma posed by the doctor. He had never told his wife about it. He had hoped that time and distraction would chase from his mind the gurgling sounds of the infant trying to breathe. He had tried to forget that he had not got up to see her, thinking she was alive and healthy, that he had never seen her alive. His regret was bitter, his heart troubled by the idea that perhaps he could have done something, even if it was just giving her the paternal blessing he had bestowed on his first three sons.

He and Félicité left the cemetery, leaning on each other, giving a last glance to the tiny patch of disturbed earth that protected Marie-Anne from the cold, and from life. As they were going home, Dosithée decided that it was time to tell his wife about his purchase of Mr. Mercure's land. Since the birth, he hadn't wanted to bang a single nail into the frame of the new house. He drove her past its bare skeleton; she remained expressionless. When he told her that he would finish it as soon as he could, she just shook her head. She didn't believe a word of it. Nor did Dosithée. He had given up on it. The frame was holding, solidly anchored in the earth. The walls of the first floor were all up. Félicité could see where the main door, the side door and the windows would go. The work had stopped at the upstairs floor, which the wind and rain had swept utterly clean of sawdust. Félicité walked around the house, followed by Dosithée. Finally, she smiled and thanked him for thinking of her. Dosithée just grunted.

Félicité never talked about the house again, except to scold her sons for keeping the secret so well. The boys, still disturbed by the fear of losing their mother and the sadness of burying a sister, made no comment.

In spite of the coming holiday, December brought no laughter to the homes of Bourdais. Emilie sat in her room and looked at the biscuits she had forced herself to bake, although she didn't want to eat them. Since the day of the burial, she had not seen Ovila. She had overheard his brothers saying that he had left the village to work in Shawinigan or "somewhere around there." After a few weeks, she visited Mrs. Pronovost and was heartened to see that she was doing well; she confirmed that Ovila had gone.

Emilie went often to get her mail, always hoping, in vain, to hear from Ovila. She realized that he probably hadn't forgiven her for leaving him alone that morning. She regretted her obstinacy in insisting on going back to the school, but she also knew that she really hadn't had any choice. Since then, she had spent many evenings drying her eyes, wracked by a pain that she felt was not entirely deserved. It would have been so simple if they could only have talked about what happened that day. But it seemed that Ovila didn't feel the same way.

Emilie wrote to Berthe, telling her about all the misfortune that had befallen the Pronovost family. She couldn't give her all the details of what had happened with Ovila, so she just mentioned that her old pupil had come to seek "comfort and a good word" and to ask her to pray. Not knowing how to describe her feelings, she wrote, "I wasn't able to pay him the attention he wished, since I had to be in class when the children arrived." She concluded, knowing that Berthe would understand, "Their son Ovila was so shaken that he left the village without telling anyone."

*B*erthe did indeed understand, and she wrote Emilie a long, consoling letter. She alluded to the "prodigal son" in such discreet terms that Emilie had to reread the letter a few times to figure out that Berthe was telling her that he would surely come back and they would straighten things out.

Emilie went home to her family for Christmas. In contrast to other years, she felt no desire to return to Saint-Tite. She drifted into 1899 with none of the excitement that comes from witnessing the last year of a century. Winter once again gave way to spring, and Emilie hoped that Ovila would return from wherever he was working. But he didn't. She devoted all her energy to her teaching, preparing her pupils for a painless end-of-year visit from the inspector. True to form, he came, covered with dust, on a hot and humid June day. He had taken pains to arrive early so that he could spend the entire afternoon in Emilie's classroom. She understood that he would never change, and she didn't forget to favour him with a little gentle flirtation.

The sun was beating down when Henri Douville arrived. He started his visit as he always did, reading the notebooks Emilie supplied. She hadn't forgotten to prepare a class plan, even indicating which students excelled in which subjects. Douville did an honest job. He had no use for the inspectors who tested a teacher too severely by questioning her students at random. In his opinion, schools were meant for learning, and he knew the difficulties faced by children who wanted to do well there. The parents didn't encourage them enough; they didn't know what he knew: that education was becoming a necessity. The proof was that the Saint-Gabriel brothers had decided to build a college right here in Saint-Tite. Douville had had the privilege of going to college, and he hoped that some of the students seated before him would want to go, too. Thus, he kept himself from discouraging even the slightest ambition.

As they did each year, Emilie's students performed well. This teacher deserved a great deal of credit, and the inspector was full of compliments. He would have found it inappropriate to tell her that he enjoyed seeing her, but he did permit himself to let her know in other ways. Each year, he strongly recommended that she receive the teaching bonus, but each year she was turned down.

The children had been out of school about fifteen minutes when a thunderstorm hit. Douville was forced to wait until the thunder rolled away and the rain let up. Emilie smiled at the poor inspector's "bad luck" and invited him to share a salad and a platter of cold roast beef, which she served in her room. She feigned polite interest when Douville asked her if she had ever travelled.

"What kind of travelling do you mean?"

"Big trips, to the United States or even Europe," he said.

Emilie's look hardened. Douville had known her for almost five years, and he knew very well that she had travelled only down the road from Saint-Tite to Saint-Stanislas, with a short excursion to Trois-Rivières for her government examinations.

"You know very well, Inspector, that I've never travelled."

Douville chewed his food slowly. He asked Emilie for a napkin, which he used after each mouthful. Emilie watched him, suddenly aware of his nice manners, which she tried to imitate. He complimented her on the meal, then he said that he had meant to ask if travelling interested her.

Emilie lit up. "Yes, of course! I'd love to see more of the country — first all of Montreal, and Quebec City." Then she told him about a cousin of her father's who had gone to the Klondike, and another who lived in Keene, New Hampshire, where he had been working in a textile plant since 1892. The inspector listened closely.

"If I never marry," Emilie added, "I'd like to save my money so that one day I can take a trip — on a steamship — to New York, then across the ocean to Europe. But why did you ask?"

Douville went to the window to watch the falling rain, discreetly picking his teeth. Emilie gathered the plates and began to wash them. She wondered what else she could do to entertain this intimidating visitor. Despite her best efforts, she kept clinking the plates in the dishpan.

He discarded his toothpick and sat down again. Emilie gave him a rapid once-over and found that, in spite of his crossed eyes, he was a good-looking man. In profile, his eyes didn't show so much. His hair was grey, true, but his shoulders were solid, if a bit stooped.

Douville let her finish washing the dishes, since she had refused his offer of help. The rain was still falling heavily. Darkness was creeping into the school, not so much because of the late hour — summer solstice was approaching — but because of the density of the downpour and the clouds. Emilie took off her apron and sat down at the table. Mr. Douville looked at her alertly. Breaking the silence that had slipped between them, Emilie offered to make tea. He thanked her, but reminded her that he didn't like to drink tea in summertime. She had forgotten this detail.

Emilie asked him to excuse her and went downstairs to the bathroom. She had installed a mirror and a shelf on which she had put some rice powder, some kohl that she had ordered from Montreal and could use without looking all made-up, a hairbrush, a comb and a small bottle of toilet water. Of course, these items were hidden from her students' view in a closed box. She looked in the mirror and spent a good ten minutes "refreshing" herself. When she went back upstairs, she was disappointed to see that Douville seemed to have fallen asleep in the rocking chair. But as soon as he heard the rustling of her skirt, he opened his eyes.

"I was relaxing," he said. "You know, these days really wear me out."

"I'm sure they do."

Douville looked at her carefully, noting that she looked different, though he couldn't figure out why. He remarked on it.

"My eyes are bright?" She feigned surprise. "It must be fatigue."

Douville leapt to his feet. "I'm sorry. I must go. You should have told me that you're tired."

"Of course not! Stay a little longer. The weather isn't cleared up yet."

"Hasn't . . ." said Douville.

"What?"

"You said 'isn't.'"

"I did?"

"Yes. You should pay a little more attention. You have an excellent vocabulary, but you mix up your verbs."

Emilie was shocked. No one had ever criticized her language. She wondered if she should be grateful or tell him frankly to mind his own business. She thanked him dryly, adding that she would try to be more careful. Realizing that he had hurt her feelings, Douville apologized. He explained that in college he had developed an obsession with — "an almost pagan worship" of — the language of Molière. Emilie reassured him by saying that he had done well to correct her (although she hadn't really appreciated it) and she would speak more slowly and pay more attention to all of her words.

The rain began to let up. Douville stood and turned to the window. "Well, I think I can get going now."

Emilie agreed. She was running short of subjects for conversation. Douville went down to the classroom to collect his papers. He thanked her again, adding that he had never eaten in such pleasant company. She smiled and replied that she had rarely dined with someone with such good manners.

He dismissed this remark with a sweep of his hand. "What do you expect," he said. "I've spent my life in institutions. I was raised by nuns and Jesuits in Montreal."

"Oh!" Emilie said, surprised at the sudden confidence. "I thought you were from around here."

"I've been here for ten years, because of my work, but I was raised in Montreal."

"Montreal! Lucky you. In fact, I have a friend who's living in Montreal now . . ."

"Do you think I was lucky to spend my childhood in an orphanage?"

Emilie bit her lip. She thought he had received a good education because he came from a wealthy family.

"I'm very sorry . . ."

"It's nothing. I thought you knew. You see, when good families came to the orphanage to adopt a child or take him as a ward, they wanted a so-called perfect child. Me, with my eyes, I stayed in the orphanage."

Emilie let him talk. She had no idea how to remedy the injury she seemed to have caused.

Douville put on his hat and went to the door. He turned toward her. "I asked you if you liked travelling and you said yes. All right. I'm not going to ask for an answer right away, but I would like to ask you to be my wife. Next summer, we could go to Paris, France, where there's a big international exposition."

"Yes, I know," she heard herself say.

"I know that you know. That's not the question," he said dryly. "I just want you to think a little about my proposal. If you have no objections, and if your parents approve, I'd like to visit you occasionally this summer. I know that I'm a little older than you, but our tastes in common — literature, the French language, children — are probably sufficient to help us form a lasting union."

Emilie didn't answer. She wanted to think. Douville left the schoolhouse without saying another word. She ran to the door.

"Mr. Douville! If you come to Saint-Stanislas, you know where to find me!"

Seventeen

*E*MILIE WENT HOME for the summer. She had again left the key to the schoolhouse with the Pronovosts, taking advantage of her visit to ask for news of Ovila. It turned out that he was still in Shawinigan; Dosithée told her that he'd spent the winter in a lumber camp, then worked as kitchen help in a log-drivers' camp. After that, he'd been hired on a construction site for an electrical switching station.

"You know," Dosithée added, "Ovila's no letter writer, and he's not big on details."

Emilie thanked them. It was clear that they didn't approve of their son's departure, especially because he was needed on the farm.

She had missed him terribly at first but, little by little, the pain had faded. A crush. She had had a crush. She might have wished for things to be different, but she knew now that Ovila's feelings for her weren't as deep as hers for him.

In Saint-Stanislas, she rarely talked about Ovila. When Caleb asked her about him, her answers were vague. Caleb figured that there was no point in twisting the knife in the wound. On the other hand, Emilie mentioned Henri Douville often, and Caleb and Célina realized that there might be a son-in-law on the horizon. Caleb had actually met him once, at some meeting or other. Douville seemed to be an educated man, perhaps the kind of man who would please Emilie. After all, she needed a man as knowledgeable as she was; a farmer might not be able to satisfy her completely.

Douville came to visit Emilie, as he had promised, and she introduced him to her family. No one commented on his crossed eyes, and Emilie didn't even notice them any more. But during their long walks in the woods, she couldn't help comparing his awkwardness to Ovila's easy movements.

Whenever he came, Douville brought her a little gift: handkerchiefs with her initials embroidered on them; a jar of preserved fruit; a bottle of real perfume. He courted her with a great deal of dignity. She began to be happy when she was with him, for he taught her so many new things. She took more and more care with her speech, and they spent many evenings talking, by the light of a lantern, about Europe and about Paris, which he was eager to visit. Paris and its sophistication. Paris and its museums. Paris and its history. Emilie imagined herself at his side, first on the bridge of a ship, then in a cabin — a small detail, which she looked forward to about as much as death in the family — then in Paris, in the cathedrals and museums. But she had trouble picturing the city — what would an underground train be like?

Summer was drawing to a close. Emilie looked at the new filly nursing at her dam's teat. Like her sire, she had a pretty blond mane. Caleb had named her La-Tite, in honour of her origins. Emilie remembered the day she had spent with Ovila more than a year ago. Berthe had been there, too. What would Berthe think of her marrying Henri? Oh, if only she could talk to Berthe, tell her how much she liked Henri's company, even though he didn't arouse a fraction of the feelings in her that Ovila did. Tell her how smart Henri was, how good his manners were; how he had never lived in a true home, and how hard she'd work to help him make up for lost time; how he wanted many children, even if he was starting his family a little late. Describe to her how he seemed to know about so many things. If only she could have talked to Berthe. Berthe would have understood.

Douville's arrival interrupted her thoughts. She smiled as she went to greet him. He had brought her a crystal vase; she had never seen anything so beautiful. After eating supper with the family, he asked Caleb if he could have a word with him. Emilie understood, and so did Caleb. The two men went outside and returned a few minutes later. Caleb asked Emilie and Célina to join them in the living room. He informed them that Douville had put on his kid gloves and asked for Emilie's hand.

"He has my consent, if he has yours," he told his daughter. "What do you say, Emilie?"

Emilie blushed, looked at Douville and said that she agreed but would like to take the year to think about it. She reassured Douville, telling him that she would be only twenty in December and that she intended to finish the school year at Saint-Tite. She added that there was no hurry, they could easily get married at the end of June, 1900. With a nervous laugh, she joked that it would simplify the arithmetic: if they got married in 1900, they would always know which anniversary was coming. Douville sighed; he had wanted the nuptials to take place at Christmas.

Caleb had tried not to admit that, between Ovila and Douville, he preferred Emilie's first suitor. Douville was a very good man, true, but his daughter wasn't the same with him. He would give her a good future, but Caleb wasn't sure that Emilie had what it took to live with such a logical, wise man. He could already see some sparks flying. Henri didn't know the fire of his daughter's spirit. In fact, Caleb wondered whether Emilie had held on to her old passion. She had become so composed, so ladylike. When Douville was around, the way she spoke almost didn't sound like French. Sure, the inspector spoke nice, but it was funny to hear Emilie talk like that.

Caleb discussed the match with Célina, who didn't seem to have the same apprehensions. She admired Douville and reminded Caleb that a woman should admire her husband if she wanted to be happy. All she said about Ovila was that he seemed to be an adventurer, and Emilie needed a stable husband like Henri. Caleb wasn't so sure. He had found Ovila's sudden departure very mysterious.

Emilie and Henri decided that it would be better if he didn't visit her in Saint-Tite; they would see each other at Christmas. On the other hand, he could write her if he wished — on official paper, of course. At Emilie's suggestion, they would not reveal their engagement to anyone. Douville understood this restriction — such news might compromise her chances of getting a bonus.

Henri and Emilie parted on the eve of the latter's return to Saint-Tite. She had permitted him to kiss her, which he had done with honourable modesty. He could have taken advantage of the absence of a chaperone to devour her lips more greedily, but he hadn't. Emilie said goodbye and watched him go. The moment he turned his back, she wiped her mouth and then bit her lips a number of times, as if to make sure they still had feeling. She had felt nothing. Nothing. But he was so good . . . so generous. And Paris . . .

Eighteen

$\mathcal{E}$MILIE RETURNED TO SCHOOL with no great enthusiasm; this year of teaching seemed a little like purgatory. There was news of Ovila, who had been gone almost a year. Mrs. Pronovost told her that he had paid a short visit home during the summer to allow an injury he had sustained at work to heal completely. Emilie pressed for details, trying to remain impassive when she heard that he had gashed his foot with a pickaxe. Félicité said that he had stayed just a few days, but he had found time to visit the schoolhouse, using the key Emilie had left. Emilie excused herself and went to unpack.

She entered the schoolhouse, put down her suitcases and looked around the classroom to see if Ovila had left her something. Nothing. She climbed the stairs, pushed open the trap door and struggled miserably into her room, dragging her heavy suitcases. No sign of Ovila here, either.

She spent much of the evening washing dishes, putting her clothes away and making her bed. This done, she went down and sat at her desk. She looked around the classroom. This year, she would have thirty-one students — the first time she would have more than thirty. It worried her a bit. She should have asked the commissioners to make sure that the extra desks they had promised her would be delivered in time for the start of classes. She would ask Mr. Pronovost to make sure they were here tomorrow, since the children would arrive the day after. Standing still, she let her eye rove freely around the classroom. She glanced at one of the windows, which had been cracked since May; her gaze fell on the plank-and-nails coatrack, which looked abandoned. Noticing that it was getting late, she went up to her room and quickly had a little supper. That night, she dreamed about Henri. They were in a boat together on a wild, tossing ocean.

❋

*I*n the morning, Emilie felt more like herself. She dressed and did her hair, then went over to the Pronovosts' to ask about the extra desks. Mr. Pronovost smacked his forehead; he had completely forgotten. He asked Emilie if she wanted to go to the village with him; some desks would surely be available in the South Concession school. She gritted her teeth — she had many other things to do — but agreed. They decided to leave as soon as Dosithée was finished his chores.

They had been rolling along about five minutes when they passed the house Dosithée had started the year before. He sighed. "I think it would have been a nice house. Now, I don't have the heart to finish it. I shouldn't complain, but since I began to buy up old man Mercure's land, Lazare started having more fits, Ovide's lung problems began, I almost lost my wife, and I've buried a fourth child. Now Ovila's gone like a gust of wind, without a word. Do you know why he left?"

Emilie was startled by the question. She hadn't realized the depth of the Pronovosts' bitterness. Now, everything was clear: he hadn't said anything to them, either.

"Why would you think I'd know anything? Ovila . . . Ovila is a . . . um . . . funny sort of fellow, although I'd still like to hear from him."

"We thought he was writing you."

"You did? Why?" She tried to sound surprised.

"Well, Miss, it's no secret to anyone that Ovila always liked you. Anyway, it was no secret to me."

He was quiet for a few minutes. Emilie didn't want to let on that he was right. He continued, "You might as well admit it. Me, I always hoped that you . . . that one day you . . . oh, well. I thought about Ovide, but then I thought about Edmond, but . . . anyway, I never thought about Lazare. Ovila, even if I thought he was a little young, I thought that maybe . . . Anyway . . . I guess my boys just aren't the marrying kind . . ."

Emilie didn't say anything, remembering Ovide's discreet advances, Edmond's special attentions and finally Ovila's declarations. She didn't even feel the tear that was trickling down her cheek. Dosithée didn't notice it either.

"Ovila didn't say anything to you this summer?" she asked, finally.

"No, not a word. He spent his evenings at the Hôtel Brunelle and his days chipping away at that piece of wood he always has in his hands. I hoped he was home for good, but he wasn't. The land doesn't interest him. He's no help to his father. That leaves Emile, Oscar, Télesphore and Edmond. But Edmond is more interested in breeding horses than in farming. That's not enough to keep the farm going."

Emilie wondered why he was confiding in her this way; she could offer nothing to ease his sadness. So taken up was she with his confession that she didn't feel her own sadness settle in her breast and her lungs, cutting her breath and softly smothering her heart.

They were able to find extra desks, which they loaded in the buggy and brought back to the schoolhouse. Emilie still wondered why Ovila had visited the school during the summer. Dosithée went in first, carrying a desk, and Emilie followed with a chair. Back and forth they went in silence, depositing everything at the back of the classroom. He offered to help her line them up properly, but she politely refused, telling him that she preferred to do it alone. In the afternoon that stretched before her, she would organize the classroom and write her words of welcome on the blackboard. Dosithée gently pinched her cheek before leaving. She smiled and wondered if she should tell him that he hadn't been mistaken, there had been something between her and Ovila. She went upstairs to change her clothes.

She came down two stairs, then sat on the steps. Had he come to sit here too? She looked down at her classroom, locating Ovila's desk. She imagined him writing, saw him raising his arm to answer a question. She remembered his smallest gestures, from his running his hand through his hair to neaten it when he arrived in the morning to his jumping up to open or close a window for her.

Emilie's heart was struck by lightning. She stood up and ran down the stairs, went to Ovila's desk and opened it. There it was — a letter! A letter from Ovila! Finally! Nervous, she sank into his chair. She turned the letter over and over in her hands. Her heart was pounding. She folded the letter and smoothed it out. Weakening, she took a deep breath and tore open the envelope, which was addressed to "EMILIE" and adorned with a drawing of a bird.

The crickets provided the accompaniment for Emilie's soaring thoughts. She retired early, contrary to what she had planned. After quickly arranging her classroom, she undressed slowly, waltzing around her room holding the letter close to her heart. She wanted to lie down so that she could let her imagination run free. Ovila was there beside her. He was talking to her, telling her about his shame and desperation. He asked if she had missed him and begged her pardon for having left her so suddenly. Then he told her about the lumber camp, and the log-drivers, and the site of the electrical switching station, the name of which she didn't yet know but which, he said, would produce enough electricity to light a large town. He then admitted that he regretted having caused her so much pain. He asked if her hair was still long and if she still put it in braids when she was tired. He begged her to wait a little longer. Not too long. Just enough for him to save the money that "we" would need. Ovila . . .

She curled up tight to quell the delicious shivers running through her body. Her spine was curled so that her knees were tucked under her chin, the letter next to her skin under her nightgown. Not for a second did she think of Henri, or of the promise she had made him. She saw only Ovila: his nonchalant walk, his clear blue eyes. Opening her eyes, she rolled over and tried to imagine his face, but it retreated before her mind's eye. In anguish, she wondered if she could have forgotten him so quickly. And did he remember her, was he dreaming of her the way she was dreaming of him at this moment? Aching for him to come back, she got up, drank a glass of water and went back to bed. Finding the little corner her body had warmed, she made believe that Ovila had slipped in next to her.

Morning surprised her asleep on her back, her nightgown shoved up to her chin. She quickly pulled it down. Feeling languorous, as if she had really spent the night with her true love, she sang as she washed her face. Downstairs in the classroom, she thanked the sky for being filled with sunshine. The floor shone, as it always did on the first day of school. She was no longer in purgatory. Ovila would be here in a few weeks. She welcomed her students and laughed as she started her fifth year as a teacher.

Nineteen

$\mathcal{E}$milie celebrated her good fortune right up to mid-October. Every morning, she told herself that today would be the day when Ovila would surprise her. Every evening, she was sure that the surprise was waiting for her tomorrow. Convinced of his imminent arrival, she wrote her parents to tell them that she would spend the All Saints holiday at Saint-Tite. But by the end of October, her spirits sank again. No word from Ovila, and four letters from Henri.

She always wrote back to Henri, not wanting to discourage his attentions. His letters were tender and full of poetry: he went into raptures over her autumn-coloured hair and her springtime eyes; he talked of birds and nests, of bits of straw and broods. He told her stories as if she were a little girl, describing, among other things, the long journey across the Atlantic of a bottle with a love message in it. At first, Emilie found such epistles silly, but Ovila's absence and her desperation finally led her to appreciate them — and even, she admitted, to look forward to their arrival. Ovila's face, his presence, his smell began to fade from her mind.

On November second, All Souls' Day, Emilie went with Mr. and

Mrs. Pronovost to the cemetery to visit the graves of their four children. She felt that she had to make up for not being at the burial of Marie-Anne. All three were kneeling and praying when they heard cries, followed almost immediately by the agonizing sound of the fire alarm and the church tocsin. Making the sign of the cross, they ran toward the convent, which was in flames. Dosithée told his wife to go home and asked Emilie to take her back to Bourdais, but Félicité wanted to stay to help the nuns and boarders. She promised to leave if there was danger.

Dosithée threw off his jacket and rolled up his shirtsleeves, then called to Emilie to find his sons and tell them to come and help fight the fire. She drove the horse like the wind all the way to the Pronovosts'. Ovide and Edmond were outside, and she told them to get Lazare, Emile and Oscar. The brothers didn't wait to ask questions; they knew that something must be seriously wrong. They got into the buggy, none of them thinking to take the reins from her hands, and she turned the horse back toward the village. The thick smoke ahead told them where they were going, and why.

They arrived at the scene of the tragedy at the same time as dozens of other villagers. The work was quickly organized, with the firemen placing the volunteers in strategic positions. The drivers were busy around their brand-new fire truck: some unrolled the hoses, others formed a chain between the convent and Rivière des Envies to fill their hundred-gallon barrel. The job of the last fireman on the scene was always to calm the horses; although they were unquestionably reliable for pulling the truck to the scene of a fire, they became dangerously agitated once they were near the blaze.

The volunteers, Dosithée first among them, formed two long chains. The men in the first chain passed along the water buckets toward the fire as quickly as possible, and those in the second line returned the empty buckets to the water source. The Pronovost boys took their place in these lines, with Ovide, because of the condition of his lungs, finding a spot away from the billowing smoke.

The women's work was organized differently. They converted the church sacristy into a huge emergency room for the nuns and the convent boarders who hadn't gone home to be with their families for the holiday. To everyone's great relief, no one had been injured; things might have been very different if the fire had broken out in the middle of the night. Many of the victims, though safe and sound, were in a state of shock. Some wept softly, others sobbed loudly, and still others turned their fear into gales of laughter.

Emilie and Félicité lit the stove in the sacristy and boiled water to make mint tea, which they served to all and sundry, both victim and volunteer. Other women of the parish emptied their larders to bring food to the church — cauldrons of soup, baked beans, boiled vegetables.

In less than three hours, enough clothing and food had been gathered to see to the needs of the entire population of the convent. The convent itself had completely disappeared from Saint-Tite. The church was full of its parishioners — men covered with sooty sweat, women wilted from the effort of bringing everything to the sacristy.

The evening was devoted to organizing a makeshift dormitory. An appeal was launched to lodge the homeless with families. The nuns refused all invitations, preferring to stay together in the church to thank God for keeping them alive, and their fellow citizens respected their choice.

But that still left the children who boarded at the convent and were taught by the nuns. Over the past five years, Emilie had opened the doors of her school to dozens of children, so she agreed to open her home now to two more, Alma and Antoinette. Moved by their predicament, she hadn't thought twice about it — nor had she considered that she was taking in not children but teenaged girls, almost as old as she was. When the Pronovosts headed back to Bourdais, at dusk, they drove the three girls to the schoolhouse before going home themselves.

Emilie didn't talk much to her guests during the ride; she felt strangely ill at ease. She glanced over at them: Antoinette was small and stocky, her hair was held back with ribbon, and she had a thin mouth and lively eyes. Alma was anxious, with a sad, pensive, faraway look. Her dimples were invisible at the moment, but they were surely pretty once her face was lit by a smile.

Emilie opened the door for her "boarders." She looked around the classroom with relief; the desks in their straight lines and the blackboard were familiar, reassuring sights. Emilie's heart beat loudly. Now she had to take them to her room. Her own room. She had to reveal who she was — her tastes, the hours spent sewing and decorating — to share her small, private domain, very different from the classroom. Would they know at a glance what she dreamed of? Would they find the place where she kept Ovila's one letter and the many from Henri? She'd better put them in a safe place. Suddenly, she had lost her teacher's self-confidence. She had become a girl, just like these two, and she regretted bringing them home with her.

Upstairs, Emilie put some water on so that all three could soak in a good, hot bath. Alma and Antoinette offered to let her bathe first, and she politely thanked them. She had wondered if they would be so courteous; she would have been uneasy washing in water that total strangers had used. She lent each girl a clean slip and apologized for not being able to give them nightgowns. The two girls thanked her for her concern but said that they were just as happy with good undergarments.

Emilie filled her tub with hot water and then slipped behind the screen to undress in privacy. In the tub, she energetically rubbed her soap holder to make foam so that the bath water wouldn't look dirty too quickly. She washed as rapidly as possible to leave the water warm for Antoinette and Alma and was careful to be as quiet as she possibly could. She would have been extremely embarrassed if, through unseemly noises, she had indicated which part of her body she was soaping.

When it was Antoinette's turn, Emilie couldn't avoid hearing sounds. Had she been so loud? Alma, the youngest, found it completely normal that she should bathe last. Emilie added warm water, which she foamed up again.

When the three girls were dressed for bed, they started to chat. Emilie didn't know what to say to interest her guests, but Alma had many questions about her years of teaching. So Emilie told her what life had been like since she'd left Saint-Stanislas — leaving out some details, of course. Alma listened innocently and intently, drinking in all of Emilie's words and asking for details. Antoinette didn't react at all; she seemed sullen and lost in thought. Emilie asked if there was something wrong, and Antoinette replied that everything was "fine, thank you." Emilie frowned. She had a feeling that Antoinette was hiding something, but she didn't prod.

Antoinette went downstairs to the bathroom. Knowing that no one would come looking for her, she opened the box in which Emilie kept her toiletries and took a good look. When she returned to the second floor, Emilie asked if there was anything she needed.

"It's been a long day," the girl answered. "I'd just liked to go to bed."

"Of course," Emilie said quickly, annoyed with herself for not having realized this. "I'm sorry. I shouldn't have kept you up talking."

Emilie spread sheets on the floor, along with the cushions from her chairs, since she didn't have extra pillows, covered the makeshift bed with a good blanket and invited the two girls to lie down. As she got things ready, she tried to make jokes to put her guests at ease — which was quite pointless, since they were obviously more at ease than she — and also to put herself in mind that she must control her dreams in case she talked in her sleep.

They finally got to sleep after Emilie and Antoinette had managed to console Alma, who suddenly realized that she had lost everything. No more books, no more clothes, no more comb or hairbrush, no more missal — not even the letters her mother had sent her had been spared.

*T*he sun tinted the windowpanes with the pink of dawn. Emilie opened her eyes, rolled onto her back, stretched and yawned, scratched her head, rubbed her eyes and heard the sound of a pot being stirred. She froze, then rapidly pulled up her covers and closed her eyes. She had forgotten that she wasn't alone.

It seemed that Alma was making porridge. Emilie cleared her throat to get her attention.

"Good morning, Emilie," Alma said. Emilie looked around for Antoinette. "Antoinette went for a walk outside to say her prayers. Antoinette is very religious, you know. When breakfast is ready, we'll just go and get her. She won't make us wait. So? Did you sleep well?"

"Like a top. I didn't even hear Antoinette get up."

"She's been gone at least half an hour. I hope my cooking didn't wake you. I imagine a schoolmistress needs her rest on the weekends. I just wanted to make a surprise for you and Antoinette."

"That's sweet of you, Alma."

Alma smiled and turned back to her porridge. As soon as she turned her back, Emilie rushed behind the screen and began to get dressed.

"Antoinette put on one of your dresses," Alma told her. "She said hers smelled of smoke. I think mine is all right."

Emilie was shocked. Antoinette hadn't asked for permission! She would have offered a dress willingly, but there were some that she could not lend — the pale blue, for example, which she had just finished making and was saving for her engagement party at Christmas.

"I imagine," she said anxiously, "that Antoinette took my brown dress, or the grey one." She stopped dressing to hear the response.

"Oh, no. Antoinette doesn't like brown or grey. She took the blue one."

"Pale blue or dark blue?" Emilie asked in an anguished voice.

"Pale, I think. Yes, pale. A lovely powder blue with lace at the collar and cuffs. My God, Emilie, did you make it? If you did, you have the nimblest fingers."

Nimble-fingered Emilie turned purple. She buttoned the top of her dress, burst out from behind the screen and flew downstairs. Alma's question — "Have I done something to upset you, Emilie?" — floated in the air behind her. She didn't waste time detouring to the bathroom for morning relief but flung the schoolhouse door open and found herself right in the middle of the Bourdais road, looking to the right and the left, spinning like a top. She didn't see Antoinette. She went behind the school, by the Montée des Pointes, and saw her at the top of the hill. Without thinking, she sped after her, and as soon as she was within earshot, she started to yell.

"Antoinette What's-your-name, little Miss Innocent! Take off that dress right now! Hurry up, you little witch! I have a thing or two to say to you, so stop that praying and take off that dress. You're so puny you'll step all over it."

Antoinette had stopped walking. She stared at Emilie, who had caught up to her. "You're all out of breath, Emilie. You shouldn't run like that in the morning before breakfast. Unless you've already eaten, that is."

"Don't change the subject, and I'll run whenever I please. What right did you have to take my blue dress?"

"I just took the first one that seemed clean."

"Liar! Triple liar! Alma said you didn't want the brown or the grey one!" Emilie was so furious that she was gasping. She took a deep breath, then continued, unable to quell her anger. "It's obvious that's no everyday dress. Do you think I teach in dresses like that?"

Antoinette shook her head slowly, looked sidelong at Emilie and shrugged before answering. "Given what you hide in your bathroom, I didn't even ask myself what you wear when you teach."

Emilie fumed. She had dared to mess around in her private things! The only response she could think of was to stamp her foot.

"Seeing you like this," Antoinette continued, "I'm beginning to think that story's true, about you dunking that boy's head in the bucket of piss."

Emilie choked with fury. Again, that cursed story coming back after all these years! "Has anyone ever told you, Antoinette, that you're a mean girl?"

"Not to my knowledge, Emilie. And you, has anyone told you that in the village people say you're a stuck-up show-off?"

"Me! Me, a stuck-up show-off? Who says that, Antoinette? Who says things like that? Tell me, if you have the guts."

"I have the guts to keep quiet. So put that in your pipe and smoke it!"

Emilie turned and started back to the schoolhouse, tears streaming down her cheeks. Who was this Antoinette to destroy her peace? Never again, she promised herself solemnly, never again will I invite strangers to stay with me. Never again will I do anyone any favours. Never again! All it gets me is horrible pain.

Antoinette, a mean smile on her lips, dropped the hem of the dress and trampled on it as she followed Emilie. Soon her smile changed to a grin, then from a grin to a grimace. Like Emilie, she burst into tears.

"Emilie," she cried, "Emilie, come back. Wait for me." She cried harder and harder, like a child who has fallen and scraped her knees. "Emilie, I'm sorry! You hear me? I'm sorry!"

Emilie wiped her eyes and turned around. Disheartened, she watched Antoinette stepping on the hem of the dress. When Antoinette finally caught up, Emilie looked at her coldly and asked her why she had done it. Antoinette, sobbing, said that she'd been hearing about her for years: everyone seemed to agree that she was above the crowd. Even the nuns said that she taught well. Antoinette had never seen her before yesterday because she rarely left the convent, but when she had gone to the sacristy she had recognized her, since she had heard her description so many times. Even Alma, her best friend, ignored her the previous evening because Emilie was telling such interesting stories. She couldn't help putting on the blue dress this morning, because she had never had one so pretty. She couldn't sew very well, and anyway, she had to sew for the convent; since she had been boarding there since her father died and her mother had to go and work in Trois-Rivières.

"Then yesterday, Alma cried because all of her things were burnt . . . she didn't even think to be grateful that her best friend hadn't died . . ."

Emilie's anger evaporated. Antoinette wasn't a bad girl, after all; she had been overwhelmed by a fear bigger than anything she could imagine. Emilie put her arms around her and patted her back.

Antoinette sobbed even harder. "I'm sorry, Emilie. I'm so sorry for what I did. Look at your pretty dress. I've torn it."

"We'll see what we can do. The hem is pretty bad. But we'll see."

Emilie had tears in her voice, tears that had nothing to do with the fact that her dress was stained and torn. Antoinette slipped out of Emilie's hug, gave a heartfelt sniff and said in a very soft voice, a little girl's voice, that she was cold. Emilie realized that she was shivering, too. She had gone out without stopping to put on a coat. She looked at the ground, white with frost.

"Why did you go out without putting on your coat, Antoinette?"

"I wanted to walk in the dress by itself, so I could hear it rustle."

They entered the schoolhouse arm in arm and went upstairs to join Alma. The porridge was stuck to the bottom of the pot, and

Alma got busy scouring it. Miserably, Antoinette gave the dress to Emilie, who examined it carefully. There was only one thing to do: quickly sew another.

❁

Antoinette and Alma went back to the village, where temporary classes had been organized for the eighth- and ninth-graders. Emilie took five sixth-grade students into her classroom; the others went to the South Concession school or to the other school in Bourdais. A convent employee brought all the girls in the morning and came to get them at the end of the day. The young convent boarders adjusted to Emilie's teaching style, even though they made some unfavourable comparisons at first.

Emilie spent her evenings sewing a new dress. Although she didn't find fabric as pretty as the pale blue, what she made was very appropriate for an engagement party. Because of her extra work and the time she had to spend sewing, she didn't make a Christmas crèche or stage a pageant. On Saturdays, she visited Antoinette when she did her shopping in the village, and Antoinette came to spend Sundays at the schoolhouse. The nuns had given her special permission, knowing that she was spending the holidays far from her mother, as she did every year.

Emilie had received two letters from Henri during December, and none from Ovila. Ovila, she decided, could go jump in a lake. When Antoinette tried to draw her feelings out, Emilie divulged nothing, saying simply that a schoolmistress couldn't permit herself "such indulgences."

The December weather was very pleasant that year. Though they had snow, it was so insignificant that people were still using their buggies. Emilie packed her suitcases and left with her brother on December 23. They stopped in the village so that she could say goodbye to Antoinette. Emilie hopped out of the buggy and told her brother to wait, she would be just a few minutes. Antoinette opened the door, happy that Emilie hadn't forgotten her, and wished her a merry Christmas.

"Here, Antoinette, I brought you a little something for the new year."

"For me?" Antoinette said, pleased and surprised.

"For you."

Antoinette took the box Emilie was holding out. She held it next to her heart and touched it all over before opening it. Emilie fidgeted impatiently. "Stop patting the box as if it were a cat and open it!"

When Antoinette finally opened the box, she burst into tears. The blue dress! The beautiful blue dress! The Trudels, with whom she was living, were enraptured.

Antoinette unfolded the dress and held it in front of her. "You fixed it completely!"

"I made the shoulders narrower, shortened the sleeves and took eight inches off the hem. Don't worry, my dear, I had plenty of time to see how it had to be altered."

"Believe me, I'll never grow another bit! If you think I'm going to give up this dress for one or two extra inches! I'm just four-foot eleven, and I intend to stay that height, even if I look like a midget beside you."

The two friends parted with tears in their eyes — Antoinette, because all she had to give Emilie was a sachet; Emilie, because she had truly made Antoinette happy.

Twenty

HE HOUSE HAD BEEN turned upside down, and Célina had spent interminable hours preparing for *réveillon*, the traditional Christmas Eve celebration. This *réveillon* was to be very special: in addition to celebrating Christmas, it would mark Emilie's twentieth birthday and her engagement. Célina's daughters offered their help, but their mother now felt more energetic than she had in a long time. At Emilie's request, the small party that was to follow midnight mass would involve just the family. Caleb would have liked the betrothal of his eldest daughter to be an ostentatious occasion, but he acquiesced.

Emilie looked radiant. She showed her dress to her mother and sisters and asked them if they thought she could wear it in the summertime. Célina told her that, in her opinion, it would be very appropriate for cool nights. Emilie smiled. She hadn't told anyone about the plans she and Henri had made for their honeymoon; she would wear this dress on the bridge of the ocean liner. She still had her regrets about the fate of the pale-blue one; this one was just as pretty, but a little less stylish.

As he had promised in his last letter, Henri arrived in Saint-Stanislas four hours before midnight mass and held his arms open to her. Emilie was taken aback at his crossed eyes; it seemed to her that when they had last seen each other she hadn't noticed them this much. Henri was carrying an enormous package, which he quietly asked Célina to hide. Then they all sat in the living room and chatted about the fine weather. Henri told Emilie that she could easily go to church without her overshoes.

Emilie laughed. "I will," she told him, "and it will be the first time ever that I'll be able to hear my own footsteps on the church floor on Christmas Eve."

Following their parents, the children left the living room to put on their good clothes. Emilie, already dressed, stayed alone with Henri.

He sat by her side and took her hand. "Emilie, I never thought I would be so lucky. When I saw you this evening, it seemed to me that I was at the opera and the diva was making her entrance."

"You never told me that you had been to the opera," she said, forcing herself to pronounce each of her words distinctly.

"In fact, I never have been, but I've read many descriptions in papers from the *métropole*."

"The *métropole* . . . ?"

"France, of course, Emilie. You know very well that people in the colonies call France the *métropole*."

"Yes, but this isn't . . . we aren't a French colony any more."

"Oh, yes, Emilie, we are. In the heart of all French Canadians, France is always our mother country and we will always be French. We speak the French language, our law is the Napoleonic Code, and we are as stubborn as the Normans, our ancestors. At least, I assume that your ancestors are Normans."

"I couldn't . . . I couldn't tell you, Henri. For all I know . . . to my knowledge, our ancestor was a soldier in Carignan's regiment, and he married a *fille du Roi*."

"Is that so? Aah! The *filles du Roi* . . . a pretty story."

"What do you mean by that?"

"Nothing at all, my dear, but I have my own ideas about it."

"Well, fine." Emilie shut her mouth. She didn't know what he meant, and she was a little put off by his rigid attitudes. She wondered if she would ever be able to hold her part in such serious conversations. But she was flattered that she had such an effect on him. She was sure that as his wife she would make him proud, and a man who was proud of his conquest, she knew, was always an attentive husband.

Caleb returned to the living room, clearing his throat to announce his entrance. He noticed that Henri didn't release Emilie's hand; she withdrew it.

"So, you two, will you be ready to go at quarter past eleven? It seems to me that would be a good time."

"It's up to you, Papa. If you think it's a good time, then it's a good time."

Caleb looked at his daughter, puzzled. Normally, she would have wanted to discuss the time of departure. He had said quarter past eleven to be sure that she would be ready to go at half past. And there was something else: when Henri was with her, she had a way of speaking that got on his nerves. Although he didn't want to criticize, he felt obliged to say something to his daughter.

"Emilie, could you come into the kitchen for a moment?"

Emilie excused herself to Henri and followed Caleb, thinking that there was something last-minute to do for the *réveillon*.

"What is it, Papa?"

"It's not my place any more to ask you this."

"I don't understand."

Caleb sat down in the rocking chair. He glanced toward his bedroom to make sure that Célina was still in there. He also listened for the sounds coming from upstairs, where the other children seemed to be keeping busy. He rocked slowly.

Emilie grew impatient. "What is it?"

"I don't know. I don't want to be a mother hen, but it seems to me, my girl, that you're not like you were before. I know you're old enough to choose your own husband, even if you're not of age yet, and I know Henri's a damned good match for you. But something's bothering me. Maybe you're not ready to get married right away."

He sighed; he had finally told her what had been in his heart since she had arrived from Saint-Tite.

Emilie blushed. Her father had no right to interfere like this; she had been getting along on her own for long enough to feel that he had no real authority over her any more. But she didn't want to ruin this evening by losing her temper.

"Thank you for telling me this, Papa, but I think that you are in error. Henri is a remarkable man, and I respect him enormously."

"That's exactly your problem, Emilie. You respect him. Does that mean you love him?"

Emilie didn't answer. She had never asked herself the question in those terms. Henri was a good choice, she knew. She would be spoiled, coddled, protected; she wouldn't even have to prepare a hope chest for her new home.

Seeing that she wasn't answering, Caleb went on. "Me, I've always wanted for my girls to marry the men that suit them. But it seems to me Henri is very different from you . . ."

"Opposites attract, Papa."

"And things alike get together, too."

He paused, looked at her and pursed his lips. Then he got up and patted her cheek, telling her that in the end it was her business, and he didn't want to spoil such a beautiful evening. "Anyway, Emilie," he added, "how's that big Pronovost boy doing, the one who was nice enough to bring his stallion to service the mare?"

"I imagine he's doing fine," she answered dryly.

"Aah, you haven't heard from him?"

"Sure I have. I just told you, he's doing fine." Her tone turned brittle.

"It seems to me you just said you didn't really know too much."

"So he's doing fine. Are you happy?" Emilie was reaching the end of her patience.

"Now, I like that better," said Caleb, a small, wry smile on his lips.

"What?"

"*That*, when you're on your high horse a little, when you talk like you were brought up to talk, not dotting your 'i's and crossing your 't's."

Satisfied with himself, he turned on his heel and went to the foot of the stairs to call up to the other children that it was time to go.

Emilie returned to the living room to get Henri, who, visibly impatient, greeted her with a sigh of relief. She invited him into the kitchen to get dressed to go. Henri asked if she could make an exception and open a little gift before leaving for mass. She told him that she would prefer to wait. He persisted; she resisted. He told her that if it weren't important, he wouldn't insist. She answered that a Christmas gift was a Christmas gift. Annoyed, Henri explained that she could consider this little gift her birthday present. Emilie finally agreed to open the package, which Célina, at Henri's request, went to get. Caleb, witnessing the argument, was amused. His Emilie was back.

Emilie sat at the kitchen table, careful not to disturb the tablecloth. Her mother gave the box to Henri, who put it on her knees. Emilie remembered Antoinette's gestures when she had given her a gift and imitated them for a few seconds, stalling. Finally, reluctantly, she opened Henri's gift. The box contained a hat and a huge muff, made of beaver. Emilie's jaw dropped.

"Hurry and put on your coat, Emilie. Forgive me my childishness, but I am frightfully eager to see if the hat becomes you."

Caleb gritted his teeth. There was no question: the way his future son-in-law talked always rubbed him the wrong way. He helped his daughter on with her coat, showing Henri that the Bordeleaus also had good manners. Emilie went and stood in front of the living-room mirror to adjust the hat, and Henri followed to admire her. She smiled at her reflection and went back to the kitchen, when she realized that she had completely forgotten to thank him. Her expression of gratitude sounded a little hollow to her ears; he answered that it was nothing.

Emilie got into Henri's sleigh and invited her sisters to ride with them. They sang Christmas carols the whole way. Henri tried to join them, but everyone burst into laughter at the sound of his voice, which was utterly off-key.

"You made a good career decision when you chose teaching over opera singing!" Emilie teased. Henri just muttered a response, and she realized that she had hurt his pride.

During the offertory, Henri slipped a magnificent diamond ring on Emilie's finger. Though he had guessed right on her hat size, he had made a mistake with the ring; it was much too big, and Emilie had to take it off for fear that she'd lose it. When they got back to the house, he had yet another gift, her "real Christmas present," a splendid cameo brooch. Emilie thanked him yet again, embarrassed by such expensive gifts. Her parents gave her a nice suitcase. She burst into tears and ran to her room.

"What a tender heart," remarked Henri, somewhat baffled.

"Emilie has always been like that," said Caleb. "Very quick, very unpredictable, very proud, very hot-headed, very stubborn —"

"Come on, now, Caleb," Célina interrupted. "You shouldn't exaggerate. Emilie is just moved by such attentions. Don't you think, Henri?"

Henri agreed. But Emilie's behaviour worried him. She had changed greatly since they had last met. Had he written something in his letters that had shocked her sensitive soul?

When Emilie returned, she was the life of the party, all traces of unhappiness gone. Célina, too, had a wonderful time and stayed up till dawn. The entire family went to bed — except for Caleb, who had to go milk the cows — after the sun had risen on a perfectly cloudless morning. A beautiful Christmas Day.

Caleb didn't want any help this morning. It was in the barn, surrounded by the warmth of his animals, that he liked to be alone to think. He milked the cows, his hands nervous and dry. The beasts showed their disapproval by stamping and swishing their tails; one expressed her discontent by knocking over a full bucket of warm, foamy milk.

"Damn, Joséphine!"

Finally, Caleb started milking the last cow, concentrating on the udder, of course, but even more on his thoughts. He was scared. Not the kind of fear he'd felt when a bull had chased him over a fence, but another kind of fear. He was scared for Emilie. Right up to last night, he had been very taken with Henri Douville. And then, without knowing why, Douville suddenly reminded him of a sad hound dog. He had a hard time figuring how his daughter, frisky as a racehorse, would spend her life with a man whose shirts she would have to wash and iron every day — the guy sweated like a pig, as Caleb couldn't help but notice.

He knew he probably hadn't found the right words to make

Emilie see that she could put off her wedding for another year, until she was twenty-one. He knew, too, that Emilie was playing a game. He knew her so well. It hurt his heart to see that she was running into the arms of her own unhappiness.

The barn door opened, and Caleb turned around. It was Emilie.

"I couldn't sleep. So I said to myself that you must still be out here thinking things over."

"Do you think I have things to think over?"

"Yes. I don't have anything to do in the barn, but I was thinking things over, too."

"Do you think we were thinking about the same things?"

"It depends. Me, I was thinking about my honeymoon. You?"

Caleb stopped for a moment. So she *was* going to get married.

"From what I know about your fiancé," Caleb said, casually, "he must have something unusual up his sleeve for your honeymoon. It wouldn't surprise me if he took you to the big waterfall in Upper Canada."

Emilie smiled. Her father had sized Henri up well. She watched him for a few minutes before telling him where they were going. She knew that he'd fall off his milking stool. Caleb waited for her to speak. Thank God, she didn't notice that his hands were trembling.

"This year, Papa, I'll have to be replaced at school for the month of June."

"Why?"

"Because Henri and I are getting married."

"You decided on the date without talking to us!"

"That's because there was no choice. We have to be on the ship at the beginning of June."

"The ship? Which ship?"

Emilie waited a few seconds to prolong the suspense. "The ship we'll be taking to New York to go to France. To see the Paris World's Fair!"

Caleb didn't fall off his stool, but that was because he had a solid grip on the cow's teats.

"Well, my girl, that's quite an idea. I hope that you don't take after me. I have trouble taking the ferry to Trois-Rivières without throwing up. And I've heard that the ocean can churn your guts up,

Miss, and no joke. I hope Henri has his sea legs, because you'll be busy cleaning up some little messes."

Emilie stopped smiling. She had never thought about this aspect of the trip. She had seen only the elegance of an ocean liner, the lights reflecting on the water at night, dinners served by the light of immense chandeliers. But either she or Henri — or both — would be seasick?

"Henri told me that in June it's usually not rough."

"They say it doesn't have to be rough for you to be seasick. Just the fact that you're not on solid land is enough. Anyway, that's what they say. Me, I've only been on the river, and if my memory serves me well the water was calm."

"Oh, you! Anytime I have an idea and you don't like it, you always make sure to . . . to . . ."

She didn't finish her sentence. She turned on her heel and left the barn, closing the door and leaning against it. She almost fell backward when Caleb opened it a few seconds later.

"I thought you'd still be here. What did you really want to tell me, Emilie?"

"Nothing special. In fact, I just wanted to tell you that Ovila Pronovost did write me. I like Douville better. At least with him, you know what's coming tomorrow and the next day."

"That's true. The big Pronovost boy, he's not the same kind of man at all. He seems to be as pigheaded as you."

"He's stubborn, that's for sure. So, two stubborn people is no good, Papa. You can't understand why Henri is the husband I need. Don't forget, it's been years since I've lived here, and you don't know me as well as you did before."

"I know that, Emilie. That's why I'm wondering why you're trying so hard to convince me. If you were sure of yourself, it would show on your face, it seems to me."

He had hit the nail on the head. Emilie had told herself that by convincing her father she would find the arguments to convince herself. She wasn't sure of her feelings, and she hated this confusion. She sighed. How would she explain to Henri that their engagement was to last only one night?

Caleb knew what his daughter was thinking. "In my time, Emilie, there was a saying that engagements served two purposes. One was to tell the intended that you would marry him; the other was to take more time to think about it. You can choose."

He rubbed his neck, then his eyes. Yawning, he stretched. "Well, okay. If you don't mind, I'm going to get some sleep, and I think you should do the same."

Christmas Day passed without mishap. Emilie chose not to talk to Henri. Not knowing how to describe her feelings, she decided not to rush into anything. Henri left Saint-Stanislas on Chrismas night, promising to be back for New Year's Eve. Nothing in the world, he vowed, would keep him away from his fiancée when they witnessed the turn of the century.

Caleb and Emilie didn't discuss her marriage any further. He was certain that she was going to change her mind, even though she wasn't sure about anything.

*O*nce again, on New Year's Eve, Henri arrived four hours before the midnight mass. Looking troubled, he asked Emilie if they could take a walk outside, even though it was extremely cold. Emilie asked no questions. She put on her coat, making sure she wore her hat and muff. He was too quiet for her to figure out what he was going to say.

"Emilie," he began, finally, "I've thought about you, and about us, for a week. I've written you ten letters, each of which I've torn up. You see, Emilie, I was wondering if the eagerness with which we are sealing our union doesn't indicate that we aren't ready. You . . . you are truly everything I've dreamed of, for as long as I can remember. But I have some . . . let's call them fears. I am a bachelor, and I don't know anything about women. You are so young, so enthusiastic about everything, that I wonder if I would cut much of a figure beside you. I beg you to believe me, Emilie, when I tell you that I am suffering greatly. I've made you so many promises that I fear I won't be able to keep."

He stopped, avoiding Emilie's eyes as she turned and gave him a hard look. If she had heard him right, she wanted to roll on the ground with laughter. It was obvious, however, that he didn't see the humour in what was happening. So she contained herself, telling him that she was unhappy and disappointed — *what a liar she was* — that she was seeing a beautiful dream die — *now, one mustn't exaggerate* — that if life meant them to be together, life would make sure it was so — *no!* — that she had had marvellous moments in his company — *especially this moment* — that she most ardently wished him the greatest happiness — *far away from her* — and, finally, that nothing would keep them from remaining friends.

Henri, moved, told her he knew she'd understand and kissed her cheek. He begged her, however, to say nothing to her parents; he would give them the "bad news" himself, like a man. Emilie asked him not to say anything; she preferred to bear the message herself.

Emilie and Henri sat together at midnight mass. At the stroke of twelve, they looked at each other. Emilie wished him much happiness in the new century. Henri whispered, in return, that he wished that for both of them. He winked at her, and she smiled back. Henri Douville was still a good man, and she was sure that if she were to reverse her decision, he would surely reverse his.

In spite of this certainty, Emilie felt a little twinge of regret. A solitary future stretched out before her. Would she be a teacher forever?

Twenty-one

WINTER THAT YEAR was absent-minded and almost forgot to send snow. What there was soon became nothing more than puddles that evaporated in the sun. April's warm rays brought hearts back to life and announced the end of Lent. Dosithée, who hated the period of penitence, was fuming on this Good Friday. He had finished his annual contract at Lac Pierre-Paul a week ago, and Félicité had made him fast and do penance, if only for the overeating he no doubt had allowed himself at the lumber camp.

"Come on, you can't imagine that after a long, hard day in the woods, we ask if the Good Lord is watching what we eat. He told us to work by the sweat of our brow, but He never told us to work on an empty stomach."

"The Good Lord told us to do penance, so you'll do what He says, Dosithée Pronovost!"

"If you want to know the truth, I think the Good Lord is secretly married, and it's His wife who invented the story of Lent just so He wouldn't know supplies were getting low, and so she could stretch things out to the first harvest. Because, between you and me, asking people not to eat for forty days, with the cold we have here, it just doesn't make sense."

Félicité made it clear that she'd rather he didn't talk like that in front of the children. It was hard enough making them understand that there would be smaller portions and no dessert. To hear their father spouting his almost sacrilegious ideas wouldn't help. Sighing, she resisted the temptation to scold him as she would a disobedient child.

"Be patient," she said. "Easter will be here in two days."

Dosithée just took a puff of his pipe and muttered an angry "Hallelujah!"

Télesphore came running into the house. His mother just had time to catch him as he slid on a throw rug and nearly went head over heels.

"Hey now, young man, how many times has your mother told you not to charge into the house as if you were racing into the barn?" yelled Dosithée.

"Ovila's coming! I saw Ovila! He's passing old Mr. Mercure's house. It's him, I'm sure! There's no one else as big as him!"

Everyone jumped up, Dosithée first. Finally, some good news to help him forget the gnawing in his stomach! Father and mother, children trailing behind, walked out to meet the son from whom they had heard nothing in months.

Ovila waved. Even from afar, they could see his smile, but they were astonished to see how much his bearing had changed. Dosithée and Félicité could scarcely believe that this grown man was none other than their determined, independent boy. Finally, they were close enough to touch him. Félicité kissed him on the lips, and Dosithée shook his hand and held it for a few long seconds.

"Good God," Ovide said, out of breath, "I guess no one tries to step on your toes."

"Especially not the foot I sliced open!" Ovila laughed.

"Does it still hurt?" Rosée asked.

"Only when it's cold and damp."

Oscar and Télesphore grabbed their brother's baggage to show him how they, too, had grown bigger and stronger. Everyone crowded into the kitchen, eager to hear what Ovila had to tell them.

*E*milie sat down with the shock. It was him! It was really him! He was back! She would have recognized his walk from miles away. Riveted to her window, she watched him calmly walking through Bourdais. She saw Télesphore run into the house, and she watched the family welcome him home. She would have given anything to be with them at that moment, but she stayed where she was. If he wanted to see her, he would have to come to her; he knew where to find her. She wouldn't rush into anything. He would have to realize that she hadn't spent all these months waiting for him. But who was she fooling? She knew very well that she had never stopped hoping he would come back; the letter he had left her in his desk was worn and faded from the many times she had read and reread it . . . and the many nights she had placed it under her pillow. My God, let him come, she prayed silently.

Henri was a hundred miles from her thoughts. Henri, the man who had made her feel beautiful and desirable. Henri, who, as it turned out, had rehearsed her in her role of lover. My God, let Ovila come, she repeated endlessly. She took a deep breath, then decided to take action. She went upstairs, heated some water and poured a bath. My God, let him come.

She lowered herself into the water, closed her eyes and tried to calm down before starting to soap herself. It was several long minutes before she washed her hair, something she had promised herself to do the following evening. She put on her old bathrobe, thinking that it was about time for her to make another, and dried her hair with a good, thirsty towel. Throwing the towel over the back of her chair, she sat on the edge of her bed and began to comb out her tresses — a hateful chore, since her hair was so long.

She was heading for the screen to put her dress back on when she saw Ovila, standing on the top step. Stunned, she stood in the middle of the room before him. Her hair was soaking the bathrobe down her back and on her breasts; she forgot that the water made the light cotton of her robe transparent.

Ovila looked her over from head to toe, smiled and went to take her in his arms. "I knocked three times. There was no answer, but I knew you were here because the door was unlocked, so I let myself in. Mind you, I never thought I'd find you so beautiful in the middle of the afternoon."

Emilie had not yet managed to gather herself. Here he was, in front of her, smiling, more sure of himself than ever. The way he was acting, one would think he had been here just a day ago. She finally found her voice.

"Stop joking. I look like a wet cat."

"A lady cat, Emilie, a beautiful lady cat."

This remark didn't ease the discomfort that was growing in her. "When did you get home?" she asked innocently.

"About an hour ago."

"Your family must have been really surprised . . ."

"Yes, very."

Emilie looked away in an effort to gain her composure. She asked Ovila to turn around so that she could go behind the screen and get dressed. Ovila begged her not to change a thing, he liked the way she looked. She let out a silly laugh — surely, he was joking — and went behind the screen anyway, where she pressed both hands to her heart. Ovila sat on the bed and watched her. She couldn't stand it any more.

"I said to turn around, Ovila Pronovost."

"It's been so long since I've seen you that I didn't want to miss a moment more."

In record time, Emilie slipped into her underclothes, camisole, petticoat and dress.

"Did you think about me while I was gone, Emilie?"

"Not often, Ovila. In fact, you made it easy to forget you. How come you only wrote one letter?"

"Because I hate writing."

"Well, you know, I hate waiting for a ghost."

"You should have trusted me. I told you I was working to make enough money for us to start out."

"That's easy to say, Ovila Pronovost. Did you really think I'd spend all that time sitting like Patience on a monument?"

"I was patient," he said bitterly.

Emilie couldn't hold back any more. She emerged from behind the screen and threw herself at him. They fell back onto the bed.

"You big fool! You have no heart, doing that to a girl."

"No, but I have the heart to do this."

He kissed her tenderly. She abandoned herself up to the very limits of decency as Ovila's passion mounted.

"Ovila . . . we should go out for a walk. It would be better if people saw us outside."

"In two minutes. I promise . . ." he said, eagerly nipping at her cheek.

They left a half hour later, after Emilie had spent much energy restraining the woman in her who cried to be let out. They took the road up the Montée des Pointes.

"I thought of you a lot," Ovila said. "I spent sleepless nights wondering if you had forgotten everything stupid I've done. I hoped you wouldn't be too angry. I don't know how to say this, but what I wanted, the morning Marie-Anne died, was for you to stay with me and comfort me."

"I know, Ovila, but I couldn't do anything but tell you to come back later. I couldn't lose my job."

Ovila scratched the earth with his toe, then gave a couple of small kicks to the pebbles he dug up. "It's because I was so ashamed that I left. Too many things happened in two days. I need time to think when everything changes like that."

"If you don't mind, I'd rather talk about something else."

"That's fine. I hope you took me seriously when I told you I went to make money for us to get started."

"It didn't seem all that clear."

"I wrote it down in black and white."

"Yes, but from what I heard about you, I thought it might just be empty words."

"You're so damned stubborn, Emilie! You're worse than me. Okay, so now you're going to listen. When I say I'm back, I mean I'm back. I'll be helping my father this summer. And in the evenings, I'm going to finish that house that's been half built for so long. If things go well, my parents will move there next year. Then we'll get married and live in the old house. Edmond and Ovide aren't interested in it."

"I can understand for Ovide, but Edmond . . ."

"Edmond wants to stick close to our parents, and to his horses. Anyway, if things go well, we'll get married next summer. Now you have to tell me, one, if that's clear, and two, what you think."

"Well, yes, it's clear. But as to what I think, you'll have to give me a little time."

"What do you mean? You don't want to marry me?"

"I don't know what I mean! This is the first time you've mentioned it."

"Seems to me it's what we said we would do."

"Ovila Pronovost, you will wait. You arrive like a hair in my soup, you see me wet as a duck, you say we'll get married next year and live in your father's house. And what about me? Is it possible that I might have an opinion about all this?"

"Don't be mad, Emilie. I've thought about nothing else since I left. I'll wait. I'll do whatever you want."

Emilie was quiet. She had been waiting for this day as long as she could remember, but now fear started to gnaw at a corner of her heart. She looked at Ovila. He was as handsome as ever, and she thanked heaven that she was no longer engaged to Henri. She wanted to believe everything Ovila said, but something frightened her. What if he left again? What if he forgot his wonderful promises? No! The look he gave her at that moment was full of such confidence, such questioning and such innocence that she wanted to shout her acceptance of his proposal. But he had hurt her. He had let her spend long hours waiting, full of doubt and anguish. Though he had never doubted her, she couldn't say the same . . .

"Do you think it would be reasonable if I gave you my answer at the beginning of the school year? I'll think about everything over the summer. That way, you and me, we'll spend proper time together and get to know each other a little better."

Ovila let out a despairing sigh. She was asking that he wait four months for her answer. Four long months during which they couldn't talk about their future together.

"If you want me to wait until September," he said, "I won't be able to start working without everyone wondering what I'm up to."

"Ovila, I want just four months to think. You thought about things for a much longer time."

"All right, I'll wait. I just hope winter isn't too bad, so I can work without too many problems."

Each lost in thought, they walked in silence back down the road. As they separated with a quick touch of hands, Emilie smiled. "Anyway, I wanted to tell you I'm happy you're back."

"I couldn't stay away from Bourdais and your little schoolhouse any longer. And, if it makes you feel better, I can tell you that I love you, forever and ever."

Spring was as perfect as Ovila and Emilie's love. Neither of them was looking forward to the end of classes, though; the two months of separation ahead seemed like an eternity. Emilie had carefully kept her answer secret, not because she was undecided, but because she liked having Ovila court her. He certainly didn't have Henri's finesse and fancy words, but he had a spontaneity that Henri utterly lacked.

Henri came, as he did each year, to inspect the school. He was very distant, without abandoning his customary courtesy. He made no reference to their brief courtship, nor did he talk of the engagement ring, which Emilie had never seen again. In fact, she had expected another inspector, convinced that Henri would have left for Europe, but she didn't ask what had happened to keep him from sailing across the Atlantic.

At the end of the school day, Henri refused the glass of water she offered, on the pretext that he was expected in Sainte-Thècle. Emilie agreed that it would be better not to keep the person with whom he had an appointment waiting. Mr. Douville put on his hat and politely said goodbye. And this year, for the first time, he didn't turn and wave once he was on the road.

*E*milie packed her bags and waited for Ovila. He didn't want to say goodbye to her at Saint-Tite, preferring the hours alone the trip would provide them with. Emilie hesitated at first, then let him convince her. It wasn't the first time a Pronovost had done her such a favour. She told her parents to expect her on June 23, and that it wasn't necessary to send her brother with the buggy; an acquaintance, she wrote, had offered to drive her.

The trip was long and tiring, punctuated by frequent, sudden thunderstorms. They had left under a threatening sky that roiled up with no warning, and they were soaked by the time they got to Saint-Séverin. Emilie proposed that they stop at her cousin's to dry off a little and get a bite to eat.

Lucie was truly surprised and delighted to see them. Emilie introduced Ovila as "a good friend," a former student. Lucie, who had a sharp eye, wasn't fooled for two seconds.

"Well, my d-dear, if all of your 'former students' l-look like him, I can understand why you like t-teaching."

Emilie shot her a look, but then smiled. What was the point of hiding something that, if her cousin's reaction was any gauge, was becoming more and more obvious? They stayed just an hour, until their clothes were almost dry and the sky had cleared again.

Emilie and Ovila didn't talk much for the rest of the trip. They just held hands, clasping more tightly as one thought or another drifted through their minds. Emilie had no fear of her father's reaction. She was less sure about her mother, who had been most annoyed that all her hard work for the special event at Christmas had been for nothing.

When they arrived at Côte Saint-Paul, Ovila recognized the road, and Emilie didn't have to give him directions.

"There's not a tree, a rock, a blade of grass, a turn, a light, a sound or a smell that I don't recognize, Emilie. This is where I began to think about our future." He stopped the horse. "If my memory serves me well, here is where I said, 'I love you.'"

"Your memory is correct."

So much time had passed since that visit. So much water had flowed down the Batiscan. She would have to find time to write to Berthe and tell her what had happened since Good Friday. She would also have to write Antoinette, whom she had neglected terribly.

Antoinette had kindly offered to help with teaching the classes, which were always overloaded with students from the convent school. Emilie told her that she would think about it. Antoinette added that she wouldn't ask for any financial compensation; she would just put a second bed upstairs and they could live as they had when their friendship started.

Since Alma had left Saint-Tite to go home to her family and Ovila had returned, Antoinette had spent long hours alone. Emilie had visited her a little less often and had even asked her, several times, to put off her Sunday visit. Emilie promised herself to think over Antoinette's proposal during her vacation. Of course, such an arrangement would make her work easier, but she wondered how she would see Ovila without letting Antoinette in on the secret. Yes, she'd think about it. She loved Antoinette as a very dear friend, but she worried that her presence would deprive her of her liberty. She'd think about it.

Ovila stopped the buggy exactly where he had when he'd made his first — and last — visit. Emilie's entire family had apparently been on the lookout, and they were all on hand to greet her — and all surprised to see Ovila. Caleb's surprise, however, was nothing compared with his wife's. Célina wished them welcome, completely unaware that Ovila was her daughter's suitor. For his part, Caleb warmly shook Ovila's hand and said, over and over, that he was "very, very, very happy" to see him again.

They took Emilie's suitcases inside and invited Ovila to spend the night at Saint-Stanislas. Although he had plenty of time to get back to Saint-Tite before dark, he accepted the invitation. Emilie blushed with pleasure. The next morning, they could take a nice walk in the woods. Alone.

Twenty-two

OR THE FIRST TIME, Emilie refused to take students during the summer. She wanted to have a real rest after the difficult year she had just been through. She also wanted to think about all the decisions she had to make. As she reviewed the plans that Ovila had described to her, she realized that he had never entertained the possibility that his parents might refuse to move. He was so enthusiastic about all his schemes that he hadn't given a second thought to their feelings. Emilie would be miserable if she felt that she was forcing the entire Pronovost family out of their home.

At the end of July, she wrote Antoinette to accept her offer. She had found three reasons to go ahead with the arrangement. First, she truly loved her young friend. Second, she didn't have the courage to undertake the coming school year without help. She knew that there would be even more students, since the nuns had asked if she would keep the boarding-school students from the previous year and take in the new sixth-graders as well, which would add up to more than forty children. Normally, this would necessitate hiring a second teacher, something the commissioners hadn't been able to do. Emilie knew that her work load would increase terribly; on top of that, she would have to prepare her hope chest. All of this meant that she would have to be very organized. The last reason for accepting Antoinette's offer was that she realized she and Ovila couldn't hide their relationship forever; having Antoinette live with her would stop tongues from wagging.

Antoinette wrote back that she was very excited about coming back to live in Bourdais. She promised Emilie that she would be as quiet as possible and would make sure that Emilie never regretted her decision.

Caleb tried to talk to his daughter about Ovila, but she didn't give him even a hint of what was on the horizon. He grumbled a bit, feeling deprived of her confidence. Nor did Emilie satisfy his curiosity with regard to her reasons for breaking off with Henri.

*I*n spite of a summer that was a bit quieter than usual, Emilie was surprised to see the end of August looming. She had missed Ovila terribly during the two months, but she had refrained from writing him. She was looking forward to the moment they would see each other again.

On the eve of her departure, a glum-looking Caleb asked if he could talk to her. She told him that she would meet him in the barn.

"Emilie, I don't think I'll be able to drive you tomorrow."

"That's no problem, Papa, one of the boys will take me."

"That's the problem. I'll need everyone tomorrow for the potato harvest."

"So I'll leave the day after tomorrow, if that's more convenient."

"Well, I promised a neighbour we'd help him the day after tomorrow."

Emilie didn't know what was going on. If he kept up like this, she'd begin to believe that he didn't want her to go. She looked at her father, frowning, and told him that she'd make her own arrangements. She'd go to the general store and ask the merchant if he knew of anyone going to Saint-Tite.

"That's a good idea, Emilie . . . except, you'll have to walk to the village, because I promised to lend the buggy to Ephrem."

Emilie saw nothing further to discuss. Her father was clearly in one of his difficult moods, and she had no time for it. Tired of all this talk, she asked if he had a solution to propose.

"Well, I might have one." He pretended to search for words. "You know that La-Tite is ready to be bred. I may be crazy, but I thought it could be real handy for my daughter to have her own buggy and horse. I asked your mother to write to Mr. Pronovost to see if he had a little room in his pasture and a stall for the winter, and he wrote back that it would be his pleasure."

Emilie jumped for joy. Her own horse and buggy! She gave her father a big hug.

"I know it's not every day a girl is so well equipped, but since you're going to be twenty-one, it may come in handy. Anyway, it's not the first time people will say I'm crazy. So one more time won't bother me too much."

Before hitching up her mare, Emilie brushed and brushed her, talking softly into her ear. She knew that most people thought it was silly to get attached to an animal, but they could say whatever they wanted. In a few minutes, she and La-Tite were the closest of friends.

Caleb had bought her an almost-new buggy for a song from a widow in the parish. It was the most beautiful buggy Emilie had ever seen. She would have been just as happy with her father's old one, but he insisted that she take the new one. It was superb, and the top went so far forward that, unless the rain was blowing directly in her face, she could almost always stay dry.

Emilie put her suitcases on the front seat, beside her, not leaving much space for her to move around.

"Why are you doing it that way, Emilie? You have the whole back seat free."

"I just wanted to see if I can organize things like this, that's all."

"Do what you like, my girl, do what you like. You're the one who's going to be aching when you arrive in Saint-Tite."

"I'm not worried about that. Anyway, Papa, if it's too tiring like this, don't worry, I'll rethink what I've done."

As they did every year, Emilie's parents, brothers and sisters gathered round to see her off.

"Don't talk to strangers," Célina said. "You never know who's travelling on these roads." She whispered to Caleb that she really didn't like this; she thought he was going overboard by giving this beautiful rig to their daughter. Caleb didn't answer. His mind had been made up since the summer began, and he wasn't about to think twice now.

"Giddyup, La-Tite. I'll show you the way."

Emilie took her mother's advice to heart. She said hello only to people she knew. But she said hello with an ostentation that bordered on exhibitionism. Her father would certainly have been very proud if he had seen her paying her respects to Elzéar Veillette, who was so surprised that he dropped his pipe, breaking it yet again.

She trotted happily to Saint-Séverin, where she stopped to see her cousin Lucie.

Lucie was astonished to see Emilie's rig. "Well, well! You're your father's d-daughter, arriving like a p-princess. Is that beautiful b-buggy yours?"

"Yes, my dear. My father gave it to me for my twenty-first birthday."

"Yes, well, I think I'll arrange to turn t-twenty-one on my next b-birthday. Maybe my Phonse will buy me a g-gift like that."

Emilie asked her cousin if she could get away to go to the village, so Lucie asked her husband to keep an eye on the children and told Emilie to wait while she got her hat. Emilie told her that she didn't need one.

"My dear cousin," Lucie insisted, "if you make my hat blow off in the wind, then we'll know that you drive just like a man."

The two young women got going. Alone in the back seat and in gales of laughter, Lucie held on to her hat. "It's a good thing it's only a little windy, b-because I'd say that you drive well."

After sharing her cousin's mirth, Emilie took a serious tone, telling Lucie that she needed her help. Lucie, realizing that this trip wasn't just a whim, asked what she could do.

"I need you to help me lift a cedar chest onto the back seat." She didn't say anything else; Lucie would figure out what she meant.

"I imagine your 'good friend' will help you empty it of its contents?"

"Yes, but no one knows it yet."

"Ahh!"

They went to the general store and bought the chest. Once it was up on the back seat, Emilie thought it looked too obvious and asked the merchant for an old cloth, with which she covered it.

"What does that look like, Lucie?"

"A chest hidden under a big cloth."

"Yes . . . so help me put my suitcases and bags on top of it. Then it'll look less square."

"Well, you always have b-bright ideas."

Finally, the chest was camouflaged as ordinary baggage that a teacher might bring with her at the beginning of a school year. Emilie drove her cousin home, thanking her over and over for her help. Lucie replied that it had given her great pleasure, and added that she had really liked Ovila. Emilie smiled. Lucie knew very well that Emilie couldn't have bought her chest in Saint-Stanislas, because the whole village would have known that she was thinking about getting married; nor could she have purchased it in Saint-Tite, for the same reason. Emilie's confiding in her made her heart tingle.

They stopped a little way from Lucie's house so that Phonse wouldn't see the cargo. Lucie hoped that the store merchant wouldn't say anything; they had been lucky to be the only customers in the store.

Emilie started off again for Saint-Tite without worrying about what she would do once she arrived. Ovila would surely come and help her carry the chest upstairs. The significance of the chest would, of course, be obvious to him. What a lovely way of giving him her answer!

Twenty-three

$\mathscr{E}$MILIE ARRIVED IN SAINT-TITE early enough to do some shopping at the butcher and the grocery store, say hello to Antoinette and invite her to move her things in the next day. Then she went to Bourdais.

As she approached old man Mercure's land, the beating of her heart matched the rhythm of La-Tite's rapid trot. As always, her little schoolhouse was a charming sight. She slowed down as she passed by the Pronovost house, to make sure that someone would see her. And, of course, someone did.

"Hey! It's the fine lady from Saint-Stanislas. Don't you stop to say hello any more?"

"Hi, Ovila! I was just going to freshen up, then I was going to ask you to help me with something."

She turned to watch him walking over, his eyes filled with smiles and pleasure. No, she hadn't been dreaming this summer. He measured up to her wildest hopes and desires.

"You don't have to freshen up, pretty lady. You look like a flower sprinkled with morning dew."

"Good God, Ovila, did you practise that sentence all summer?" she teased, to cover her surprise at his greeting.

"Come on, Emilie, how could I have known that you'd have a little drop of sweat on your brow?" he answered, laughing. "If you want, I'll come and help you right away."

"That would be fine."

He sat beside her, without asking to take the reins. "Your father really bought you something nice." He looked at her, and his eyes crinkled. "But I'd have to say that without the mare, the buggy wouldn't look half as good."

When they arrived at the school, Emilie asked him to open the door. While he did so, she made sure no one else was in sight, then hurriedly pulled back the cloth. When Ovila returned to the buggy, he saw the cedar chest. He looked at the chest, at Emilie, and at the chest again. He was speechless.

Emilie was moved. "My Lord, Ovila, if you had a hat on your head, you'd have to take it off like you do at church."

"Between you and me, Emilie, I'm not seeing a chest, I'm seeing a cathedral."

"Watch out, you'd better not get delusions of grandeur."

"Don't worry about me. I've been having delusions for a long time. And you've just given me the grandeur!"

As the school year started, Emilie was busier than ever. She got up early to prepare her day's work, while Antoinette made breakfast. Antoinette was a big help, and Emilie didn't once regret her decision. At mid-morning break, she began to smell the lunch Antoinette was preparing. They had agreed that she would give food to the boarders at the convent, as she had the previous year. She would also continue to provide lunch for the few students who discreetly remained at school. The commissioners had blinked at this practice because, after all, it was an act of Christian charity, and also because Emilie had never asked for an increase in pay to cover the extra food.

Most of the morning was devoted to the little children. In the afternoon, Emilie concentrated mainly on the older ones, whose powers of concentration were better, while Antoinette took charge of the little ones, helping them with their homework and sometimes taking them outside. The classroom was rearranged so that Antoinette could talk to them in a low voice without disturbing Emilie.

Autumn passed quickly. The trees kept their magnificent colours only a few days before frost obliged them to drop their leaves. As planned, Ovila had begun to finish the house. Dosithée was ecstatic when he was finally let in on his son's intentions for Emilie. A few parishioners regarded the situation with a sceptical eye, but Emilie's high morals, Antoinette's presence and the success of the students kept the murmurs from multiplying.

If they didn't have visitors, Emilie and Antoinette spent their evenings correcting schoolwork and preparing Emilie's trousseau. Antoinette had patiently learned to sew, starting with simple things: making pillowcases, hemming sheets. Under Emilie's careful tutelage, she had started to embroider. She was almost always even-tempered; the only thing that made her sad was that she didn't seem to attract suitors.

Emilie teased her gently, telling her to be patient. "You shouldn't take the bit in your teeth, Antoinette. The young men of Saint-Tite are much more interested in bricklaying and the Hôtel Brunelle than in the friend of the Bourdais schoolmistress. Besides, if you want my opinion, the young men of Saint-Tite sometimes need glasses."

Antoinette laughed and felt better. She had boundless admiration for Emilie, who felt the same way about her friend.

"Sometimes, Antoinette," Emilie said, "I wonder what I would have done if you hadn't come to stay. I even wonder how I managed before you came."

Antoinette blushed and continued to work her needle wordlessly. Never in her life had she felt so useful.

Emilie had written home at the beginning of September to announce that she would become engaged at Christmas. She joked about how happy she was, but added that this time she thought she had truly found the right man. She begged her mother not to start thinking of extravagances, but she allowed her parents to announce that their eldest child was getting engaged. When Caleb received this letter, he grinned from ear to ear. Here was Emilie's true match.

Ovila visited Emilie in his role as bashful suitor. He couldn't sit still for counting the days until the wedding, which had been set for the first Saturday in July. Every evening, he put another notch in a piece of wood with his knife, telling Emilie that he was counting the days until he became "the prisoner of her liberty." Emilie's response was to give him a little punch on the shoulder, and Antoinette laughed up her sleeve. She would so have loved to be adored the way Emilie was by Ovila.

December sneaked in under cover of a huge snowstorm. Ovila was forced to halt construction on the house for more than a week because the gusting wind took his breath away. Following his mother's advice, he spent this time shopping for the holidays. Emilie offered to accompany him, but he refused, saying with a laugh that his mother was already meddling enough, telling him what he needed, and he didn't want to give his fiancée the opportunity to "play the schoolmistress with him."

Antoinette helped Emilie sew the lace onto her engagement dress. It was a much prettier dress than the one she had made the previous year, flattering her generous bosom and square shoulders, and adroitly camouflaging her thick neck and waist and her slightly chubby thighs. When Emilie invited Antoinette to Saint-Stanislas for the engagement party, she accepted right away. Emilie offered to sew her something new, but Antoinette had refused; she wanted to wear her pale-blue dress. Lucie was also planning to be there with Phonse and their children. She wrote to Emilie to accept her invitation and also to ask whether the chest was a third full, half full or overflowing.

On December 21, all the Pronovosts came to the schoolhouse to celebrate Emilie's twenty-first birthday.

"It's my lucky year," she said, looking at Ovila.

"Wait till you see what's ahead," he retorted.

A veritable procession left Saint-Tite. Only Edmond stayed behind, to take care of the animals. The trip was long and tiring, but no one complained; warm hearts made up for the biting cold.

The celebrations started on the morning of Christmas Eve. Célina and Caleb invited the entire Pronovost family to stay with them, but Dosithée and Félicité declined the offer, having already arranged for half of the family to stay with their cousins, the Bédards. Ovila, of course, would stay under the same roof as Emilie, in spite of the teasing of both fathers, who made much of the fact that the priest had better not find out or he'd force the two turtledoves to change their engagement day to a wedding day! Antoinette, Rosée and Eva agreed to stay together; Lucie and Phonse were expected only for *réveillon*.

Célina got busy putting the final touches on all the preparations, her heart light and her hands flying. Caleb teased her that the more work she did the better she looked. She responded that it was because the work kept her from eating, and she was always in better shape when she just nibbled.

Those in the Pronovost party who were staying with the Bédards left the Bordeleaus' at about ten o'clock that evening, promising to meet in the church square at a quarter to twelve. Félicité took Ovila aside, reminding him one last time to take care putting on his shirt collar. Ovila laughed and told her that he had enough women around him to make sure he passed inspection. Everyone knew that he hated to get dressed up; he had a decided preference for work clothes over his Sunday best.

The night was a dream. A light snow dusted Emilie's shoulders. Out of respect, she didn't wear her beaver hat and muff, covering her head with nothing more than a scarf.

Driven by Ovila, the sleigh slid smoothly, its blades singing on the thick snow. Emilie cuddled up to him, whispering all sorts of sweet-nothings in his ear. As they approached the church, they heard more and more sleigh bells and cries of greeting.

Caleb and Dosithée made a grand entrance, both walking a step behind the soldier of the parish guard. They were followed by their wives and children. Walking arm in arm, Emilie and Ovila brought up the rear.

Isidore Bédard, the choirmaster, began the "*Minuit Chrétien*," using a faster beat than usual. Emilie and Ovila didn't smile, however; they had ears only for each other's tender words.

Once the second mass was over, most of the women left the

church to go prepare for *réveillon*. Some of the men went with them to drive the rigs, but Emilie and Ovila stayed for the dawn mass. After the priest sang the *Ite missa est*, the parishioners hurried to the door, then lingered in the church square to exchange Christmas greetings. Many remembered having met Ovila before. Joining them, the priest congratulated all the couples that had become engaged.

Célina and Caleb welcomed more than thirty people to *réveillon*. Once the third sitting had eaten their fill, all the furniture was pushed against the walls and the musicians got out their instruments: Jew's harps, violins and accordions. The newly engaged couples were invited to dance the first steps, and the others applauded them before joining in. Lucie, in fine fettle, got her husband sweating in the first dance. Antoinette found a dancing partner; her pale-blue dress, for which she received numerous compliments, did her proud. But Emilie was the queen of the night. With her arms sometimes around Ovila's shoulders, sometimes linked through his, she whirled in a mist of joy.

The people of Saint-Stanislas issued a challenge to the people of Saint-Tite, and a jig contest was organized. Lucie tried to convince Phonse to hold high the honour of Saint-Séverin, but he refused to participate, although he offered his services as a judge. Caleb started off, followed by Dosithée. All the Pronovost sons put in their best turn, except, of course, Ovide, who joined Phonse as a judge. Folly overtook the celebrants to such an extent that the jury couldn't name a victor. Their task was made all the more difficult by the fact that their view and their judgment were clouded by the vapours of pure alcohol.

The sun had come up by the time the last guests left Côte Saint-Paul. Lucie tried to convince her husband not to take the reins, but Phonse was beyond advice. However, he fell asleep even before they reached the banks of the Batiscan, and Lucie had to drive the rest of the way back to Saint-Séverin.

After all the excitement, Emilie couldn't get to sleep. She changed and went to help Caleb, who was trying to milk his cows. Caleb told her that he had never seen such a wonderful *réveillon*, and she pointed out that he must have had a great time, because he was trying to milk the same cow twice. He burst out laughing, toppled backward into the hay and fell asleep. Emilie woke him after she finished the milking.

At noon on Christmas Day, the party started all over again. In another departure from tradition, some gifts were exchanged. Ovila gave a mother-of-pearl necklace to Emilie. She gave him a weather-proof jacket that she had made out of a thick serge, and a picture-frame with a photograph of herself in it. Ovila put on the jacket and slid the picture frame under his shirt. Everyone laughed. Antoinette received a bracelet from Emilie and Ovila. She thanked them warmly, saying that she had never had one so beautiful.

Once the gift exchange was over, the eating and drinking began again. That evening, Emilie, Antoinette and Rosée took care of milking the cows, since the men were too busy playing checkers — or picking up the pieces that they kept dropping.

The Pronovosts left Saint-Stanislas on Boxing Day. Emilie promised that she would be in Saint-Tite for Epiphany. Ovila took the reins of one of the sleighs, leaving La-Tite in the barn, and waved goodbye to Emilie, saying, "Whether you can sleep with the pea under your mattress or not, you're going to be the queen, Emilie." He reminded Antoinette that she was also invited, and she thanked him.

After the Pronovosts left, Célina and her daughters spent two entire days scouring the house. The most difficult task was scrubbing away the black marks left on the floor by the dancers' heels.

As he had promised his daughter in a letter, Caleb gave her a sleigh as an engagement present. Emilie and Antoinette returned to Saint-Tite alone on January 3, the first day of good weather. During the trip, Emilie wondered if she should tell Antoinette about her romance with Henri Douville. She had never talked about it to a soul, for the sake of both her pride and discretion. She decided not to do so now; let the story die a quiet death.

They took their time, making a long stop at Lucie's, who told them all the problems she had had waking Phonse and getting him into the house after *réveillon*. "It wasn't f-funny. I looked like a little sardine t-trying to move a whale!"

In Saint-Tite, they stopped at the Trudels' to offer their best wishes. The Trudels were enchanted with this thoughtfulness.

The last part of the journey went by in silence. Emilie was thinking about the new year and about Ovila, who had seen it in with her. She felt as though she was exuding joy through every pore. Unable to contain herself, she turned to Antoinette.

"Antoinette, the more I think about it, the more I think it's impossible."

"What, Emilie?"

"It's impossible to be this happy."

Part Three

1901–1913

Twenty-four

HE WINTER OF 1901 made up for the mildness of its predecessor. Even when the air wasn't thick with snow, the sky was still full of clouds overburdened with storms yet to come. Ovila abandoned work on the house his father had started; the cold was so intense that the nails split the wood. Emilie and Antoinette continued to spend their evenings on schoolwork and needlework, filling the hope chest with cottons and linens.

The earth began to warm up only in May. Ovila started work on the house again, with the help of his brothers and father, who had returned from Lac Pierre-Paul. He was worried; the work wasn't going as quickly as he would have liked. Dosithée offered to let him and Emilie stay with the family until the new house was ready, but Ovila refused. He wanted to bring his bride to "their home." Though Dosithée didn't understand his son's stubbornness, he promised he'd do everything he could to make his dream come true.

Seeing problems ahead, Ovila mentioned to Emilie that it might be necessary to put off their wedding for a few weeks. If nothing could be done, she would adjust to this delay, she told him, though she still hoped that the work would be finished in time.

In mid-May, Emilie told Antoinette that she was going to start making her wedding-night negligée. Antoinette blushed as she watched her unfold a length of fine, translucent linen.

"You're not going to make your honeymoon nightgown out of that!" Antoinette said.

"Why not? It's a lot more appropriate than thick cotton. I'm getting married in summertime, Antoinette, not in winter."

"Yes, but still, it's almost transparent!"

"Almost . . . Anyway, do you think I'm going to have it on for long?"

Antoinette said nothing more, but watched Emilie cutting the pattern. To her great surprise, Emilie cut it so that it would open in front. Antoinette had never seen anything like this. Emilie admitted that she had been inspired by a picture she'd seen in an advertisement. Antoinette was even more surprised when she realized that Emilie didn't intend to put buttons on it.

"I think little ribbons, six little ribbons that'll make nice bows, will be a lot prettier," Emilie mused.

Antoinette was beginning to wonder if Emilie knew what she was doing. She was even more perplexed when she saw that the nightgown would have no sleeves. The fabric was simply gathered at the shoulder.

"Isn't it a bit too much, Emilie? No sleeves, no collar, no buttons, no lining. Just transparent fabric with little ribbons and some lace. You could never wear it again. It'll fall to pieces."

Emilie replied, smiling, that she hoped so. Antoinette was scandalized!

*I*n early June, it became obvious that the house wouldn't be ready. Emilie wrote her parents that she'd be home for the summer, reassuring them that this time it wasn't because the engagement was cancelled. Antoinette declined her invitation to spend the summer at Saint-Stanislas; she was going to Trois-Rivières to stay with her mother, whom she hadn't seen for at least five years. The two friends were saddened at the prospect of parting. Thanks to Antoinette, this had been Emilie's best school year ever, and Antoinette herself had never been happier.

Ovila came to visit the schoolhouse every day. Now that their engagement was common knowledge, the village turned a blind eye.

Emilie and Antoinette worked hard to prepare their pupils for the inspector's year-end visit. Emilie described Henri to Antoinette as faithfully as possible.

Antoinette pursed her lips. "From what you tell me, the poor man doesn't cut much of a figure."

"Make no mistake — he isn't handsome, but he's a very special man."

"How do you know that?"

Emilie cut short this dangerous turn in the conversation. "Come on, Antoinette, I've known him since 1896."

He arrived a little earlier than usual, so Emilie introduced Antoinette and then offered him a glass of water. Antoinette, to Emilie's surprise, seemed more animated than usual, and Henri was apparently taken with the lively young woman. Emilie asked him to stay for supper.

Antoinette spent the afternoon cleaning upstairs, getting rid of every trace of the sewing work — bits of thread, scraps of cloth and especially cuttings from the negligée. She started to cook supper very early, hoping to awaken Henri's appetite. Her mother had taught her that a well-fed man rarely went looking for other kinds of fulfilment. She thought of what Emilie had said about Henri and decided that her friend had exaggerated both his crossed eyes and his mannerisms.

As usual, the children were allowed to leave school very early after the inspector's examination. Henri and Emilie went upstairs.

"Miss Antoinette," Henri said, "Emilie told me just now that you helped a great deal with the younger children."

"Well, really, I'm not sure it was that much. Let's just say I did everything I could to help Emilie with all her work. I don't know if you noticed, Mr. Douville, but Emilie has the largest class in the county. Mind you, the new convent is going up quite quickly. With a little luck, the nuns will be able to start up their school again this year."

As she spoke, she stirred the pot, straightened up some things that hadn't found their way back to their proper places, returned to the stove and asked Henri yet again if there was anything she could offer him. She refilled his glass the moment he wet his lips.

Emilie could hardly keep from laughing; never had she seen Antoinette make such a fuss. Finally, the table was set and they sat down to eat.

"It's delicious, Miss Antoinette," Henri said.

"Oh, my God, it's nothing complicated. Just an old recipe for chicken soup handed down by my grandmother."

"Yes, perhaps, but there's something special in it."

"Maybe it's because I added some marrowbones. That changes the taste of a soup quite a bit."

"Either that, or it could be your personal touch," Henri countered.

Emilie didn't want to deprive Antoinette of the obvious pleasure of spending time with Henri, but try as she would, she couldn't come up with a reason to leave. Finally, she suggested that Antoinette show Mr. Douville the beautiful view from the top of Montée des Pointes.

"Show him where we had our first fight, Antoinette." Fortunately, she had never told him the story of the pale-blue dress.

Antoinette asked him if he was interested in admiring the view.

"I've been waiting to see it for years" he replied.

Emilie stifled a laugh. "Take your time, Antoinette," she said. "I'll do the dishes."

Ovila happened by while Emilie was still putting away the last pots.

"What's going on? Isn't Antoinette here?"

"Just think, she's gone for a walk with Henri Douville."

"The inspector? I always wondered what kind of woman would attract a man like that. Now I know!"

Emilie didn't pursue the subject. As she did daily, she asked Ovila how the work was going.

"We're still working on the inside," he said. "It always takes the longest. All that detailed finishing takes forever, and I won't be happy telling my parents to move in if the house isn't perfectly finished."

Emilie agreed, even though her heart was aching for the new wedding date to be set. She whispered in his ear that she couldn't wait. Ovila kissed the nape of her neck from bottom to top, which, he knew, drove her wild.

When Henri and Antoinette returned, Henri was in the best of moods and Antoinette was red with pleasure and breathlessness. She had invited Henri to stay a little longer.

"Henri, I imagine you remember Ovila Pronovost," Antoinette said. "He's one of Emilie's old students. He's also her husband-to-be."

Henri's grip tightened around Ovila's extended hand. "That's very romantic. You're going to marry your former teacher."

"I don't know how romantic it is," Ovila replied, "but we've known for a long time that we were meant to be together."

"Oh! That's very interesting. A love hidden for years. And you, Miss Emilie, how long have you known that this was the man of your dreams?"

Emilie cleared her throat. She wanted to keep her composure at any cost, but Henri had started a little game that only the two of them could understand. She just shrugged and smiled, hoping to suggest that men — and Ovila in particular — were uninformed.

Ovila, who had no idea what was going on, explained, "I was gone for almost two years, then I wrote Emilie to ask her to wait for me. When I came back, last year, Emilie was waiting."

Ovila spoke with such pride, tenderness and love that Emilie didn't know where to look.

"And you, my dear Antoinette," Henri asked, "have you also had such feelings?"

"Oh, no. As I told you, I've spent a good part of my life as a student in the convent. But you, Mr. Henri, with all your charm, you must have made the girls cry."

"Not really, my dear. To tell the truth, I've only been interested in one woman. I even asked her for her hand. But, you see, I realized that she didn't love me as much as I loved her. So I pretended to be scared of marriage, and I gave her her freedom."

"Poor you! That's a sad story, isn't it, Emilie? You must have been so very hurt."

"Yes, terribly hurt, to the point that I put off a trip to Europe. We'd been planning to go there on our honeymoon."

"To Europe!" Ovila cried. "She must have been very flighty, your fiancée. I don't know many women who would refuse such a trip."

"What can you do, dear fellow? Somewhere, there was a lucky man who loved her in secret. One man's sorrow is another man's joy."

"Are you still devastated?" Antoinette asked, mindful of his romantic nature.

"Occasionally, particularly when I see her."

"Oh," Antoinette said, "that must be horrible. Don't you think, Emilie?"

Emilie had become more and more upset. She looked at Antoinette, at Henri, at Ovila, then back at Henri, not knowing what to say. She realized suddenly what pain she had caused. She had to find a way to say she was sorry.

"I understand, poor Mr. Douville, that this woman hurt you horribly. But I find it difficult to believe that an honest woman would go so far as to become engaged just for fun. Personally, if I knew a woman who had done such a thing, I would never speak to her again."

Henri hung on her every word, and she felt the tension growing in the room. Nevertheless, she had to say her piece.

"I know a girl who went through, let's say, something similar — "

"You do?" Antoinette said. "You never told me that!"

"That's because it's a girl from Saint-Stanislas, Antoinette." Emilie launched into her story, forgetting to mind her language. "So, this girl, it seemed she got engaged for the wrong reasons. She was sure she'd make her fiancé happy. Then it seemed — anyway, this is what people said — it seemed she realized that perhaps he and she didn't have so much in common. Then the man realized the same thing, or so he said, and he told the girl it would be better if they split up. It also seems that when the girl later found out the man had lied, she was heartbroken."

"That's a stupid story," Antoinette said indignantly. "If only people talked to each other."

Douville blew his nose noisily, sneezed twice to hide his tears and blew his nose again. Emilie remembered how Father Grenier, at the Christmas pageant, had hidden his laughter that way. If she could have, she would have comforted him. She tried to let him know with her eyes that she appreciated the generosity behind his decision to break off their engagement.

Henri changed the subject, turning his complete attention to Antoinette, who, steadying her emotions, suggested a game of cards. Ovila heartily agreed. Something in Emilie's mood troubled him, and he was glad to have his hands and his mind occupied.

The evening passed with no further clouds. Both Emilie and Henri recovered their good humour, and Antoinette was beaming.

Ovila reminisced about Henri's first visit as an inspector. "*Series*. Who can spell the singular of *series?*" he said, imitating Henri's accent. "Believe it or not, Henri, I've always remembered the answer: 'There's no singular for series.' You remember? A series is always more than one thing."

Antoinette's pleasure nearly overflowed when Henri made a suggestion.

"I know that I'll have to go to Trois-Rivières a few times this summer. With your permission, Antoinette, I'd like to visit you."

Once the card game was over, Henri took his hat and asked Antoinette for a last glass of water.

"Emilie," he said, "could I speak with you for just a minute? There's something I want to check in your attendance book."

Henri and Emilie stayed behind in the classroom, while Antoinette and Ovila went out to hitch up his horse.

"I'm very sorry I hurt you, Emilie," Henri said. "I imagined that your feelings toward me were very cruel — and I see now that I let my imagination run away with me. I've been thinking about it for so long that I've probably warped the facts."

"I should have talked to you about it sooner."

"The incident is over, my dear, and, as the philosopher says, life goes on." He went toward the door and looked out the window at Antoinette.

Henri and Antoinette, thought Emilie, two orphans, raised by the Church. Yes, perhaps Antoinette and he could discover the joys of family life together.

"Emilie," he turned to look at her, "you were a falling star in my life. People say that when you see a falling star, you should make a wish. I made my wish this evening." He tilted his head toward Antoinette. "My wish is to find a harbour. I feel that I am a ship that has been sailing with no anchor for many, many months, and which has finally sighted the North Star." He cleared his throat, smiled wryly and added, "Was that, Emilie, a sufficiently poetic turn of phrase?"

They burst out laughing. Yes, Henri Douville was definitely a special man.

"One last thing, Emilie. If perchance you were to see Antoinette wearing the ring that you wore for a few minutes, would you mind?"

"Which ring is that, Henri?"

*A*ntoinette had known for a long time that she would be sad to leave the Bourdais concession school, the first real home she'd known in years. But she left much more easily than she had believed she would, for she was moving quickly toward another life — a life, she hoped, with Henri.

Emilie had been careful to keep his remarks to herself. She simply rejoiced to see that Antoinette had strong and sure feelings for Henri and was happy that her friend had never seen her own torment.

Antoinette offered to stay with Emilie until the day she left the school for the last time, but she understood when Emilie replied softly that she preferred to take her leave of the school alone.

Henri came to get Antoinette and arrived looking sweatier and dustier than usual. He lifted her few things — a suitcase and a small iron bedstead — into the back of his carriage as Emilie and Antoinette were upstairs saying their goodbyes.

Antoinette was excited about travelling with Henri, but her happiness was clouded. "I don't know how to say it — it seems wrong — but I've never been so happy as I've been since the fire at the convent."

As the two friends hugged, they heard Henri calling Antoinette's name, and they brushed away their tears.

"Just think," Antoinette said, "all of this started because I was jealous that you were prettier and taller than me."

"I've always been jealous of you, too."

"You, jealous of me?"

"Yes. People are always envious of people with hearts as big as yours."

"Oh, Emilie, stop, you'll make me bawl."

With these words, the two friends burst into tears, to the chagrin of Henri, who had come to join them.

"If I were a painter," he said, "I'd call this scene 'The Weepers.'"

"Don't joke, Mr. Henri," Emilie said.

"But I'm not joking at all. The only problem is, I'm not a painter. So, I beg you, dry your tears."

Ovila came to say goodbye to Antoinette. He knew that he had a lot to thank her for; if she hadn't acted the part of the schoolhouse chaperone, he wouldn't have been free to visit Emilie there. And his intuition told him that this was no time for Emilie to be alone.

Henri helped Antoinette climb onto the seat of his buggy, then he climbed up beside her and clucked at the horse. Antoinette held on to Emilie's hand for a few moments, then let go as the buggy picked up speed. Emilie watched the dust settle on the Bourdais road.

*E*milie turned in a circle. She had closed her suitcases and her many trunks, having risen with the sun to make sure everything was in order. She had eaten her last breakfast, washed her cup, her plate, her knife, fork and spoon, and then put everything on the shelf, upside down, to keep the dust from getting in. She had removed her bedding, aired her mattress and opened wide all the windows in her quarters and in the classroom. Taking in deep breaths full of the familiar smell of the walls and the floors, she remembered six years of laughter and tears. Six years of work and pleasure. And boredom, too.

After bringing downstairs everything she could carry, she went to her desk, sat down and looked at the classroom empty of children, empty of herself. Six years of teaching. Six years of her life. Six years that she would never have back. She was quitting teaching, for good. She had no regrets; of course, the teacher's life had often been hard, but it was the life she had wanted.

Now, she wanted another life. To be with Ovila, have children and think about the future for a change. For five years, the future had always looked the same: a classroom, desks, windows that she struggled to keep clean, children who changed but all bore a family resemblance. This year, she had welcomed Charlotte's little sister, and it had been as if she were reliving the arrival of Charlotte herself. Except that Charlotte's little sister didn't have to be reminded of the time. Charlotte . . . she had seen her only rarely, since she didn't leave home much any more. She had visited her on her birthday, at Christmas, at Easter. She would never forget Charlotte.

For six years, she had taught the same things, but never really the same way. She had always adapted her teaching to the children. Some years, they were curious, eager to learn; other years, they were fidgety, distracted. No group of students was ever like those of the year before.

She opened one of the boxes that she had already closed tightly. It contained her most precious mementos: a drawing; a dried flower; a twisted sprig so yellowed and dried that it had no odour left; the composition Ovila had written on "respect"; another composition by Ovila, this one on "wood"; a prayer that fat Marie, now married, had written to thank her parents for their kindness, entitled "My Fourth Commandment."

Emilie smiled through her tears. She would miss school, even though she knew that she wouldn't be far away. She would miss teaching, even though it had been heavy going this last year. She would miss the laughter, the tears, the disappointments and successes of her students. And the seasonal variety teaching offered: ten months of work, followed by a summer that she could sit and watch go by. She would miss that, too.

She went back upstairs to close the windows. She had tried to make the room as attractive as possible for the new teacher, who would arrive in September. The commissioners had asked her if she would be willing to substitute if the teacher fell ill, but she recommended Rosée for this work. It would be better if she never again touched a stick of chalk, a correction pencil, a schoolbook. She wanted teaching to remain a memory — a time that she could always bring back to life by saying, "When I was young, I was a teacher . . ." Not one day had she failed to be at her post. Through colds, woman troubles, laryngitis, she had always been there. By sleeping upstairs while her students worked and giving them lessons to study in silence, she had always managed to be with the children, even when she was under the weather.

Ovila would arrive any minute now. She went back down to the classroom and began to close the windows, one by one, taking her time so that she could engrave every detail on her memory. The first one squeaked. The second one required a sharp hit two feet from the bottom. The third was missing a screw in the hinge. The glass in the top-right frame of the fourth had a star-shaped crack from a stone thrown by an unknown student. The glass in the bottom of the fifth had always been warped, as if it had melted in the sun. Every year, the caulking in the sixth shrank, for some mysterious reason, more quickly than that in the other windows.

She ran her hand along each desk, suddenly aware of the graffiti the children had written across them and couldn't erase: "Charlotte + Lazare"; "Emilie, my beauty"; "Cockroach"; "I love Jesus"; "J.C. is stupid." She had always told the children that they shouldn't damage other people's property, but this lesson obviously hadn't stuck.

Then she turned her attention to the floor. Still the same splintery floorboards, with the same chinks between them. Still the same stains that it was impossible to get out — especially the one in the shape of a bear that little Oscar had inadvertently created when he'd dropped his inkpot. The stain had paled a little under the onslaught of bleach, but it was still there.

Emilie went outside. She walked around the school, stepping back for a better view, but the building seemed out of focus, so she went back inside. Sitting down again at her desk, she looked at each of the places in front of her. She could still hear the children's voices, see their faces — sometimes serious, sometimes smiling. In fact, she concluded, she was the only one who had changed: she had arrived here when she was sixteen years old, and now she was twenty-one. She had aged. No, she couldn't have!

Feverishly, she plucked all the hairpins out of her bun, and her hair spilled down her back. She ran to the bathroom and did her hair in braids, much longer and heavier ones than she had made that first winter after the Christmas pageant. Looking in the mirror, she gave herself a toothy smile. The smile changed to a short-sighted squint as she leaned closer to the mirror. No, she wasn't seeing things! Clear as day, there was a white hair on her head. Her first white hair! She yanked it out.

When Ovila saw her, he burst into laughter. "You look very young, my morning mist."

"I hope so. I'm leaving here without too many wrinkles . . . and just one white hair."

"A white hair! Well, my love, it's high time we start getting rid of your problems."

He put his arms around her waist and kissed her on the neck. Emilie let her head fall back. "It's not the summer I wanted, Ovila."

"It's just a few weeks, Emilie. It won't be any easier for me. But anyway, I'll be proud to bring you to our home, under our own roof."

"The only roof I want, Ovila, is the shelter of your shoulder."

After a few minutes, the two went upstairs.

"Are you going to leave your hope chest in Saint-Tite?" Ovila asked. "I don't see the point of carrying it all the way to Saint-Stanislas."

Emilie reflected for a few minutes. She would need it for her wedding day; all her things were in it. "I'll take it for the wedding, and for the days when I miss you."

"If that's what you want, we'll put it in the buggy." Ovila started to say something else, but stopped himself.

Emilie sensed his hesitation. "What did you want to say?"

"Nothing."

"Nothing?"

"You'll laugh at me."

"Say it anyway."

"Do you have something that, that . . . something that's yours, something that would remind me of you? So if I miss you, I can comfort myself a little?"

"Would a handkerchief and a comb make you happy?"

"If you promise not to laugh at me, it would make me happy."

"I'd never laugh at missing someone, Ovila. Missing someone hurts so much."

Ovila carried the hope chest, and Emilie lugged the rest of her things. She left her school without shedding a tear. Ovila kept her company on the drive to Saint-Stanislas. Most of the time he followed her, but when the road was clear, they drove their buggies side by side.

They made a short stop at Lucie's, as had become their habit. Lucie welcomed them with open arms and asked when the wedding was. Emilie told her that she'd let her know as soon as possible.

Just before they arrived in Saint-Stanislas, Emilie reminded Ovila to let her know the wedding date at least three weeks in advance so that they'd have enough time for publication of the banns.

They arrived at Côte Saint-Paul at dusk. Célina and Caleb were relieved to see their future son-in-law in tow. Deep down, Caleb admitted to himself, he wouldn't have been too surprised if Emilie had broken off her second engagement.

Emilie and Ovila parted the following morning, their hearts on their lips. He promised to write this time — she promised that she would answer each letter as quickly as she could — and that he'd come and see her several times during the summer.

"Don't tell me when. That way I'll always be surprised," she said.

"Two months, Emilie, just two short months, then we'll be together for a good, long time."

"I hope I won't have to wait two whole months."

"Me too, but it'll depend on the weather."

Ovila turned back to wave a thousand times. Emilie had the feeling that she was always the one who stayed behind. With Berthe, with Antoinette, and now with Ovila. Berthe had never come back; Antoinette came back occasionally; Ovila, she hoped, would come back forever.

She went into the house, smiled sadly at her parents, then sat at the kitchen table and began to undo her braids, staring into the distance, as if she could still see a buggy trotting somewhere between an already blurred past and a future that caught at her heart, it seemed so far away.

Twenty-five

*T*HE SUMMER SEEMED TO LAST FOREVER. The days stretched out, one after the other, like old, worn-out rubber bands. Emilie spent her days reflecting on the past six years and turning her adventures into stories for her young brothers and sisters. After a few weeks, they knew her favourites by heart.

Finally she received a letter from Ovila, asking her if September 9 would be a good date. She wrote back that it was perfect, and that she would not put it off any longer for any reason whatsoever. In his next letter, Ovila asked her to go to the church and take care of the details for the wedding. Caleb went with his daughter to fill out the forms. The priest was extremely kind, even though the groom was absent.

Emilie went into the woods to find a nice, straight, dry branch. Using one of her father's knives, she stripped it of the few flakes of bark that still clung to the wood, then made a little notch.

"What are you doing, Emilie?" Caleb asked.

"I'm counting the days."

"Wouldn't you rather cross the days off the calendar?"

"No, because I know that Ovila is counting the days with a little piece of wood, too."

This was how she kept Ovila close to her heart — notching her piece of wood every day, as he was probably notching his. Caleb didn't say anything to her about it, but one evening he mentioned it to Célina.

"Is it me who's gotten older, or were we more serious at her age?"

"I'd say it's you who's gotten older," she answered. "Sometimes people do silly little things that are important to their heart. For sure, you've never notched a little piece of wood, but I've drawn flowers on the calendar."

"You did that?"

It turned out that Ovila was unable to come even once to see Emilie. Deep down she had known that he would not be able to keep this promise. But he did keep his promise to write, and she was grateful for that.

*W*aiting for September 9 had been torture for Emilie, but she was a bundle of nerves, nevertheless, when the day finally arrived. She had told Ovila that she would prefer to see him only at the church. The mass would be sung at 9:00 a.m. At 8:15, Caleb quietly asked one of his sons to go to the church to see if the Pronovosts had arrived from Saint-Tite. The boy made the quick trip and came back to whisper in his ear that they were all there. Caleb sighed with relief: the wedding really would take place.

"Emilie!" Caleb shouted. "Emilie, by God, are you going to make your man wait on his wedding day?"

"I'm coming, Papa. You don't have to yell. Mama is just putting the flowers in my hair."

"You're not putting flowers in your hair!"

"Just little ones. You'll see, it's very pretty."

Caleb shrugged. What would she think of next?

Emilie tiptoed down the stairs, motioning to her sisters to stay upstairs. Her brothers, sitting at the kitchen table, saw what she was up to and didn't say a word.

Caleb was busy in front of the mirror above the water pump,

parting his hair for the thousandth time, never quite managing to get a straight line. "The furrows in my fields are straighter," he grumbled. "Damn fool business! I'll get it yet."

He tried with clumsy fingers to get a rebellious cowlick to lie flat, but it kept springing up. When he wet his scalp, it stuck up even straighter.

"Now, here's the trick — glue it down with a little bit of soap." So calm and and ironic was Emilie's voice, Caleb thought for a moment that he had found the solution himself. When he finally saw her reflection in the mirror, he slowly turned around. For the first time, he realized how beautiful his daughter was.

"If I didn't know it was you, Emilie, I'd have thought it was the ghost of your mother when she was young."

"It seems there is a resemblance," she replied softly.

"You're her spitting image." He looked at her for a few moments, telling himself it was truly a miracle that heaven had sent him a living portrait of her mother. It was also a miracle that he had been given such a beautiful wife.

"So, now, are you going to stand there looking at my hair-do or are you going to show me how to glue it down with soap?"

Emilie wet three fingers, rubbed them on a bar of soap and then on his unruly hair. The part was perfect and the hair didn't budge.

"You see? It's as simple as that," she told him. Caleb finally smiled at his image in the mirror.

Célina came downstairs and adjusted the buttons of his false collar. "Now, don't touch it or you'll mess it all up. All right, everyone outside, we're on our way."

Caleb, Célina and Emilie got into one buggy. The other children piled into the other buggy and took the lead.

"You're lucky to have such a nice day, Emilie," Caleb said. "Look at the Batiscan, it's shining like it got all dressed up for your wedding."

Emilie looked at the river, then at her dress, then back at the water. "It's funny, I just realized my dress is the same colour as the river."

The church steeple dodged between the houses, sometimes visible, sometimes not. Finally, it had no choice but to reveal itself fully.

When they saw the Bordeleau children's buggy pull up, the Pronovosts and all the guests entered the church. Emilie felt her throat tighten, and she took her mother's hand.

Célina looked at her daughter and smiled. "I wonder if our parents were as nervous on our wedding day as we are now," she said to Caleb.

"I'm not nervous. It's been a long time I've been waiting to get rid of that girl."

"Oh, stop teasing her."

"It's all right, Mama, it makes me look forward to getting married when I hear such nonsense."

"*What* nonsense?" Caleb blustered. "And I'll tell you something else, I think I was even *more* nervous when I married your mother."

He stopped the buggy and got down, going around to help Célina and Emilie descend. Emilie energetically patted down the front of her skirt to get rid of the wrinkles that had formed during the ride, while Célina patted down the back.

"The velvet's not too bad," Célina said. "That's good quality. Now, I'm going in. I want to see you walk up the aisle. Hold your shoulders and head straight. And you, Caleb, don't walk faster than her. Let her lead you."

"Go on, go on, hurry up," Caleb said. "We have to go in a minute."

Célina waved to the most familiar faces as she walked up the aisle to the front of the church. She nodded at Dosithée and Félicité, who seemed to be at least as nervous as she and Caleb: Dosithée was chewing on his moustache, and Félicité was biting her lower lip.

Ovila was standing proudly in front, his back to the altar, the priest at his side, and he greeted his future mother-in-law with a full smile. Célina wondered how he could be so calm. Then she saw a little vein beating in his forehead. A tiny blue vein. Discreet. Yet revealing.

A murmur started in the back of the church, rolling forward like a wave. Caleb and Emilie had just made their entrance. Célina stood on tiptoe and craned her neck to catch a glimpse of them. Félicité and Dosithée smiled. The little vein in Ovila's forehead beat faster.

Emilie held her father's arm and looked up the aisle at Ovila.

Caleb felt her steps get faster and faster. He held her back a bit, and she slowed down. For Emilie, it took an eternity to walk up the aisle. She didn't recognize anyone; she saw only Ovila's eyes melting into her own. At last, she was by his side.

The rest of the ceremony was a blur, right up to when the priest asked her if she took Charles to be her husband. She was about to say yes when she suddenly realized what name the priest had said.

"Charles?" she repeated, stunned.

The priest looked at his paper again. "That's what's written here."

Emilie turned to Ovila. "Charles?"

"That's my baptismal name," he whispered. "It never occurred to me to tell you." He was on the verge of laughter.

Emilie said yes. The fog slipped back in, parting only to show her the wedding band he had slipped on her finger.

She signed the register, unaware of what she was doing; Ovila and the two fathers signed as well. Then she found herself in the endless aisle once more, hanging on to Ovila's arm, seeing only smiles — reflections of the smiles that she and her husband wore. Finally, the sun broke through the fog.

"May I kiss my bride?" Ovila asked.

"Oh, yes, as much as you want!"

Ovila's kiss was more enthusiastic than the customary peck people were used to seeing.

"Congratulations, Mrs. Pronovost."

Emilie turned around, thinking that people were talking to her mother-in-law, then realized that they were talking to her.

Catching sight of her dear friend, Emilie cried, "Antoinette! Look, Ovila, Antoinette came!"

The two friends hugged, and Emilie's emotions spilled over. Only after a few moments did she catch sight of Henri's smile.

"Henri! How nice of you to come!"

"But Emilie, did you think I would let my wife make the trip all by herself?"

"Your wife?"

"Antoinette."

"Antoinette! You're married?"

"We got married last week, Emilie." Antoinette beamed.

Awash in happiness, Emilie didn't think to be offended that her friends hadn't invited her, and Antoinette didn't leave her time to reflect on it. "My mother isn't well at all," she said, "so Henri and I decided to do it quickly. We even managed to dispense with the banns, thanks to the priest in my mother's parish. Our honeymoon started last night when we hitched up to come here. This evening, we're going to stay at the Hôtel Grand Nord in Saint-Tite." Her voice dropped to a confidential tone. "Because it's romantic. To-morrow, we're off to Lac aux Sables, and next year, Henri's going to take me to Niagara Falls."

So caught up was she in her friend's news, Emilie didn't realize that people were waiting to congratulate her. Antoinette noticed, and she left Emilie with her parents, telling her she'd see her at the celebration afterwards. Everyone got in line to kiss the bride. Ovila, who couldn't resist the joke, cut in almost every minute. After a while, Caleb interrupted to remind his guests that they were ex-pected at his house. The newlyweds led the procession in Ovila's buggy.

"What would you think," Ovila asked, "if we stayed just long enough to be polite, then went to Saint-Tite? I can't wait to show you my surprise."

"If you think we can do it, I couldn't ask for more."

The wedding had been perfect. A radiant Emilie took time to talk to each guest, spending a few extra minutes with Lucie and Antoi-nette. Then, when Ovila began to show his impatience, she went to her room, took off her velvet gown and put on a dress more suitable for travelling. It had been agreed that the Pronovosts would take all her luggage later, including the hope chest, from which she had already taken a few clothes and other necessities.

While she was upstairs, Emilie's parents put all the wedding gifts on the floor in the middle of the living room. When she was ready to come back down they made her close her eyes. She entered the living room on Ovila's arm, her eyes shut tight and an easy laugh on her lips.

"Why do I have to keep my eyes closed?"

"Because there are gifts we couldn't wrap," her mother answered. "All right, now you can look."

When Emilie opened her eyes, she cried out. Before her were a spinning wheel, a warping frame and a loom to be assembled. The Pronovosts had bought the spinning wheel and made the warping frame; Caleb had ordered the loom from the Leclerc store in L'Islet.

Emilie and Ovila unwrapped the other presents. Lucie, unpredictable as always, had given Emilie a whip. "Now, don't m-misunderstand," she explained. "It's for your m-mare, not your husband."

From Antoinette and Henri was a swan-necked vase. "I know how much you like flowers," Antoinette said, "so I thought a really nice vase would make you happy." Emilie gave her a warm smile, remembering that it was Henri who had given her her first vase.

Soon there was only one package left to open. The postmark showed that it came from Saint-Tite. Emilie undid the wrapping carefully, since "Fragile" was hand-printed in several places. The package contained a tiny slate, a piece of chalk, a little eraser and a note saying that this slate was a reminder of her six years of teaching. On the slate, sent by Charlotte, was written the cryptic message, "Thank you! And I never betrayed our secret!"

The newlyweds left Saint-Stanislas in mid-afternoon. Following Ovila's instructions, Emilie took a suitcase — the one she had received as a gift from her parents the year before — filled with everything she would need for one week. He wouldn't tell her why.

"Now, Ovila," she teased, "you don't want to keep me in the house for a whole week without going out, do you? Without seeing anyone?"

"Be patient, Emilie. You'll understand when we get to Saint-Tite."

"Mind you, I'm not saying I'd have anything against it . . ." she added, mischievously.

Ovila let go of her hand and slid his fingers along her thigh. She put her hand on her husband's and sighed. He gave her a sidelong look, thinking of the pleasures ahead.

As they crossed the bridge over Rivière des Envies, Emilie grew nervous. Her little school was just around the next curve. When she finally saw it, though, she was relieved to find that she wasn't stirred by the familiar excitement she once felt after a long summer away. No regrets, she thought.

Ovila watched her out of the corner of his eye. "Emilie, you haven't even looked at the new house."

"I'm sorry, Ovila, I forgot. It's not very nice of me, especially since it was because of that house that we had to wait to get married."

"I'll forgive you, as long as that's the real reason you didn't want to see it."

When they arrived in front of their house, Ovila asked Emilie to get down. She grabbed her suitcase, but he stopped her.

"Leave it there, Emilie," he said. "I just want you to take a look at the inside to see how it's changed. My mother didn't want to put up curtains or anything like that. She said you'd have your own taste and it wasn't for her to decide for us."

"Why shouldn't I bring in my suitcase?"

"Be patient, Emilie, be patient."

Ovila took her hand and led her to the door. He swung it open. "Welcome home, Mrs. Pronovost."

He kissed her, lifted her up in her arms and carried her into the kitchen. Emilie burst into laughter.

Without putting her down, he spun her around once. "Have you seen everything?" She replied that he had turned too quickly. Then he sat her down in a chair, without letting her feet touch the floor. "You stay still while I put some things in the buggy."

He opened the icebox and took out some packages, which he added to a box that was already almost full, then took the box out to the buggy. Emilie sat very still, wondering where he was taking her.

Ovila came back in and, with a gallant bow, said, "Now, if madam will follow me, her coach is ready."

Playing along, she gave a dignified nod as he escorted her to the buggy.

"Enough with the secrets, Ovila! Tell me where we're going."

"No questions. The secret stays secret till I tell you we've arrived."

They went back along the road as far as the new house; this time,

Emilie gave it a good look and complimented him on the magnificent work he had done.

"The house has just one little fault," he said. "The upstairs floor will always be a little warped because of all the winters it was unprotected."

Emilie thought that they would go back toward the summer road and then turn left, but Ovila turned right and started down a path faintly traced by a few buggy wheels.

"We're going into the woods?" she asked, taken aback.

"That's where we're going, Emilie, but to a special place you've never seen."

"I've already been up there."

Ovila looked at her, suddenly fearing that his surprise wouldn't be such a surprise. "You have? How far?"

"I couldn't tell you."

He sighed with relief. They bumped along for quite a while, with Emilie warding off the branches that constantly threatened to hit them.

"We're getting there," Ovila assured her. "Just ten more minutes at the most."

Finally, he stopped the horse and unhitched it while Emilie, following his directions, emptied the buggy. He tethered the horse with a long rope so that it could graze, then he covered the buggy with a large cloth. Emilie still didn't understand.

"Now, we walk for five minutes and we're there."

Grabbing the box of provisions, he told her that he'd come back for her suitcase. She answered that she could carry it herself.

Ovila stopped at a point where the woods became denser. "You wait for me here. I have two little things to do, then I'll be back."

She obeyed. Not for anything in the world would she sneak through the trees to find out what he was hiding. She loved surprises, and she knew that Ovila had to make some little detail perfect. A chipmunk hopped by her without seeming to notice her, then stopped, twitching its tail. Emilie held her breath so she wouldn't scare it off. The chipmunk turned, looked at her and scurried away, its colour flickering from dark to light as it passed through shade and sunshine.

A rustling of leaves and the cracking of a branch announced Ovila's return. "Are you still there, Emilie?"

"I didn't move an inch."

He appeared before her, a colourful scarf dangling from his shirt pocket. He took it and held it before her. "This, Emilie, is a little gift. But before I give it to you, I need you to lend it to me for a minute." Before she could say a word, he tied it over her eyes. "Can you see anything?" he asked, waving a hand in front of her face.

"Not a thing."

He took her arm and told her to follow him, promising to tell her where to place her feet so she wouldn't trip. Yet again, she obeyed him unquestioningly. They walked for about three minutes. She heard a brook burbling and smelled water. She was confused; as far as she knew, there was no water around here. When Ovila undid the blindfold, she saw a lake — a marvellous little lake with clear, shimmering water! Standing behind her, Ovila put his hands on her head, just behind her ears. She held his wrists.

"But, Ovila, how come I never knew there was a lake here?"

"Because it's on old man Mercure's land — it's called Lac à la Perchaude. I guess no one ever mentioned it."

"It's a little jewel hidden in the woods."

"And now . . . " He spun her around. Before her was a tiny log cabin, newly built. Ovila gently pushed her forward, and she went to the door. The moment she opened it, Ovila lifted her up.

"My pleasure, ma'am." With a little kick, he opened the door and carried her in. "A large room for you, ma'am, with all the comforts. A stove, a table with tablecloth, four chairs, a little chest of drawers, dishes, an icebox that'll hold ice one of these days. Oh, I forgot! A mirror so you can look at your beautiful eyes and your beautiful hair and, the best of all comforts, a big, beautiful bed with a pallet full of good fresh hay, two pillows, sheets and a bedspread, which it was Eva's pleasure to make."

He laid her down on the bed gently. She put her arms around him and began to explore him with her hands. His thick hair tickled her tender body like a feather. He stood up and started to unbutton his shirt, but she pulled him to her and pushed his fingers away so that she could do it herself. He didn't resist.

The evening drew off the heat of the day. Frogs and fat toads were singing to the moon when Emilie and Ovila left the little cabin, wrapped up together in a blanket. They went to the lake and sat with their feet in the warm, inviting water.

"Wait here, Ovila. I'll be back in a minute."

Emilie ran to the cabin and lit a lamp. Flinging her suitcase on the bed, she opened it and pulled out her negligée. She slipped into it, tying the six ribbons without taking the time to make bows. Then she plucked out the few hairpins that were still entwined in her hair and gave it a vigorous brushing. She took a quick look in the mirror, and smiled.

Ovila heard her coming and turned to watch. Moonshadows played in each fold of the negligée. She came toward him without saying a word. Once she reached him, she didn't stop, but kept going toward the lake, not even slowing down to feel the sand sliding between her toes. She kept walking, without turning around. When she was in water up to her waist, she bent her knees and immersed herself up to her shoulders. She turned around and stood up. Ovila was standing, the blanket at his feet. She opened her arms and he joined her in the water. Hugging her, he whispered that she was completely crazy and completely beautiful, and that beautiful, crazy women always drove him mad.

The birds had been singing in the sun of the new day for hours by the time Ovila opened his eyes. He turned and contemplated Emilie, smiling in her sleep. He bit her ear. She sighed and turned her back to him. He bit her other ear, and she woke up.

"Good morning, sleepyhead. Would you like something to eat? Your mother is a damned good cook, but her kitchen is quite a ways away."

Emilie got up and put on her negligée, wrinkled but dry. Ovila got up too, but he didn't put anything on. He went out to answer nature's call, and she did the same. As they ate, they laughed with pure happiness. He teased her that not many people knew the hidden talents of schoolmistresses!

"Ovila Pronovost, I've been looking at your shoulders, your neck, your legs and your backside for six years. The only talent I've shown is the patience to wait for them." She let out a little victorious, teasing laugh.

"And it's been six years I've been watching you grow up faster than me," he went on, "scared you'd never look at me. For six years, I've been dreaming of you every damn night, since you're the prettiest girl around. For six years, I worried you'd fall in love with someone else. And now here I am, scared to wake up because I'm scared I'm still dreaming."

For five days, they slept, ate the food Ovila had brought, watched the moon rise and continued to discover the intimacies of married life. They didn't swim any more, though, for the heat of summer had definitely departed.

*O*n their sixth day of solitude, they heard someone coming. Ovila quickly got dressed and left the cabin, telling Emilie not to move. So she stayed in bed, completely hidden under the covers, stifling laughter at her childish predicament. She heard Ovila talking and thought she recognized Lazare's voice. What's he doing here, she wondered vaguely, figuring that he had probably come to see if they needed anything. She strained her ears but didn't hear anything more. Finally she got up, tiptoed to the window and peeked out. Ovila was standing alone with his back to the cabin, his head buried in his arms, leaning on a tree.

She went to the door and whispered, "Ovila, can I come out?"

He nodded. As he watched her picking her way toward him between the pebbles and the dry twigs, he searched for the words he needed.

"What's going on, Ovila?" Emilie asked.

"It was Lazare, Emilie." He searched for words. "My darling, I have something to tell you." He put his arms around her.

"You're scaring me, Ovila. What's going on? Is someone sick?"

Ovila sighed. "It's Charlotte. She's been asking for you. She's very sick, and the doctor has given her only a few more hours to live."

Emilie ran into the cabin and grabbed a large bowl. She filled it with fresh water from the lake, then rushed back inside, telling Ovila to hitch up the horse.

"Lazare's taken care of it," he said. "The buggy's ready to go."

"Are you going to shave?"

"It's better not to waste time heating the water."

"Is it that bad?" she asked, suddenly very worried that she would arrive too late to embrace her little Charlotte.

"I think it is, yes."

She threw on a dress, took her comb and hairpins to make a bun as they drove and told Ovila she was ready.

When they arrived at Charlotte's, Emilie ran to the house, relieved to see that the priest's buggy wasn't there. She knocked on the door and went right in. Charlotte's mother greeted her, her face wet with tears.

"Charlotte is waiting for you, Miss . . . Mrs. Pronovost. It seems there's something she wants to tell you."

Emilie followed her to Charlotte's room. The entire family was kneeling around the bed. As a path was cleared for her, Emilie felt a sudden chill: she'd never before made a deathbed visit. She took a deep breath, clasped one of Charlotte's hands in her own and leaned over to whisper that she was there.

Charlotte, emaciated, jaundiced and waxen, batted her eyes. "Emilie," she asked weakly, "did you get my gift?"

"Yes," Emilie said, trying to put a little gaiety into her voice. "It was the most beautiful and practical gift of all."

Charlotte's smile was more of a grimace. "I've never given away our secret," she whispered.

Emilie didn't know what secret she was talking about. A number of times since her wedding, she had tried to figure out the enigma of this little sentence, promising herself to ask Charlotte when she returned from Lac à la Perchaude. But she didn't have the courage to ask her now about the famous secret that seemed so important to her. Her eyes welled up with tears. Little Charlotte had such a big place in her heart; why had she neglected her so over the past year?

Charlotte's head fell heavily back on the pillow. She opened her eyes once more and looked all around the room, trying to fix each person there with her gaze. Then she looked at Emilie and let out a gurgling sound. Aware that she was taking Charlotte's mother's place, Emilie leaned over to put her ear next to Charlotte's mouth. All she heard was a little sentence, weakly breathed. "It's time, Charlotte."

With that, Charlotte passed away. Feeling faint, Emilie turned to Charlotte's mother to tell her that she thought it was over. Charlotte's mother placed a little mirror under her daughter's nose. No mist. She knelt and made the sign of the cross.

Emilie spent part of Sunday at Charlotte's house, where Charlotte was laid out in a corner of the living room, on a plank of wood. She had been clothed in her best dress and covered with a white shroud. At her head, on a table, was a statue of the Immaculate Conception. At her feet, a Sacred Heart sheltered with open arms a baptismal font and an aspergillum. On the wall just behind her, a crucifix was nestled in the folds of embroidered tablecloths affixed to the wall, which made a sort of alcove around the body. Oil lamps burned constantly; the red globes, meant to lend some reflected colour to Charlotte's pale face, were blackened and served instead to protect the mourners from too bright a light, as their eyes were gritty from lack of sleep and floods of tears.

Emilie looked at her poor little pupil, whose kidneys had finally succeeded in mortally poisoning her. Charlotte had never complained. She had lived with her constant humiliation without a murmur. Every year, Emilie had calmly, gently explained to new students the concept of respect, always using "Charlotte's little hourly problems" as an example.

The sun on this Sunday, September 17, shone rudely with all its might. Emilie went outside to tell it what she thought of it. She raged, fumed, cried, and Ovila's best attempts to console her were in vain.

Lazare arrived alone, looking completely crushed, while his brother and sister-in-law were pacing on the porch. He started to go into the house, but instead he turned to them. "Emilie," he said, "can I talk to you?"

Emilie asked Ovila to wait where he was and went to Lazare. She knew that there had always been something very special between him and Charlotte; even after they'd left school, they continued to see each other. Emilie remembered Lazare's first seizure and Charlotte's refusal to leave him until she was sure he wasn't dead. From that day on, little Charlotte had always protected big Lazare, as if she knew that they both suffered from the same fundamental problems: difference and loneliness.

"Emilie, does Charlotte look bad?"

"No, Lazare, she looks like she always did. I'd say she even has a little smile on her lips."

"I don't know if I have the strength to see her . . . like that. I don't know if it's better to keep a memory of her as she was, thin and sick, but . . . alive . . . " He stopped to hide the trembling in his voice.

Emilie found it pathetic that a man of his age was so torn by the death of a thirteen-year-old girl. But because of his affliction, Lazare had never matured as he should have. In some ways, he was still Charlotte's age.

"Do what you think best, Lazare. If you think you want to see her, go in. I'll go with you if that'll help. If you don't want to see her, go home and try to remember her as you want to remember her."

Finally, Lazare went in. He stayed just two minutes, long enough to offer his condolences and quickly take and kiss Charlotte's hand. But the shock proved to be too great for him. As he left the house, he let out a cry and collapsed on the porch, hitting his head on the stairs and his mouth on the unpainted planks of the floor. Ovila quickly turned him over and asked people to stand back so that when he came to he wouldn't feel that he had made a ridiculous scene. That was his problem: he always felt ridiculous instead of accepting his malady.

*E*milie didn't want to leave the lake. She and Ovila had gone back there the night of Charlotte's death, and again the next night. She knew that she would be able to see the school from the window of her new house, and she didn't want to see it before Charlotte's funeral. Ovila didn't argue. They took Lazare home and left for the cabin. Once supper was over and the dishes were washed, Emilie spent long hours looking at the lake and sighing. Ovila didn't talk much; he just kept his arm around her shoulder and wiped away her tears with his big, gentle thumbs.

On Monday, they packed their suitcases, cleaned and closed the little cabin and took everything to their house. After that, they went to the church. The funeral was sad as only the funeral of a child can be. Ovila couldn't stop thinking of the ceremony for the infant Marie-Anne. As for Emilie, she promised herself that she would never bring a child into the world only to see it die. She would die first. It wasn't right when a mother had to bury her child. A child was the only guarantee of immortality.

Twenty-six

*O*VILA WAS THRILLED. The nuns had asked him to make most of the furniture for the refectories in the new convent, which was almost finished. He set up a workshop in an outbuilding and eagerly attacked his task. Everything had to be delivered by December 8, the date set for the blessing of the convent.

Most of Emilie's time was spent weaving comforters and blankets. In secret, she went to see the doctor, who confirmed that she would be a mother in June of the following year. Whenever Ovila was out of the house for a few hours, she got out her wool and crochet hook and her fingers flew to make little blankets, booties and bonnets. She didn't want to tell Ovila yet; he hadn't noticed that there had been no rags on the clothesline since their wedding.

Emilie hung lace curtains patterned with birds and flowers. She moved the furniture around, just to give Ovila's childhood home a different look. Meanwhile, he worked on the tables, chairs and sideboards for the convent, which he decorated with carved flowers or diamonds.

"That's beautiful, Ovila," Emilie told him. "It looks like the chair is lighter, just because of the flowers."

"I'm glad you think so. Sometimes I'm not so sure. The nuns didn't ask for anything so fancy."

"Well, I hope all this extra work won't mean you'll be late with your delivery."

"I've calculated everything, and I've organized my work to go fast. I prepare all the crossbars, I cut all the pieces for the legs, I make all the holes for the pegs, and then I make the seats. Then I line up all the pieces and assemble them. That way, I'm sure that all the chairs are the same size. All this, ma'am, leaves me time to carve in the evenings, sitting next to you, which, as we both know, is what I like to do best."

Emilie smiled, catching a glimpse in her mind's eye of a student building an immense crèche in a little classroom.

*A*utumn and the first frosts passed almost unnoticed, for the sun kept the house warm. Every morning, between bouts of nausea, Emilie revelled in her happiness.

Three days before the convent blessing, Ovila delivered the furniture. The nuns congratulated him for work done "more than perfectly, Mr. Pronovost." When he returned, Emilie told him not to put his tools away. "I have a little job for you to do," she told him.

Ovila frowned. What could she want? He had already told her that he would make something nice for their bedroom, and a new table for the kitchen was under way. The chairs had been done at the same time as those for the convent.

"I want you to make a nice little crib, Ovila." She tossed off the words in such a casual tone that it took a good two minutes before he realized what she had said. When he finally got it, his jaw dropped. Then took her in his arms, bursting into laughter. Emilie laughed too, with delight.

Without a second thought, he hustled her into her jacket, boots and hat, then threw his own on and dragged her to his parents' house, saying, "Don't ask me to keep a secret like this, Emilie!"

The Pronovosts' excitement matched their own. Sitting at the supper table with two extra places set for the impromptu guests, Dosithée was beyond joy: he was going to be a grandfather!

*E*milie and Ovila spent Christmas at Saint-Stanislas. Emilie had to put up a good fight with her father and her husband before she was allowed to dance; they were worried for her health. They finally gave in when she began to dance a jig to the music in her head.

Caleb gave Emilie a present, making her promise not to open it before the new year. She tried, in vain, to guess what it might be.

"The only hint I'll give you, Emilie, is that it'll keep you busy nights."

Emilie and Ovila returned to Saint-Tite for New Year's Day. Before making their way to the Pronovosts', Emilie opened Caleb's present. She howled with laughter. She had been expecting something with which to prepare for the arrival of her baby: supplies for embroidery or sewing, perhaps. Instead, Caleb had given her an accordion!

"Can you figure out where my father gets his ideas?" she asked Ovila, trying to pick out a few notes.

"We'd better get going," Ovila urged. "You'll have lots of time to learn."

At the Pronovost home, Dosithée blessed his entire family, joking that he was blessing someone "who isn't even here yet."

The party on the evening of New Year's Day was a great success. Emilie laughed when she was teased about her growing girth. "I'm eating for two!" she insisted. "I spend all my time nibbling."

"Nibbling," Ovila snorted, "that's a laugh! Do you know what she nibbled on last night? A chicken wing, then a leg, along with two fat slices of bread dipped in pan drippings."

"What Ovila doesn't know is that I had another little snack in the middle of the night. But I didn't overdo it. I just had one big slice of bread, dipped in nice, thick cream with good maple sugar. It was delicious!"

Félicité smiled. "You'd better watch what you're doing — many women never lose the weight they gain during pregnancy."

"I exaggerated a bit," Emilie answered, "but it's true — I should be more careful."

The men left the room, as they always did, to talk politics and farming. Dosithée took the opportunity to ask Ovila and Edmond if they wanted to join him at Lac Pierre-Paul to help finish up his cutting contract for the railway beds.

Edmond, embarrassed, told him that he'd rather stay in Bourdais. Seeing his father's disappointment, he hastened to add that Ovide and Lazare really needed him.

Dosithée turned to Ovila and tilted his head.

Ovila was uneasy. He really didn't want to leave Emilie, especially while she was pregnant. On the other hand, the money he had received from the nuns wouldn't last until the baby was born. He promised his father that he'd discuss it with Emilie and give him an answer as soon as his mind was made up.

"Anyway, we'll be going right after Epiphany," Dosithée said. "If you want to go with us, be ready by then. No one's going to run after you."

Ovila pussyfooted around the subject for two days. He had promised Emilie so many times that he would never go away. He didn't sleep well. He knew that he couldn't always stay by the hearth; few men did. And yet he was a little angry at his father for having brought the matter up.

Dosithée should have understood that he wanted to be at home, near his wife. He had already been down so many roads, worked in so many lumber camps, that the only thing he wanted now was the tranquillity of his own home. He wanted to hear the wood stove roaring, the knitting needles clicking. He wanted to curl up next to Emilie, in their bed, listening to the wind howl. He wanted to spend hours in his workshop making the cradle and the wash stand for the baby, while Emilie made curtains, mattress covers and swaddling clothes. He especially didn't want to be far away.

But at the same time he wanted to show his father that he had changed, to be the son who could take up the slack from Edmond. He wanted to prove that he could please his father, even though he'd broken so many promises.

In the end, he broached the subject with Emilie. She listened to all his reasons for going and all the ones for staying. He seemed to want her to make his decision for him. She understood his dilemma well. She also knew that he hadn't told her everything.

The fact was, life in the woods attracted him. Maybe he didn't know it yet, but she did; a woman felt these things. When Ovila wasn't in the woods, he had to work with wood, touch wood. She had known it was so when he admitted that he had constructed the cabin at Lac à la Perchaude at the same time as he was finishing work on his father's house. He had made it for her, so that she would have a beautiful place near the water. But it also had a lot to do with his being in the woods. He had lived at the lake for almost the entire month of August, so absorbed in building that he hadn't had the time to go and see her in Saint-Stanislas. She had understood all of this during their week at the lake. She had realized that Ovila would always be torn, and she couldn't be angry with him.

Since her wedding, she had found the days very long without her thirty children to teach. Happily, Ovila's presence had been ample compensation. Now, he was talking about going away. Just for three months, he said. Three whole months. She hadn't the courage to tell him to stay; nor could she bear to tell him to go. He had to decide for himself. If he left, she'd wait. If he stayed, she'd be much happier.

"Listen, Ovila," she said, "I think you have to do what you want. Three months won't kill me. When a woman lives in a country that's mostly woods, she has to figure out that sometimes the woods are very important. And it's not for nothing — you'll be earning money . . ."

Ovila wasn't sure that he understood what she was saying. Perhaps she was trying to tell him that she didn't want him around all the time, since she was used to solitude. The next day, he told her he had decided to go with his father. She smiled to hide the pain in her heart. Her great rival, the forest, had just won a battle.

The next day, Epiphany, he left, his heart torn. Emilie had packed his clothes while he had sharpened his saw and his axe. She walked him to the sleigh, holding his hand, forcing herself to smile.

"I'll be back by Easter, my love — take care of the little one," he said, patting her stomach.

"I'll tell him about you every day, don't worry . . . I miss you already, Ovila."

Dosithée told them to stop their cooing and hurry up. When Ovila kissed Emilie, what he kissed was mostly teeth, she was smiling so hard. Nevertheless, as he turned away, his cheek was wet with her tears.

Emilie declined to spend the evening with her in-laws, eager to be at home. But as soon as she crossed the threshold, she felt the emptiness in her house. She ran to her room, threw herself on her bed and wept. And it was just at this moment that the baby decided to give its first kick.

Her cravings for snacks disappeared when Ovila left. She spent her evenings learning to play her accordion and quickly picked up a few tunes to accompany herself as she hummed or sang, a faraway look in her eyes. Ovila wrote her often, but his letters brought him no closer. Ovide came over every few days to keep her company. Seeing that she was always lonely, in spite of her apparent good humour, he made a suggestion. "What if I take you to Lac Pierre-Paul next Sunday? You'll be a surprise for Ovila."

Emilie jumped for joy. "Ovide," she said, "you must be the best brother-in-law on earth!" She spent the rest of the week cleaning the house, making fudge for Ovila and finishing the shirt she had started sewing before he left, which she hadn't had the heart to finish once he was gone.

Finally, Sunday arrived — but it was impossible to see it, the snow was so thick. They couldn't go anywhere, and the trip was put off for another week. The next Saturday was a memorable one for Emilie: her parents came to stay for the night. She made up her mind that she'd finally go on the following weekend, but Antoinette and Henri, who judged from the tone of her letters that she needed company, decided to come and see her. Ovide was feverish the fourth Sunday, and he had to postpone their outing. By then there were only two weeks left before Ovila was due back, so Emilie decided not to surprise him after all.

It was he who surprised her the following Tuesday, in the middle of the night. She was startled out of a deep sleep by the sound of someone coming in, but she didn't have time to panic.

"Hello, my love!"

"Ovila?"

"I hope I'm the only man who comes round in the middle of the night . . ."

"Ovila!"

"No, it's Charles."

"Ovila . . ." she purred. Her dream had come true.

He flung off his clothes, dove into bed and drew her close.

"I couldn't stand missing you any longer, Emilie."

"I couldn't wait any longer, Ovila."

He kissed her belly; she kissed the back of his neck.

"I've been trying to come and see you for the last four Sundays. How come you're back before Easter?"

"The work was almost finished, so the foreman said that some men could leave. I said I'd go, and I took off like greased lightning."

"You have the best foreman in the world!"

The June sun had mixed up the months, pounding down with incessant, hot July rays. Emilie dragged her feet from the bed to the kitchen, from the kitchen to the baby's room, from the baby's room back to bed. She didn't think she could carry her pregnancy much longer. The closer her due date, the more she trembled with fear. She knew that nature had made her misshapen and heavy so that she would wish for the birth to take place, but she still couldn't make up her mind. She wished she were a slate, so that Ovila could simply erase all traces of her pregnancy.

Their nights were troubled by insomnia. Every few minutes, she got up to relieve the pressure on her bladder, then she came back to bed and tried to cling to her husband. She was scared. Ovila made feeble attempts to calm her, but anxiety was gnawing at him, too. The chasm of fear within each was not shared with each other. Ovila didn't want to relive the hours he had gone through when Marie-Anne was born. No, he would never accept the thought of making a little white coffin for his child!

The doctor had reassured Emilie that everything was going very well, that she was made to bear children. He offered to assist with the birth, but she joked that she would prefer the midwife. "I promise, Doctor, that if it takes too much time, I'll send Ovila to get you so you can use your ice tongs. I want to do everything right, but I don't want to suffer." The doctor repeated that she could count on him.

On June 9, exactly nine months after her wedding day, Emilie felt something tighten in her stomach and rip through her kidneys. She didn't tell Ovila about it. These pains lasted a few hours, then stopped. The next morning, at dawn, the phenomenon repeated itself, but this time, it didn't stop.

She tried to stay calm, telling herself that she was young and healthy, but her heart jumped as soon as her stomach clenched. In a very composed voice — where had she found the strength? — she told Ovila that she thought it was time. Ovila rushed off to his parents' house, asked his mother to come right away and sent Oscar for the midwife.

Félicité laughed at his nervousness. "Calm down, my boy. The first time, it takes hours. It's the first one that breaks the path for the ones to follow. I'll go over after I get dressed and tidy the house a little."

Ovila didn't understand. His soul had been turned inside out with the troubles she had had, but she didn't even seem to remember.

"While you're waiting for the midwife, make yourself useful," she continued. "Clean the kitchen, and keep some hot water ready."

Dosithée didn't say a word. Births always made him edgy. He wanted to be a grandfather, but he wished that the process took minutes instead of hours. He squeezed Ovila's shoulder. At least his father hadn't forgotten, Ovila thought. No, Dosithée would never forget the terrible choice he had had to make. Ovila left, telling his mother again that he was expecting her.

Félicité went into her room and closed the door slowly. When she was alone, she gave way to her trembling and knelt by her bed. She didn't have the courage to go to Ovila's. She didn't have the strength to hear Emilie cry out. She didn't want to see the blood of a birth ever again. Four times, for her, that blood had been the blood of a dead baby.

"Good God, help me to help Emilie. Another Pronovost is about to be born. Dear Lord, let it be born in peace!"

She left her room as calmly as she had entered it. Looking her husband straight in the eye, she said, "I'm going, Dosithée. Keep her in your thoughts."

Dosithée knew that Emilie was all he would think about. He promised his wife that he would have a word with the Holy Ghost.

Félicité knocked before entering her son's house. To her great relief, Emilie was sitting in the kitchen, almost smiling. Félicité looked at Ovila, wondering if he hadn't sent for the midwife for nothing.

Emilie read her thoughts. "It's me, Mrs. Pronovost," she said, "who wants to stay out here as long as possible. I don't really want to lie down, because my kidneys hurt."

Félicité told her that she would stay with her the whole day if necessary. Emilie wondered how she could endure this pain for a whole day.

When the midwife arrived, she took Emilie into the bedroom to examine her. She asked her all the usual questions and went back to the kitchen, satisfied. "Things are going well," she said, as she washed her hands. "She's already two fingers dilated."

Emilie rejoined the group in the kitchen. She paced back and forth, leaning on Ovila's arm, preferring to stand up through the contractions.

When the sun was high in the sky, she was still walking. The midwife had examined her twice more. It was slow work.

"She's still at two fingers."

Emilie was worried. Why was it taking so long?

When the sun began to go down, Dosithée came for news. He hadn't allowed the children to go, because he'd kept hoping that he'd soon see his wife returning. He retraced his steps with none of his worries relieved.

Finally, the midwife announced to Emilie that she was at almost four fingers and asked her to stay lying down. Emilie didn't argue. She had delayed this moment for as long as possible, thinking that she would feel miserable stretched out on her back. She heard the clock strike eleven times and calculated that the storm in her belly had been going on for eighteen hours.

The midwife had the water heated and started to apply hot towels to her private parts. "It's not to wash you, ma'am," she explained, "it's to keep the skin from tearing."

Emilie let her do her job without asking any questions. The storm was getting more and more violent. The midwife examined her yet again.

"You're four fingers dilated! When you feel like pushing, push."

She left the room to tell Ovila and his mother that the delivery would start any minute now. Ovila blanched. Félicité closed her eyes.

Emilie thought she had screamed. She couldn't catch her breath. Her hair was in wet strings on the pillow. The midwife talked to her softly. She wondered how long it had been since she had lost all sense of reality. Had she just screamed again? She mustn't scream. Ovila would worry.

Each time Emilie screamed, Félicité jumped as if a pain she had forgotten, but one etched deep within her, had jabbed her. And each time Emilie screamed, Ovila held back his tears and squeezed his mother's hand. The sounds were the same, and he was sitting in the same place. It was all the same. If only he could, even today, run to the schoolhouse to seek comfort on Emilie's shoulder . . .

The midwife frowned. What was it with these Pronovost women? Mind you, this one wasn't a Pronovost, she was a Bordeleau, and she'd told her that her mother had never had problems giving birth. "Go on, push one more time. This time, we should see the top of its head."

The clock lugubriously tolled midnight, followed, an eternity later, by one o'clock. Ovila paced the room, stepping toward his mother every time he heard a new cry. Finally, there was one that was deeper and longer than the others.

He bowed his head, weeping. "I can't take no more, no more. Please let it be over."

He heard nothing. His heart stopped pounding. He looked at his mother, who was staring at the bedroom door, her ears pricked.

Inside the bedroom, a tense drama unfolded. The child had

suffered too much. It wasn't breathing yet. The midwife didn't waste a second. Emilie watched her, her eyes wide and filled with tears.

"What's going on?"

The midwife didn't answer. Then the miracle happened. Emilie saw the little grey baby take on colour, unfold like a flower in the sun, turn pink and begin to cry. Ovila entered the room immediately. Since the silence had fallen, he had been lurking by the door, every muscle tensed, ready to leap.

"It's a girl. Small, but pretty," the midwife told him.

Ovila looked at the infant, who was flailing as if she was angry that her sleep had been disturbed. Emilie wept hot tears, her thighs trembling with fatigue.

The midwife put the baby down beside her and told her not to worry. "It's the shock, and your muscles are exhausted from all that work. Put the baby on your breast. It'll calm you down, it'll calm her down, and it'll help the rest come out."

Emilie obeyed. Ovila laid his head beside hers on the pillow. She had another contraction and expelled the placenta.

Félicité helped the midwife bathe her daughter-in-law, who was now only aware of one thing: she was alive and Ovila was with her! The baby, all pink, was already nursing.

*E*milie and Ovila decided to name their daughter Rose; Emilie had described to Ovila the instant when the baby had changed colour and told him that only Rose would do.

Félicité said that her own daughter, Rosée, had been given her name because she had been born at dawn. "We mothers have a strange way of remembering the births of our children. I've always said that behind each name is a little story. Sometimes it's just a feeling, other times it's a memory, and other times it's the face of the baby. But I'm sure that there's always a little story behind a name."

Emilie held Rose good and tight. Her mother-in-law was right. Before the birth, she had promised herself that if it was a girl she would name her Charlotte. But when she saw the baby, she changed her mind. She wondered now if she hadn't been scared to call her

Charlotte. Charlotte was a memory of softness and gentleness, but also of death. She had tried to convince herself that Charlotte was just the feminine version of Charles, but she hadn't really succeeded.

Exhausted by the birth, Emilie couldn't attend the baptism. She stayed home alone, refusing all offers of company. She told Ovila that she was sure she'd hear the bells. "The wind is blowing in the right direction. I'll know when you're coming back."

When she heard the bells, her heart swelled with love.

Her parents had come from Saint-Stanislas that morning. Antoinette and Henri were there too, because Henri was making his annual visit to the area. Antoinette helped her friend with the diapers, saying that it would be good experience for her.

"When will you decide to have one yourself, Antoinette?" Emilie asked.

"It's decided already. Can't you see I'm a little fatter than usual?"

Emilie looked at her closely, then burst into laughter. "Are you trying to make me believe there's a baby in there?"

"I don't have to make you believe it, Emilie. For five months it's been making a comfy bed in my tummy."

"Well, nothing's showing. Why didn't you tell me?"

"Because I've never been regular, and I didn't notice that I was getting fatter either. I've known for just three weeks."

"You're five months along and you didn't know you were pregnant!"

"Don't tell anyone. I don't want to look totally silly. But between you and me, I'm finding a four-month pregnancy something special."

Everyone came back from the church, and Emilie hurried to give a bottle to the baby, who was crying with indignation and hunger. She had had to resign herself not to breast-feed, since she didn't have enough milk to satisfy her baby.

Ovila passed out glasses of wine to everyone; even Emilie accepted one. Caleb and Dosithée, the new grandfathers, couldn't stop congratulating each other.

Emilie had already forgotten her labour pains. "It's true that it hurts," she reassured Antoninette, "but it's not so bad."

The day was very long, beyond Emilie's strength. Before supper, she grew pale and went to lie down. The guests did their best to be as quiet as possible to let her sleep, but it was no use. At eight o'clock, her parents decided to go to the Pronovosts' to play cards. Antoinette gave Emilie and the baby a good sponge bath and went to bed with Henri. Ovila stayed home with his wife instead of going to his parents', for which Emilie was grateful.

At midnight, back from the Pronovosts', Caleb went upstairs, opened his bedroom door, went in without looking, came back out to ask Célina if she was coming, went back in with his lamp and got undressed. Only then did he notice Henri on top of Antoinette in the bed, and Antoinette staring at him, her eyes full of surprise and laughter. Caleb excused himself, picked up his clothes and left the room without bothering to cover his rear end.

He closed the door behind him, trying not to make a noise. Then he went to the other bedroom, sat on the bed, took a deep breath and burst out laughing. Antoinette, in her bedroom, did the same thing. Célina, intrigued by all the commotion, ran upstairs. Caleb was laughing so hard that he couldn't explain why.

"Be quiet, Caleb," she scolded. "Emilie's feeding the baby."

Ovila came up to see what was going on. He knocked on his in-laws' door. "What's going on?" he asked.

"Everything's fine," Célina said. "But don't come in. Caleb isn't presentable."

Caleb was laughing so hard that he had to wipe his eyes. Ovila knocked at the door of the other bedroom, but the only responses he got were Antoinette's giggles and Henri's shushing. Ovila went back downstairs to Emilie.

The next morning, Henri was the first to go downstairs — or so he thought. He wanted to leave without meeting up with Caleb. But when he went to the bathroom and opened the door, Caleb was sitting on the throne, a newspaper in his hand.

"Are you doing this on purpose, Douville? You always seem to catch me with my pants down."

Henri quickly closed the door. Then he burst into uncontrollable giggles. Caleb did too, hoping to hide the embarrassing noises of his business in the process, though Henri heard them quite well anyway.

"It's starting again," Ovila said, leaping out of bed.

Henri was sitting at the kitchen table. When he saw Ovila, he got up and went to the back door. "Excuse me, Ovila, but I must go outside to urinate. I'll try to be as discreet as possible." He burst out laughing again. Caleb came out of the bathroom, doing up the last button on his fly.

"I've never seen such a thing, Ovila. Douville and me, we have lots of problems with very natural things."

Douville came back in. When he saw Caleb, he started to titter, and Caleb joined him.

"Are you two going to tell me what's going on?" Emilie was standing in the door of her bedroom, the baby in her arms. Caleb and Henri laughed even louder. Antoinette came downstairs, followed by Célina. Antoinette was already laughing, even though she didn't know exactly what was going on.

Caleb finally caught his breath enough to speak. "Well, it's just that yesterday evening, I went into the wrong room, and I got undressed in front of these two."

"You are too polite, Mr. Bordeleau." Henri chuckled. "Since we're all laughing about it, why not tell the whole story?"

"If I have your blessing, Henri . . . What Henri wants me to tell you is that while I was in his room with my trousers around my ankles, he was making love to his beautiful Antoinette." He stopped to see if Antoinette was blushing, but she was laughing. "Then, this morning, I thought I could take a quiet look at the paper. But no, Henri had to open the door and find me with my trousers around my ankles yet again!"

Henri roared with laughter. Célina pursed her lips. Emilie tried to comfort Rose, who was frightened by all the noise. Ovila slapped his thighs, and Caleb ran for the toilet again.

Rose's baptism was not soon forgotten.

Twenty-seven

O GIVE EMILIE AND OVILA a chance to have a proper first-anniversary celebration, Rosée offered to take care of little Rose. Ovila, who had found regular work as a carpenter with Mr. Légaré, asked Emilie if she wanted to take a trip.

"Where to?"

"You choose. Montreal or Quebec City."

Emilie thought it over, licking her lips. She chose Montreal.

"For how long?"

"As long as you like, if Rosée can stay with the baby."

Emilie went to look at Rose, who was sleeping peacefully. Could she leave her for a week without missing her? Would the little one notice that she was gone? Her mind was clouded with doubt. And what would people say? No, they could say what they liked. She wasn't going to let that worry her, and ruin her chance for some fun.

"If you twist my arm, I'll have to say yes."

Ovila got up, took her right arm and twisted it behind her back. Emilie winced. "Are you crazy? I didn't want you to twist it for real!"

Ovila twisted a little harder.

"All right. Yes. Yesyesyesyesyesyesyesyes . . ." Emilie said, shaking with laughter as she slipped out of his painful grip.

Rosée agreed to stay with the baby for as long as they were gone. Emilie packed their suitcases; in secret, Ovila counted their money. They had enough to last for a week they'd never forget.

*W*hen Emilie kissed Rose goodbye, her heart was pounding. But her heart beat even more wildly at the idea of spending a week alone, far away, with Ovila.

She let herself be rocked by the train, resisting the temptation to rest her head on his shoulder. She was trying to act like a true lady and didn't want to spoil the illusion. So eager was she to arrive in Montreal that the train seemed to be going at a snail's pace.

"Where do you want to stay?" Ovila asked as soon as they arrived.

"The Windsor Hotel." She had seen photographs of it and had promised herself that at least once in her life she would stay there.

"The Windsor! If it's the Windsor you want, it's the Windsor you'll get!"

They got into one of the calèches waiting in front of the station. Ovila asked for the hotel in a loud, self-assured voice that Emilie didn't recognize. She looked at him and held back a ferocious desire to laugh.

He leaned toward her and whispered that that was his lumber-camp voice. "When you talk like that, no one steps on your toes."

The driver turned and asked Ovila to repeat the name of the hotel. Ovila did, certain that he had impressed him.

"Are you tourists?"

"How did you know?" Ovila asked.

"It's easy to tell. You have a couple of suitcases, and only tourists would hire a calèche to go to the end of the block."

Emilie looked around, biting her lips hard so that she wouldn't giggle at Ovila's embarrassment, and also to convince herself that she wasn't dreaming. Finally, she let her head fall onto her husband's shoulder, having noticed that many other women allowed themselves this gesture.

"It's ugly, eh, Ovila?" she observed.

"Montreal?"

"No, the posts full of wires."

"Wait till you see the lights they make before you complain. Apparently, it's really something!"

They were in front of the hotel, and Emilie had to keep herself from crying out with pleasure. Since the hotel wasn't too crowded, they got a room on the third floor, with a view onto Dominion Square. Emilie rushed to the bathroom, where she flushed the toilet repeatedly and then turned on the taps, fascinated to note that there was running hot water. She washed her hands with a scented soap that was there just for guests. Back in the room, she went to the window to join Ovila.

"It's a real palace."

"Nothing's too good for you, my morning mist."

For two long hours, they tested the bed to make sure the mattress was comfortable, and then they went downstairs to the magnificent dining room. Sitting in splendour at a table for four, they studied the menu and chose the least expensive items.

Emilie's eyes weren't big enough to take everything in. She spent the entire meal exclaiming over the extravagances around her.

"I count at least twenty-four," she told Ovila.

"Twenty-four what?"

"Lights in each candelabra."

"Electricity is really something. Did you notice, the light doesn't even flicker."

She couldn't stop crying out, and soon Ovila was caught up in her excitement. "Did you see the lovely paintings painted on all the walls all around the room?" he asked.

"I'm not sure what they're supposed to be."

"I think they're scenes of the old country."

"Maybe that's why I don't recognize anything."

After the meal, they decided to take a walk. They didn't stray far from the hotel, as they didn't want to get lost. They decided that the first thing they would do the next day was visit Berthe. And they would take a ride on the streetcars.

*T*he sky was threatening rain when they left the hotel after a rather disturbed night; they had woken up every time other guests had arrived. "It's crazy, when do people sleep in the city?" Ovila had grumbled. "It's past eleven o'clock. Maybe they go to parties every night."

But now Emilie's heart skipped a beat. They were in the convent parlour, a white room featuring a grille with a curtain behind it. She didn't dare say anything to Ovila while they waited, fearing that a nun would overhear their remarks.

Finally, they heard a door opening, and then someone pulled back the curtain. Two veiled nuns were sitting behind the grille. Emilie looked at one, then the other. Which one was Berthe? She didn't wait to guess, sure that Berthe would react as soon as she spoke. Ovila took off his hat and turned it in his nervous hands, finally placing it on his knee.

"Hello, Berthe. We're so happy to see you," Emilie began.

One of the two nuns nodded. Would she not talk at all?

"Your friend, ma'am, is in a period of penitence. During this time, she has decided to isolate herself and live alone, in silence, in one of the places intended for this purpose at the end of the garden. You should have let us know you were coming. In this case, considering that you have come from so far, our mother superior has allowed your friend to come to the parlour. However, your friend does not have permission to talk to you. I hope you will understand that this is a choice she has made and not a rule that has been imposed on her."

"Can Berthe at least nod her head?" Emilie asked.

"Yes, she can," the nun answered.

Emilie was sure that, with these explanations having been delivered, Berthe would be left alone with her, but it was not to be. Emilie dug into her handbag and pulled out two photographs.

"Berthe, a photographer passed through Bourdais, and Ovila and I hired him to do our marriage portrait." She laughed nervously. "It's not a real marriage portrait, since he just came around two months ago. It's a good thing I'd already had the baby." She put the photo up to the grille so that Berthe could see it. She would so have liked to see her expression. "We'll leave it here in the parlour, where you can get it. We brought it for you."

Berthe shook her head "no." Emilie raised her eyebrows and looked at the other nun.

"Your friend has vowed not to attach herself to things of this earth. She prefers not to have the portrait in her possession."

Emilie put the photograph back in her handbag and took out another, this one of Rose in the arms of her grandfather Pronovost. Berthe looked at it for a long time, and Emilie thought she heard a little sigh. To fill the silence, Emilie began to describe the photograph as if Berthe had lost her sight as well as her tongue.

"Rose's hair is quite long for a baby her age. As you see, it's a little curly. I made her dress. It's a little white dress with lace and sewn pleats. She was wearing white socks and nice black shoes with a strap and little round buttons. You don't know my father-in-law. That's him holding Rose. But you can't see him well because his hat makes a shadow over his face."

Berthe leaned close to the grille and stared at the photograph for several minutes. Emilie would have given anything to know what she was thinking. Then Berthe turned her veiled head away.

"You don't even want this one, Berthe?"

Berthe shook her head. The second nun fidgeted in her chair. Emilie looked at Ovila, who seemed to be just as ill at ease as she was. The second nun got up, followed by Berthe. Emilie and Ovila did the same.

"Well, Berthe, I guess we'll get going. We're here for the week, so we're going to see the city."

She didn't know what else to say. If only Berthe could speak. Fearing that she had done something wrong, she tried to redeem herself in the eyes of the other nun.

"May we visit your chapel?"

*O*vila and Emilie had two extraordinary days. They went to the top of Mount Royal, visited the magnificent city hall and went down to the port, with Ovila checking the merchandise offered by the farmers as they passed through Place Jacques-

Cartier. Once they reached the port, he headed for the Bonsecours pier. Outside the market building were other farmers, with their wares set out under awnings. When they arrived at the pier, they saw the *Terrebonne* and its great paddle wheel.

"It must be something to go to Trois-Rivières on that," Emilie said admiringly.

Ovila made a rapid calculation and asked Emilie to wait a few moments. She sat in a cart between the boat and stacks of wood, which would feed the steamship boilers. Ovila came back half an hour later.

"Now, listen. If you like, we could change hotels and take a room right near here. There are four or five hotels in this area that cost a lot less than the Windsor. They're not as nice, that's for sure, but they're quite decent. Especially the Rasco. If we stay here for two days, we'll have enough money to go home by boat. What do you think?"

Emilie thought it was a wonderful idea. The Rasco had no vacancies, so they took their things to the Canada Inn. After two more days full of sightseeing, they embarked on the *Richelieu*, since the *Terrebonne* had already left port. As they pulled out of Montreal, their minds were still reeling from all the wonders they had seen. They saw Ile Sainte-Hélène and, along with all the other passengers on the *Richelieu*, waved at the people on the ferry chugging toward town.

Emilie took deep, full breaths. Her stomach was hovering somewhere between its normal spot and the bottom of her throat.

"I don't feel good, Ovila."

Ovila looked at her. She was green. "You should probably lie down."

He took her to their cabin, where she stayed for the entire trip. She couldn't help thinking of the trip to Europe. She could never have made it — she was her father's daughter all the way. When they finally reached Trois-Rivières, she was the first down the gangplank.

"You're some traveller!" Ovila laughed. "Anyway, as soon as your feet touched dry land, your colour came back."

He shook his head, then asked her if she wanted to take the train or a buggy the rest of the way home.

"Let's take the train to Shawinigan and a buggy home from there," she said.

In Shawinigan, they paid a surprise visit to Antoinette, who was plumper than ever. They stayed for a day, during which Emilie described her trip to Montreal in great detail, enjoying her friend's naïve reactions. Henri arrived a few minutes before they left, just in time to hear Ovila joke about Emilie's sea legs. He looked at Emilie and smiled. She shrugged her shoulders, as if to say, "Just imagine what would have happened! You're lucky things turned out the way they did." To everyone's great pleasure, Henri told them that he had to go to Lac aux Sables to meet with the commissioners. Emilie and Ovila would sleep over and travel with him in the morning.

*B*ack home, Rose sulked for two days, reproaching Emilie with doleful looks for having abandoned her for so long. Emilie and Ovila invented all sorts of faces to make her smile and, to Emilie's great relief, she finally relented. Emilie had begun to tell herself that she must never leave her child again, and she felt a little cloud darkening her light heart. But this shadow was nothing compared to the one that followed.

Ovila was prowling around as if he had something to hide. Emilie could feel it.

"What is it, Ovila, that you don't want to say?"

"Mr. Légaré doesn't need me for a few months. That means, if I want to earn enough money, I'll have to go to Lac Pierre-Paul with my father."

Ovila would leave, and she would wait . . . again. Sunless days. Cool evenings. Freezing nights.

"You told me you would never go away again, Ovila. You told me that you never wanted to be far away from me. We have the little one now, and you can see how unhappy she is when we're not here."

"I know all that, Emilie. I know Rose probably won't recognize me when I come home at Christmas. But I don't have much choice. Légaré has no work, and our trip made a big dent in our savings."

She was in no mood to be cheered up. The air in the house grew very chilly. The two spent entire days turning away from each other in anger.

Emilie felt weak. She needed Ovila so much; why couldn't he keep his promise? She would never have the courage to live far away from him. If only he could find a little contract, even at the brickyard, and give up the woods for one winter. Rose, of course, chose this time to cut a tooth, and her crankiness cost her parents their sleep.

Ovila resigned himself to going up to the lake after trying every means, reasonable and unreasonable, to find some work that would have kept him home. It wasn't that he wanted to be far away from his wife, yet she acted as if he had chosen to go. She turned her back to him at night, and didn't let him near her. Why didn't she understand?

He was sitting near the stove, whittling a new piece of wood. Emilie had put down her accordion and was busy hemming a blanket. The north wind rattled all the windows, trumpeting the first, early frost. Rose had finally fallen asleep after Emilie rubbed her gums with a clove. Ovila looked at Emilie, his throat tight. He missed her already. From time to time, she glanced over at him and their eyes met. Then she broke the spell, sighing and returning to her work.

Ovila had had enough. He got up, grabbed his coat and left the house, slamming the door. Emilie jumped. She left enough time for him to get away from the house, then ran to the window to see where he was going.

Emilie knew that she had gone too far. Ovila was furious. What had she done? She pulled on her coat, ready to go after him, when she realized that Rose held her prisoner. She began to weep in frustration.

Ovila came back in the small hours of the morning, obviously drunk. He gave Emilie a raffish look, then got undressed, forgetting to remove one sock. She watched him, confused and upset. He wasn't in the habit of getting drunk.

"Where did you go?" she asked after a bit.

"To the Hôtel Grand Nord. At least there people are in a good mood. I won an arm-wrestling contest. Four dollars, ma'am. Four nice new dollars."

He laughed savagely, then burst into tears. He told her, hiccuping, that he didn't want to see her so sad any more, that he didn't want to go away, but he had to, as a good family man with two mouths to feed. She was doing her best to make him miserable, while he was doing his best to make her happy. She opposed him constantly, and he felt like she was scolding him. She had to stop playing the schoolmistress with him: he was her husband, and she was his wife.

Tears ran down Emilie's face. All she wanted to say was that she loved him and that she suffered terribly when he wasn't there. She held his head and stroked his hair.

Both of them were awash in tears when there was a violent knock on the door. It was Ovide. Ovila wiped his eyes and looked at the time, while Emilie quickly opened the door.

Ovila grumbled that five in the morning was no time to come visiting. "Go milk the cows, Ovide, and let my wife and me sleep." He was about to chuckle when he saw his brother's silhouette framed in the doorway.

"Ovila, it's Lazare, " Ovide said in a hoarse voice.

"He doesn't want to do the milking?"

"Even if he wanted to, Ovila, he never will again. He's suffocated for good this time."

It took a few minutes for what Ovide had just said to sink in. When he heard Emilie crying, Ovila's head cleared.

"What did you say?"

Ovide told them how they had been on their way to the barn when Lazare had suffered a fatal seizure.

"It's impossible," Ovila said. "He was fine yesterday. And it's been months since he's had a fit."

"I'm telling you, Ovila. What do you want me to say? Lazare died this morning."

Emilie and Ovila's quarrel was drowned in the depths of their grief.

*D*osithée pushed Ovila to pack his things. "We'll leave right after the funeral," he said, in a sharp tone that left no doubt as to the depth of his pain. "Make sure you're ready."

Emilie packed Ovila's suitcase while he went to his parents' home to view the body. She couldn't be with him, as much as she would have liked to, for Rose was feverish yet again.

Ovila and his brothers carried Lazare to his grave while Félicité, almost succumbing to her grief, bathed Rose's little coat in tears.

"Give her to me, Mrs. Pronovost," Emilie said. "After a while, a baby grows heavy in your arms."

"I know," Félicité said. "But even when a child isn't a baby any more it still grows heavy. It aways does, in other ways. So let me hold Rose. It makes me feel like I'm still holding onto life."

Emilie and Félicité watched the men change their clothes and leave for the lake. Dosithée didn't want to spend a single second looking at the void that had opened up, once again, in his house.

Back at home, Emilie struggled with Rose, who was grumpy from the changes in routine. After Emilie managed to put her to bed, she sat at her kitchen table and wrote a long letter to Berthe. She had put off this moment since her return from Montreal, not knowing how to tell her friend how she had felt in her presence. She knew that she'd be unable to recapture the casual tone she had always affected in her letters. Berthe was so far away from her now. In fact, she wondered, was Berthe still there?

*F*rom her window, Emilie watched a feeble autumn go by, offering no resistance to winter's grip. She kept busy with Rose and with carding, weaving and sewing. She started on a Christmas dress for the baby, who had already grown out of her pretty white one.

Rosée fell ill with a virulent flu while she was filling in for the teacher, who had caught the same bug, and Emilie was asked if she would reconsider her decision not to teach. She agreed to return to the classroom once Eva promised to look after Rose.

Her heart in an uproar, she found herself once again at her desk, chalk in hand. She gave each pupil a long look, smiling at the ones she recognized and even more at those she didn't know. Their features were clues to their family names. She told them about their older brothers and sisters whom she had known so well. Only a young Crête, a second-grader whom she'd never met before, glared back at her.

"You must be the youngest in your family, eh?" she asked.

He answered with a short, dry "Yeah," like a twig breaking. Emilie shrugged her shoulders. Even after seven years, it seemed, the Crêtes were still telling the story of how she had put their eldest son in his place.

The teacher told the commissioners that she could come back to work after Christmas. Although she was feeling better, Rosée asked Emilie if she would stay on for the last two weeks of the term, because her mother needed her help. Emilie didn't have the heart to refuse. Finding herself in the classroom every morning made her forget some of the unhappiness in her heart. She also felt closer to Ovila: when she sighed over his absence, she could look at the desk he had occupied for so long and take refuge in memories of her adolesence. As well, the small amount of money she was earning would help her buy her husband a modest gift for New Year's.

Ovila came home on the eve of her birthday. Emilie was going to bed, alone with her twenty-three years, when the door burst open so suddenly that she thought she hadn't closed it properly and the wind had blown it open. She went to the kitchen to shut out the wintry blast, which would soon be sweeping across the floor.

"I thought, my love, that if I slammed the door two or three times, you'd get up to see what was going on."

Ovila! Joyously, wordlessly, she threw herself into his arms. In spite of the cold he'd brought in with him, Ovila's welcome was warm.

"Happy birthday, Miss Bordeleau," he said when she let go of him. He put a finger to his lips, took off his outer clothes and tiptoed to his daughter's bedroom. Emilie followed him. He stood for a minute watching Rose sleeping peacefully, a smile on her lips, her eyelids fluttering when a dream visited her. They went back to the kitchen.

"Would you like some hot tea?" she asked.

"Only if you have some, too. You know, tea always keeps me awake," he teased. Emilie put two cups on the table and filled them to the brim.

"Before we talk about serious things, my love," he continued, "I have a little something for you. I didn't come back just before your birthday for nothing. I wanted you to see what I have for you. You know me, I can never wait when I have a surprise."

"Another surprise? Just having you here is a wonderful present," she said, touched and intrigued.

True to form, Ovila made her close her eyes and wait while he prepared everything, and Emilie played along with his game. She heard paper rustling. Thick paper, she thought, not fine paper. Then she heard him bustling around the chairs and table. Every time he passed her, he stopped to kiss her on the forehead or the cheek or the hair or the nape of her neck. She laughed; she had no idea what he was doing. Finally, he covered her eyes with his warmed-up hands and helped her stand up.

"Ta-da!" he sang, letting his hands drop.

"Oh!"

On the backs and seats of the chairs, on the table, everywhere, there were beaver skins laid out. Beautiful skins, well tanned and very lustrous.

"First thing tomorrow, I'm going to the village to see the lucky person who'll have the pleasure of making the most beautiful beaver coat in the village. And not just any beaver! Beaver I trapped myself!"

Emilie touched all the skins, rubbing the fur the wrong way to feel the thickness, then smoothing it to feel softness. Ovila must have been thinking of her hat and muff. What a set she'd have now: the cold could knock at her door, but it would never again get in.

They celebrated their reunion until Rose woke up. At her first morning gurgle, Ovila ran to get her and brought her back to bed, where Emilie swaddled her. They played with her until she stopped smiling and made it clear that she was hungry. Emilie, eyes puffy with love and lack of sleep, got busy preparing a sumptuous breakfast. All three ate voraciously: Rose, her hot cereal; Ovila and Emilie, eggs.

"I think the little one remembers me," Ovila said.

"I think so too. Lately she's been pretty wild, but she doesn't seem to be scared of anything you do."

Ovila spent every spare moment making a sled for his daughter, stopping only to celebrate Christmas. He wanted the sled to be ready for New Year's Day. But he still found time to take his skins into the village, accompanied by Emilie, who had a picture she'd cut out from a newspaper of the style of coat she wanted. They went to see Mr. Tourigny, who told them that he wasn't in the habit of doing such big work, preferring these days to make shoes and boots. He told them to ask Marchildon. "But don't worry if Marchildon has too much work. There are a lot of people who work with leather here in Saint-Tite, and you won't have any problem finding someone who works with fur. After all, it's just hairy leather."

The Marchildons weren't eager to take on the work at first, fearing that they lacked the experience to do the finishing. Emilie asked them just to sew the skins, and she would make the lining. They agreed, and they promised Emilie that she would have her coat before the end of February.

The holidays flew by like lightning. Ovila had just got back into a daily routine when once again Emilie had to pack his suitcases, including a pipe she had given him, the bowl of which was already black. Both of their hearts were in turmoil.

"With a little luck," Ovila said, "next year I'll find something that's not so far away."

He kissed her one last time, climbed up beside his father and cast a long, last glance at her. In one hand she was holding the handle of a red sled in which Rose was sleeping, her breath making little puffs of steam in the cold, biting air.

Twenty-eight

ROSE STILL COULDN'T SIT UP. Emilie had tried to show her how, propping her up in a chair surrounded by cushions. She wanted to be able to write Ovila that their daughter had accomplished this feat. Instead she wrote, at the end of March, that Rose was still sleeping almost all the time, that she ate all her food, that she had cut two more teeth and that she smiled a lot, although she often looked pensive — almost anxious.

Then she told him that she was still finding her fur coat very useful. What she didn't mention was that there had been enough extra furs to make him a jacket. Never, she'd thought, would he wear a fur coat, so she'd asked the Marchildons to turn the skin inside out so that the fur would show only at the collar.

She also related the latest news from the village, pointedly mentioning the rumour that the municipal council was planning to build an aqueduct. When Ovila read this, he understood that she was suggesting he try to find work on the site. He promised himself to do so, and hoped that the aqueduct project would prove to be more than just election rhetoric.

For the first time, Emilie found the winter passing very quickly.

Rosée announced that she was going to marry Arthur Veillette in September, so Emilie spent most of her evenings helping her sew, knit and weave items for her hope chest. Rosée's wedding-night outfit was less revealing than Emilie's — but then, Rosée didn't seem to have Emilie's audacity.

Félicité was so nervous at the idea of marrying off the older of her two daughters that she convinced herself time was playing tricks on her and grinding to a halt two or three times a day. "It's not the same when a son gets married," she complained. "You know you'll get an extra daughter. But when your daughter gets married, you lose her for good. Her in-laws get the best of the deal."

Rosée had noticed that her sister-in-law was languishing; Emilie seemed to think about nothing but Ovila, to talk only about him, to live through her days waiting only for his return.

"It's funny, Emilie," she said. "When I spend a lot of time with you, I can't help but notice that you're not all that happy when my brother's away." Emilie said nothing. Rosée looked at her and blushed. "Sometimes I think you're very romantic. I wonder if you love Rose for herself or because she's Ovila's daughter."

"I love Rose because I love her, it's as simple as that," Emilie answered. "But it does make me laugh to see how much she takes after her father. I always promised myself, Rosée, that I would marry a good-looking man so I'd have good-looking children. When I got to know your brother, I thought he was good-looking." She paused a few seconds to bring Ovila's face to her mind's eye. "You know, he's got under my skin."

Rosée smiled. "I hope Arthur and I will be as happy as you and Ovila. What's your secret, anyway?"

"There's no secret," Emilie said. "We love each other. We love to be together, to go to the lake together, to eat together, to make projects for the future. And, of course, we love sleeping together." She thought of the nights that belonged just to her and Ovila, the nights that gave her goose bumps when she dreamed about them.

ℛosée's hope chest was almost full by the time Ovila came back. A week after his return, he was rehired by Mr.

Légaré. This time, he thought, there would be enough work that he wouldn't have to leave Saint-Tite the following fall.

He worked the entire summer, and Mr. Légaré's contract was far from finished. There were still a number of pieces of furniture to make for the Saint-Gabriel brothers' college, construction of which had long since been completed. The brothers were waiting to accumulate some capital before finishing the furnishings. Ovila got an extraordinary opportunity to use his talents, for the brothers asked him to sculpt the Stations of the Cross.

"Are you sure that you don't want it to be painted?" he asked. "The Stations of the Cross made out of wood would be very unusual."

"We're sure. We figure we'll save money over the long term. We won't have to touch up the paint every ten years. They have to do that a lot in the old country."

"If that's what you want, that's what you'll get."

Ovila announced the good news to Emilie. They danced with joy in the living room, to Rose's great amusement. This commission meant that Ovila could stay home for the entire year.

"Anyway, Charles Pronovost, if you change your mind and go away, I'll crucify you myself."

"If you're planning do it with one of your hatpins, I'm not worried. And don't call me Charles, I don't like it. It feels like you're talking to someone else."

*R*osée's marriage was celebrated with great pomp, Dosithée having spared no expense. The very next morning, she left her family to go with Arthur to Cap-de-la-Madeleine. Félicité and Emilie both promised her that she would get used to living in a new parish.

"You see, my girl," Félicité said, "myself, I came from Sainte-Geneviève-de-Batiscan, and I'm doing all right."

"It's not the same. You came with your whole family."

"But *I* didn't," Emilie said. "I came all alone. I must say, it would have been a lot easier if I'd had a husband with me, but I managed anyway. Now I can hardly remember what it was like to live in Saint-Stanislas."

Rosée swallowed her apprehensions and was radiantly happy when she left. As soon as she was out of sight, Félicité looked at her husband and saw that he felt the same way she did.

"It's hard, eh, my dear, to see the young ones go."

Dosithée took Rose from her mother's arms and held her to his chest. "Life is good anyway," he said. "Now, little Rose will take her place."

*E*milie and Ovila spent most of their days off at the lake. They took Rose with them when her grandparents didn't ask to keep her, but most often they were alone and took full advantage of the slowly, softly passing hours.

Ovila bought a gun, and he showed Emilie how to use it. They always came back home with a hare or a partridge. To Ovila's surprise, Emilie was a good shot.

"Are you sure, my love, that you never used a hunting rifle before?" he asked.

"Never. But it's so easy to aim."

"Easy? Careful you don't exaggerate!"

"Ovila, look! What is that bird over there?"

Ovila looked up where Emilie was pointing. The bird was climbing in spirals with stunning speed, making use of its impressive wingspan. Without taking his eyes off it, Ovila sat down on a rock and watched it soar.

"Look how beautiful it is, Emilie. It's only the second time in my life I've seen such a sight."

Beside him, Emilie was watching the bird too. It circled above them one last time, then disappeared into the woods.

"I think we'll hear it one of these nights."

"You still haven't told me what it is."

"An eagle owl, Emilie. A damned beautiful eagle owl. Almost white. I know people who would pay a lot for one of those killed and stuffed. But I could never kill a bird like that."

That night, they slept close together, listening for the eagle owl's hooting.

✳

*T*he tranquillity of their days left but a thin trace on the winter ice. They got along so well. Emilie always got up first and washed Rose. Then Ovila got out of bed and stoked the stove and heated the water. If he knew that his brother was tired, he would go and help with the milking. But if Ovide was well enough to supervise the younger ones, Ovila stayed home with Emilie and Rose, sipping hot tea and munching toast.

Now that Rose was a year and a half old, she demanded a great deal of attention. When the day was sunny, Ovila went earlier to his workshop so that he would have time to take a break and play with her on her sled. Emilie sometimes went with them, when her hands weren't wet with dishwater and detergent or if she wasn't busy soaking a piece of fabric in dye. Having waited for months to hear Ovila complain about the cold, she finally got the beaver jacket out of mothballs and gave it to him. Ovila was surprised that she'd found a way to make two garments out of the pelts.

The cold was too bitter for them to go to Saint-Stanislas for Christmas. Célina wrote that she understood their reluctance to take Rose on such a long, chilly trip. Instead, Caleb and Célina paid them a surprise visit on the eve of Epiphany. Emilie greeted them and rushed them inside. As they warmed up, she played a few tunes on her accordion.

Then Caleb played horse with Rose. He crossed a leg and sat the toddler on his rubber boot, holding her firmly by the hands, then bounced her to the rhythm of his rhyme: "Off to Paris we will go, on our horses white as snow. First we walk, walk, walk . . . then we trot, trot, trot . . . then gallopy gallopy!" Rose smiled as she was rocked gently at the walk, giggled as she was jiggled at the trot and shrieked with laughter as she was bounced at the gallop.

"Do you want to start again, my Rose? Grandpa's horse never gets tired."

"Aaooo," Rose replied.

"Did you hear, Emilie? The child said 'gallop.'"

Emilie chuckled at Rose's red cheeks. "I don't want to disappoint you, Papa," she said, "but Rose says 'aaooo' for everything. 'Aaooo' for up, 'aaooo' for water, 'aaooo' for booboo, for cake, for sled and now for gallop. All you have to do is look where she's looking to know which 'aaooo' she means."

Caleb pretended to be terribly disappointed, and he kept trying to teach Rose to say "gallop."

"Seems to me she doesn't talk a lot for her age," he remarked.

"She's just like that. She doesn't talk, she walked late, and she's not at all interested in the potty."

"You don't take after your grandpa, my Rose, being lazy like that. Look at your grandpa. He's not lazy, and he's living to be an old man anyway."

Célina refrained from comment, except to remind Caleb not to bounce the baby in the galloping game right after meals. "Stop for two minutes now, Caleb. You'll upset her stomach."

"Célina, I never had the time to play with our children because I was too busy. Now that the milk goes in the buckets even when I'm not around, I'm not going to deprive myself of playing with my granddaughter. Rose only knows her Grandpa Pronovost. I have to upset her stomach a little if I want her to remember me."

*E*milie and Ovila watched spring arrive from their bedroom window. She told him that there was also a bud about to blossom within her. Once again, Ovila danced with joy; the agonies of Emilie's first labour had already faded from memory.

"This time, my love," he promised, "I won't leave your side the whole time the little one is growing inside you. I'll be here to watch it pushing your belly out. Uh . . . exactly how long do I have to wait?"

"Till autumn. Don't worry, you'll finish your Stations of the Cross before I finish mine."

Emilie wondered whether it was Ovila's presence that made this pregnancy easier or whether her body had now grown accustomed to motherhood. "This baby's an angel. It lets me sleep at night and it doesn't give me backaches."

"It must be a boy."

"I'd say no. I'm the same shape I was the last time."

"Don't tell me you believe those stories, Emilie, as educated as you are. Whether they're boys or girls, you have the same shape."

"Say what you like, I'm sure it's another girl."

"And I think a boy. Do you want to make a bet?"

"Yes. We'll bet that if it's a girl you won't go up to the woods next winter." Emilie threw out this challenge triumphantly, as if she had found a foolproof way to keep Ovila far from the forest and by her side.

"Well . . . you don't beat around the bush!" Ovila joked that the stakes were too high.

Emilie hoped he was joking. "When we make a bet, we bet, my boy," she laughed.

"Done!"

The leaves had long taken over the branches and abandoned them again by the time Emilie felt the first labour pains. She asked Ovila to go get the midwife. He wanted to send Oscar or Télesphore, but Emilie asked him not to.

"I would prefer if you went yourself. If you go to your parents', everyone will get worried. This way, we can let them know at the last minute."

With Rose on his knee, Ovila drove to get the midwife, taking his time as Emilie had asked him to do. When they returned, an hour later, the midwife knocked on the bedroom door, but Emilie asked her to wait while she got ready.

Then Ovila knocked. "Is everything all right?"

"Everything's fine," she reassured him. "This time's much easier than the first time. Why don't you take Rose outside to play?"

"I don't want to leave you all alone."

"I'd like it better if Rose isn't in the house."

"So I'll take her to my mother's or Eva's."

"No! I want you to stay close to home."

"Emilie, it's crazy to talk like this, through a door. The midwife is ready to come and help you."

"I'll let her in as soon as you're outside with Rose."

Ovila looked at the midwife, who was heating the water and tearing old sheets into long strips. "A woman in labour has her strange ways," she said, a wry smile on her lips.

Ovila left the house, with Rose in tow. The midwife knocked on the bedroom door and went in. Emilie was red-faced — a sure sign of fever, the midwife thought anxiously. Emilie asked her if she had brought the string. The midwife reminded her that they weren't at that stage yet.

Emilie burst out laughing. "The baby's here. I just need the string to cut the cord."

The midwife stared at her, incredulous, then quickly lifted the sheet. A baby girl was wriggling on Emilie's breast. Emilie laughed again, and the midwife realized that she was blushing with happiness. As the midwife tied off and cut the cord, Emilie looked out the window at Ovila, who was trying to distract Rose but was obviously having great trouble doing so.

"When was she born?" asked the midwife

"Well before you arrived. That's why I didn't want you to come in, and I didn't want Ovila to see her until she's bathed."

"Why didn't you send for me sooner?"

"Because I knew that everything was fine. Actually, I was a little surprised to feel her coming so fast."

"It doesn't make sense. When did you have your first pains?"

"Two hours ago!"

"Now I've seen everything! The first time it was never-ending, and this time it was over almost before it started!"

Emilie asked her to get Ovila, who was pacing back and forth outside, counting each step out loud as if teaching his daughter her numbers. When he saw the midwife, he turned pale. She smiled and told him to go to the bedroom.

Ovila frowned as he knocked on the door. The crying of a baby announced that he was expected.

"Not already, Emilie!"

"Oh, yes! And I won our bet."

"Another girl?"

"Yes, sir. Pretty as an angel. The spitting image of your mother."

Ovila kissed Emilie before leaning over the baby. He studied the little wrinkled forehead and the large, blindly staring eyes. He counted her fingers and toes and jokingly checked to make sure that she was a girl. When he took her in his arms, she didn't make a peep.

"I think I know what to name her, Ovila."

"Félicité? Like my mother? It's true she looks like her."

"Maybe the next one. I want to call this one Marie-Ange."

Ovila looked at the infant, repeating the name in various tones. Then he smiled at his wife. "The name suits her well."

Twenty-nine

$\mathcal{F}$ALL CRADLED MARIE-ANGE in long, sunny days — an Indian summer to remember. With the arrival of her sister, Rose began to suck her thumb. Emilie and Ovila tried everything to get her to stop this habit.

"Don't suck your thumb, Rose. Your teeth will be crooked."

"Tas'es good, my t'umb."

"I know it tastes good," Emilie replied patiently, "but you're not a baby any more. You are still your mother's beautiful Rose, but Marie-Ange is the baby. And Marie-Ange will start to suck her thumb if she sees you sucking yours."

"Tas'es good, my t'umb."

Emilie sighed and decided not to mention Rose's new habit at all. Ovila ignored it too. Rose still continued to suck her thumb eagerly.

"For twenty-seven months, Rose never sucked her thumb," Ovila said one evening. "She's only started now."

"And she made a mess in her pants today."

"No!"

"Yes. Here I am with two babies in diapers."

Ovila was furious. It had taken what seemed like forever to

potty-train Rose, and he wasn't about to start all over again. Emilie asked him to be patient; Rose was probably jealous of the baby. "It happens almost all the time. My mother told me that I stopped feeding myself when my brother was born."

"That's no reason to let Rose do the same thing."

To Emilie's chagrin, Ovila undertook to "train" Rose by leaving her sitting on the potty for hours. Rose cried, wailed and tried to stand up, but Ovila sat her back down. She also started to wake up at night and ask for water when Emilie got up to feed Marie-Ange.

"We're going to go crazy, Emilie," Ovila complained. "We have only two children and our arms are full. Can you tell me how mothers manage with more than two?"

Emilie sighed and shrugged. She had lost quite a bit of weight and was feeling more and more harassed. Luckily, the new baby was easy, crying only when she was hungry or her diaper needed changing.

By the time Marie-Ange was three months old, Rose still hadn't stopped sucking her thumb or soiling her pants. On top of that, as her mother had done years before, she had stopped feeding herself.

For several days, Emilie and Ovila refused to spoon-feed her. Rose fasted. Finally, Ovila couldn't take it any more. "I don't know what her problem is," he said, "but I'm going to see the doctor today. Rose is two and a half years old, and she's worse than a baby." He bundled his daughter up and took her straight to the doctor.

Emilie stayed home, crying softly. She didn't recognize Ovila any more: he was impatient, irritable, nervous. Too many sleepless nights, she thought. Too many problems with Rose. Perhaps Félicité was right when she said that he was too wrapped up with the children, that it wasn't a man's work. Emilie rocked Marie-Ange, drying her tears before they could fall on the baby.

Ovila returned two hours later. He quietly entered the house, a sleeping Rose in his arms, and laid her in her bed, carefully unwrapping her from his jacket. Marie-Ange was sound asleep, and Emilie got busy washing diapers, scrubbing them energetically on the washboard. She smiled at Ovila, who came to stand behind her and put his arms round her waist. As she leaned her head against him, she realized that he was trembling.

"What's the matter?" she asked.

He took her hand and led her to the living room, where he sat her down directly in front of him.

"Ovila, stop looking so grim. You look like you're going to a funeral."

He looked into her eyes, then looked away. "The doctor asked how long Rose didn't breathe after she was born." His voice was hesitant, almost toneless.

"So you told him it lasted a couple of minutes, that's all."

"That's what I said."

"And?"

"He examined Rose for quite a while. He said that she doesn't talk a lot for two and a half years old. He even asked me if we talk to her from time to time."

Emilie was annoyed. "I hope you told him that we talk to her all the time." Did the doctor think she didn't know how to look after a child?

"I told him all that, Emilie, don't worry. Then the doctor made her walk in his office."

"So?"

"He found that she walks on her tiptoes."

"She's always walked like that."

"I know. But the doctor told me that at two and a half years old, she should be walking on her heels."

"You told him it's because she only started walking at eighteen months?"

"I told him that, Emilie."

"So then what happened?"

"After that, he asked her some questions, like what was her name."

"She said her name."

"No, Emilie, she didn't."

"Come on, Ovila!" Emilie was feeling worse and worse. She felt as though she was being judged, although she didn't know exactly what she was guilty of. She was sure that Ovila would soon accuse her of some sin.

"'Ose Ovo.' That's what she said. 'Ose Ovo.' We know she means 'Rose Pronovost,' but that's not what she says. Emilie, the doctor thinks Rose has little problems because she didn't get enough air when she was born."

Emilie blanched and couldn't catch her breath. She wet her lips over and over. "What does he know about babies?" she cried. "He's never seen Rose in her life, because Rose has never been sick, and now he tells us Rose isn't right! Who does he take himself for? God? Rose not right! What a laugh! Rose just isn't quite as fast as other children."

"That's it, Emilie, not quite as fast, that means slower. Rose is slow."

Emilie had always known it. She had tried to hide it, teaching Rose as much as she could. Now she had to face her worst fears. She gritted her teeth, breathed deeply and tried, in vain, to hold back her tears.

"Listen to me, Ovila Pronovost. I swear on Rose's head, and on Marie-Ange's, that my daughter will read, write and count. Believe me. It'll take as much time as it takes, but Rose will be like the others. Rose will grow up to be beautiful, and one day she'll get married. Do you understand, Ovila Pronovost?"

"Don't be angry at me, Emilie."

"I'm not angry!"

"So stop yelling. It hurts me to see you like this."

He was crushed. He had tried to spare Emilie this pain; he knew that she wasn't responsible for what had happened. The way she was acting, you'd think it was all her fault. She continued to rage against the doctor until Rose came into the kitchen crying. Emilie took her in her arms and rocked her. Rose, comforted, eagerly sucked her thumb and hummed a nameless tune while her mother whispered millions of little promises in her ear.

"I don't think you're going to help her by treating her like a baby, Emilie."

"I didn't ask you, Ovila Pronovost. In fact, I never asked you to make babies with me. On top of that, it might interest you to know that there's another one on the way."

⚜

*O*vila went to the Hôtel Grand Nord to drown his sorrows. He felt Emilie had gone too far when she blamed him for having made the children, as if it was all his fault that she was pregnant again.

"Hey, big guy! You look like you just came from a funeral!"

"Could be."

"So who died?"

"Me."

"Ha, ha, ha! Always the joker!"

"Leave me alone, Joachim Crête."

"Hey, guys, look at Pronovost's face. You look like your wife beat you up. That's what you get, Pronovost, for marrying a schoolmistress, especially the lovely Emilie . . ."

With one punch, Ovila sent Joachim sprawling over the neighbouring table. Then he gave him another blow in the stomach. Joachim howled. Two men grabbed Ovila and threw him out of the hotel, saying, "Crête was just teasing you, big guy. If you want to start a fight, do it in somebody else's parish." Then they threw his fur jacket and his hat out after him.

Ovila tried to get up, but he couldn't. He was foaming at the mouth, and his saliva made icicles on his chin. He shook his fist and saw, through the fog of his drunkenness, that his knuckles were bleeding. Struggling to his feet, he made his way back into the hotel. He didn't get far before he was again escorted to the exit, but he had time to see that Crête was still stunned and that ice was being applied to his face.

"Hey! Crête!" he yelled. "Don't they know you like to have your head dunked in a bucket of piss?"

Crête lifted his head, threw the ice down and headed for the door after Ovila. Turning to the men sitting at the neighbouring tables and laughing, he said, "There's no one to keep me from beating him up outside. We'll settle this with our fists."

"Be careful. Ovila's a tough guy. And this evening he isn't in what you'd call a good mood."

No sooner had Crête gone outside than the men began to bet on the outcome of the fight.

"The big Pronovost boy'll knock him out right quick."

"No, he won't. He's too drunk! Crête'll have him crying 'uncle' in no time."

"Pronovost hates Crête so much he'll sober up fast."

"I wouldn't bet my shirt on it."

They went to the window and saw Crête grab Ovila by the shoulder. Ovila tried to get into his sleigh but tripped and fell on his back. Crête jumped on him and pummelled him with his fists. At first, Ovila didn't resist, but when he heard his nose crack, he got mad. He threw Crête off and kicked him in the head. Crête grabbed his head with both hands. Ovila kicked him in the ribs, then fell over himself, too drunk to stay standing.

The men rushed out of the hotel and ran over to Crête. "Quick, get the doctor! He's out cold!"

Ovila burst out laughing. Then, to everyone's astonishment, he began to cry like a baby.

"Can someone wipe him off?" one of the men asked. "His nose is running and bleeding at the same time."

The men backed away from Ovila and Crête to let the doctor through. Furious, he leaned over Crête first. He shook his head reprovingly as he lifted the unconscious man's eyelids and took his pulse. "Put lots of snow on his neck. Make him walk."

The men did this while the doctor examined Ovila. "Your wife won't be happy," he said. "Don't you think one piece of bad news a day is enough?"

Ovila didn't react, but the doctor's remark about Emilie hurt more than Crête's fists had.

"Bring both of them to my dispensary," the doctor said.

The hotel customers took the two largest men in the village and left them with the doctor, who spent the night changing Ovila's dressings and keeping Joachim awake. At dawn, he took each of them home. At Ovila's, Emilie opened the door right away, and the doctor could see that she hadn't slept a wink.

"I was waiting for you, Doctor," she greeted him. "They told me Ovila was at your place. Is he really banged up?"

"A broken nose, a swollen eye and bruised cheeks. It'll be a couple of weeks before he looks like himself again."

She helped him bring in Ovila, who was still staggering from the effects of alcohol but more from fatigue and weakness. He let himself be taken to the bedroom, undressed and put to bed. The doctor told Emilie that he would be back later in the day, and in the meantime she should apply ice to Ovila's face.

She returned to Ovila's bedside and stared at him. When she heard him groan, she put her head on his chest and cried. "What were you thinking about, Ovila?"

"About you."

She didn't need to ask any more questions. She knew that she had pushed him over the edge. But he should have understood her pain. How did he think she would react to his bad news? Then, suddenly, she was angry at him. He had left her for the entire night, without saying a single word about where he was going. He had come home completely drunk, with a face that looked like chopped meat.

She stood up and looked at him contemptuously. "Ovila, whenever I need you, you're not there. You only think of yourself. Well, from now on, you're on your own. I already have two babies. I don't want to change your diaper, too."

She slammed the bedroom door. Ovila began to sob. He heard Marie-Ange crying, awakened by the noise. Then he heard Rose babbling as she did every morning. Finally, he heard Emilie's soft, maternal voice as he found sleep through his pain.

Thirty

*E*MILIE WAS EXHAUSTED, and her belly was growing day by day. Rose was getting bigger, but she didn't seem to want to learn. On the other hand, Marie-Ange always behaved herself, and she was the pride of her parents and grandparents. Emilie and Ovila never spoke again of Rose's "little problems," or of their quarrel. Ovila explained that he had got drunk only to drown his sorrow and his inability to console her. For her part, Emilie apologized several times for having been so cavalier with him after his fight with Crête.

And so they returned to their daily routine: Emilie on the Bourdais road doing the wash, planting her vegetable garden, keeping an eye on the girls, watching the children going to school and preparing her family's meals; Ovila on Notre-Dame Street in the village, wielding a pick and shovel, working long hours to install the pipes for the aqueduct. When he came home in the evening, dog-tired, Emilie hurried the children off to sleep after supper. Then, with a salve she had purchased in Montreal, she massaged Ovila's muscles, which were sore from labour and burned by the heat.

"It's not possible, Emilie," he sighed. "I'm more tired after a day working on the aqueduct than after a week in the lumber camps."

"Don't talk, Ovila. I know you're working hard, but it must feel good to have something steady that lasts a while. I think you've forgotten how tough it was in the woods."

"Maybe," Ovila said, closing his eyes to concentrate on his wife's hands on his body. "And in the lumber camps, no one rubbed my back like this."

❀

Toward the end of May, Emilie received a letter from her mother inviting her to Saint-Stanislas for a welcome-home party for her uncle, Amédée Bordeleau, who was returning after thirteen years in the United States. Ovila urged her to go, so she could help her mother; Eva could look after the children. Emilie packed her things, but on the morning she was to leave, Rose woke up with chicken pox.

Emilie left Marie-Ange with her grandparents so that she wouldn't catch her sister's virus. She unpacked her suitcase and wrote her mother a short note apologizing for her absence, promising to pay a visit as soon as she could.

The illness made Rose so irritable that Emilie prayed for the patience to stick it out till the last itchy spot disappeared. For three days, she sat at her daughter's bedside singing lullabyes, applying cold compresses, keeping her from scratching herself and coating each blister with an ointment that the doctor had prepared. She wouldn't allow Eva and Ovila in the house. Ovila said she was being ridiculous, that he had already had chicken pox and she knew he couldn't get it twice, but Emilie still wouldn't let him in. If he couldn't catch it, he could still carry it to the village.

Her precautions were in vain. An epidemic attacked the village and the concession, hitting every second household. The doctor came to see Emilie twice, reassuring her that her daughter would be fine and confiding that he had never seen so many bedridden children. This round of chicken pox seemed quite serious; any more blisters, and he'd have suspected smallpox. "We've been lucky," he added.

Rose's spots finally faded, much to Emilie's relief. Now she could get some rest and open the door to Ovila and to Marie-Ange, who was grumpy because of the long separation from her mother.

✿

*E*milie's daily rhythm reestablished itself, ever slower, beaten down by the heat. She welcomed Henri Douville, as she did every year, but this time he came alone. Antoinette, also pregnant, had decided to stay home. Concerned by the circles under Emilie's eyes, Henri decided not to tire her by staying overnight but to go straight on to Sainte-Thècle.

Ovila tried to get home as early as possible to check on his wife. Rose was stuck in a bad mood, which, to Emilie's despair, was beginning to rub off on Marie-Ange. They had celebrated their elder daughter's third birthday, sadly admitting to each other that she wasn't much brighter than Marie-Ange, who wasn't even a year old yet.

At the end of July, Emilie was forced to ask for Eva's help. The doctor had strongly suggested that she stay in bed, and she had wept with frustration and fatigue. This third pregnancy felt heavy. Ovila tried to encourage and reassure her, but he could hardly hide his own fears. She seemed to be feeling the same way she had during the first pregnancy, and he worried that she would have another difficult birth. Emilie didn't even have the strength to smile to reassure him that she was all right. From her bed, she heard Eva trying her hardest to be the perfect aunt to two nieces who had become impossibly wayward now that they rarely saw their mother any more.

Even so, Marie-Ange gave Emilie the most wonderful present for her own first birthday. At dawn, she walked all the way to her parents' room, all by herself. Emilie burst into laughter when she saw her daughter's little face in the doorway. Ovila, woken by her laughter, opened his arms, and Marie-Ange ran tottering into them, a smile on her lips and excrement running down her thighs.

"She stinks, our little walker!"

Emilie struggled to her feet and took Marie-Ange by the hand to make sure that she was following her and that she wouldn't soil anything else as she went. On her way to the water pump, she found Rose smearing the walls with her own excrement.

"Rose!"

The little girl didn't even turn around; she continued her malodorous work.

"Ovila, come here right away!"

Ovila heard the urgency in his wife's voice and jumped into his pants. His jaw dropped when he saw what Rose had done, and anger overcame him. "I've had enough of these games. This morning, I'm going to give you what for."

He gripped his daughter by both arms, put her nose in the excrement and gave her a spanking. Then, not knowing what else to do, he picked up a cloth, wet it and ordered her to wash everywhere she had soiled. She smiled, happy to have something to do. Ovila didn't like this, and he changed his tactics. He took her by the arm again and propelled her to her room. She began to whimper, looking at her mother, who looked back at her reproachfully, and at her sister, who was gurgling with pleasure at the morning's activities.

"No sleep. Rose no sleep!"

Ovila made her lie down and ordered her not to get up. Rose kicked her legs. Ovila held her down and repeated that she would be very sorry if she disobeyed.

"No sleep, Papa! Rose outside!"

Ovila firmly put her back on her bed, and Rose stopped yelling. She sucked her thumb and picked at her blanket with her free hand. Ovila went back to the kitchen. Emilie looked at him, and he asked how she would have reacted. Ever since the doctor had told him about Rose's problems, he had tried to let Emilie do what she wanted with the child. But Emilie had no energy to answer, for her pregnancy was making it hard to breathe. Ovila looked in her eyes for some sign of anger or reproach, but he didn't see either. Instead, he thought he discerned amusement.

"Why are you laughing? It seems to me that mornings like this aren't very funny."

"So you say. I find it quite amusing to see you lose your patience like that. And . . ." She closed a safety pin fastening Marie-Ange's diaper and took another one out of her mouth, then continued, ". . . I'm glad you got angry. At least you stayed in control of yourself. If I had been that angry, Rose would have bruises on her bum."

"I know it's not easy for you, Emilie," he said, hugging her after she let Marie-Ange down on the floor. "Rose still wants to be a baby, Marie-Ange is beginning to copy her, and the doctor makes you stay in bed all day . . ."

"Stop talking and make me some tea."

Ovila kissed her neck, then her shoulder blades, then the small of her back. He put his arm around her and patted her belly. Emilie purred with pleasure.

"Yes, it's been difficult these last few months," she said, "and this is a heavy burden to carry."

Ovila understood what she was trying to say and pressed up against her a little tighter. He too missed the passion of their nights. He knew that for a few months yet he had to be satisfied just to lie close to her and breathe in her scent — it was something he would never grow tired of.

"I'm sorry, Emilie."

"What for?"

"Well, it seems to me that it would have been better if you hadn't got pregnant right away. We might have had time to go away for a little while, you and me."

"You know we can't really think about vacations now that our family is well and truly started. And you don't make babies all by yourself, Ovila Pronovost . . . So, are you going to make the tea before you head for town? It would be nice if we had breakfast together, like lovers, before your sister arrives."

Ovila made tea and toast while Emilie played with Marie-Ange on her knees. Rose had gone to sleep, which gave them a few moments of respite. Ovila played waiter, serving his wife with a dishtowel folded over his arm, elegant gestures and a fixed smile on his lips. Emilie burst out laughing, and Marie-Ange imitated her.

"You're almost as good as the men at the Windsor."

"You think I have a future as a waiter?"

"No, you're a little too tall."

"That has nothing to do with it."

"I know."

$\mathscr{E}$milie, swollen but happy, welcomed October with open arms. Ovila had finished his contract with the municipality for construction of the aqueduct and now he was home helping Eva, who was beginning to weary of playing mother. Rose had stopped exercising her special talent for wall painting, and Marie-Ange trotted around with confidence. Emilie wrote her mother that she didn't think she'd get to Saint-Stanislas for Christmas, provoking a worried response from Célina. Emilie assured her that she was perfectly healthy, adding that she would soon be able to announce the birth of her grandson.

The grandson was born on October 8 and was baptized . . . Louisa! In spite of everything, Ovila was overjoyed at the birth of a third girl. But Emilie was mortified; she had hoped to deliver a boy to her husband. She would ruin him with so many hope chests!

Louisa slept poorly; she was fretful and agitated. Emilie spent long nights rocking her in the kitchen so that Ovila could get a little sleep. But it was no use; he got more and more tired. Fatigue was a normal state for a new mother, she thought, but a man had a right to some sleep. So she was very serious when she asked him if he wanted to go away to Lac Pierre-Paul or somewhere else until Christmas.

"Are you crazy? Do you think I'd leave you alone with three infants in diapers?"

"It seems to me that it's precisely because the house is so full of babies that you'd like to be in the company of men."

"It's out of the question. I don't want to be with men. I want to be with you. Emilie, my days of going to the lumber camps are finished."

"Think about it. It might be a good thing. Then, when you come back at Christmas, things will be quite a bit better. Louisa will be two and a half months old, Rose three and a half years and Marie-Ange fifteen months. Things'll be a lot easier."

Ovila insisted that he didn't want to go, but Emilie all but pushed him out the door. She didn't know what was making her act like this. Only a little while ago, she would have been furious if he had talked about going away. But things were different now. She wanted to lose weight and make herself beautiful again, and for this she needed rest — sound sleep, without worrying that a child would wake Ovila. She needed to be alone for a while, to devote her days entirely to her children without feeling that she was neglecting her man; it was bad enough that nature prevented her from satisfying him at night. It made her feel bad to think that he'd be gone, but suddenly she wanted to miss him. She wanted to spend long evenings sighing by the window. She especially wanted to see him again after two months, to welcome him and open her arms to him.

Reluctantly, Ovila agreed to leave. He had the sharp feeling that she was pushing him away, and he didn't know why. But the moment he was in the woods he found, to his great surprise, that he breathed more easily. He sighed when he thought of Emilie, telling himself that she had known he would feel this way. He spent these days of waiting torn between his happy freedom and missing his wife.

*T*he first days of winter were pitiless. Emilie watched the snow falling on people's heads like powdered sugar on the doughnuts she had made for *réveillon*. Ovila wouldn't be home for another two weeks. Although she had many times regretted her decision, her mirror told her that she had been right: she now recognized in herself what had first seduced him. She made a new dress, with a lace bodice that she could draw tighter if she lost more weight. Félicité and Eva offered to keep the children for a few days, but she turned them down, saying that the little ones would be unhappy to be taken from their familiar surroundings.

"If that's your only problem, Eva and I will even look after them here," said Félicité. "Ovila said he'd be back for your birthday. *Réveillon* will be almost ready by then. Why don't you two go to Lac à la Perchaude for a couple of days?"

Emilie refused vehemently. Leave them with all the work? Never. It made no sense. But still, the thought of being alone with Ovila, the thought of sleeping late in the morning, warm in the crook of his arm, the thought of not hearing children crying, of watching time go by instead of chasing it . . . In the end, she accepted her mother-in-law's offer. Félicité just smiled and reminded her that she would only be young once.

"Young? You make me laugh, Mrs. Pronovost. I'm going to be twenty-seven, I'm not so young any more."

"Maybe not you, Emilie, but don't forget that Ovila is younger," Félicité teased.

Emilie stared at her image in the mirror even more desperately. She had more white hairs, and even Ovila had a few mingling in his thick hair. But she had no wrinkles — not one.

Six days before Christmas, Emilie had a feeling that Ovila was coming home; on the morning of the 19th, she took a long time doing her hair, put on a dress that she hadn't worn for two years, scrubbed the house mercilessly and managed to get all the diapers off the clothesline. Fortunately, Rose had regained her toilet training and sunny character. Even baby Louisa took her bottle well; she was almost over the colic that had kept her awake nights.

Emilie's instincts were right. Ovila arrived in early afternoon. When she, Rose and Marie-Ange threw themselves at him, he couldn't hide the emotion he felt at seeing them all. The house seemed full of good feelings and welcome. Eva didn't let her brother take off his coat; as soon as he put the girls down, she filled his arms with provisions and told him to go hitch up a cutter.

"If it's to take these to Papa's, I can walk. And there's no hurry. Why are you so eager to send me away when I just got here?"

Eva just pushed him outside. The minute he was out the door, Emilie put on her coat and took out the suitcase that had been waiting under the bed for two days. She hugged her children and her sister-in-law and went outside to join Ovila. He jumped when she tapped his back; he'd been busy bridling the horse and hadn't heard her coming.

"What are you . . . ?"

She didn't let him finish his sentence, silencing his lips with hers. When they stopped for air, she told him where they were going.

"The children?"

"Well taken care of by your mother and sister."

"*Réveillon?*"

"It's ready. Women without men have lots of time to bake from morning to night."

"My things?"

"In the suitcase, which you're about to put in the cutter before I get annoyed."

And so they left in gales of laughter. Ovila took one more minute to hug his girls while Emilie held the horse. When he came back, he put down an enormous, poorly wrapped package.

"You are a strange mother, my love," he said.

"Not at all. I wouldn't be a mother if I weren't a woman first."

Ovila's young brothers had gone ahead to the lake earlier that day and fired up the stove. When Ovila and Emilie arrived, they shed their coats, then Ovila immediately got to work on Emilie's dress.

"You've got thin. Haven't you been eating?"

"Not a crumb. It's a well-known fact: when a woman misses her man, she loses her appetite."

"You sent me away because you wanted to lose weight?"

"No, I sent you away because I wanted to miss you. Because I knew that there's nothing better than missing someone for . . ."

She didn't get a chance to finish her sentence. Ovila was groaning with the pleasure of seeing her more beautiful than she had been since the birth of Marie-Ange. They didn't bother to eat but went straight to bed after Ovila made her close her eyes and open the badly wrapped package he had brought. "Under the circumstances," he insisted, "you should have your birthday present right away."

The package contained two pairs of snowshoes. Emilie thanked him warmly. "We'll try them out first thing tomorrow, right after breakfast," she promised.

The next day, she and Ovila spent hours walking through the bush. She quickly figured out how to use the snowshoes and loved the feeling of being suspended on top of the snow.

Being alone together worked its magic, and neither Emilie nor Ovila thought about the three little ones they had left behind. They had eyes, ears and thoughts only for each other and spent more than two days beyond the reach of time. It was an interlude so heavenly that they had trouble bringing themselves down to earth. They went home the day after Emilie's birthday, and Eva scolded them for not making a longer escape.

Knowing that their children had missed them, Emilie and Ovila hurried inside. Emilie worried about the effects on Rose of her absence, while Ovila was eager to get to know Louisa better.

Fortunately, Rose kept up her good behaviour, and her parents dared to hope that the doctor had made a mistake or, at least, had exaggerated the effects of the circumstances at her birth. Marie-Ange was beginning to assert her personality, and Louisa was a splendid baby.

The Christmas holidays were simply perfect, and Emilie wondered if she mightn't have gone to Saint-Stanislas after all. Ovila reminded her that it would have been a long trip with two babies and Rose all excited, and Emilie conceded that he had a point.

"Next year, Emilie, we should be able to go."

"If there's not another baby between now and then."

"Don't worry. Mother Nature has been playing tricks on us for the last two years. She should leave us alone for a while."

*M*other Nature, however, didn't listen to Ovila, and Emilie told him in February that she was to be a mother again. She had to laugh when she saw the guilty look on Ovila's face.

"I don't understand, Emilie. We waited forever for our second one, and now we seem to be making one a year."

"I guess Mother Nature's decided to give me all the children I need before I turn thirty."

Emilie was thrilled when Ovila found work at William Dessureault's new door and window-frame factory, which meant that he wouldn't have to go back to the woods. Serene in her pregnancy, she didn't feel the need to be apart from him any more. On the other hand, Ovila found his days and evenings a little long. He got into the habit of stopping at the hotel after work to bend an elbow with the other men before going home. Emilie didn't reproach him, except on the rare occasions when it was obvious he had stayed too long.

"It doesn't bother me when you stop at the hotel from time to time, but when you get home, I'd like you to be here."

"What do you mean? When I'm home, I'm here."

"Sometimes yes, sometimes no, Ovila. Sometimes you sit in your chair, but your thoughts are far, far away."

Ovila grimaced. The rest of the winter, he tried to limit his conversations at the hotel to one glass of beer.

Thirty-one

SPRING ARRIVED WITHOUT FANFARE at the end of March. By the beginning of April, the snow had melted away as if by magic, and grass that had wilted for long months under the weight of the heavy white blanket sprang up. Emilie didn't feel as heavy as she had during her last pregnancy. Her health was excellent, and Ovila was pleased to see that she kept her spirits up. The three girls were doing wonderfully; Louisa, who would be six months old the next day, had already cut four teeth.

Ovila went to the hotel to toast the arrival of spring. Emilie had asked him to come home early, since she had to take Rose and Louisa to the doctor; seeing how well Rose had progressed, she had decided to confront him. Ovila thought she was looking for reassurance. She spent an hour a day with Rose, using the little slate that Charlotte had given her as a wedding gift to teach the toddler her numbers and letters. Ovila told her that Rose was perhaps a little young for such things, but Emilie didn't give up. She felt that if Rose knew these basics before she went to school, she would get through first grade with little problem. Ovila just shrugged. As well,

Emilie wanted the doctor to confirm that Louisa was in good health, despite a few digestive problems.

Ovila looked at the clock, saw that he still had time and asked for a second glass of beer. He thanked heaven for his good luck as he listened to the other men complain about their wives. One man said his wife couldn't get to sleep if she hadn't recited a rosary. Laughing, he said that ever since she had taken up this habit they had stopped having children — he was always asleep before she finished the five decades.

"But I can hardly ask her to be less devout," he concluded.

"You could remind her of her duty, though."

"Don't make me laugh! My wife is thirty years old and we have eight children. She's done her duty."

Another said that his wife nagged him about his tough beard. He could go to her only when he was freshly shaved, and he shaved only on Sunday mornings. "Is there anyone here who has the time to service his wife before Sunday mass? I've never managed to do it."

Ovila listened without saying a word. It was beyond him how they could discuss their conjugal life so openly. He asked for a third glass, curious to hear everything they said. Emilie would laugh her heart out when he told her all their stories.

"Mine has a new idea," another man piped up. "Now, I can only sleep with her once a month. And not just anytime, boys, but only when she's started her period. Have you ever done it during her period? She says it's the time when we won't make babies. I say it's the time when I'll stay on my side of the bed."

Ovila chuckled. He thanked all the saints in heaven for giving him a wife like Emilie. She never had problems in this respect.

"That's nothing. Mine went to see a doctor in Trois-Rivières to get a medical exemption. And do you know what? She got it! Now, every time I try to cosy up to her, she gets her damned paper out from under her pillow. It kills the passion, I can tell you . . ."

Ovila was having more and more fun. He even got into the conversation, asking a question from time to time.

"It's crazy. The Creator made it pleasurable so that we would multiply. Me, I think He forgot to tell Eve."

"What exactly do you find pleasurable about it?"

"What do you mean? Don't you like doing it?"

"Not at all. I even find it . . . uh . . . quite disgusting. Fornicating is not my strong point."

"Are you sick? Hey, fellows, he doesn't like doing it!"

"Is it because you can't get it up?"

"Hey, I got it up often enough to have three children."

"Are you trying to make us believe that you only got it up three times?"

"In fact, yes. I'm just beginning to see that you guys get it up for something besides duty. Me, I got it up on my wedding night, and two other times. My wife doesn't complain. I don't have your problems. My wife doesn't need an exemption. She doesn't recite rosaries every night. When I service her, she doesn't say no."

"You've only serviced her three times?"

"Three times, I swear on her head."

"And you had three children?"

"Yes, sir. And three boys, too."

Ovila frowned. Perhaps he had just found out why he'd had only girls.

"What do you say to that, big guy?" one of the men called over to him. "To hear him talk, you'd think that boys are children of duty while girls are children of pleasure. If my memory serves me, you have three girls, right?"

Ovila calmly swallowed the dregs of his glass and signalled to the waiter. He wiped his mouth on his sleeve and smiled. "I don't believe in that."

"You mean you do it for duty? Don't make me laugh! That's the last thing on your mind. Are you still taking those little vacations at the lake?"

"Why? Is it bothering anyone?"

"I hear your wife's pregnant again."

"That's none of your business."

"Well, let's see. If you have a boy, we'll think maybe you did it out of duty for once. But if you have another girl, we'll begin to believe what that guy said."

"You can believe what you like. I think it's a scandal that you talk about your wives this way. You have good women and healthy children. I can't see as how you have any reason to complain."

"Listen, big fellow, if you don't like men's conversations, all you have to do is go home and listen to pretty Emilie talk about diapers and temperatures. We like to sit around and talk. If you don't like it, all you have to do is shut up."

"Exactly. Good night, everyone."

Ovila got into his buggy and tried to read the time. Nine o'clock! He looked again, not believing his eyes. It was worse. It was midnight. The hand that had misled him had now joined the other two hands. He winced. There'd be no smile for him when he got home.

Emilie was sitting in the kitchen, asleep in her rocking chair, her accordion still on her lap. Ovila approached her, trying to discipline his steps.

"Hey, my morning mist. You'd be better off in bed," he said, touching her shoulder.

Emilie opened her eyes and smiled at Ovila. Then she remembered that he had kept her from going to the doctor, and a cloud passed over her face. She turned away. Ovila took the accordion from her hands and tried to lift her up. She jumped to her feet.

"Don't touch me! I sat around all evening waiting for you! Did you forget that I had an appointment at the doctor for Rose and Louisa?"

"Yes, I forgot. I'm sorry. The guys were telling such funny stories, I wanted to hear everything so that I could tell them to you."

"I don't care about their damned stories. What I care about is to see my husband come home sober, then to go see the doctor with my girls when I've decided that I have to see the doctor with my girls."

She went to the bedroom, indicating with a glance that he should look in on the children. He decided to let her fall asleep before going to bed himself; it made him so uncomfortable to see her this angry that he didn't have the courage to take more scolding. He lit his pipe and rocked gently. He would go check on the girls before going to bed.

Ovila woke up at three in the morning. His pipe was on the floor and the tobacco had burned the floor. It's a good thing there's no carpet here, he thought. He stretched and belched. As he opened the bedroom door, he remembered that he had to check on the girls. Leaving the lamp in the kitchen, he went to Rose's room. She was sleeping peacefully. He kissed her and sighed. What would become of his Rose? Then he tiptoed to the other room. Marie-Ange was sleeping on her back, her arms crossed and her legs askew. He smiled and went to Louisa's crib. As always, she was curled up, her head a little to the side and framed between her arms and her two little fists.

Ovila left the room and softly closed the door. He smiled at the thought that he was a father, then grimaced when he thought of Emilie. He would have to apologize the moment she opened her eyes. He went back to the kitchen, troubled by something he couldn't put his finger on. The kitchen was bathed in silence, disturbed only by the ticking of the clock. This is the heart of our house, Ovila thought. The heart of our house, filled by Emilie and me. He sat down in the rocking chair and listened. He was listening for a sound, but he couldn't figure out which one. He smiled again — this reminded him of hunting. He kept listening, his ears alert. Without knowing why, he noticed that his throat was tight. What was troubling him? Emilie's anger? Her eyes heavy with reproach? No, her eyes weren't so very disapproving this evening. Well, a little, but not enough for him to feel this strange unease.

He closed his eyes and tried to recall everything he'd done, everything Emilie had said when he got home. His heart began to beat faster. He saw Emilie leaving him to go to bed. Then he saw the black stain made by the burning tobacco on the floor. He saw Rose, then Marie-Ange. He thought about Louisa. Louisa. His heart beat even faster. Louisa. All curled up as usual. Louisa . . . He leapt to his feet, grabbed the lamp and ran to the baby's room. Marie-Ange, disturbed by the light, rolled over and mumbled a bit. Ovila tiptoed to the cradle and lifted the lamp over Louisa's head.

"Emilie! Emilie! Oh, no . . . Emilie!"

Marie-Ange, surprised into wakefulness, looked at her father and echoed his cries. Rose got up and came to the door. Emilie surfaced from her sound sleep in a second, terrorized by his shout, and came running. Without knowing how she got there, she was at the door to the babies' room. She pushed Rose out of the way and was inside.

Emilie froze before the shadow the lamp was throwing on the wall. Ovila had a doll in his hands, a broken doll with the head falling backward and one dangling arm moving in a rhythm imposed by his rocking. Emilie's eyes left the shadow and slowly moved to Ovila. He was in a heap on the floor, the lamp beside him, Louisa in his arms. Rose pulled on her mother's nightgown. The only response she received was a cuff. Crying, she took refuge beside a weeping Marie-Ange. She gave her little sister a tap, as her mother had just done to her, and Marie-Ange, shocked, fell silent.

Emilie slowly went to Ovila. It took hours, days, nights to cross the room. Then she was beside him. She bent over, looked at his face flooded with tears, and then looked at Louisa. She felt as if she was suffocating. Then, seized with a sudden madness, she punched Ovila violently and ripped Louisa from his arms. She shook the baby energetically, holding her by the legs and letting her head fall toward the floor, then turned her right-side up and hit her back harder and harder, screaming, "Wake up, Louisa! Wake up!"

She opened up her nightgown and uncovered a breast. Ovila looked at her grief-stricken face. Though she knew very well that she had never had milk, she put one of her dry nipples in the mouth of her dead baby. Crying hot tears, sobs coming from unexplored depths, she tried to make Louisa nurse. Ovila went to her, but she roared for him to get away. He backed off, terrified. Hearing Rose and Marie-Ange crying, he took them to Rose's room. Trying to smile, he asked Rose to protect Marie-Ange and left them quietly curled up together.

Emilie had hidden Louisa under her nightgown, telling her that she would warm her up. Ovila went to her once more, and again she ordered him to keep away, but he kept coming toward her. She backed up, on her knees, tripping on her nightgown. In her haste to get away from him, she dropped Louisa, who fell to the floor with a dull thud.

Ovila's tears burned his cheeks as he pleaded, "Emilie . . . Emilie, give me Louisa . . . Get up, Emilie . . ."

"Get away! Damn you! Get away!"

Ovila backed out of the room and closed the door. He went to see Rose and Marie-Ange, who hadn't gone to sleep. He picked them up and began to dress them with nervous, feverish hands. Amazed at his own calm, he buttoned up their woollen sweaters, then he took them by the hand and went out into the black night, heading for his father's house. His sobs caught up with him before he was halfway there. He tried to speak softly to the girls to ease the terror on their faces.

At his parents' house, he entered the kitchen and called his mother for help. Félicité came running, her husband at her heels. Then Eva came downstairs, followed by all of her brothers. She took her nieces and began to undress them. Ovila hiccuped and sobbed so much that no one understood what he was saying. They heard only the words "Emilie," "Louisa" and "crazy." Then Ovila abruptly left the house and ran home. Félicité hurried after him, not stopping to put on her coat, followed by Dosithée and Edmond. Eva kept the others back.

Ovila carefully opened the door, scared of what he might find. Emilie was there, in the kitchen. She had put Louisa down in the middle of the table and was sitting beside her, playing a song on the accordion.

"See, Ovila! I tried to put Louisa to sleep while I was waiting for you. I didn't want to make the doctor wait."

Her voice was high-pitched and strained. Ovila looked at her, incredulous. She had erased the hours she had spent waiting that evening. She was waiting for him so she could take Rose and Louisa to the doctor. She had waited for him while he . . .

Félicité pushed him aside lightly. Taking in the situation at a glance, she went to Emilie and said, softly, "Dosithée and Edmond will take Louisa to the doctor, Emilie."

"No, I have to go. I asked Ovila to stay here with Marie-Ange. Rose is ready too."

"Rose is already at our house, with Eva. Now, Dosithée has to take Louisa."

She went to the baby and took her in her arms. Emilie ran to her room and came back with a baby blanket. "Do you think I'd let her go like that? Come on, Mrs. Pronovost, a baby doesn't go outside in just a diaper and an undershirt."

Ovila watched, dumbfounded, while Emilie swaddled and clothed Louisa, even putting on her shoes. She talked ceaselessly. "Mama will put on your nice little dress with the English lace that she made for Rose. You'll be as pretty as a little angel. You're a good girl not to move. Rose wriggled all the time when I put on her little socks."

As the others looked on, their hearts in their throats, she wet a washcloth and wiped Louisa's hands and face gently, as if she were playing with a porcelain doll. Finally, she picked Louisa up and gave her to Félicité.

"It's nice of you to look after her. Don't forget to tell the doctor that Rose can count to fifty. That's not bad for a slow child."

Ovila burst into tears. Emilie looked at him, frowned and went to him.

"Don't worry, Ovila, I'll take care of Rose. I told you. Rose will be just like the other children."

She accompanied Dosithée, bristling with recommendations. "Be careful. Louisa is still so small. Hold her head. Cover her well so she doesn't get cold. But above all, keep an eye on her so she doesn't suffocate. That's very important. Louisa mustn't suffocate."

Dosithée and Edmond left with Louisa's rigid body. Félicité made a pot of herbal tea and took Emilie to her room. Emilie laughed at having so much attention paid to her.

"You're carrying a baby, Emilie. You have to stay in shape if you want him to be healthy."

Emilie looked at her belly and began to giggle. "I had completely forgotten. Thank you. Are you coming to bed, Ovila, or are you waiting for the girls?"

"The girls are sleeping at Mama's, Emilie."

"Oh, yes? Well, good. I'd forgotten. Good night."

She went to sleep. Ovila collapsed at the kitchen table and wept pitifully.

Félicité wrapped her arms and her soul around him. "What happened, Ovila?"

"I don't know."

"When did Louisa die?"

"I don't know."

"How did she die? Did she have a fever? She was very blue. It looks like she might have suffocated."

"I don't know anything."

Félicité stopped asking questions and waited for Dosithée to come back.

Dosithée came at seven in the morning. Ovila had sat, unable to sleep, smoking one pipe after another. Félicité had made coffee, although she wasn't sure how to use the apparatus.

"So?" she asked Dosithée.

"According to the doctor, Louisa suffocated when she spat up. He's coming over. I said that Emilie was . . . uh . . . that she didn't seem to be counting all her buttons."

The doctor arrived as Emilie was waking up. She called for Ovila, who went to the bedroom. When she saw her puffy eyes in the mirror, she realized that it hadn't been just a nightmare. It was all true. She opened her arms, and he threw himself into them. Together they cried as neither of them had believed possible.

Emilie and Ovila buried their daughter the day after her death. Emilie insisted on going to the funeral, saying that if she didn't see her put in the earth, she would never believe that Louisa was dead. Ovila didn't leave her side for a second, fearing that her mind would give way again under the burden of pain. But she held up. She remembered the night of Louisa's death only vaguely, although a bitter taste still stuck in her throat.

When she got home, she isolated herself in her bedroom. Félicité packed a suitcase and told Ovila that she'd keep the girls for at least a week, to give him and his wife time to sort things through. He knocked on the door of their room, but Emilie didn't reply. He knocked a second time. Still no answer. He went in and sat on the edge of the bed, staring blankly out the window. When he put his arm around her shoulder, she brusquely shrugged him away.

"What's the matter, Emilie?"

"It's your fault, Charles Pronovost. It's all your fault."

The blood drained from Ovila's face. Since Louisa had died, he had been telling himself the same thing. He sat at the other end of the bed, waiting for what she would say next. Without looking at him, Emilie told him that she blamed him because he hadn't come home when he had promised, leaving her alone and waiting for him. Her voice was dry and brittle, like a breaking window. "If I had seen the doctor with Louisa, she would still be alive."

"No, Emilie, she suffocated in her sleep."

"Let me finish!"

Ovila swallowed his remorse.

"First of all, if you hadn't been drunk when you came in, you might have heard something."

"Like what?"

"I don't know. You might have heard her coughing or crying."

"You can't say that, Emilie. She may have been dead already when I got home."

"No! No, she wasn't dead. I'm sure of it."

"Anyway . . ."

"And if you hadn't slept the sleep of a drunkard, you would have heard her. If you had gone to look at her when I went to bed, maybe it wouldn't have happened either."

"If, if, if . . . Emilie, it doesn't solve anything to talk like that."

"I will never forgive you, Ovila. Never!"

On the second "never," she finally turned and looked at him. Ovila lowered his head, then stood up. He couldn't talk to her. The doctor had told him that Louisa had probably died between ten at night and two in the morning. Ovila asked how he could confirm such a thing.

"You say the body was cold when you found it at three in the morning," the doctor had said. "That means she had been dead for at least an hour. A little baby like that grows cold quickly."

"Does that mean that she could have been alive when I got home?"

"That, Ovila, will always be a question. Yes or no? Only the Good Lord knows, and the Devil takes a guess."

Ovila left the bedroom, paced through the kitchen then turned around and went back. In vain he tried to speak to Emilie, to tell her that he loved her, to talk about fate. She wouldn't listen. Defeated, he took a suitcase from under the bed and filled it with his things. She watched him without asking what he was doing. He stood before her, hoping that she would make a gesture, some little thing to make him stay. He didn't want to leave her alone with her grief. She didn't move; she just sat, twisting and untwisting her hair, which she had let down from its prison of hairpins. At the bedroom door, he turned and tried one last time.

"You have nothing to say to me, Emilie?"

"I have nothing more to say to you, Charles."

Ovila walked to the village. He heard his mother and sister calling after him, but he didn't turn around. Then he heard a horse galloping and the squeaking of buggy wheels, but still he didn't turn around. His father and brother caught up with him.

"Where are you going, my boy?" Dosithée asked.

He didn't answer and continued to walk straight ahead. Dosithée and Edmond could only watch. They turned back, convinced that they would find him at the hotel later.

That evening, they went to the Hôtel Brunelle. Ovila wasn't there. They went to the Grand Nord. He hadn't even stopped there. They searched the entire village. Ovila was nowhere to be found. They went back to Bourdais empty-handed.

At their house, they found a downcast Emilie. She questioned her father-in-law with her eyes. Dosithée shook his head. Emilie shrugged, completely uninterested in what they had to tell her. She rocked Rose, who was enchanted with so much attention. When she went home, having declined to stay overnight, Félicité offered to go with her, but she wanted to be alone, to think things over.

She didn't sleep at all that night, or the next, with Ovila's voice echoing in her ears. She got up in the middle of the night to change the sheets, which were redolent with Ovila's smell.

On the third day, the priest, to whom the Pronovosts had gone for help, paid her a visit. She listened politely as he talked about life and death, but she remembered only two sentences: "I will come upon thee like a thief" and "The Lord works in mysterious ways." She thanked him for his kind words and saw him to the door, and, though he hadn't expressed any desire to leave, he didn't object.

The next day, she went to get her children. She had dreamt that they had died in a fire at the Pronovosts'. Feeling guilty for not having had them with her, she caressed them endlessly as she brought them home. In a long letter to Berthe, she asked her to pray for her and for Louisa, and in a letter to Antoinette, she laid all the blame for what had happened on Ovila and his irresponsibility.

No one could find Ovila; he had completely disappeared. Félicité and Dosithée had mixed feelings: on the one hand, they worried about their son; on the other, they were angry at him for having left his wife alone after the tragedy. Emilie never let them know what she was thinking, nor did she talk about Ovila's departure. She continued her daily routine without ever referring to him.

People talked. Men who had spent the fateful evening at the hotel with Ovila said that he had left completely drunk. Certain parishioners even began to say that Ovila had perhaps killed Louisa. The doctor had to intervene, letting all and sundry know that the baby had died in her sleep, suffocated. "And suffocated by natural causes!" he specified.

People admired Emilie's courage. In two days, she had lost both a child and a husband. Emilie didn't listen to them. It no longer hurt when people disparaged Ovila as if he were a rank criminal. She had begun to wonder about him herself.

*E*milie sat on her porch and watched the men bale hay. As far as the eye could see, hay bales lay in huge piles, making the people look like little ants walking among giant anthills. Ants. Were people really that much more important than ants? she asked herself. She got up, then quickly sat down again.

"Rose! Come here, Rose."

Rose went to her mother.

"Go get Grandma. Mama needs Grandma. You understand, Rose?"

"Oh, yes. Rose go get Grandma with Marie-Ange?"

"That's a good idea, Rose. Take Marie-Ange with you. And Rose, take your doll, and take Marie-Ange's too. You understand, Rose?"

"Yes, my doll and Marie-Ange's doll."

"Now, when you find Grandma, tell her the Indians are coming. Can you do that?"

"Of course. I'm not a baby."

"Tell me what you're going to say to Grandma."

"I'm going to tell Grandma that the Indians are coming."

"That's right, Rose. Come and give me a kiss before you go to Grandma's. Now, go and get Marie-Ange and the dolls. This evening, there'll be a surprise."

"What?"

"Maybe you'll sleep at Grandma's tonight. But don't tell Marie-Ange. It's a secret."

Rose and Marie-Ange left, holding hands. Ten times a day, they made this walk. Ten times a day, Emilie watched them.

Félicité hurried to find Edmond, who rushed off to get the midwife. Emilie went inside and lay down. The midwife had barely arrived when Emilie gave birth to a big baby boy.

*A*nger was rumbling at the Pronovosts'. September had come and gone, and Emilie still had no news from Ovila. Dosithée and Félicité didn't say anything, sure that something had happened between their son and his wife that they didn't know about. For the six months Ovila had been gone, Emilie had talked to no one about him. She was unfathomable. She had even refused to have her son baptized. Not knowing what to do, Dosithée decided to write Caleb to ask his advice. Caleb hadn't been able to come after his grandson was born, and Dosithée wondered if an impromptu visit now might help.

Caleb arrived unannounced. He hadn't seen his daughter in such a long time that he had no idea what to expect. He saw her out in the garden, pruning dead branches. Her two daughters — so big, now — were playing nearby. She had strapped her son up against her chest. Caleb frowned. Her hair was in braids, and she looked exactly like an Indian. When she saw him, she called the girls and pointed to Caleb. He thought she was smiling. The two little girls ran to meet him as he gave a broad wave with his hat.

"Be careful, you little monsters. Grandpa doesn't want his horse to knock you down."

The girls laughed and followed his buggy behind the house. Caleb hugged them fiercely as he watched Emilie approaching, and his heart skipped a beat. He didn't recognize her. He went toward her, holding out his arms, but Emilie didn't take refuge in them, so he let them fall heavily to his sides.

"Hello, Papa," she said. "What brings you? The last time I saw you, Rose was only a year and a half old."

"That's because you've always told us the bad news late and you never come to Saint-Stanislas."

"It's a lot easier for you to come to Saint-Tite than for me to take the children down to Saint-Stan'."

"We're not getting any younger, Emilie."

"Do you want to stand out here or come inside for some coffee?"

Caleb followed her slowly, mentally registering all the changes. She must have put on at least twenty pounds. She no longer had crow's-feet around her eyes. Her hair had lost its lustre, and the white streaks weren't just reflections from the sun. He shook his head, trying to hold back all the questions that wanted to tumble out.

In the kitchen, Caleb sat his granddaughters on his knee. He had never seen Marie-Ange.

"Forgive my poor memory, Emilie," he asked, "but how old are the girls?"

"Rose will be four in June. Marie-Ange turned two a few weeks ago, and the little one was born the fifth of last month. Louisa . . . Louisa would have been a year old this week."

Caleb looked over to the baby she was carrying on her chest. "What's the new one called?"

"He doesn't have a name yet. I'm waiting for Ovila to come back to choose a name."

Caleb put his granddaughters down and told them to go look in his buggy. "If you've been good," he told them, "you'll find some surprises in there."

As soon as they had left the house, Caleb coughed, then tried awkwardly to ask Emilie about Ovila's absence and Louisa's death. Emilie was mute. Caleb changed the subject.

"You wouldn't recognize your brothers and sisters now . . ."

"It would be difficult for me to recognize them, Papa, because I can't say that I ever really knew them."

Caleb searched for another topic of conversation. "Have you heard from Berthe?"

"I got a letter after Louisa died."

"So you haven't heard the latest news?"

"What?"

"About her health?"

Emilie put her cup down. Caleb sighed. At last, she had reacted to something.

"What's wrong with her health?"

"Well, she doesn't have any to speak of."

"What do you mean?"

"Her sister went to see her because the mother superior at her convent had written that she was sick, and no one, not even the doctors, could figure out what was wrong."

"And?"

"Apparently, her sister came back very depressed."

"I'll write to Berthe tomorrow."

That closed the discussion. Caleb got up and went to the window. He saw his granddaughters playing with the gifts he had brought them.

"I have something to ask you, Emilie. I hope you'll say yes."

"You can ask, Papa. We'll see what my answer will be."

"Your mother isn't feeling good these days . . ."

"My mother has never felt good in her life."

"That's why she didn't come with me. We wondered . . . well, I wondered if I could take the children to spend some time with their old grandpa." He turned and looked her in the face.

She went to the window and looked out at the girls. "I'm not sure I'd like that. It makes me nervous when I'm not with them, ever since . . . "

"I know, Emilie, but it seems to me it would do you good. You could rest and take care of the baby. And the girls would get to know a bunch of their uncles and aunts." He paused, keeping his eyes on her. "So? What do you think?"

Emilie told him she'd think about it. The offer appealed to her. She had lost touch with her family so completely that she sometimes forgot they existed. Her daughters would have a good time in

Saint-Stanislas, and she shouldn't keep them from knowing their grandparents.

The next morning, she told her father that it was a good idea. Caleb was pleased. Emilie packed a suitcase for her girls and watched them get into the buggy. Marie-Ange looked so small.

"Papa, are you sure you can take care of Marie-Ange on the road? I think it would be better if Rose went alone."

"Don't worry. With everything you gave us to eat, all I have to do is keep her mouth full to Saint-Stan'. If she's her mother's daughter, as soon as we're moving, she'll sleep like a princess."

With the girls away, Emilie was able to catch up on her sleep. She thought of her father tenderly. He had tried to comfort her, but his famous tactlessness had once again undercut his efforts. However, she thought long and hard about one unimportant little sentence he had pronounced: "If she's her mother's daughter, as soon as we're moving, she'll sleep like a princess."

Yes, Emilie had slept. Since Louisa had died, she had refused to open her eyes. She had closed them — even blindfolded them. Ovila's absence was starting to weigh heavily on her. She knew that he was in La Tuque. She hadn't told the Pronovosts this, preferring to play the martyr, the abandoned woman. They would be furious when they found out that she'd known all along. How would she explain to them that Ovila had deposited money in the bank? No. Yes. She would tell them. She would even ask one of her brothers-in-law to go get him. He was probably waiting for her to say she wanted to see him. Surely he was waiting.

When Caleb brought the girls back, two weeks later, he found his old Emilie. She even announced that Ovila would be home soon. Edmond had already taken the train to La Tuque, but Emilie didn't let her father in on this detail, preferring to let him believe that she had heard from her husband.

Caleb left for Saint-Stanislas with a promise to visit Emilie more often. Now that he knew his granddaughters better, he added, he wouldn't be able to stay away.

Dosithée came to tell Emilie that Edmond would be back the next day. Emilie jumped for joy.

"I said Edmond, Emilie."

She stopped smiling. "And Ovila?"

"Ovila will be back a little later."

"How much later?"

"It depends."

"Depends on what?" asked Emilie impatiently.

"It depends on him, Emilie. Ovila isn't . . . how can I say it . . . isn't ready to come back. Anyway, Edmond will talk to you about it tomorrow."

When she questioned Edmond, he was as vague and reticent as his father had been.

"Will he come back, at least?"

"Of course, Emilie. Maybe even faster than you think."

"But he doesn't want to come back right away?"

"It's not that he doesn't want to . . ."

"What is it, then?"

Edmond didn't answer. He didn't want to tell her that he had looked for Ovila everywhere and had found him, dead drunk, in an Indian camp. He had been sober only rarely since he had left, for he was drowning, in all senses of the word, in grief. Edmond had to wait for him to emerge from the worst of his depression to tell him that he had an unnamed son, and that Emilie was waiting for him before she would have the boy baptized. He had driven him to a church where he could stay until he had cleansed his body and soul.

"Emilie . . . Ovila says you practically accused him of killing Louisa . . . and he says the doctor said Louisa may have died before he even got home, while you were sleeping. Is it true, Emilie, that you said that to my brother?"

Emilie stopped holding back the tears that had been dammed up in her soul. She sobbed for a long time. Edmond tried to console her, even though he was beginning to understand why his brother had left. Emilie's burden of sorrow seemed quite light compared to what he had seen in Ovila's eyes. He told her Ovila's version of the story, and about his incomprehensible unease the night Louisa had died.

"Ovila says he sat in the kitchen trying to hear a sound. He thought what he was hearing was Louisa's breathing."

Emilie asked him to stop. She didn't want to hear any more about Ovila's suffering. She hadn't even given him a chance to explain himself. She had accused him, but he hadn't even suggested that she was as responsible as he was. No, he had saved her that guilt.

Emilie watched the death of autumn and the birth of winter without news of Ovila. Her soul was in waiting, and Ovila must have known this. She went to sleep on the eve of her birthday thinking that, if she knew her man, he'd come home during the night. She slept with one eye open. Ovila didn't come home.

She spent the evening of her birthday with her in-laws, who had made her a cake. After the girls had supper, Emilie put them to sleep at the Pronovosts' and went home alone with her son, disappointed and bitter. She put him to bed and walked around the house, looking through each of the windows. Ovila was nowhere to be seen. She resigned herself to going to bed alone. After taking a last look at her son, she went into her room.

"Close your eyes . . ."

She shrieked and dropped the lamp she was holding. Fire began to sweep across the floor. Ovila grabbed a blanket and threw it on the flames, quickly snuffing them out. Emilie was still frozen with surprise when he came back and sat on the bed surrounded by all the gifts he had brought.

"This, ma'am, is a little doll for Rose. As you can see, it's made by the Indians. And here's a little wooden game for Marie-Ange, also made by the Indians. And this is a rattle for the little one. When you shake it, it makes noise because the Indians put kernels of corn inside it. And this is for you. I know that you won't want to wear it out of the house, but if you'd like to put it on, I'd love to see you in it."

He handed Emilie a magnificent Indian dress, made of skins sewn together and linked by fine laces. Emilie held the dress to her face and sniffed it. She smiled. She had always liked the smell of skins.

"And this," Ovila said finally, leaning over to take something from under the bed, "this is for the two of us. When you've got this on, you'll never lose sight of our papoose."

"I was thinking the same thing, Ovila. Since the little one was born, I've been carrying him with me in a shawl."

There was a long silence. Ovila looked at the floor; Emilie looked at Ovila.

"I wasn't fair, Ovila."

"I never want to talk about it again."

$\mathcal{T}hirty\text{-}two$

$\mathcal{F}$ INALLY, EMILIE AND OVILA WERE ABLE to enjoy months
of long-hoped-for happiness. Their son was baptized, to
everyone's relief. Emilie wanted to call him Ovila, after his father,
but Ovila resolutely refused, preferring the name Emilien. After
some discussion, Emilie yielded, but she thought it was funny to
have a son whose name was so similar to hers.

Ovila stayed close to his wife and children. Emilie didn't complain. There was only one shadow on their life: since Louisa's death,
Emilie found herself incapable of letting Ovila touch her. She
suffered as much as he did from this abstinence. He understood her
reticence and didn't complain. In fact, though he was happy to
watch his son grow strong and mischievous, he wondered if he really
wanted any more children.

But the daily fact of their love eventually overcame their most
painful hesitancies. Emilie conceived once again at the end of May,
during a night full of laughing, crying, sighs and lunacy. Expectation
of another child filled them with as much joy as if this child were
their first. Emilie's pregnancy passed without incident. Ovila teased

her as she grew big, but, in spite of the extra pounds, he found her as beautiful as always. And so she was.

That autumn, Ovila had to resign himself to leaving Bourdais to work in the lumber camps; they both knew that they really had no choice. But this time, Ovila departed with a light heart, knowing that all was well with his family. Rose was going to school and getting along fine, thanks to her mother's perseverance. Marie-Ange, sharp tongued and short-tempered, was one of the most comical children he had ever known. Emilien was growing by leaps and bounds, and Ovila had fun roughhousing with him, even if he was only a year old. And, with a little luck, he'd manage to put enough money aside to be back in mid February to help Emilie with the birth of their next child. They couldn't count on Eva any more, as she had now married and left the family home.

When Ovila left, Emilie promised to wait for him. "I hope you will, my morning mist. In any case, it doesn't look like you have much choice!" he laughed.

"Oh, I don't know about that," Emilie replied. "If I get the feeling that you've stopped thinking about me, I might just have to forget about you altogether."

Ovila pretended to be stricken and begged her to do no such thing.

Emilie spent four months looking out the window every evening, going through the ritual of her daily wait. Missing him wasn't a terrible trial, for she knew that his return would make everything better. She devoured the letters he wrote and, as always, hid them under her pillow. She didn't want to lose the habits she'd had as a teenager, even if those days were now a part of the distant past.

The winter was mild enough that she didn't have to weigh herself down with her heaviest clothing. Ovila had told her that he would be back by February 15 at the latest, in case she went into labour earlier than anticipated. By February 10, she was finding it hard to be patient. Every day, she had to pinch herself to combat the dreaminess that took hold of her, making her do the strangest things. Under its spell, she forgot to put wood in the stove, to close the door tight or to wash Emilien's diapers. February 15 passed without word from Ovila, and she began to get nervous. She reread his last letter a hundred times. There it was, in his own writing: he would be back by the 15th.

By the 20th, Emilie was sombre and anxious. She was worried that Ovila had had an accident. Her in-laws tried to calm her down, but in vain. She got more and more upset. Edmond just knit his brows; he had his own fears.

On the morning of February 27, she had her first labour pains. She wanted to think that they were just in her imagination, but they persisted. At the end of the afternoon, when daylight was giving way to winter night, she put the children to sleep and took to her own bed. The pains grew sharper. She got up, panicking at the idea of giving birth without help, and decided to get her mother-in-law. She regretted not having made this decision earlier, when Rose could have fetched her. Now it was too late. She didn't want Rose to go out in the dark — and besides, she was asleep. She trembled at the idea of leaving the children alone. Perhaps she wouldn't give birth until the next morning?

A violent contraction convinced her that she had to do something. She had to go for help. She wrapped herself up in her coat, took her muff, clamped her toque down on her unkempt hair and stepped out into a night full of snow squalls and gusts of wind.

A blade of wind hacked at her swollen belly and tore the breath out of her. She would never make it. The wind blew even more cruelly. She cursed her predicament, then decided that everything that had happened was Ovila's fault.

"Damned Ovila! Damn you! Why didn't you come like you said you would?"

Tears started to roll down her cheeks. Her labour was becoming more and more urgent. She looked in front of her and couldn't see the Pronovost house; looking behind her, she couldn't see her own, either. She wondered if she should turn back or keep going. Her sobs were now so violent that they were louder than the howling wind. She decided to go home, frightened that one of her children would wake up and come outside to find her. She tried to retrace her footsteps, but they were already blown away by the wind and impossible to find. A stronger contraction forced her to stop. She had the horrible feeling that she would never get home. If only she hadn't tried to go for help.

The contraction was immediately followed by another, even more violent one. Emilie let out a cry; her waters had just broken. She felt the fluid turn from warm to cold as it ran down her leg. She tried to walk faster but tripped and fell.

As soon as she felt the snow sweeping in under her collar, she fell into a pit of despair. Resigned, she stopped fighting and abandoned herself to her pain, the cold and the wind. As she turned on her side, the snow quickly covered her. She stopped crying. She needed all her energy to get through this crazy birth — the craziest birth she had ever got herself into.

Now she was panting as loudly as the wind. In the shelter of her fur coat, her body expelled the baby. She took her muff and, unbuttoning her coat, managed to contort herself to curl around the little warm, sticky mass, still attached to her by the umbilical cord. Worried about the consequences for the baby of this birth on the hard ground, she dragged herself to her feet and finally saw a glow from a window that she recognized as her house. Painfully, she made her way toward it, losing her footing several times. Finally, she staggered to her door and, with a trembling hand, managed to open it without letting go of her precious bundle.

She rushed to her room, hunched over with the supreme effort of not dropping the muff and its vital contents. She grabbed a pair of scissors and some thread on the way and closed the door behind her. New contractions warned her that she was about to expel the placenta. She managed to smile, grateful that her body had waited until she was ready. Without even taking the time to take off her coat, she lay down on the bed and unwrapped the baby from the muff. She then knotted and cut the cord.

All alone, she did the work of both mother and midwife. She expelled the placenta, took off her coat and washed herself, then washed the baby and placed it in the bassinet waiting beside her bed. She lay back down, leaving her lamp lit, and spent long hours gazing at the baby girl, who already had a twinkle in her eye and was blowing bubbles with her saliva. Emilie sighed with relief that nothing was obstructing the infant's lungs. Finally, she took the baby in her arms and regretted that she couldn't nurse her. Why had she never had milk in her breasts? She got up and, baby in her arms, went to the kitchen to heat up a bottle. She returned to her room after checking on the other children. Thank God, they were all breathing.

The baby was still nursing eagerly when Emilie was joined by her children. She took the nipple from the baby's mouth so that Rose, Marie-Ange and Emilien could take a good look at her. Then she asked Rose to get dressed and go find her grandmother.

"Is it a stallion or a mare?" asked Marie-Ange.

Emilie burst out laughing and told her it was a girl. Marie-Ange was definitely Edmond's niece — much as Emilie might have preferred to think that she was first her father's daughter. She gave the nipple back to the newborn and reminded Rose to go get her grandmother. Rose went off, all alone, tiny among the mountains of snow.

When Félicité arrived, less than half an hour later, she scolded Emilie for not sending for help. Emilie didn't answer. She didn't want to tell her mother-in-law about her adventure. She wouldn't tell anyone, not even Ovila. This birth would be a secret which, for a little while longer, would be just between her and her daughter, then, as the memory faded from her daughter's mind, for herself alone to remember.

"One might say, Mrs. Pronovost, that Ovila and I only make children that look like you."

"You think so?"

"Oh, yes, this one has your features too."

Félicité went and took a good long look at the little bald head. "That means she looks like Marie-Ange."

"I think so, though Marie-Ange looks more like your husband as she grows."

Félicité smiled at her daughter-in-law and dared to ask if she would wait for Ovila before choosing a name. Emilie told her that she wouldn't wait, the name was already chosen.

"This one, Mrs. Pronovost, I'm going to name Blanche."

"How did you decide on that name? Do you know someone named Blanche?"

"No, but it's her name, and I'm sticking with it."

Félicité looked again at the infant, who had fallen asleep. "Do you know, Emilie, I think it suits her. Did you choose it because of the snowstorm?"

"I can't hide anything from you, Mrs. Pronovost," answered Emilie, a private smile crinkling the corner of her eyes.

*O*vila came back only at the end of March, to his parents' despair. As for Emilie, her gentle waiting had changed to rage. She greeted him coldly and granted him little time to look at Blanche before she changed her and put her to sleep. Ovila made no comment. He unpacked his bag by himself, a new phenomenon: usually, Emilie did it. He had prepared any number of answers to her questions, but she didn't ask any, only inquiring if he'd brought back enough money to buy food until autumn. He was deeply hurt.

Emilie ignored Ovila for months. One morning she woke up and decided that he would never hurt her again; she would never let him. If he had nothing to say to her, then he didn't merit her attention and her love. Little by little, she switched her concentration from her husband to her children.

Ovila tried many times to explain why he'd been late, but she didn't want to listen. So he couldn't tell her that there had been an accident at the lumber camp. A sleigh filled with logs had overturned on a dozen men, killing three instantly. He had escaped death only because he had gone to urinate; one of the victims, three minutes before he died, had even teased him about not "freezing his future." Nor could he tell her that he had agreed to stay three weeks longer at the lumber camp to complete the work undertaken by his foreman, a man who reminded him of his father, or how they had had to free the bodies caught under the blades of the enormous sleigh. He kept all these nightmares to himself, images he couldn't get out of his mind, like when the head of one of the men had rolled right to his feet and he had bent over to pick it up.

Now that he was back, Emilie seemed like a stranger. He had lost his wife somewhere under the logs in the lumber camp. He accepted his error; he should have written her. But he had known that the letter probably wouldn't arrive before he did. Now he realized that a letter, even one that arrived late, would have forced Emilie, if not to listen, at least to read. He would thus have proven that he hadn't acted carelessly but compassionately.

In despair, he tiptoed around her. She went on as usual, always kind in front of the children, but the minute they were put to bed she built a wall of silence around herself. She sewed, embroidered, wove or, if she didn't feel like working, played her accordion, which she had mastered. When the weather was nice in the evening, she went to her garden to pick out stones and weeds or stake plants.

Twenty times Ovila went to the hotel to slake his thirst for Emilie. Twenty times he came home sober, refusing at the last minute to plunge himself back into the hell he had known. But when the shadows began to stretch out in the early evening and Emilie still hadn't opened her mouth or her arms, he disappeared. He broke all the promises he had made to the good priest in La Tuque and to Edmond, drowning his soul in a sea of gin.

*E*milie was at her window. For five days, she had been waiting for Ovila. For five days, she had gone through a rainbow of emotions, from the red of anger to the pink of sorrow to the green of hope. She should have talked to him. She should have told him about Blanche's birth and laughed about it, now that she was able to. She should have listened to him when he was obviously trying to talk to her. She was angry at herself for pushing him away and rejecting him. But she told herself that he needed a good lesson. Even though they'd been married for almost seven years, he shouldn't take her for granted. She wanted him to continue courting her. She wanted him to take her, just her, to the cabin. They could have found someone to look after the children. He had proposed nothing, said nothing. She was furious to see that he acted like an unhappy victim, when it was she who was the victim, the unhappy one.

She waited for him, more and more impatiently. She couldn't stand any more days without sunshine, any more endless nights. She heard the last breaths of summer and was in despair at the idea that

Ovila would have to leave again soon and they wouldn't have taken advantage of the time they had at their disposal.

It was twelve days before she finally saw him, tipsy and dirty, stumbling toward the house. At first she jumped for joy, but when she saw how drunk he was, she rushed inside and locked the doors. He had to understand that she was happy to see him but that she didn't want him back like this.

Ovila tried to open the door, but he couldn't. Obviously, Emilie was still mad at him. He didn't push matters; he headed for his workshop. He flopped down in a corner, curled up and wept bitter tears. It was Rose who came and woke him, telling him that her mother had made some strong coffee.

He opened one eye and saw her, slightly out of focus. "What did your mother say?"

"Mama said you were back from a trip, and you were playing bogeyman, and she locked the door because you scared her, and she went to sleep."

Ovila scratched his head to stimulate the circulation. Rose seemed to be quite amused at the story that Emilie had told her. Emilie had never lacked for imagination when she had to cover for someone in the family. Conquered by his daughter's smile, he laughed along with her and continued the story that Emilie had started. Then he painfully stood up and headed for the house.

When he opened the door, Emilie, Marie-Ange and Emilien threw themselves at him with wooden spoons. "Bogeyman! Bogeyman!" they cried in chorus.

When Ovila looked at Emilie, he realized that she had found a good way to welcome him home. He also saw the joy in her eyes. Keeping the game going, he growled and pretended to grow claws, running after the children and never quite catching them.

"I told you the bogeyman slept here," Emilie shouted, laughing. Blanche, awakened by the noise, cried to get her mother's attention, but it was her father who went and carefully picked her up.

*E*milie and Ovila spent several days trying to make up for lost time, but neither one of them talked about what had pushed them apart. Ovila avoided the hotel for a while, then he went back, hoping to convince himself that he had mastered the force that had mastered him. Emilie refrained from saying anything at all, considering that he was never so drunk that he deserved her reproach. It was only on the eve of his departure, when he came home in the gathering night, that she looked at him sternly.

"Don't stare at me like that, Emilie," he protested. "You know I won't have a chance to raise a glass in the lumber camps. I'm just stocking up, that's all." He found this funny, and he chuckled. But Emilie didn't join him.

"You'll have to explain this to me, Ovila," she said. "When you come home, you say you need time to recover, and when you leave, you say you have to stock up. If I understand you, when you're not in the woods, you always have a good reason to drink."

"Come on, Emilie, I don't drink that much. Just every once in a while."

"I think you're being easy on yourself. It seems the only thing you don't know how to count is the number of drinks you order."

"Don't be so dramatic, Emilie. It's not that many."

"That's what I'm saying, Ovila — you don't know how to count."

Ovila left the next day, holding his suitcase in one hand and his head in the other. He had forgotten Emilie's words. He gave her a long look, waved a number of times and promised that he would be back as soon as he had enough money for them to survive until the next lumber camp. Emilie nodded and smiled, but she wondered whether he would now figure his hotel bills as part of their household expenses.

To everyone's surprise, Ovila came back at the beginning of January, stepping alertly in spite of the cold, impatient to surprise Emilie and the children. Emilie laughed with pleasure when she saw him. They spent an excited, happy night together — a night like those they had always loved.

The next morning, Emilie asked him when he had to go away again. Ovila was evasive. When she pressed him, he admitted that he wasn't going back to a lumber camp but to a log drive. "That'll mean almost two and a half months away."

"A log drive? That's too dangerous, Ovila. I'd rather you didn't go. I'll be too worried. You have no experience with that."

"Whether or not you're worried," he responded dryly, "that's where I'm going, since we don't have enough money to last until autumn."

Surprised, she asked if the salaries had gone down, and he said they hadn't. She kept probing until he lost his temper and asked her if she worked for the police, and if he had to account to her for every dollar he earned and spent. Emilie was shocked to see him so irritable. He had never talked to her this way. Then she had an idea that she tried, in vain, to push away. But the more she thought about it, the more she was sure she was right.

"Tell me, Ovila," she said, "when exactly did you leave the lumber camp?"

"Why do you ask?"

"I just want to know."

He turned purple and shouted that he had left the lumber camp a week before he came home. Emilie waited a couple of minutes before telling him, coldly, that she didn't believe him. Ovila got even more furious. She continued to needle him until finally, losing all control, he told her that he had left the lumber camp before Christmas!

Emilie swallowed painfully before she was able to speak. This time, she was the one who was furious.

"Charles Pronovost! I bet you were fired from the lumber camp. And I bet you don't have a cent in your pocket, and that's why you're going to the log drive. You drink away all your earnings and tell me barefaced lies! While I'm here at home being a good wife, you, instead of acting like a responsible husband, you're wallowing somewhere in a seedy hotel. The more time goes by the less reliable you are. How can I trust you now? What can I count on? I don't want to live with the fear of not having enough money, especially with four children to feed. I have no peace of mind left."

Ovila dismissed her with a wave of his hand; she could go jump in a lake and he would do whatever he liked. He got up, put on his coat and left. Emilie didn't see him again for two months. The one thing she was grateful for was that the children didn't seem to understand that he had come home and left again in less than twelve hours.

Thirty-three

*D*URING THE ENTIRE time Ovila was away, Emilie refused to wait for him to come back. She swallowed her anger and didn't breathe a word of his short visit, except to her father-in-law, who thought he had seen him on the road. Dosithée frowned and noted that Ovila had changed a lot. Emilie cried only when the doctor told her that she was pregnant again. She couldn't believe that in one night, one short night, they had created a new life.

When Ovila returned, Emilie ignored him almost completely, simply telling him that his bags had been packed for a long time. Ovila took a bath and played with the children. Then, with his suitcase in one hand and the doorknob in the other, he said, "I hope you'll forgive me, Emilie. There are things that even I don't understand. Take care of yourself and the little ones."

"When I married you, Ovila, it was because you wanted to take care of me. If it was too difficult a task, you should have stayed a bachelor. I would have survived. As for the children, I don't want you to leave without knowing that there will be another one sometime in November. I know you won't be here, but this way when you come back between jobs in the lumber camps, you won't be shocked to see me fatter than usual."

Ovila shook his head, put down his suitcase and went to kiss the top of her head. "I know that you can't understand, Emilie, but I love you. It's sad, but I love you, my love."

Emilie watched him through the window. She had read his grief in his eyes swollen with tears. Where was her Ovila, her big, crazy man? And she, where was she?

*O*vila wrote Emilie to tell her that he had found work in a lumber camp owned by Laurentide Pulp. To reassure her, he told her that he was spending most of his time constructing a dam and docks. The foreman had asked him to watch the river to make sure there wasn't a logjam. He was living in a tent with other men. He also told her that when this work was over, he would work on the "sweep," which consisted of pushing back into the water logs that had washed up on the river banks. Then he wrote that he would work seven days a week until the end of summer and that he hoped to put quite a bit of money aside, since he was earning fifteen cents an hour and working from 5:30 in the morning to 8:30 at night. He asked her to add it up for herself.

Emilie looked at the calendar. She knew that he would probably be back at Christmas. On All Saints' Day, she brought another son into the world, baptized Joseph Paul Ovide. She wrote to Ovila, asking him if he would prefer to call his son Paul or Ovide. Ovila answered that he preferred Paul. And so Paul began life fussed over by his mother and sisters, not knowing that his father was, at that very moment, working as a labourer in a new camp.

Ovila didn't come home for Christmas. Emilie was only slightly saddened, for she was beginning to rediscover the joys of solitude and the simplicity of days spent with children and without the company of adults. Her hands were full with her five little ones, and she wondered how she would have found time to devote even a few minutes in her day to her man. This year, he would be home at the end of May . . . without a cent and without a job. Emilie wept in despair. How would she manage to feed all her children?

"You told me to calculate how much we'd have . . . well, according to my calculations we should have quite a bit more than what you've brought."

Ovila didn't contradict her but apologized and promised that the next time he wouldn't spend a cent before he got home.

"You drink too much, Ovila. You drink all the time. It's not the first time you've lost a job. We have five children. You have to start thinking of them."

"Why do you think I'm working my tail off, eh? Why do you think I let myself get eaten by mosquitoes, blackflies and deerflies if it's not for you all?"

"You may leave on our account, but when you come back, you give the impression that you're more interested in buying rounds for your buddies."

Ovila groaned. He knew that Emilie was right. How could he make her understand that he worked constantly to earn money for the family but, in spite of all his good intentions, he didn't manage to put aside a single penny?

"I don't like to make rules, Ovila, but I would like you to send me money every week. That way, I won't worry as much."

"You have no confidence in me, my love?"

"No, Ovila, I don't. But you can win my confidence back. All you have to do is show me that you want to change. I'll believe in you again."

"It's a promise."

When Ovila headed off three weeks later, he left behind Emilie, pregnant with a sixth child; Dosithée, furious that he'd refused to help out on the farm; and five children, the three oldest deeply saddened by his departure.

Emilie sent him news as regularly as possible, hoping that in return he would think of sending a few dollars. He didn't.

And so life went back to normal — a life without a man, in the midst of a multiplying brood of children. A life following the turning of the seasons. She grieved for the first years of her marriage and wondered if Ovila would have changed so much if he had stayed on the family farm, working the land. She was a little angry at herself for having declared then that she didn't like farming. What had she been thinking of? With almost no effort, the land put more food on the plate than the invisible salary of an absent provider.

At the end of February, 1911, she gave birth to a third son, whom she baptized Georges Clément. This time, she told Ovila that he would be called Clément, without asking his opinion. Three boys and three girls made a nice family. She hoped that she would keep it at this number.

At the beginning of June, she was surprised not to see Henri Douville. He had found a new job in Montreal and had left the job of inspector to a young, pimply man with blond hair who, Emilie learned, let the children do whatever they wanted. He spent long hours reading their work, comfortably ensconced at the teacher's desk, while the teacher leant over his shoulder to decipher the poorly written words for him. Emilie received a long letter from Antoinette, who seemed delighted at living in the big city and invited Emilie to visit her there. Emilie smiled bitterly. Never would she see the day when she returned to Montreal.

At the end of June, she attended, all alone, the marriage of Edmond to Philomène Beaulieu. Her father-in-law took her aside to tell her that, if he wanted to, Ovila could make amends now that Edmond had left home. To his great astonishment, Emilie was pleased with this idea. She couldn't sleep for days, imagining a new life with Ovila never going away again and having no more reason to be bored and to drink.

She dreamed of springtime, of clearing and sowing. She dreamed of summer, of hay and the harvest, of the preserves she would put up while Ovila brought in the grain for the animals. She dreamed of autumn, of the colours and smells, of the flax Ovila would cut and she would mill. She dreamed of the winter she would spend alone, waiting for him, her heart tight in her chest every time she heard footsteps on the porch. Then sugaring-off time. Now their children would have work to do. Rose and Marie-Ange would be big enough to wash the buckets, and Emilien could follow his father.

She dreamed so much that she began to believe the dreams, and she still believed them when Ovila came back at the end of the summer. She talked to him for an entire day and night. Defeated, Ovila finally promised his father that he would take Edmond's place. Dosithée gave him a big hug and asked Félicité to prepare the veal he had just butchered to celebrate the return of his prodigal son.

Ovila brought in the hay while Emilie joyfully preserved tomatoes, corn and peas. He reaped the flax while she threw herself into the milling with the other women. Later in the autumn, when her belly was heavy with a seventh child, she began to spin her flax while Ovila and his father repaired all their tools and put them away for the winter. She cured the meat when they butchered the animals. And when Ovila left for the woods during the winter, she sighed as she thought of his return.

She was still waiting for him in May 1912 when she gave birth to a fourth girl, Emma Jeanne. When Ovila returned, he would decide if it was Emma or Jeanne who was sleeping peacefully, suspended on her mother's back in the Indian pouch that he had brought her six years before.

In June, she and her father-in-law spent an almost funereal evening talking about their disappointing wait. She wept long and hard. Never again would she believe in miracles.

*J*eanne was three months old when she was finally introduced to her father. He didn't really see her until two days later, when the fog of alcohol dissipated. As soon as he could walk, he went to tell his father that he didn't want to work the land any more. Dosithée sighed — his own private way of crying.

Ovila went home to explain to Emilie that he couldn't live the life of a farmer. "I'm suffocating on the farm, Emilie. I need air."

"And I suppose the air is better in the woods?"

"It's just not the same air."

That afternoon, Emilie asked him to go to the butcher for two dollars' worth of beef. She gave him the money, neatly folded. Ovila told her that he would be gone no more than half an hour.

Suppertime was long past when Emilie, taking inventory of her provisions, had to admit what her eyes told her: she didn't have enough meat to feed her children. She looked once more out the window to see if Ovila was coming. To her great relief, she saw him. She ran to open the door for him. Ovila came in and stumbled toward the bedroom. Emilie paled.

"The beef, Ovila. Did you bring the beef?"

"What beef?"

Emilie tried to swallow her anger. She looked at her children, waiting as patiently as they could.

"Give me the two dollars, Ovila."

"What two dollars?"

Emilie slammed the door of their room. She told the older children to dress the younger ones and themselves. Then she left with them, drying her tears as discreetly as possible, and knocked on the Pronovosts' door. She tried to make a joke of it, telling them that, absent-minded as always, she had forgotten to buy meat and hadn't made anything for supper. Félicité put a hand on her shoulder and invited the children to sit down at the table. Dosithée left his rocking chair and hid in his room.

Emilie went home late. She put the children to sleep and made herself up a bed in the living room. The next morning, Ovila woke up alone. He went into the kitchen, where Emilie was already busy.

"What's going on that you're not sleeping with your husband?"

"Nothing's going on. That's the way it is. When I have a husband, I'll sleep with him."

Ovila laughed. "You'll have to find one who likes fat women."

Emilie threw down the dishrag she'd been using and turned to face him. "The only fat I'm carrying," she said, in a voice strained with anger, "is the fat from when I was pregnant."

"Hey, now you're losing your sense of humour."

"I've lost a lot — me and the whole family — we've lost you."

Ovila stopped laughing and went back to bed. As he lay down, he punched his pillow with his fists.

For the next two weeks, he didn't leave the house. At first, Emilie thought it would only last a day or two. But seeing that he didn't even talk about going out in the evening, she slowly eased up on him. They spent many evenings talking about the lumber camps and about family life. Emilie clearly saw a sparkle in Ovila's eyes every time he talked about the woods. She knew that he had sap running in his veins, not blood.

The third week began with a short courtesy visit to the general store, followed by a long catching-up visit to the hotel. Emilie didn't wait up for him. She knew that the man who came home that evening would be a perfect stranger. She knew that she would detest him. So she rocked Jeanne, not because Jeanne usually fell asleep in her mother's arms, but because her mother had a desperate need for warmth.

Ovila left for the lumber camps when the first red leaf appeared. Emilie wasn't surprised, nor did she complain. These departures were no longer determined by the seasons, but by Ovila's thirst. As soon as he left the house, Emilie changed the sheets on their bed. That evening, she moved back into the bedroom, sure of at least one thing: she wasn't pregnant.

Ovila came back nine months later, on the eve of Rose's birthday, with a gift for her: a notebook. Rose thanked him politely and showed the notebook to her mother, who promised that she would fill it with letters and numbers. Rose was ten years old and still didn't really know how to write, but Emilie didn't despair. She spent much time hiding or minimizing Marie-Ange's and Emilien's progress; even though he wasn't yet at school, her son knew all his letters and could count to a thousand. In fact, he showed more talent for numbers than for letters.

Ovila didn't visit his parents. When Emilie reproached him, he admitted that he didn't feel strong enough to face them. Emilie knew that he felt remorseful for not having accepted his father's offer.

"Each time I see my father," he admitted, "my heart leaps out of my chest. I know what I would have to do to make him happy, but I just can't put down roots on a farm."

"You could at least go and see him."

"Tomorrow. I'll go tomorrow."

The next day he went over, but his father had gone to the village. Ovila told his brothers that he'd come back. He decided to visit Edmond and his wife, Philomène, whom he didn't know very well. He arrived in the middle of a scene. Philomène was in tears. When she saw him coming, she hid in her room.

"She doesn't seem to be in a good mood," Ovila remarked. "Is it her delicate condition that makes her like that?"

"Ha! Imagine — she wants me to move to the village. Ever since she's known she's pregnant it's been worse. To hear her talk, this is no way to raise a family, what with the smell of the manure and all the flies around. Can you see me in the village? I'd go crazy right quick. People living beside me and in front of me and behind me. People spying on me. No thank you, not for me. I'm not moving anywhere."

Ovila didn't ask any more questions. If Philomène hated farm life as much as he did, he understood why she was so desperate to leave.

"I haven't been to the movies at Saint-Tite," Ovide mentioned. "Do you want to go take a look?"

"Would it bother you if Philomène came along?"

"Of course not."

Philomène declined the invitation, alleging that she was too ugly to be seen in public. Edmond looked at Ovila, making a face to say that he'd known she'd refuse. After watching the movies, the two brothers went straight home. Ovila had never dared to go for a drink with Edmond. It was still fresh in his memory what his brother had done for him when he'd disappeared, and he tried to preserve the illusion that he had stayed on the right path.

Emilie was so surprised to see Ovila when he came home that she threw her arms around his neck to embrace his sobriety. "Your father came," she said. "He told me he was sorry he missed you. He said he'd expect you tomorrow."

"So I'll see him tomorrow."

After a night without alcohol, Ovila got up feeling well and told Emilie that he would have coffee and breakfast with his father. Emilie smiled encouragingly.

Ovila left with an alert, confident step. This particular morning, he knew that he would find the words to make his father understand why he couldn't live on the farm. He knew that his father was almost in despair when he thought of the future of his land. Ovide lay around like a lizard, spending much of his time stretched out on a hammock strung between two posts on the porch, or between two trees at Lac à la Perchaude when he found the house too noisy. He had also cultivated the art of falling into a fit of apparently very painful coughs whenever he was asked to do anything. Edmond had left the family farm to live with his wife in old Mr. Mercure's house, which he had bought. He helped to seed and gather the hay needed for his horses, but he spent the rest of the time at the race-track with other young village men, all of them bitten by the gambling bug. As for Oscar, he had made it known that he intended to make his career on the railways, using the English he had learned at the business college. He preferred wireless telegraphy to barbed wire. And Emile was interested in working the land, but he was still too young and so short that Dosithée wondered if he would ever be strong enough to carry hay bales. Télesphore had only one passion: jewels, watches, clocks and anything that had to do with them. He dreamed of one day having his own jewellery store and spending his days with a loupe to his eye, replacing watch springs, tightening screws so small they were almost invisible and listening to the constant tick-tock of all the clocks around him. He also dreamed of having a bunch of jingling keys, each opening a drawer lined with gems and precious metals nestled in velvet.

Ovila frowned. He understood his father's fears very well. But maybe Ovide would regain his strength. Maybe Edmond would return to work his father's land. Maybe Oscar would get tired of spending his days sitting and deciphering messages, filling and emptying mail cars, selling tickets and carrying suitcases. Maybe Emile would grow another inch or two. Maybe Télesphore would wake up from his colourful dream of sapphire and emerald. Sure, and maybe Lazare, who had been gone for ten years, would rise from the dead. Ovila knew only one thing: he could never give up the freedom of the woods.

This morning, he would tell his father that he loved the land, but the wild land, crawling with life, rich with peaty soil, rocks and brush, the beauty of weeds. He would explain that he had finished with alcohol and that never, ever would he leave Emilie without resources. Never again would he leave his father to feed the mouths his son had produced. He would explain how much he respected him and how proud he was to tell the men in the lumber camp that everything he knew about wood his father had taught him, that his father had been and always would be the best woodsman in the world in his eyes.

He arrived at the door. A quick glance at the house brought a smile of pride to his face. Not a single plank or nail out of place after eleven years. Already eleven years. Eleven years since he had worked like a dog to surprise his love. He had butterflies in his stomach. Emilie deserved better than him. He would prove to her that she hadn't made a mistake, starting today. As soon as the estrangement between his father and him had dissipated like a morning mist, without a trace.

He wiped his feet on the mat that his mother always left at the door and put his hand on the knob. It turned and left his grip. His mother was standing before him, ashen-faced.

"Your father just died, Ovila."

Ovila slumped against the door frame and wailed.

Part Four

1913–1918

Thirty-four

NEVER HAD A FUNERAL been more painful. Ovila had long believed that Louisa's death, both revolting and absurd, was the worst he would ever have to confront. But his father's brought with it the bitterness of regret, remorse and powerlessness, and an aching need for forgiveness that would remain unfulfilled for the rest of his life. All the "ifs" crowded in on him: if I had gone to see him the night before . . . if I hadn't been a disappointment . . . if he could have counted on me . . . if . . .

From the cemetery the family went straight to the lawyer, where Ovila had to face his shame. From beyond the grave, his father shouted his rejection: Emile, known in the family as "Ti-Ton," inherited the property and was charged with taking care of his mother to the end of her days. To Ti-Ton also went responsibility for Ovide. Edmond, Oscar and Télesphore would all get some money. And to Emilie went all the money that Ovila had never deserved.

Emilie's face reddened as Ovila's grew pale. He stood and excused himself. Not knowing what else to do, she followed him. As they trailed out, the lawyer cleared his throat to cover his embarrassment.

Félicité was the first to regain her composure. "Are you sure you read it right?"

"Absolutely, Mrs. Pronovost. There is no error."

"Thank you," she said, weakly.

"There's one other little detail." The lawyer cleared his thoat again. "Your late husband made certain arrangements with me. As you know, I am the executor of his will. The money deposited in the name of his daughter-in-law cannot be touched by . . . anyone but her."

"He left nothing to Rosée or Eva?"

"No, nothing."

Félicité thanked the lawyer coldly, more uncomfortable to have him mixed up in family affairs than shocked or even surprised by the terms of the will. Once outside, her sons in tow, she noted that Ovila's buggy was gone. No, she corrected herself, Emilie's buggy was gone. Ovila had always considered it his, but everyone knew that it was Emilie's. Old and faded, but hers.

Emilie cried as Ovila drove, his mouth clamped shut and the little blue vein in his temple pounding. Staring straight ahead, he pushed the horse much faster than usual. Emilie feared that he somehow blamed her for this "punishment" — as indeed it was — meted out by her father-in-law.

"Stop crying," Ovila said. "Mind you, he must have loved you a whole lot."

Emilie didn't respond but blew her nose noisily.

"Listen, my love," Ovila went on, "my father followed his conscience. It's hard to swallow, but he followed his conscience." He couldn't bring himself to say more.

Finally, Emilie said, "The will is unfair. I'll give you my share."

"No, you won't! I don't need that money. I'll earn enough to feed my family."

Instead of going home, Ovila took the road to the lake. Emilie made no comment. She would go wherever he needed to go.

"Emilie, I have to talk to you," Ovila said. Seated at the cabin window, Emilie indicated that she was listening.

"I'm finished with life in the lumber camps," he told her through his tears. "I'm thirty years old. I can't play in the woods like an Indian any more. I love the children, all seven of them, no matter what you think, and I mean to stay near them and their mother." His sobs grew heavier. "I swear, on my father's grave, that I'll be like I was before . . . you have to have faith in me." After a pause, he added, "You haven't seen your family in years because of me."

Emilie's heart grew heavier; she knew how much her father missed her. Caleb had come to realize that his daughter's marriage was a purgatory — he had never dared say a hell — and he didn't know how to console her. With no words to help her, he had stayed silent. This distance was painful to Emilie, and she wrote him a long letter telling him how much she needed to see him. Through Célina's pen, he had answered, a little coldly, that she never came to visit him. Emilie could not forgive him for this reproach.

Since then, she hadn't written him; her letters were addressed to her mother. She had seen her brothers — Hedwidge, Emilien and Jean-Baptiste — when they'd stopped in Saint-Tite on their way to Abitibi, where they had gone in search of adventure. Their meeting was brief, but not brief enough to hide the depths of the misery into which Emilie had sunk. Her brothers were so troubled to see their oldest sister living this way that they began to send her little bits of money. For the first time in fifteen years, Emilie was rediscovering her family ties.

Ovila continued to weep as he spoke, telling her that he knew he had made her very unhappy, that she was starting to have more wrinkles than laugh-lines around her eyes, and many more than one white hair. He wanted to spoil her, the way he had done long ago . . .

They spent the afternoon at the lake. On the way home, Ovila explained that he had lost the courage to face life the night Louisa died. "Do you realize, Emilie, that of the first three children, only Marie-Ange gives us hope for the future?"

"Yes, Ovila, but after Marie-Ange, things didn't stop. We had Emilien, Blanche, Paul, Clément and Jeanne. If there's no future with our three handsome sons and our four daughters, what more do you want?"

Her sentence put a mirror to Ovila's soul. He didn't like what he saw.

That evening, for the first time in years, Emilie slept with Ovila in their bedroom. She rocked him as she had rocked each of his children, whispering all of their hopes in his ear. She swore to him that she still loved him and always would.

"I can't say I've given much to my children, Emilie," he answered, "but at least I can say that I gave them a damned good mother."

*O*vila spent the summer at Saint-Tite, helping his brother Emile. Télesphore went to Grand-Mère to learn to be a jeweller, and Oscar kept working at the telegraph office. In the autumn, Ovila found work on Moulin Street, at the Massicotte bottling company. Emilie was happy that he had come to his senses.

The year 1914 began marvellously. Emilie and Ovila conceived their eighth child. The village now had electricity, and there was no lack of work. Leather-making shops sprang up like mushrooms, and everyone was invited to the opening of Acme Glove Work Limited. The village prospered, and the town council even voted a special budget to pave the streets. The women said that this would improve things immeasurably; now, they wouldn't have to dust more than once a week.

Edmond and Philomène never seemed to agree. One day, Philomène gave Edmond an ultimatum, and Edmond didn't budge. And so, to everyone's surprise, she left him. One morning when he got up, she was gone. Félicité scolded her son; he should have been more understanding. Edmond refused to bestir himself, so Ovila went to see Philomène in the village to try to reason with her. After all, she couldn't leave her husband in the eighth month of her pregnancy. It wouldn't be right for Edmond to live in Bourdais while his wife lived in the village. But Philomène answered that she would never return to the country; if Edmond wanted to see his child, he'd just have to come and join her. When Ovila delivered this message, Edmond laughed disparagingly and said he was sure Philomène would be back.

Once Philomène heard of his response, she decided to take the next step: back to her mother's in Shawinigan. And it was in Shawinigan that she gave birth to her daughter, Marguerite, about whom Edmond heard only weeks later. No one outside of the family knew of the quarrel. People even found it normal that Philomène would go to her mother's to give birth. However, when she didn't return, the whispering started. The handsome Edmond was considered above reproach, but Philomène — now, that was another story.

The rumours were drowned out by the faraway boom of cannons ripping through the air and the flesh of Europe. A number of Saint-Tite's young men signed up for the Canadian army, attracted by the pay — and also by the promise of travel and adventure. Oscar volunteered for the American army as a telegraph operator. The road out of Saint-Tite was sprinkled with his mother's tears.

"Don't worry about Oscar, Mama," Ovila tried to console her. "Oscar knows what he's doing. Think about it for two minutes. The danger isn't in the American army; they've never been involved in the war. The danger is in the Canadian army. Oscar would never have volunteered for our army. You see, he knows better than that."

On March 4, the town council voted in prohibition, but people complained so much that the law was amended to permit sale of liquor "under special circumstances."

Emilie worried that the war would have terrible consequences for Canada. She feared for her children, especially the one she was still carrying — a war baby! To reassure her, Ovila said that he wasn't worried, and she shouldn't be either. After that, Emilie said no more about her anxieties regarding the war, or about her anxieties as a mother. Since her father-in-law had died, she felt like she had lost her protector. Also since his death, however, she had once again learned to smile when Ovila was around, to the point that she had almost lost her fear of seeing him succumb to his strange, unquenchable thirst. She no longer had the strength or the courage to relive years like the ones she had endured.

As appealing and charming as when she first knew him, Ovila seduced her all over again. He reclaimed the right of ownership that he had always held over her heart, soul and body — and she freely gave it to him. She closed her eyes on the few evenings when he partied a little harder than he should have, for he now drank much less on the whole. He didn't stay out all night any more, and now she was even used to the smell of fermented alcohol that he exhaled when he slept. However, on those nights she didn't let him near her.

Their life was back on the right track. They all went together, the whole family, to Sunday mass. People started to say once again that they were the handsomest couple in Saint-Tite. Emilie once again held her head high with pride for herself and Ovila. On his parish visits, Father Grenier told her that he was full of admiration for them: they had faced many trials, and their love had grown. He remarked again that "God works in mysterious ways." Emilie agreed. Ovila smiled. All the debts Emilie had accumulated at Mr. Léveillée's grocery store were paid off, and she was no longer embarrassed to shop there. She even wrote her father that she was very happy, that God had given her a miracle. Caleb answered that he would come to see her, for he was intrigued by his daughter's sudden religiosity. Never before in his memory had Emilie mixed God up in her marriage!

In mid-October, Emilie gave birth to Alice. It was an extremely painful labour, and she told Ovila that she hoped Alice would be their last child; she was too old to bring any more into the world. Remembering the painful birth of Marie-Ange, Ovila agreed. Alice would be the birth of their rebirth.

They decided to go to Saint-Stanislas for the Christmas holidays, since Célina was sick and Caleb couldn't come to Saint-Tite. Emilie didn't tell her parents; she wanted to surprise them. After Christmas in Saint-Tite, the whole family, including Alice, went to Saint-Stanislas on New Year's Eve. When Célina answered her door, she nearly fainted.

"What an idea, Emilie! You should have warned me. I don't even have enough for you all to eat."

It wasn't the greeting Emilie had expected. She was hurt.

"Come in! Come in!" Caleb shouted from the kitchen. "We thought we'd have a quiet holiday because of your mother's health, and Napoléon was the only one who could come. But this is a damned nice surprise! So we'll kill a big goose right away." He took a long look at his daughter and gave her a big hug. "What brings you, my girl?"

"Ovila and me, we just wanted to receive my father's blessing."

"I'll bless you, I'll bless you. At least ten times for all the years I've missed."

Célina lay down for a rest while Ovila and Caleb went to butcher the goose, with Emilien trailing behind. Caleb gave the boy the important job of sitting on the bird to keep it from moving too much while they slit its throat. Emilien hated feeling the agitation of the bird in agony under his weight.

Later, Caleb took each of his grandchildren in turn to sit on his knee.

"You're the biggest. You must be Rose."

"No, I'm Marie-Ange."

"Marie-Ange. Are you as good as your name?"

"No, I've never been good."

Caleb burst into laughter. Emilie, her hands full of blood and feathers, turned and agreed. "That one, Papa, she doesn't live up to her name. Marie-Ange has changed a lot. She was a good little baby. But all that changed when Louisa died."

"So you must be Rose," Caleb continued.

"Yes."

"And how old are you, Rose?"

"Twelve and a half."

"You're not too big for your age. Are you still in school?"

"Yes."

"You must know a lot now. Are you going to be a teacher like your mama?"

Emilie banged her knife down on the counter to attract her father's attention. He seemed to have forgotten Rose's problems. Caleb looked at her, surprised; then he remembered.

"Uh . . . my pretty Rose, would you like to help your old grandpa? I can never remember names or ages. Now Marie-Ange, how old is she?"

"Almost eleven. And you know him, that's Emilien. He's eight. And the shy little one is Blanche. She's six."

"Almost seven," Blanche retorted, offended.

"Me, I'm five years and two months, less one day," Paul said. "I was born the first of November, 1909."

The adults laughed. Paul asked if he had said something funny.

Caleb pulled him over and perched him on his knee. "You're good with numbers, little guy. I bet you'll work in a bank when you get big."

"No, Grandpa. I'm going to be a priest."

"That's a good idea. You won't have any problems counting the hosts, or the money from the collection, or adding up indulgences."

"And Papa, Paul draws very well. He can already write all his letters, and even words."

"You take after your mother. Even when she was small, your mother said she would be a teacher. Are you as stubborn as she was?"

"I'm not stubborn, but Mama says I always get my way."

"Me too, Mama tells me that," Blanche piped up.

"Me too," Marie-Ange said nonchalantly.

"And the other day, Paul and me were in the street," Blanche continued. "You see, Grandpa, Paul and me, we were doing what we wanted. Mama told us not to go there."

Caleb frowned and looked at both of them sternly. He said, in a deep voice, "You disobeyed your mother?"

Paul looked at Blanche, furious. Then he glanced toward his parents, who seemed lost in thought. "You don't have to talk to us like that, Grandpa. The frog told us already."

"The frog?"

"Of course, the frog," Blanche said. "Paul and me, we saw the frog. Poor little frog, all squashed because it was in the street. Paul and me, we ran home to tell Mama we would never disobey her again."

Next, Caleb picked up Jeanne and Clément.

"You must be Clément."

Clément nodded.

"Cat got your tongue?"

Clément shook his head "no."

"How old are you?"

Clément showed three fingers, then pointed at Jeanne and showed two fingers.

"Do you ever talk?"

Clément frowned and made a fist at his grandfather. Then, to the adults' shock, he hit him, hard, right in the eye. Caleb was so astonished that he pushed Clément off his knee, and the toddler landed on his backside on the floor. He promptly got up and kicked his grandfather's right shin. Ovila quickly grabbed Clément by the arm and swatted the back of his head.

The sound of Clément's howl brought Caleb to his senses. "Good!" he said. "I'm very happy to hear your voice. I was beginning to wonder."

Emilie prepared the New Year's dinner all alone — her mother was too tired to help — but she was happy to do it. She was surprised that she was having trouble finding things; after all, she'd lived here for sixteen years. But she had been gone for twenty, and her hands, which had once automatically found what they were looking for, now had to open many cupboard doors and drawers to find knives, forks, dishes and glasses.

It was a pleasant, peaceful meal. Taking advantage of a few minutes alone with his daughter, Caleb told her how much he had missed her, how stupid he'd been not to help when he knew she needed him, how much he regretted having intervened in her engagement to Douville. Emilie smiled and told him that she was happier with Ovila than she would have been with a nicer, more proper man like Douville.

"It's hard to explain, Papa, but I was always trying to attract Ovila. Ovila's independent. Whenever I'm with him, even now, I have the feeling I've won a little battle . . . or sometimes a big war."

Ovila, Emilie and the children sang Christmas carols all the way back to Saint-Tite. Alice slept for almost the whole trip, warmly bundled in her mother's arms. When they passed through Saint-Séverin, they stopped to visit Lucie, but the house was empty. Lucie and Phonse must have gone to celebrate elsewhere.

"It's been such a long time since Lucie's made me laugh," Emilie said, disappointed. "I don't hear her giggle in her letters, so they're not as funny."

It was late when they arrived in Saint-Tite, but Paul stayed up to count all the money that Grandfather Bordeleau had given the grandchildren. The next morning, he convinced his father to drive him and Blanche to the new Provincial Bank so that they could open an account and deposit their fortune. Ovila smiled as he watched his son shake the hand of J.B. Lebrun, the manager, and sign his first deposit slip. Paul said that he would use all the money he put in the bank to pay for his schooling. Blanche was saving up for a trip to Montreal, and Emilien was planning to buy a store.

The moment she saw the telegram, Emilie knew it was bad news. She took scissors to slit open the envelope instead of tearing it along the side. The words burned her eyes. The message was brief and indisputable. Her mother had spent a troubled night struggling against the weight of her father's body, which kept rolling over to her side of the bed. All night long she kept telling him to move over, but he didn't move. In the morning, she realized that she had been sleeping with death — that her body, warm with life, had been trying in vain to keep away the great cold that had taken over her husband's.

Emilie didn't read the telegram a second time. Marie-Ange and Emilien hitched up the cutter while Emilie put on her coat. She drove to the village to get Ovila, sliding dangerously on the snow that had turned to ice after a night of rain. Her tears fell so fast that she thought she would flood the already treacherous road.

She said just one sentence to Ovila. He took off his greasy apron, wiped his hands with newspaper, went to say something to his boss and quickly left the building. Emilie passed him the reins of the cutter and took refuge with her thoughts under the bear skin.

"I'll pack the bags," she said.

"The roads are too slippery, Emilie. We'll never get there in one piece."

"If you're scared, Ovila, stay here. Nothing's going to stop me from going."

Ovila knew his wife well enough to know that all the arguments in the world wouldn't keep her from her father's funeral, even if she had to walk the entire way.

"Go see Edmond," she said. "Ask him to lend us his Model-T. If we have bags of cinders, bricks and good shovels, we'll get there."

Ovila had never dared ask to borrow his brother's beautiful automobile. He could barely imagine himself driving such a machine. But he went.

Edmond agreed, but only if he drove himself. That was fine with Ovila; if they slid into a ditch, it wouldn't be *his* fault.

They got to Saint-Stanislas in half the time it would have taken them by sleigh. Emilie's sisters, and her brothers Rosaire and Napoléon, were already comforting their mother, who was still sobbing away the horror of her last night as a wife. Caleb was resting peacefully in the living room. Célina hadn't even dusted the house, so overwhelmed was she by Caleb's sudden demise.

Emilie ran to hug her mother. Then she went and looked at her father, unable to keep a smile from finding its way through her tears. She stood there for a long time, thinking about this man whom she had so feared and so loved. Her ambitious yet timid father, who had always reproached her for her stubbornness, as if unaware that she had inherited it from him.

She drew closer to the lifeless body. Unconsciously she smoothed back the cowlick that, even in death, remained rebellious. She went to the kitchen and wet her fingers, rubbed them on a bar of soap, then glued down the cowlick, as she had done the morning of her wedding. Digging a comb out of her handbag, she made a new part in Caleb's grey, greasy hair. She centred the knot in his necktie, dusted the back of his suit collar and placed the rosary in his stiff fingers. The index finger of his right hand showed the mark of his last act of clumsiness; he must have cut himself. She narrowed her eyes to see if she had missed anything. Reassured that her father looked good for his arrival in the hereafter, she placed a kiss on his forehead and silently asked him not to judge her too harshly, not to make her laugh too much, and to help her, his big mule, during the days left to her. She thought she saw him smile, but it was her own tears that blurred his face.

Elzéar Veillette came into the living room, leaning on a cane, and Célina found the strength to stand and greet him. Veillette had come to visit Caleb for the first time in his life. He knelt before the body of his oldest and dearest enemy and wept like a child whose favourite toy had broken. Célina moved away, thinking that

Veillette would want a private moment. Emilie went to him and put a hand on his shoulder, murmuring that her father must have been very sad to be the first to bow out of the funny little war they had been carrying on for half a century.

Veillette shrugged and began to laugh through his tears. "That damned guy will chuckle when he sees me weeping like a lamb. We spent our whole life hating each other, because if the world knew we didn't hate each other there would be no stories to tell. But, between you and me, ma'am, your father and me, we always shook hands. No one ever knew that."

Caleb was placed in the cemetery burial vault, since the earth was frozen too hard to welcome him. Emilie asked the parish beadle, one of her cousins, to let her know the date of his burial, even if it was to take place several months hence. The beadle promised — though he completely forgot when the time came.

The return trip was almost as quiet as the trip out had been. Emilie burst into tears, rocking with sadness at not having seen her father enough since she'd left home. Then she burst into laughter and recounted some comical memory to Edmond and Ovila. Then she was quiet, reliving moments, emotions, images, sounds, even conversations. She would miss her father terribly, in spite of the curtain of quarrels that had fallen between them, in spite of their misunderstandings. Even though things had been less than perfect, her father had left her with many good memories: the freedom he had allowed her; the respect and pride he had shown in her, even through gritted teeth; his innumerable surprises wrapped in humble or great joy.

Emilie thanked heaven hundreds of times for having brought her to Saint-Stanislas at the beginning of the year to see him and receive his blessing, which had turned out to be his farewell. On the first of January, Caleb had used his hands to form a cross over his children and descendants. That same day, Caleb had used his eyes as an aspergillum, sprinkling them with his sentiment and his recognition. On the fifth of January, he had departed; he hadn't even had time to relive the precious minutes he had spent with them.

Together, Ovila and Emilie learned to fly with just one wing. In eighteen months, they had each lost a father. At least, Ovila thought, he and Emilie had avoided living through another death like his father's. Their short visit to Saint-Stanislas had enabled both of them to avoid the burden of remorse. Ovila envied his wife, who'd been given the chance to say goodbye.

When Emilie received another inheritance, he didn't say anything. He knew that she now had fifteen hundred dollars in the bank. He also knew that she would never give him any, even if he stayed as sober as he'd been since the day Dosithée died. He had sown mistrust, and it had eaten into his wife's soul like a worm.

✸

*A*t the beginning of April, Télesphore arrived unannounced to celebrate Easter with his family. Félicité cooked a plump, well-smoked leg of ham, which she studded with cloves. Watching her children satisfying their healthy appetites, she smiled at life. At least Dosithée hadn't left her completely alone.

"So, Télesphore," she asked, "is school going well?"

"Well? It's going better than well. I know enough now to open my own jewellery store!"

"Here in Saint-Tite?"

"No, I don't think so. Not that I wouldn't like to, but there aren't enough people with enough money to buy jewellery around here. I think I'll open up in Shawinigan. With all the pulp-and-paper plants, there are lots of families, lots of salaries — and lots of buyers."

On Easter Monday, Télesphore spent the evening with Ovila and Emilie discussing some work he wanted Ovila to do. He took a creased piece of paper out of his pocket and unfolded it on the table. It was a drawing of a jeweller's cabinet. Pipe in mouth, Ovila studied the drawing for a long time, then took out another piece of paper and a pencil. From Télesphore's awkward sketch, he drew a magnificent cabinet with a glass front. For the back he sketched a mosaic of drawers of different sizes.

"Damn, Ovila, I don't believe it. You've drawn the most beautiful jeweller's cabinet I've ever seen. And what gets me is, I know you'll make it even more beautiful than the drawing. It's amazing the talent you have! Don't you think, Emilie?"

"Ovila's talent is a bottomless well. I've never tried to understand it."

They talked about the cabinet for a long time. Ovila asked Télesphore what kind of wood he wanted.

"White pine with no knots, wouldn't that be nice?"

"Never! A jeweller's case has to look rich. For that we need oak or maple. Hardwood, not softwood. Come on, Télesphore! Do you want to look like a jeweller or a farmer?"

"Use whatever wood you like, Ovila. In fact, I don't even know why you're asking my opinion."

Emilie was amused to see the genuine astonishment that wrinkled Ovila's brow. He cleared his throat and spoke more softly. "It's just that . . . I don't know how much you want to pay for this piece. It's true that pine costs nothing. Now, maple isn't the same story. There's some that was chopped down years ago. I could cut and plane it. Oak is even more expensive. But if you want my advice, I'd say you want a cabinet that'll last a lifetime, don't you? Pine will get marked up much faster than maple. And maple, I think there's something in the colour of the wood that I would get tired of. I don't mean it's not a nice wood, that's not what I mean at all. But the grain of oak . . ."

"Forget it, Ovila. I can't afford oak."

In the end, the brothers settled on maple. Télesphore said he'd be back on May 10 to see how the work was going. Ovila mentally added up the time he had and said that the piece would be almost finished by then.

The next morning, he got up very early to clean his workshop before heading off to work. Emilie was moved to see her husband pick up his tools again. For a long time now, she hadn't wanted to go to his workshop, for it had symbolized the faded image of a happiness long past. As soon as he was gone, she hurried out there. After all the cleaning Ovila had done, it seemed that he had hardly made a dent.

She went back to the house. "Rose, Marie-Ange, Emilien, Blanche and Paul, come here. You too, Clément, you can come."

The six children came quickly, hearing a tone in their mother's voice that meant "right away."

"Today," she told them, "we're going to give your father the best Easter present ever."

"Easter is over . . ."

"I know, Paul, but sometimes holidays last longer. After all, school's still closed, isn't it? All right. Marie-Ange, you'll take care of Jeanne and Alice, and you'll make the meals."

"I don't want to. I want to help make the present with you."

"That is part of the present. The others — even you, Clément — you'll come with me to the workshop. Bring all the brooms, mops, old empty boxes, rags and buckets you can find. Everyone put on your oldest clothes. And you girls, put scarves on your heads to keep the dust out of your hair."

"Me too?"

"Don't get on my nerves, Marie-Ange! You know it's not necessary in the house."

Emilie clapped her hands and her children skipped around like elves. In ten minutes, they were standing at attention in the workshop. Emilie assigned a task to each, telling them that they had just one day to clean everything. Excited, the children rolled up their sleeves and worked without stopping until Marie-Ange came to get them for lunch. They ate quickly and got back to work.

Clément, the youngest, filled the jars and cans his mother had given him with nails and screws. He gathered them carefully, one by one, and laughed as they tinkled when he dropped them into the glass or metal containers. Paul rearranged the contents of all the shelves over the workbench in order of size. Blanche washed the windows and wiped them with old newspapers. Emilien took all the garbage outside. Everything that could be burned was put in a metal barrel, and the rest was piled behind the building. Rose swept the workshop three times, then dusted everything she could find. Emilie took all the tools out of the drawers they had been thrown into. The ones that had rusted she cleaned with steel wool and oiled, and she sharpened saws, planes and chisels on the grindstone, which had been wiped clean of cobwebs.

When Marie-Ange came to tell them that supper was ready, she cried, gleefully, "Everything looks brand new!"

Emilie and the children wiped their brows and dragged themselves back to the house, reeling with fatigue and carrying buckets, rags and Clément. After the children wolfed down their food, they asked to take a bath. Emilie washed first, then put on her housecoat, leaving the tub to Rose. Marie-Ange passed, saying she wasn't as dirty as the others. Emilien and Paul bathed together, then Blanche scrubbed Clément's back and ears. At the same time, Emilie got Jeanne and Alice ready for sleep; Clément followed them to bed without complaint.

The others sat in the living room, impatient for their father's arrival. Emilie let Paul and Blanche stay up till seven o'clock. "If your father isn't home by then, you'll go to bed. But he should be back. Emilien, you can stay up to eight o'clock; Rose and Marie-Ange, until nine."

The children were too tired to argue. They sat in silence, watching the clock. Emilie prayed that Ovila wouldn't decide to come home late tonight.

The clock chimed seven o'clock, then the quarter-hour. Paul and Blanche exchanged an anxious look — they didn't want to miss the party. At seven-thirty, Emilie, her throat tight with disappointment for them, said that it was time to go upstairs.

"I knew it," Paul said sadly.

Blanche held back her tears. Emilien, then Marie-Ange and Rose, went upstairs in their turn. Emilie tried to mitigate their disappointment by telling them that their father had been held up by something very important.

"Oh, yeah, we can guess what," Marie-Ange said.

"Marie-Ange, I don't like what you're thinking!"

"I don't like what I'm thinking either. Good night, Mama."

Stunned by her daughter's remark, Emilie just frowned and pointed her toward her room.

When she was sure that the children were asleep, she began to pace. And she paced. And she raged. She imagined the entire conversation that would take place when Ovila got home. Oh, she would tell him! She would tell him about the pain he had caused the children. She would tell him that he had just lost six friends — seven, including her. Oh, she would tell him!

Her steps were so heavy with anger that she didn't hear Ovila come in. When he opened the door, she jumped. Then she turned toward him, fury pinching her lips, her eyes red with fatigue and the pain of all her children. She took a deep breath, for she'd decided that her first sentence would take as long as the time she had waited. But before she could say a word, Ovila shouted, "Emilie, come see! Come see what I bought for Télesphore!"

She froze on the spot. "What do you mean, what you bought for Télesphore?"

"Come see! I put it all in the wagon." He tugged on her arm, grabbing an oil lamp as he led her outside.

"Look at that, Emilie. There's not a single knot in these planks. There's not a crack. They're all the same colour. And the wood was press-dried."

Emilie looked at the wood, incredulous. "That's not maple. That's oak!"

"Yes, ma'am. Good, solid oak. Oak like my brother the jeweller needs!"

"He wanted maple, Ovila. He can't afford oak."

"That's what he thinks. I'm sure he can't afford the oak because he wants to pay me. But there's no question of him paying me. And on top of that, I got this oak at a bargain, for the price of maple, or even less!"

Emilie sat on the porch steps as Ovila continued. "One of the men at work, he cut down an oak tree and took it to the mill. He had it sawed into planks, and he dried them at his father-in-law's in Sainte-Thècle. Emilie, you won't believe it, but this wood has been dry for three years. There's not a plank that isn't straight. The wood has darkened a little, but that'll go away with a good sanding. And it won't cost me that much because I can use the extra to make kitchen shelves. Nice shelves over the oven, where you can put the pots. So, what do you say?"

"I don't know. You really caught me by surprise."

"I'll bet my life you thought I was at the hotel. I fooled you! Well, now I'll go put all this away in the little corner I cleaned this morning."

"No! Go into the house, sit in the bedroom and wait."

"Are you crazy?"

"No. Do what I tell you."

Joy radiated from each of her words. Ovila! Oh, my big-hearted Ovila! She put him in their room and told him to block his ears with a pillow.

"My ears? Not my eyes?"

"Your ears!"

She roused all the children, even Clément. Groggily blinking sleep from their eyes, they asked her what was happening. "Just be quiet and follow me," she whispered to them. The children walked softly, carrying their shoes in their hands. She took them outside and stood them beside the wagon full of wood, then lit a candle for each of them.

"I'll bring your father outside. He'll be wearing a blindfold. You mustn't say a single word. I'll drive the wagon to the workshop, and you'll follow quiet as mice — your father mustn't know you're awake. Then I'll lead him into the workshop. I know he'll ask what we're doing there. When I make a sign, you come in. That means that your Easter present will be almost like a *réveillon* present. Are you happy?"

The children, now totally awake, wriggled with impatience. They followed the wagon silently to the workshop. At their mother's signal, they burst into the workshop, shouting with pleasure. Ovila was flabbergasted, and they saw that two more candles lit up in his eyes and melted softly down his cheeks.

*O*vila worked like a madman for the next four weeks. Every night when he came home from the village, he gulped down supper and rushed to his workshop to work on Télesphore's cabinet. Once the children were in bed — Alice in the bigger girls' bedroom, for safety — Emilie wrapped herself in a shawl and went to watch him working.

She was amazed at the fine quality of his cabinetmaking. "I'll never understand how your hands, all hardened and scarred with handling heavy logs, can be so delicate," she told him.

Ovila smiled quietly, absorbed with measuring, cutting and fitting a strip of wood. The case was truly a masterpiece, and Ovila began to wonder if he might make a living as a cabinetmaker.

"If we went to Shawinigan, Emilie," he mused, "and the rich people went to Télesphore's to buy their pocket-watches and diamonds for their wives, maybe they'd notice my cabinet and I'd get contracts. I'd love to make beautiful dining-room sets, and furniture for lawyers and doctors."

As Télesphore had predicted, Ovila modified the design he had sketched out. Not only was the front of the cabinet in glass, so was the top. Frowning, Emilie told him that it was too fragile.

Ovila tapped his forehead. "I've thought of that. I've put three pieces of glass together."

"Won't the glass get scratched?"

"Maybe, but it's easier to change a single piece of glass than to sand and refinish a wood top. With time, Emilie, wood changes colour. And since I'm not going to stain it, putting on a wood top that would need sanding every year means that the piece would be all different colours. With glass, Télesphore will never have problems, except for changing the top piece of glass. But if you look here, I've made grooves for the glass to slide in, and here I put a little wood bar to hold them in place. Télesphore just has to open it if he wants to change the glass or dust it from time to time. Anyway, I hope he won't have to put cheap watches in such a beautiful cabinet."

Ovila constantly found new ways to make his brother's work easier, including little partitions in the drawers and slots into which he could insert rings. He had even thought to make tiny holes for earrings.

"A person would think you've been making jewellers' cabinets all your life, Ovila," Emilie said.

"No, ma'am, but to make one, you have to think like a jeweller. You have to think about what he's selling, and make a place for it. If Télesphore were a doctor, I'd make another type of cabinet. If he were a butcher, it'd be different again."

Emilie learned more about working with wood than she had ever thought possible. She even dared to suggest that he cover dowels with velvet so that Télesphore would have a place for bracelets.

Ovila thanked her with a kiss. "It's not for nothing you're my wife. There's just one little problem, Emilie. I don't have any velvet. And velvet costs a fortune."

Emilie lowered her head and narrowed her eyes, trying to find a solution to this problem. The next day, she went to the village bank, then to the general store to buy the expensive fabric.

"I'm sorry, ma'am," the merchant told her, "I sold all the velvet I had before Christmas. You're not buying at the right time, not at all. This is the season for canvas, cotton and fine linen."

Emilie went home. Standing on a chair, she pulled down a well-sealed, dusty box from where it was languishing on the top shelf of one of her closets. She opened it, took out the dress that was folded there, the colour of the Batiscan River in September, and laid it out on her bed. She looked at it for a long time, struggling with her decision, then put it back in the box. Soon she took it out again and looked at it more closely.

That evening, she went into the workshop armed with scissors, thread, needles, glue, tacks and the wedding dress. She put everything down except the dress, which she held up in front of her, holding the collar in her right hand and the waist in her left.

"Look, Ovila."

It was a few seconds before Ovila realized what she was holding. "That's your wedding dress, Emilie!"

"Yes, and if you want my opinion, it's gone out of fashion. Anyway, I'd hardly get one arm and one leg in it now."

"Why are you showing it to me?"

"If we're making a jewellery cabinet, we're making a jewellery cabinet! I've been been thinking about it too, but I've been thinking like a customer. If I saw gold or silver on beautiful velvet like this, it would make me want to buy."

"Are you crazy? You told me you'd keep that dress all your life, or you'd give it to one of the girls to get married in."

"It's out of fashion, and I have so many girls I wouldn't know who to give it to."

Emilie would brook no more discussion. She began her work, sitting on a wobbly chair beside her husband. She liked it better here than in the kitchen. Aside from the children, this was the first time in almost twenty years, since the crèche for the Christmas pageant, that she and Ovila had made something together. Thanks to her dress, the display case would express the hope that both of them had for the promising career of Télesphore, the baby of Ovila's family.

Télesphore arrived on the evening of May 9 and went straight to his brother's house without even dropping his suitcase at his mother's. Seeing that the light was on in the workshop, he headed over and slipped through the open door. Emilie and Ovila, busy buffing the cabinet with steel wool and petroleum jelly, didn't hear him come in. Télesphore put down his suitcase slowly, his eyes riveted on the piece. He was dazzled. The cabinet was a dozen times more beautiful than the sketch Ovila had made. And then he noticed that it was made of oak; he swallowed painfully and unconsciously jingled the change in his pocket. He sat in a dark corner of the workshop, amused that his brother and sister-in-law hadn't noticed his presence yet.

When Emilie and Ovila finished buffing, they rubbed the piece vigorously with old flannel rags. After this, Ovila pulled open each of the drawers, holding them while Emilie rubbed soap on the sides.

"You'll see, Emilie, with a little soap they'll slide well. When Télesphore opens a drawer, there won't be any squeaking. Do you have the keys?"

Emilie took two dozen little keys from her pocket and matched them with various locks in the cabinet. This done, she and Ovila stepped back and stood, arms around each other's waists, looking at it in silence. Then they slowly walked around it, Ovila caressing the wood as he went.

"There's no rough spot on it, not one. It's as soft as the glass. But it's warm to the touch. The glass is cold. Damn! I can't wait to see Télesphore's face! Do you think he'll like it?"

"I'm sure, although it's rare to see unstained oak. Oak is always dark. You'll laugh at me, Ovila, but I always thought oak was a dark wood. I never knew it was almost the same colour as pine. But it's much richer."

Emilie took two sheets and covered the cabinet, telling Ovila that they would have the pleasure of making Télesphore wait. "We'll keep him in suspense. We'll tell him you just got started. We'll tell him it's a hard thing to make, it'll take a lot of time — "

"And then I'll make a face like this, and I'll say what I have here is just the skeleton and I couldn't do more because I was waiting for the wood."

"Then Télesphore will say it's all right, but he'll ask to see how much you've done."

"And then we'll uncover it. Télesphore will fall over backwards!"

Télesphore wondered how he could leave without attracting their attention. He didn't want to disappoint them, or to deprive them of the pleasure of their surprise. When their backs were turned, he sneaked out, taking his suitcase and grimacing with the effort of moving silently. Outside, he moved away from the workshop, walked around a bit to put a spring in his step and then resolutely headed back toward the workshop, whistling loudly.

The next morning, Félicité, Ovide, Edmond and Emile came to see the cabinet. Félicité walked around it a number of times and opened each of the drawers, thrilled with Ovila's handiwork.

"You can't know, Ovila, what it does to a mother's heart to see the talent of one of her children show itself like this. Talent is something I'll never understand. Dosithée and me, we didn't have much talent, but our son is full of it. We always knew you loved wood, but we never thought wood would let itself be loved by you like this."

Ovila was jubilant. Time had given him a great gift — the chance once more to become a man who made his mother and his wife happy.

Clearing his throat, Ovide mumbled his admiration — though, as the older brother, he felt he had to criticize a little. "You didn't think about staining the piece?"

"I didn't want to stain it. What makes wood beautiful is its grain. If I had stained it, it would look like pine or maple — how would you see the difference?"

"Anyway," Ovide said, "I guess Télesphore still hasn't gotten over it, because he didn't want to get out of bed this morning. He told us he'd come this afternoon to pack it up for the trip."

élesphore wasn't feeling well. He could hardly move. Félicité felt his forehead and confirmed that he was running a fever.

"It must be because I was caught in the rain," Télesphore said. "I think I'm getting a cold."

The next morning, to Ovila's relief, Télesphore came to help pack up each of the little drawers. He discovered other marvels in his cabinet, and he couldn't thank Ovila enough. They settled their account, Ovila agreeing, after interminable discussion, to accept a small fee.

"I don't like it, Télesphore. Forty dollars is too much."

"Whatever I could pay you, Ovila, it wouldn't be enough. A cabinet like this is priceless. I'll never give it up in my life. Never!"

Early the following morning, Ovila packed the cabinet securely in a wagon. They had arranged to have it transported by train; Télesphore didn't want to take the risk of damaging it on the bumpy roads.

Ovila saw the doctor's wagon go by and gave him a big wave. The doctor didn't wave back. Just then, Ti-Ton arrived on the run. Ovila put down the cable that he was using to secure the cabinet. One look at his younger brother's face and he knew there was bad news.

"What's going on, Ti-Ton? Is Télesphore still under the weather?"

"It's not a cold, Ovila. We don't know what it is, but he's too sick to travel today. Mama had the doctor come. She says there's something wrong and she doesn't like it."

Ovila brought the wagon into his workshop so that the cabinet wouldn't be damaged by the light rain that was starting to fall.

"I'll go see him," he told Ti-Ton. "Give me two minutes to tell Emilie where I'm going."

They arrived as Félicité was collapsing into a chair in the living room. In a voice trembling with worry, she told them that the doctor was with Télesphore. He had told her that she had done the right thing to send for him, and then asked her to leave the room. Ovila couldn't wait. He went to his brother's room, knocked and went in.

The doctor was pulling a sheet over Télesphore's face. He made the sign of the cross, then turned to Ovila.

"I don't know why or how it happens, Ovila," he said, "but when it happens, there's nothing I can do."

"When what happens?"

"The lungs fill with blood. The patient suffocates, just as if he was drowning . . . uh . . . in his own blood. It doesn't happen often, but it's like he drowned in his own blood."

The doctor was upset. He hated it when medicine couldn't push death away — especially from a young man like Télesphore, a man at the threshold of his life, his head full of plans and dreams of success. Ovila didn't say a word. He left the room, descended the stairs and went to the door, without saying a word to his mother. Getting up, she saw that Ovila's face was grey with grief, the earthy colour of pain.

Ovila ran to his workshop. By himself, he unwrapped the heavy cabinet and slid it down the planks. Then, slowly, carefully, he began to take it apart, board by board, joint by joint, nail by nail. When Emilie came in, he was sobbing as he worked, letting out soft, low moans that were much more heart-rending than great wails. She went back to the house and told Rose and Marie-Ange to take care of the other children, and to make sure that their father wasn't disturbed for any reason whatsoever. Then she went to Félicité's house.

Ovila left only the bottom and the front of the frame intact.

A cabinet six feet by two-and-a-half feet. I'm a damned fool, Ovila thought. A damned fool! I should've made a cabinet five feet long, or four feet. Then Télesphore would never have tried to get in it. I'm a damned fool!

Télesphore was buried in a coffin the likes of which had never been seen in Saint-Tite. It was made of blond oak and had two dozen of what seemed to be little drawers on the side, sealed up. Télesphore was dressed in his parish guard's uniform, and he was wearing shoes, because the top of the coffin was three pieces of glass, glass that Télesphore had never smudged with a fingerprint or misted with his breath.

It was when he heard the glass shatter under the stones from the first shovelful of earth that Ovila finally opened his mouth.

"I'm leaving, Emilie. I'm going away. I can't stay here in this unlucky town any longer. Come with me. We'll move to Shawinigan. We'll take everything except my tools. I never want to see them again. I never want to touch them!"

Ovila went to Shawinigan the very day of his brother's burial, after emptying his room of its contents. It took him two days to cancel Télesphore's lease for the jewellery store and find a purchaser for all the equipment that he found there. He then walked through the streets of the town and found a new apartment, big and well lit. He rented it for his family. The lease in his pocket and Télesphore's money — two hundred dollars — folded in his sock, he went back to Saint-Tite to help Emilie pack. He gave the money to his mother, but she took only enough to cover the cost of the funeral and burial and insisted that Ovila keep the difference.

"That money, Ovila, it's your father's money," she told him. "I think he would have wanted you to have it. Now that you seem set on leaving" — she stopped to blow her nose — "you'll need it. If you change your mind, I don't want you to be embarrassed to come back. Your house will stay empty. I'll never sell it."

On the first of May, Ovila, Emilie and their eight children moved to Shawinigan.

Thirty-five

MILIE DIDN'T STOP to think about this sudden move. She simply followed Ovila, and all his torments. She pulled the children out of school, promising the teacher that she would complete the year's curriculum herself if she couldn't find another school for them so late in the term.

Then she took the train to Shawinigan with seven of the eight children. Emilien and Ovila, who had gone ahead by wagon to move all their furniture into the apartment, met her at the station. Her fleeting feeling that the family was on vacation disappeared when Emilien and Ovila began to describe all the work they had done on the apartment.

"You'll like it, Mama," Emilien said. "It's not as big as the house in Saint-Tite, but it's big enough. And everything's new. It smells of wood, fresh plaster and paint."

"And," added Ovila, "the landlord said that if you want to paint it a different colour, you can."

Emilie smiled. How very kind of the landlord to permit them such liberties. She wondered if she could ever get used to having to ask someone's permission before living the way she wanted to in her own home. She had always lived in a house of her own, except when she was at the school, but even there she had never had to ask for anything, except the addition of the bathroom.

When she entered the apartment, she sighed with relief. Ovila had really found something nice. She walked from room to room with him, first checking where the sun came in, then opening all the closets to check their size. Ovila smiled as he watched her; not once did she think of turning on the lights that were suspended from the ceiling.

"Have you noticed anything special, Emilie?"

She listed everything that struck her — first the toilet, then the sink and the tap in the kitchen — but she didn't mention the electricity. Finally, Ovila took her by the hand and, going around the apartment again, turned all the switches on and off. Catching on to the game, Emilie called the children to show them the lights. The ones who were big enough went to a light switch and turned the lights on and off. But they soon lost interest — in less than five minutes, this novelty held no more attraction or mystery.

Emilie quickly found a grocery store where she could buy the basics for her new, small pantry. They ate supper around their table, which, to Ovila's astonishment, seemed to have grown on the trip between the old kitchen and the new one. He told himself that he'd have to make a new one, round, with two leaves. But then he remembered the promise he'd made himself never to touch cabinet-making tools and swept the idea from his mind. Their table stayed as it was — cumbersome.

Emilie didn't sleep a wink the first night, tossing and turning, wondering if she would ever get used to the constant noise of the city. Bourdais seemed so far away — Bourdais, where only the lowing of cows, the occasional whinny of a horse, the cries of nocturnal birds, the singing of crickets and the croaking of frogs disturbed the night silence. This symphony of nature, which had always rocked her to sleep, was nothing like the faraway rumbling of the pulp-and-paper plant and the bursts of voices, punctuated by shouts, that came in through her window every night, the noise of cars constantly rolling by, the doors slamming so hard that, twice, she thought it was her own bedroom door, and the gurgling of the plumbing that invaded the apartment every time one of her upstairs neighbours turned on a tap in the kitchen or flushed the toilet.

She turned to Ovila. He was breathing so lightly, she knew he wasn't sleeping.

"Ovila?"

"Hmm?"

"You can't sleep either?"

"I can't sleep because my wife won't lie still."

"Will there always be so much noise?"

"What noise, Emilie?"

She knew that he had experienced nights other than those in the tranquillity of the country. He had slept many nights in the lumber camps, surrounded by other men who probably snored loudly. He was used to strange coughs, throat-clearings, gas from baked beans, the rumbles of poor digestion, the rhythmic creaking of beds accompanied by gasping breaths. He was used to hearing the younger men stifling the sobs of their loneliness under smelly sheets, the more sensitive ones calling their loved ones in their sleep or crying out from fear of a supervisor or an accident.

It was so late by the time she finally got to sleep that she missed the first rays of sun on Shawinigan the next morning. Ovila woke her with a kiss and told her that the children were running amok. She got up and made oatmeal and toast; then she fetched Alice and prepared her breakfast.

Ovila came into the kitchen, laughing. "I've been waiting to pee for five minutes. The children are hanging from the toilet chain."

Emilie smiled, remembering how fascinated she'd been in the bathroom at the Windsor Hotel.

"What would you say, Emilie, if I stayed with the children while you look around the neighbourhood and find the school?"

"Don't you want to go ask for work at the pulp-and-paper plant?"

"I'll go see the man at Belgo tomorrow. School is more important. If you can register them, they could start this afternoon."

Emilie agreed. Not wanting to look like a country woman who'd just arrived in town, she put on one of her better dresses, and a straw hat and lace gloves.

The school was just a street away. Inside, a nun greeted her and asked her if she had come to register her children. She replied that she had, and the nun pointed to a door. When Emilie entered the little room, she was surprised to see that it was crowded. She had to wait, standing, until she was called.

The principal's assistant didn't seem to be bothered by the arrival of so many new students. "It's not unusual at the beginning of May," she explained. "There are just as many who leave because their families move away. For May and June, with all the departures and arrivals, we have about the same number of students."

"Can my children come this afternoon?"

"Of course, if they have everything they need. Under what name?"

"Pronovost."

"What first name?"

"There are quite a few."

"If you like, we'll start with the oldest."

"Rose, thirteen years old, fourth grade."

The assistant raised her eyes from her book and looked at Emilie, who said nothing further. She didn't want to explain Rose's difficulties right now. The assistant put a question mark beside Rose's name.

"And . . ."

"Marie-Ange, eleven years old, sixth grade."

"Then . . ."

"Emilien, nine years old, fourth grade. If you have two fourth-grade classes, I'd prefer that he and Rose be in different rooms."

"We only have one fourth-grade class. And . . ."

"Blanche, seven years old, second grade."

"And . . ."

Emilie decided to take a risk. Paul hadn't started first grade, but she knew he could keep up. Once he had proved himself, it would be difficult the next year to keep him back.

"Paul, six years old, first grade."

The assistant raised her eyes again. "He started early?"

"Yes. He's very smart, and as I was a teacher myself for six years . . ."

"In a concession school?"

"Yes, at Saint-Tite-de-Champlain."

"Well, the programs are much more difficult here, ma'am. Paul must wait and take his first grade again next year. You know, we keep children back a year when they come from the country."

Emilie took a deep breath. She mustn't make a fuss on her first visit. She knew the curricula, and she knew that her children were perfectly well prepared.

"Sister, by permitting Paul to finish the year in first grade, you'll be in a position to judge if he can go on to second grade next year. And if you have no objection, I would ask you to leave each of my children at the grade I've indicated."

She talked dryly, silently thanking Henri Douville for having taught her to speak clearly and articulate each word. The nun shrugged, glanced behind Emilie at all the people still waiting and decided not to argue. This mother, like all mothers from the country, would soon realize that it was useless to be stubborn. Rarely did country children meet town standards.

"One last thing, ma'am. Next year, there will be only girls here, except for boys in first grade. You'll have to register Paul and . . ." she looked for the name in her register ". . . Emilien with the brothers."

"That's also policy?" Emilie bit her lips.

"No, ma'am, it's not policy. We just feel that it is preferable to separate the boys from the girls. Next year, the number of pupils registered will finally be high enough for us to do so."

"Where is the boy's school?"

"A little farther. But I imagine that boys from the country won't mind a walk morning, noon and evening."

Emilie's mouth twitched. This nun was getting on her nerves. Who was she to decide arbitrarily that all new arrivals would lose a year of school? Especially her children, who were at the top of their respective classes?

"Thank you, Sister, for your kindness. I will be here this afternoon with my children. What time should we be here?"

"At one o'clock."

"We'll be here."

As Emilie left, the nun rolled her eyes. They were all the same, these country mothers. And at least eight out of ten of them said they had been teachers themselves. The nun shook her head. Most of these "teachers" had trouble signing the register. She looked at Emilie's signature and pursed her lips. At least this one had good handwriting.

Deep in thought when she left the school, Emilie lost her way. Mortified, she had to ask a passerby for directions. When she got home, she pulled off her hat and gloves and assembled the children in the living room.

"I've seen your school," she told them. "It's big and it's full of students, and the principal's assistant says the work is hard. Here in Shawinigan, children are very studious."

She told them that she had tried to get them registered in the same grades they'd been in in Saint-Tite, but this wasn't done in Shawinigan. Ovila was surprised. She just gave him a knowing look.

"Between now and the end of the year, I don't want to see any laziness. If you're not as good as the others, you'll have to work twice as hard. That's how it is here in Shawinigan. Starting today, we'll have a family secret." She lowered her voice to make sure that they would pay attention. Even Ovila was intrigued. "I registered Paul in first grade."

"Yippee!" Paul jumped up and down, a broad grin on his face. "I'm gonna be . . ."

"Here in Shawinigan, Paul, we say, 'I am going to be.'"

Paul stopped, thought about what he wanted to say and started again. "Mama, am I going to be in a real first grade?"

"Yes, Paul. The secret is I said you'd . . . I said that you had started in September. I am sure that you'll be able to finish the year with no problem. Now, the rest of you." She looked at the other children, a severe look on her face. "There are three things I want from you. The first is to never tell that Paul's not . . . that Paul didn't go to first grade in Saint-Tite. The second is, I want you to say that you come from Saint-Tite-de-Champlain and not from Saint-Tite. Do you understand me so far?" All the children said yes, even Clément. "The third thing is, I want everyone to give Paul a pencil. An old pencil, not a new one. For the notebooks, I'm gonna — "

"'I'm going to,' Mama. Here in Shawinigan, we say 'I'm going to.'"

"That's true, Paul. Thank you for correcting me. As for note-books, I'm going to buy new ones for everyone. Now, you all get ready while I find a store for the notebooks."

The children went back to their rooms, all of them excited. Emilie told Ovila about her meeting with the principal's assistant.

"What's this silly rule about putting country children in a lower grade?"

"I imagine, Ovila, it's because they think country children go to school only when they want to. And between you and me, you know that's how it works in many families. All right, now, I'm gonna . . . I'm going to find a store."

Emilie searched the streets in vain. Wearily, she asked for infor-mation and was told that stationery was sold at the school. She winced at the prospect of being forced to invent a story to justify such a purchase in the month of May. She went home, made lunch, and then, holding Paul and Blanche by the hand, went to the school, making the children look around them and memorize the route they were taking and look in both directions before crossing the street.

"Here in Shawinigan, there are a lot more automobiles than there are in Saint-Tite. In Saint-Tite . . . de-Champlain, there were just your uncle Edmond's and two others. I really don't want to turn into an old mother hen here in Shawinigan. Is that clear, children?"

"Yes, Mama."

Blanche began to cry. Without letting go of her mother's hand, she began to slow down. "I want to see Grandma Pronovost," she sobbed. "I don't like it here in Shawinigan . . ."

"You'll get used to it, Blanche."

Emilie left them outside the school, telling them to stay together while she went to buy the notebooks they needed. In the hall, she bumped right into the principal's assistant.

"Mrs. . . . Mrs., uh . . ."

"Pronovost."

"Pronovost. This morning, I forgot to tell you that your husband must sign the registration papers. I also forgot to ask you for the children's baptismal papers."

"The baptismal papers are at Saint-Tite-de-Champlain, Sister."

"That's a bother . . ."

"Do you mean that the children — "

"The rule is that we must have a copy of the baptismal papers. But since your children have arrived right near the end of the year, we can make an exception. The principal will ask you to have them for next year's registration."

"That's very kind of you. Don't worry, we'll have them."

She was furious with herself. How could she have forgotten this detail? "Could you tell me, sister, where to buy notebooks for the children?"

"You don't have to buy new notebooks. They can use the notebooks they have been using this year."

Emilie forced herself to smile pleasantly as she wracked her brain for a plausible excuse. "Well, you see, my mother-in-law asked to keep the children's notebooks. They're her first grandchildren, and it made her sad to see them go. So I left her all the notebooks so she could look through them and think of us."

She wondered if the nun had swallowed this story. She kept smiling, trying to look wistful.

"Poor woman! It must be difficult to see one's son and grand-children go away." Emilie noted that the nun had left her out of the family. "In that case, follow me. I'll show you our little store."

Emilie returned to her children with the new notebooks. Paul hugged his as if it were the most wonderful gift. Emilie then asked them to give her the ones they had brought. "I completely forgot, but your grandmother asked to have them, so she'd have something to remember you by."

They accepted this explanation. Emilie stuffed the old notebooks into her large handbag. The children were being called to class. She told them one last time to be good and attentive, to raise their hands before speaking, not to pick their noses, not to answer all the questions and to wait their turn, not to argue, not to talk about Saint-Tite without mentioning Champlain county, not to scuffle or fight, always to sit up straight, to make sure they knew what homework and lessons they had to do, and to try to set a good example. Almost out of breath, she smiled and winked at them as they went inside — especially Paul, who was practically skipping.

When she got home, she told Ovila that he had to go to the school and sign the registration papers. Shaved and dressed in good clothes, he waited until the end of the afternoon so that he could take the children home with him. All of them came back happy and excited. Emilie was waiting for them on the sidewalk, with Alice in her arms and Jeanne and Clément playing beside her. Paul ran toward her, his face lit up with a big smile.

"It's easy, Mama. I knew everything! The nun asked me lots of questions and I knew everything! The nun asked me to count, and I counted. I think the nun wanted me to to count slowly, so I counted slowly, then she asked me to go faster, so I went faster. The nun told me to stop when I was at one hundred. She asked me if I knew all the hundreds, and I told her I did, and all my thousands, too."

"Your what?"

"My thousands! I told her I knew my thousands. And I even knew millions! Anyway, the nun didn't seem too happy that I knew so many numbers. The children here in Shawinigan don't know as many numbers as the ones in Saint-Tite-de-Champlain."

Emilie bit her lip to keep from laughing. She could imagine the expression on the nun's face when she saw Paul's self-assurance.

They went inside so that Ovila and Emilie could hear all the stories about the first afternoon at school. Paul started, telling everyone what he had just told his mother. To Emilie's relief, no one laughed.

Blanche interrupted him. "The nun asked me what my father does. Since I didn't know whether Papa is still a cabinetmaker, I said he was a mover. Right now, that's what he's doing. He's moving. But I made sure to say that we come from Saint-Tite-de-Champlain. Then the nun asked me which town I lived in now. I looked at her and wanted to say, straight out, that was a stupid question. But I remembered that you said to be polite, so I answered."

"What did you say, Blanche?" asked Emilie, suddenly uneasy.

"Well, of course, Mama, I said that we lived in 'Hereinshawinigan."

Emilie closed her eyes for a moment, then opened them. She asked Emilien if he had had any problems.

"No, it was easier than at home. The pupils are smarter, though.

I had some trouble in dictation. I didn't know how to spell Shawinigan. Now, I know."

"How did you spell it?"

"C-h-a-h-o-o-i-n-a-g-a-i-n."

Emilie made all the children spell out Shawinigan. Blanche knew, as she said the letters, that she hadn't answered the question in class properly, and she hung her head.

Rose and Marie-Ange had nothing special to tell. Marie-Ange observed that most of the girls had nicer dresses than hers, and Rose said that she was seated in the back of the class and the nun didn't ask her any questions. She made only three mistakes in dictation.

*O*vila burst into the apartment, red-faced and out of breath. Emilie jumped. She still wasn't used to all the noises in this new house. "Good Lord, you scared me!" she scolded. "Don't come in so fast next time. Look, even Alice is scared."

"I got it! I got it, Emilie! One day and I got it! Ah, the city! There's no searching and waiting here. I got it!"

"You got it?"

"I got it, I got it! And not for peanuts. For a good salary."

"You got it!"

Emilie put Alice down on the floor and threw herself into Ovila's arms, and he waltzed her around the room, banging into the corners of the table.

"Youch! Ovila! Don't turn me so fast!"

"If you think we're turning fast, you haven't seen anything. This morning, at the plant, I saw the 'breast rolls' and the 'guide rolls,' and those things, ma'am, *they* turn fast."

*E*very morning, Emilie made Ovila's lunch. He left early, walked to Belgo and began his long day. He was as fascinated by the machines at the plant as by the wood. He was almost apologetic as he told Emilie that the plant was full of the smell of wood. "It smells almost as good as my workshop. But here, it's wood pulp we're smelling. It doesn't sound possible, but to make ordinary paper, it takes 99.5 percent water and just a half of a percent of wood pulp. We call it fibre."

"Water?"

"Yes ma'am, paper is made with water. And just a little wood, of course."

A month after they arrived in Shawinigan, Ovila was still not over his wonder. Emilie discovered all the stores that were useful to her, and she also finally found sleep. The children brought home report cards and, except for Rose, they had succeeded beyond their mother's highest expectations. Paul had even managed to pick up two first places.

Although Emilie had found sleep, she hadn't found peace. She hated to see the children playing in the tiny yard or running on the narrow sidewalks. Her worst fear, which she kept herself from blurting out, was that they might trip and fall into the street. She missed Saint-Tite's serenity — the familiar faces and the daily gossip. She spent much of her day writing letters: to Félicité; to Célina; to dear Antoinette; to Berthe, who never answered; to her cousin Lucie, who promised to convince Phonse to pay a visit; to Father Grenier, to give him news about his little flock; to the Bourdais schoolteacher; and she would start another round without waiting for responses.

Ovila always came home late. He worked constantly. In June, he announced that he was getting some kind of promotion. Now he would look after the dryers. Emilie rejoiced, though she didn't understand how this work was different from what he had done before. When he had worked in the lumber camps, she'd known exactly what he was doing. When he'd had a job in Saint-Tite, at home or in the village, she'd been able to see him working. Here, she had no idea what he was doing. She knew only that he had an unprecedented ardour for making sure that the dryers functioned properly. She had never seen a dryer, and she had to admit that she didn't even *want* to see one.

She was suffocating in her seven new, pretty, freshly painted rooms. Seven pretty rooms identical to the seven rooms of her neighbours, and of their neighbours, and of the neighbours across the street, and those around the corner, and those across the back yard. She missed a house with a past, a present and a future.

***

The summer was torrid, and it arrived without warning. Emilie had lost track of all the signs of the seasons. In Saint-Tite, she felt summer coming for weeks and weeks; she saw the green darkening in all the new leaves. Here, she could observe one lonely tree, but one tree didn't beat with the pulse of the seasons. In Saint-Tite, she would have known that it would be a hot summer by the song of the cicadas, by the position of the leaves on the trees, by the colour of sunrises and sunsets, by the way the vegetables grew in her garden. Here, the heat took her by surprise, one fine morning, the same way she was surprised, still, by the wail of a siren or the cry of a mother calling her children when they chased a ball or a hoop into the street.

When school let out, the seven large, sunny rooms were darkened with all the heads filling the windows. Emilie had no choice but to send the children outside, but the minute they were out the door, she ran after them to make sure they didn't play in the street. Several times a day, she tucked Alice under an arm and rushed out to call one of her children back.

Ovila was away all day, and he came home late in the evening. He admitted, in words both clear and soft, that the presence of the children, the crowded apartment and the novelty of the city were to blame for his many absences. Emilie proposed a solution to his problem: "I'll take all the children to Lac à la Perchaude."

"Thanks," Ovila said, "but I don't want you all to go away."

Emilie's temper flared. "You say that we take up too much room! I offer to empty the house and you don't want to hear it!"

"Emilie, all I said was I can't spend all my time at home. That's all."

"Have you ever wondered if I like being at home all day? I'd rather go to the lake."

Belgo came to Emilie's rescue; the company offered to increase Ovila's salary and pay for installation of a telephone so that he could be on call at night. With this arrangement, he was able to spend evenings at home with the family. Now that his skills were known, however, Emilie often had to sleep alone. She didn't understand why, at a big plant like Belgo, there was always something breaking down, especially during the night.

Ovila finally suggested that she leave Shawinigan for the rest of the summer. She and the children left with supplies and luggage for five weeks. The youngest — Alice, Jeanne and Clément — stayed at the lake with her, while the older ones slept at their grandmother's and joined her during the day.

$\mathcal{E}$milie and the children returned to Shawinigan for the beginning of the school year. The only good news that greeted her was that the children would all still be in the same school, since the nuns and brothers had underestimated the number of families moving away. Paul went into second grade, but Rose stayed in the fourth grade.

Ovila celebrated their return with great pomp, taking them all to a restaurant. Ostentatiously, he unfolded a great wad of money, to impress Emilie and the children, of course, but also to convince himself that he wasn't dreaming, that this money was really his. If everything went according to plan, he would be able to buy a house for Emilie the following year.

Emilie prepared to spend her first winter in Shawinigan. She made new clothing for the children, since pride kept her from letting them wear the clothes that had been perfectly fine in Saint-Tite. Clément swam in a coat handed down from Paul, and Jeanne's coat now fit Alice.

Winter attacked Emilie on every possible front. The first assault wrapped Célina, her mother, in its cold. Emilie couldn't even get to the funeral, since she couldn't find anyone to look after the house and the children. She was angry at Ovila because he couldn't find a way to take off the three days that she would have been away.

Then winter insinuated itself through all the doors and windows of her apartment, until the pipes froze and burst. For weeks, Emilie and the children had to fill pots with snow for water. Emilie complained bitterly. Furious, Ovila took down a wall in Alice's bedroom, only to discover that the landlord had put in no insulation. The landlord feigned innocence, threatened to sue Ovila for wrecking the apartment and forced him to repair what he had damaged. Emilie then took it up with the landlord, since Ovila was working so much that he never had time to fix the broken wall.

In the end, Emilie shivered through her first winter in Shawinigan alone under the bedcovers, as Ovila had had another promotion and now worked at night and slept during the day, the telephone ringing at all hours to claim his services. Emilie jumped up at the first ring, not wanting Ovila to wake up for no reason, but the call was always for him, from Belgo. He woke up like a bear struggling out of hibernation, threw on his clothes and ran to the plant to help out an engineer stumped by a new problem. Sometimes he didn't come back all day, straggling in at night even more exhausted, only to fall into the freshly made bed.

The year 1916 slipped in on ice: ice in the sinks, ice in the toilet bowls and ice in Emilie's heart. Every cent Ovila earned was going to buy wood for heat. The children were sleeping in wool sweaters, socks and mittens. If any of them complained, Emilie laughed and told them that the city was the city and they had to get used to it. On one of the rare occasions when she had time to talk to Ovila, they decided to move when their lease was up.

"I can't spend another winter freezing," Emilie told him. "We didn't come to the city to be miserable."

"It's cold, you're right. But I've never earned so much money."

"You spend your time doing the engineers' jobs, but they're the ones who are getting well paid, not you."

"I don't have their diplomas. And I don't speak English."

"They don't have your brains! You should ask for a raise."

"I just had one."

"That's true. But how many engineers are working at night and on stand-by during the day?"

Ovila didn't reply. Emilie knew the answer as well as he did. He was the only employee working these hours. But how could he explain to Emilie that he was also the only French Canadian responsible for a work shift?

*W*hen winter finally loosened its cold grip, Emilie began to search the streets, her three youngest in tow, for a better apartment. She looked for two weeks. Ovila had told her that they could afford to buy a house, but, after thinking about it long and hard, she told him that she'd rather live in an apartment for another year. Ovila understood that she still lacked confidence in him. She wanted to be absolutely sure that he'd keep his job, without getting bored, before taking on a mortgage.

In May, Emilie had all their things moved to a new apartment, a bigger, brighter one — more expensive, closer to the river and to Belgo, and one floor up. She had resigned herself to living on the second floor, for the sake of an apartment with central heating. The children had to change schools; she wasn't happy about this, but she hadn't found a suitable home in their old neighbourhood. She had to endure the same questions all over again when she registered the children, for the new principal's assistant was as much like the old one as two peas in a pod. Even though Emilie had been in Shawinigan for a year, she still felt the slight contempt they had for her, as though it were her fault she hadn't been born in town.

Ovila had promised to take care of the move, but he was at work almost all the time. Emilie and the children carried what the movers had left behind. As she made the trip to the new apartment, Emilie noticed that the trees were budding. This year, she decided, she would spend the entire summer at the lake.

Ovila didn't object. He knew that she would never change her mind. She didn't understand that he needed her, and he couldn't blame her, he was away so much.

Emilie stopped off at Saint-Stanislas to see her brothers and sisters, and also stopped at Saint-Séverin for a long-overdue dose of Lucie's laughter.

"When I saw a b-big hen coming with eight little chicks hanging off her skirt," Lucie chuckled, "I said to m-myself that it could only be my c-cousin Emilie."

The summer sun brought Emilie much-needed warmth, but the fact that Ovila couldn't find a few days to come and be with them left a cold spot in her heart. She missed him terribly. Perhaps in Saint-Tite they would have found the time to talk, to rediscover each other. They could have taken long evening walks in the moonlight, listening to the lapping lake and searching the skies for an eagle owl. He wrote only one letter, with the news that he had officially been named night foreman. Emilie was reminded that she had always underestimated Ovila's ambitions.

*I*n September, she returned to the city, resolved to learn all the details of Ovila's work and to be more supportive. As they arrived at the station, Ovila ran beside the train until the heavy locomotive rolled to a stop. Looking at his radiant face, Emilie didn't have the heart to tell him about how the war had affected the village. Later there would be time to tell him that Amedée Trépanier had died, and that Armand Gignac and Jean-Baptiste Marchand had left for Europe. But she did say that Henri Davidson had volunteered for the medical corps, and the latest news was that he was on his way to Siberia.

Once she had fixed up the new apartment, Emilie spent much of her time sewing for herself and the children, cleaning Ovila's oil-stained clothes — often missing the wood shavings she used to find in the bottom of his pockets — preparing special schoolwork for Rose and keeping the children quiet while their father slept. Happily, Clément had joined the ranks of the schoolchildren.

Emilie wrote to Berthe several times but never received an answer. Berthe had given her up, and so she gave up on Berthe. Never in her life had solitude weighed so heavily on her. Both of her parents were dead. She didn't see Antoinette, who had a busy life in Montreal, and of course Henri no longer visited Mauricie County. She left the house rarely, so she hadn't made any friends in Shawinigan. She didn't even see Philomène.

Ovila had changed. Once the euphoria of his family's return had settled like dust behind a buggy, he had returned to the rhythm of his work, leaving the house as soon as he finished his last bite of supper, coming home in the morning after the children left for school. Emilie got into the habit of falling asleep hugging a pillow. Ovila was always dog-tired; whenever he had a day off, he spent it sleeping. Sometimes, when the older children were playing outside and the younger ones were napping, she stretched out beside him simply to feel him next to her, to run a finger over his eyebrows, to hear him breathe and to whisper in his ear that she loved him. When her need for him was unbearable, her fingers found their way to the fly of his trousers, but usually he just rolled over, as if something were tickling him.

Thirty-six

$\mathcal{E}$MILIE CONSOLED HERSELF as best she could, through Ovila's work and the children's successes. She refused to think of the days when she had had reasons to be proud of herself. That time was long gone, and she had chosen love over teaching. But even if this love almost filled her up, it left her with an appetite for learning never quite satisfied by the constant reading of newspapers and books.

Once again, winter sneaked up behind her. She was still unable to decipher the rhythm of the seasons in Shawinigan. Luckily, the apartment was warm and she and the children could sleep without their coats on over their night clothes.

Her mother-in-law wrote her that the rumour of conscription was more and more persistent. Emilie smiled. In Shawinigan, too, this rumour was making the rounds. Félicité seemed to think that Shawinigan was at the far end of the world, while Saint-Tite was in the centre of the universe.

Christmas would have been very sad if she hadn't managed to pull things together at the last minute. She and the children celebrated *réveillon* alone, since Ovila was working.

"You can't work on Christmas, Ovila!" she pleaded.

"I know, my love, but tell yourself that the money I'll make will buy presents for the children."

Emilie began to hate the money that kept Ovila away from her and the children. She would have preferred to have less. She would happily have paid six dollars a week to have him spend five or six hours with her. But he would never understand that she saw the days when they had "made sacrifices" as a happier time. He still had so much to prove. He had never forgotten the humiliation of being disinherited and wanted to show Emilie that she had every reason to walk with her head high.

At the beginning of 1917, the rumoured recruitment became a reality. On every public wall, Canadian army posters invited young men to share the "adventure" overseas. Emilie shivered. Men aged eighteen to forty-five years, measuring over five-feet two, were being recruited, with the bright prospect of free room and board. The conditions were easy: a simple signature held a man for the duration of the war and six months following the end of hostilities.

Emilie took comfort in the fact that no one in their two families had gone to the front. This war, which was supposed to last just a few cannon shots, was never-ending. Since she wasn't feeling at home in Shawinigan, Emilie sometimes imagined that she was living in Europe. She read the newspapers every day, poring over the casualty lists, fearing that she'd find a familiar name. She didn't discuss it much with Ovila; he was much more interested in his perforated rollers, his suction boxes and their filters and his hundreds of gear wheels.

A mild March finally lit up her windows, speckling them with spring showers and mud. She began to count the days until she could leave for Saint-Tite. More than three months . . .

The children came home from school all excited. "Mama! Mama! Guess what?"

"What?"

"We're going to where they make maple syrup tomorrow!"

"All the pupils?"

"Yes! With the parents who have automobiles or carts big enough to take everyone!"

"We'll have to wear our old clothes."

"And boots!"

"And we have to take eggs!"

"And a snack!"

Emilie spent the evening preparing for the children's outing. She got out the old clothes she'd told them they could wear only on certain occasions, usually for playing outside. The next morning, she watched them go off in single file and couldn't help smiling at how much they looked like country children. These were her own children from Saint-Tite, dragging their "cow boots" through the Shawinigan snow dirtied with sand, cinders, pebbles and droppings.

From a window, she watched until Clément caught up to the older ones and they all turned the corner. Then she saw Ovila arriving from the opposite direction, his hands in his pockets. His step was jaunty and he had a carefree twinkle in his eye. She returned to the kitchen as she heard the downstairs door close. He ran up the stairs three at a time and bounded into the apartment.

"Emilie?" he called.

"Here, in the kitchen."

He came up behind her, dropping on the table the lunchpail in which, the previous evening, she had put potato salad and pickles. He put his arms around her and bit her right earlobe.

"You seem very happy this morning," she said.

"I have every reason in the world to be!"

Emilie disengaged herself, turned and looked directly at him.

"Another promotion?"

"No!"

"A raise?"

"No!"

Now she was scared. She hoped he hadn't done something crazy.

"You didn't buy a house, I hope . . ."

"No!"

"Don't keep me waiting, tell me!"

"Are the children out on their field trip?"

"Of course, you know that."

"They won't be home for lunch?"

"You know they won't!"

"Do you think the neighbour's daughter will look after Jeanne and Alice until two or three o'clock?"

"Where are you taking me?"

"It's a secret! Go take the little ones next door. I'll tell you what's up when you get back."

The gleam in Ovila's eyes promised one of those big surprises he was so fond of. Asking no more questions, Emilie told him to keep an eye on the girls while she went next door. She was back in eight minutes, put the coats on the girls and went out again. When she returned, out of breath, Ovila wasn't in the kitchen.

"Ovila?" she called.

He didn't answer. She went to the living room.

"Ovila?"

Still no reply. She frowned and went to the bedroom. Ovila was lying in bed, his hands behind his head, his face lit up with a big white toothpaste smile. The thin sheet hid neither his nudity nor his desire.

"I have a day off!"

Emilie burst out laughing, looked at the time and calculated that they had seven hours of solitude in front of them. She took the hairpins out of her bun and began to unbutton her dress.

"Nononono, ma'am, not like that. Come here. I'll show you how a grown-up is supposed to unbutton her dress . . ."

They had six wonderful hours alone together, laughing as the springs on the bed squeaked. They made up a story of a fatiguing night that would explain to the neighbour's daughter why Ovila needed a day of deep sleep, undisturbed by the cries of the little ones.

Emilie quickly got dressed to pick the girls up at two o'clock, but the neighbour's daughter told her that both had just gone to sleep. Emilie pretended to be annoyed.

"I'm sorry, Mrs. Pronovost, but I took them shopping. Would you like me to wake them up?"

"No! No, I'll come back in an hour and a half. It's better to let them sleep."

She went back home and kept Ovila from sleeping for another hour of Saint-Tite-style folly.

Thirty-seven

ℰMILIE AND OVILA WERE STAGGERED to learn that she was pregnant with a ninth child, at the age of thirty-seven. To Ovila's relief, Emilie was delighted. "At least no one will ever blame this one for not being born in town," she remarked.

"Are you really glad, Emilie?"

"Yes. When Alice was born, I swore I'd never have any more children. But this one's different. This one, Ovila, will be my last little baby. And I'll have the time to make a fuss over it. That's what I want."

Ovila said nothing. Emilie was about the same age his mother had been when Marie-Anne was born. Silently, he prayed that he'd never have any reason to regret that day off in March.

At Belgo, he was still working full steam ahead. He had a reputation for being tough with the men, but they seemed to have no complaints. The job was going well: he'd had the incredible luck to get another promotion, and now he was responsible for day-shift maintenance. The news was particularly welcome to Emilie and the children, who'd be able to see more of him in the evenings. But now Belgo brought something new to Ovila: companionship.

For the first few weeks of his day shift, he could hardly wait to get back to his family. Then, one day, he agreed to stop on the way home. He knew that he still had to stay away from alcohol, so he refused all the drinks he was offered. To fill the minutes — then the hours — he spent with his workmates, most of them men on his crew, he began to play cards. Fortunately, luck was on his side.

Emilie complained about his increasingly lengthy absences. He tried to make her see that these few card games were important for the men's morale. Emilie, thinking that this phase would pass, said no more. The child growing inside her was more important than reprimands that fell on deaf ears and only drained her strength.

With her pregnancy proceeding so smoothly, Emilie decided to spend the summer at the lake. When Ovila took her to the station, he made her promise to be careful. "I won't be there to look out for you, my love. So be a good girl."

"In any case" — the words tumbled out before Emilie could stop them — "you haven't been looking out for me very much since I got pregnant. You're too busy with your flushes, straights and pairs."

"I'll never figure you out, Emilie," he replied angrily. "We've got beautiful children. I've got a job no other French Canadian has. I've got men working under me. I live in a town where nobody treats me like a goddamn farmer! We've got money coming out of our ears. And you're not happy! You're never happy! You've never been happy!"

"That's not true, Charles Pronovost! I've been happy lots of times."

"At Saint-Tite! When I wasn't off in the camps! When I was doing lousy jobs for starvation wages! When my father was spoiling you rotten! When you had your little house and your little garden and your little things that were always there in the same place!"

"Have you been drinking, Ovila?"

"No, I haven't been drinking! And quit asking me if I've been drinking every time I say what's on my mind!"

The children had boarded the train, so they didn't hear their parents' argument. Only Emilien and Marie-Ange had the feeling that something was wrong when they leaned out the window to wave to their father one last time and to urge their mother to get on board.

Emilie turned on her heel and climbed the few steps into a train car filled with vacationers, each one as ugly as the next. Slipping into the toilet, she splashed cold water on her face to wash away her tears. Finally, she joined her children, who had saved two seats, one for her and one for their provisions. When she looked out the window, Ovila was no longer on the platform.

"Is something wrong, Mama?" Emilien asked, in a voice calculated to reflect all the manliness of his eleven years.

"No. Why?"

"You look like you were crying."

Emilie laughed. She patted his face, pinched his cheek and told him that he had a lively imagination. She'd just splashed her face with cold water because of the heat. Emilien, looking at the sweater she was wearing to protect herself from the cool air, said nothing.

That summer, there were no letters from Ovila. Though Emilie wrote him often, she never mentioned the moments leading up to her departure, filling her letters with soothing anecdotes of daily life. She told him that she'd bumped into Alma, the young boarder she'd put up along with Antoinette after the fire in the convent. He'd never met her, she added, as he'd been away in the lumber camps at the time. She wrote that Félicité seemed more determined than ever to move out of the family farm so that Ti-Ton and his new wife wouldn't have to bring up their children in the company of an old lady creaking with rheumatism. She ended each of her letters with the news that her pregnancy was still going well, and that the summer of 1917 would probably be her last at Saint-Tite, especially if his mother went to live with Eva at Lac à la Tortue. In her last letter she told him the date of her return, adding that the children could hardly wait to see him.

They waited an hour at the Shawinigan train station before Emilie decided to take the children home on the bus.

Ovila had obviously been delayed. "I don't know what I was thinking about! Your father told me he couldn't meet us. We'll surprise him by going home on our own, like grown-ups."

Inwardly, she winced with anxiety every time they hit a bump. Alice, sitting on her knees, shouted "Boom in the air!" as they bounced along, her turquoise eyes sparkling and her small, white, beautifully straight teeth gleaming.

When they got home, the children hurtled up the stairs. Emilie brought up the rear, gasping from the weight of the bags and six months of pregnancy. She wasn't even at the landing when the children passed her on the way back down to play outside. Marie-Ange followed more slowly, disdaining, at almost fourteen, to show so much enthusiasm.

Emilie pushed open the door and sighed with relief. She could never get used to living on the second floor. Now that Ovila seemed happy in Shawinigan, it was time to buy that house he'd promised her.

When she went into the bedroom, she froze. The smell alone was enough to explain why Ovila hadn't been at the station. He was lying on his back, arms crossed, unshaven, hair dishevelled. A heavy sleep had him pinned to the bed.

"Oh, no! No, no, no!"

The more she tried to deny what she saw before her, the more her knees gave way, until she was huddled on the floor, her hands over her eyes. She stayed there until she heard the downstairs door slam. Stung into action by the noise, she got up, quickly left the room, shut the door behind her and locked herself in the bathroom.

She heard Blanche calling her and replied instantly, before her daughter had a chance to look for her in the bedroom. "Mama's here, Blanche."

"Are you nearly finished? I have to go."

"Give me two minutes. Can you wait two minutes?"

"Only if I squeeze my legs together."

"Then squeeze them!"

She blew her nose quickly, dried her eyes, flushed the toilet and went out, looking toward the kitchen to avoid meeting her daughter's gaze. But Blanche rushed into the bathroom without noticing the puffiness that marred her mother's face.

Ovila didn't wake up that evening, and the children didn't miss him, thinking that he was at work. The next morning, Emilie shook him.

"Ovila . . . Ovila, wake up," she insisted. "You have to go to work."

He opened one eye and took his head in his hands, moaning with pain. When he saw Emilie, he shut his eyes and opened them again, stunned.

"What are you doing here?"

"We got back yesterday, just like I wrote you."

"You wrote me that?"

Rather than answer, Emilie left the bedroom and went to the table where they usually dropped the mail. Rummaging through the papers, she found three of her letters, unopened, including the last one telling the date of their return. Grabbing it, she marched back to the bedroom, her anger getting the better of her sorrow and disappointment. She threw the letter at him.

Ovila frowned with confusion as he took it in his hands. "I guess I didn't notice it when I went to the post office."

"There are two more that you didn't notice. You'd better get moving or you'll be late."

"It doesn't matter. I've got a good boss."

"What do you mean, you've got a good boss? I thought you *were* the boss!"

"One day you're a little French boss, and the next day you're not a boss any more. Besides, I'm not working today. Or tomorrow either. And the day after that? No. And next week? No. And next month? Next month, we'll see. I say next month, 'cause by then most of their machines will be on the blink, and then they'll call me . . . No, they won't call me 'cause there's no more phone, but they'll send someone to get me. Anything else you want to know?"

Emilie realized that Ovila still hadn't slept off all the alcohol he'd consumed. Curtly, she told him to go back to sleep. He thanked her with a courtly nod and a flourish of his hand, then rolled over and was dead to the world.

Over the next week, Emilie realized that Ovila had been telling the truth. The bills hadn't been paid since mid-July. He confirmed that he'd been let go from Belgo two weeks after she'd left for Saint-Tite.

"The English have no sense of humour, Emilie. I just showed up a bit tight one morning, and they said, 'Bye-bye, Mr. *Prénovo*. Don't call us, we'll call you if somet'ing really wrong 'appens and if our *ingeneers* cannot control it. Bye-bye, Mr. *Prénovo*.'"

"There must be some English blood in my family, Ovila, because I don't have a sense of humour either, not one bit."

"That, my love, I've known for a long time. That's nothing new."

As Ovila had predicted, Belgo eventually called on him to solve some mechanical problems. Emilie found herself wishing that all their cursed machinery would give up the ghost. When he wasn't putting in his few hours of work every week, Ovila saw his friends as usual, and they all bragged loudly about how "those smart engineers from McGill University in Montreal" couldn't deal with the simplest kind of problems you'd find around the house.

By the end of October, Emilie had faced up to the hard realities. There would never be any house. Ovila had drunk up and gambled away the foundations, the walls and the roof. That wouldn't have been so bad if there weren't serious financial problems as well. He didn't bring a penny into the house — when he bothered to come home — and she resigned herself, in secret, to sending for her inheritance, which she'd left in Saint-Tite, out of harm's way.

The more her child grew within her, the more her love for Ovila diminished. He was relegated to a corner of her heart that was filled with dust and ashes. And yet, each time he came teetering in, she caught her breath, not because of the smell he gave off, but because of his beauty, which even alcohol couldn't destroy. She learned to breathe without the oxygen he had brought her for the last five years, but her body still cried out for him, despite the life that he had, one last time, created within her.

The cold attacked in November, and she had to turn on the central heating. But her heart didn't warm up, nor did those of her children, who had seen their father replaced by a disjointed puppet suspended from invisible strings.

In December, Emilie gave birth to her sixth daughter. Ovila wanted to be there with her, but he fell asleep in his armchair and missed seeing the baby, a perfect likeness of her mother, being brought into the world. The next day, he went to the cradle and gazed into it for a long time.

"I've never seen anything like it, Emilie!" he said. "If I'd been drinking, I'd say you disguised yourself as a baby and crawled into the cradle. If I didn't remember being with you in March, I'd swear you did it all by yourself."

Emilie smiled, almost scornfully. "Your contribution, Ovila, amounted to a few short hours — no more, no less."

*I*n January of 1918, Emilie was walking along the bank of the Saint-Maurice River with Rolande bundled up in the red sled, which was now sixteen years old. Alice skipped along beside her, making snowballs. The turbulence from the Shawinigan power plant kept the river from freezing, and the steam bubbled up as though hellfire were at work beneath the icy waters. Emilie looked at Alice's threadbare coat and wondered how, in just a few months, she and Ovila had joined the ranks of the poor and almost starving.

Suddenly, she stopped, her eyes drawn to a piece of cloth floating on the river. Telling Alice to watch the baby, she climbed down the bank and hooked the heavy cloth with a dead branch. She pulled it to shore and lifted it partway out of the water: it was a thick, matted wool, the colour of yellow cotton. Another piece of cloth floated by in the seething water, then a third.

Picking up the handle of the sled, she headed for home. Ovila was sitting in the kitchen, a pipe in his mouth, a knife in his hand, whittling at a piece of wood.

"Ovila," she asked, "what are those blanket things floating in the river?"

"They're Belgo covers."

"Belgo covers?"

"The covers they put over the rollers when they're finishing the paper. When there's too much pulp stuck to them, they take them off and dump them in the river."

"Ovila, you're going to find yourself a boat, and tonight and tomorrow night and every night you've got nothing to do, you're going to go and get me all the covers you can find."

"Are you crazy? I'd kill myself in the whirlpools. Those covers, when they're wet, they weigh a ton. You want me to tip over and drown?"

"I want you to take a good lantern and do what I say. I'll be able to make coats for the children, and blankets to keep us warm. You'll go tonight. That means today you drink not a drop, my friend. Not one drop! Because that's what's going to drown you, not the river."

Ovila waited for nightfall, so he wouldn't be seen; then he found a rowboat and set off, terrified of the thundering waters, to fish for the Belgo covers. When he came back, some hours later, with two covers, he dropped them in a large washbasin and curled up in bed beside Emilie, chilled to the bone. He tried to hug her for warmth, but she pushed him away. Sighing, he fell asleep with his teeth chattering.

For three nights, he repeated the process. Then he told Emilie that he'd have to stop for ten days or so, to leave time for the new covers on the rollers to become unusable. She didn't believe a word of it, knowing that he was burning up with thirst. She was right: she didn't see him for the next week, as he filled his days with lamentations and gloom and his nights with smoke, alcohol and debts.

Emilie spent all her time working on the Belgo covers. For hours, she sat at the kitchen table scraping away the paper pulp that was stuck to the wool. With patience and concentration, she used a little knife to get at the bits that were most deeply embedded. When she finally finished the first one, her nails were broken, her fingers red, and she had blisters on her thumb and forefinger, but she went right on to a second, then a third.

When the children asked what she was doing, she told them that she was making them coats. They didn't question her further. She counted her money and bought some dye: blue, wine-red, brown and beige. For the boys, she made pants and jackets from the brown and beige covers. For the girls, she cut coats from the others.

Marie-Ange watched her work, a contemptuous look on her face. "Really, Mama, do you think we're going to school dressed like that?"

"Use your imagination a little. Forget the covers and just look at the material. Isn't it nice?"

"Well, yes, it's nice material, but here in Shawinigan everyone will know what it is."

"Trust me, Marie-Ange. You'll have the most beautiful coats you've ever owned."

And she kept her word, working late into the night sewing, lining, stitching collars, making belts, putting on buttons opposite identical buttonholes.

By the beginning of February, all the school-age children were able to wear their new clothes for the first time. It had taken her four full weeks to dress them with what little was left of her pride.

Ovila was called into Belgo three or four times a week. It got to the point that Emilie was forced to lie to the messengers because Ovila couldn't get out of bed. On those days, she let him know what she thought of him, and Ovila, unable to endure her reproaches, promised her another nocturnal fishing expedition. When she'd cleaned a good five dozen covers, Emilie told him she didn't need any more.

At the beginning of March, Emilie counted the money they had left and added up their debts. Ovila hadn't been home for two days and two nights, so she left him a note on the bathroom sink, where he couldn't miss it.

She woke up to a sun-filled morning and felt Ovila sleeping beside her. She looked at him, sighed and got up to make breakfast for the children: stale bread dipped in milk and liberally sprinkled with cinnamon. She presented this dish as a treat, one that few children had the opportunity to savour. The children, their appetites sharpened at the thought of such a privilege, smacked their lips in anticipation of this breakfast fit for a king. Emilie watched them eat while she rocked Rolande. She hummed all the songs that made the baby smile, especially "*J'ai du bon tabac.*"

Ovila got up in excellent spirits and silenced her with a wave of his hand before she had a chance to open her mouth. "I know, I know. You haven't seen me in two days. But there's a good reason. I have to talk to you."

"Talk, Ovila. I can't leave the room."

"Emilie, I've had it with the city."

Emilie raised her eyes, unbelieving, then realized that he was perfectly serious. "Have you been drinking, Ovila?"

"No, I haven't been drinking. I haven't had a drop in two days. I've spent these last two days walking in the woods. I miss the woods, Emilie. I can't do without them any more."

"I knew that."

"How did you know?"

"You've started whittling again."

Ovila burst out laughing. He went over to Emilie and put his hand on her shoulder.

"I'd just as soon you didn't touch me, Ovila," she said.

He withdrew his hand and nodded his head. "I haven't had a drink in two days and I'll never touch another drop as long as I live. Every time I drink, I make everyone unhappy. I know I disappointed my father, and you as well. The worst thing is, I can't bear to disappoint myself any longer."

Emilie listened, humming all the while. If it bothered Ovila, he didn't show it.

"I know you've always been happier in the country," he continued. "Even the children talk about it all the time."

Emilie continued rocking, but the more Ovila talked the more her heart pounded in her ears. He swore he loved her as much as ever, and she raised her eyebrows.

"Don't look at me like that," he said. "It's true. I drank because I could see you weren't happy and I didn't know how to make you smile."

"Don't blame me for your vice, Ovila."

Ovila left the kitchen, and Emilie heard him rummaging in the pockets of his coat. She closed her eyes and brushed her lips over the fuzz that covered Rolande's head. She breathed deeply, to persuade herself that she was still alive and to give herself the strength to believe what Ovila, her Ovila, whom she couldn't look at without going weak in the knees, was telling her. Could it be that these months of hell were to be her last? Just a little relapse? A desire on Ovila's part to have one more look at a side of himself that he'd left behind years ago? Rolande gurgled at the tickling of her mother's breath. Emilie opened her eyes and shifted the wriggling baby in her lap.

Ovila came back into the kitchen, a wad of papers in his hands. "Next week, Emilie, I'm off to Barraute."

"Where's that?"

"In Abitibi."

"To do what?"

"Buy land . . . lease land, anyhow, to cut the trees and clear it. Do you still have a taste for adventure?"

Emilie stopped rocking. She looked him full in the face — was this some new form of madness? All she saw were his pleading eyes and a hopeful smile.

"Ovila, I can't live where there's nothing but mosquitoes! There isn't a soul up there! I don't even know if there are any schools. Our children are bright, Ovila. They have to study, so that — "

"So they won't end up like their father?"

"That's not what I was going to say."

"No, but it's what you were thinking."

Emilie got up, laid Rolande on the table and held her with one hand while she groped in a drawer with the other for a fresh diaper. She changed the baby, murmuring to her all the while.

"You're spoiling her."

Emilie shrugged, tucked Rolande under her arm and went to the stove.

Ovila followed her with his eyes. "Are you just going to keep bustling around so you won't have to answer me?"

Emilie took the kettle and poured some water into a pot. She immersed one of the baby's bottles, and Rolande started to squirm. "Look out the window and see if Jeanne and Alice are still in the yard," she said.

Ovila took a look and told her that they were. Emilie sat back down, checking the temperature of the milk on her left wrist, and gave Rolande her bottle.

"So? You have nothing to say?"

"Not for now, Ovila. You'll never change. When you wanted to marry me, you worked everything out in your head, without even asking my opinion. And now it's the same thing. You've arranged my whole life, without even asking me what I want."

"What do you think I'm doing right now?"

"You aren't asking my opinion, you want my blessing. If you wanted my opinion, Ovila, you would've talked to me about the possibility of going to Abitibi instead of turning up with all those pieces of paper. You always come to me with something you've decided in advance."

"That's not true, Emilie! For the last hour I've been busting my gut trying to get your opinion."

"Why Barraute, Ovila?"

"Because there's a future there."

"If I said I didn't want to go to Barraute, would that change anything?"

"Well . . ."

"Well, no! Because you're dreaming about Barraute. Someone, somewhere, must have been talking to you. It's not in your nature, Ovila, to look at all sides of a problem. You get your mind set on one thing, and everyone else has to follow. Barraute, Ovila, doesn't mean a thing to me. I couldn't even tell you where it is — and I was always good at geography."

Ovila poured himself a big glass of water while Emilie went to put Rolande to bed.

When she came back to the kitchen, Ovila said, "You always make everything complicated, Emilie. I keep trying to tell you that I want to leave Shawinigan. And about that, my love, you can't tell me we don't agree."

"You're right. I'd leave this place without shedding a single tear."

"The second thing is, I want to go back to the country. And so do you."

"I'm sorry, Ovila. You aren't talking about the country. You're talking about the back of beyond."

"Don't exaggerate, Emilie. You've got three brothers up in Abitibi, and they send you money. If it was that far out of the way, there wouldn't be a cent up there."

"My brothers aren't in Barraute!"

"So? One village or another, it's all the same."

"Not for me and the children, Ovila."

"I'll talk to the children. Maybe they have a taste for adventure, like their father."

"Don't bring the children into this! They've hardly seen you for a year, so don't go mixing them up with your stories!"

For weeks, Ovila tried to reason with Emilie, but she didn't want to hear a word about Abitibi or Barraute. The only thing that made her waver a little was that he didn't touch a drop of alcohol. By mid-April, she began to wonder if Ovila wasn't right. Maybe he was offering them a chance to forget all their troubles and make a fresh start.

*E*vents soon helped her untangle her feelings. It started with an unexpected visit from strangers. They arrived in the middle of the night and knocked at the door. Her first reflex was to open it, thinking it might be a messenger from Belgo. Then, remembering that there had been no messenger for days and days, she became suspicious.

"Who is it?"

"Ovila's buddies."

"Ovila isn't here."

"We can see that."

"Come back tomorrow."

"No, little lady. We want in, now!"

One of the men started hammering on the door. Emilie opened it immediately, terrified that the noise would wake the children and the neighbours. Four men burst into the apartment and quickly searched it, even checking the bathroom. The one who had talked to her from behind the door went up to her and took her chin in his thick, grimy fingers.

"Listen to me, little Mrs. Ovila," he growled. "You're going to give your husband a message from Ben, Bob and the gang. You're going to tell the big fellow we want the money he owes us, not in three months, but by the end of the week. Understand?"

Emilie looked him straight in the eye, hoping that he wouldn't feel how much she was trembling. She lifted one hand and pushed him away.

"How much does he owe you?"

"Three hundred bucks!"

Emilie wondered if they could see how wide her eyes opened. Her heart pounded, her legs turned to jelly, and her throat went dry.

"Come tomorrow night. I'll have two hundred dollars for you."

"It's three hundred!"

"Two hundred will have to do!"

Bob looked at Ben, who nodded his assent. "We'll be here tomorrow at noon."

"Two o'clock."

"Noon!"

"If you come at noon, I'll be feeding the children. I won't have time to deal with you."

"No tricks. We'll be here at two o'clock."

The four men left as noisily as they had come. Emilie circled her bedroom three times, furious and humiliated. How could she stay with Ovila in Shawinigan one day longer? How could Ovila stay here?

She rushed to her closet, pulled down a suitcase and threw in Ovila's clothing any which way. Scouring the apartment, she gathered up everything she could see that belonged to him. She looked at the time: one o'clock, and Ovila still wasn't home. She piled all his belongings by the front door and went back to her room. She took out a second suitcase and filled it with her own things. She had no choice.

Ovila came in just as she was packing up all the Belgo covers. At a glance, Emilie saw that his new-found sobriety had abandoned him.

"What's going on, Emilie?"

"You're leaving, Ovila. You're going to the station, and you're catching the first train for Abitibi. You're off to Barraute!"

Ovila had trouble making sense of what he saw before him. "What's wrong with you, Emilie? I've just been saying goodbye to the guys from Belgo. I'm not tight, I've just had one drink."

"That's one too many, Ovila. Now, get out!"

"Are you mad at me?"

"Yes, I'm mad! Out!"

She loaded him down with all his belongings and pushed him to the stairs. Ovila looked at her, unbelieving, trying to figure out what was happening.

Emilie lost her patience. "Go, or Bob and Ben and their gang will be taking care of you."

Ovila went white. He looked at Emilie, and then sheepishly asked if she could lend him a few dollars.

"I'm going to lend you what you owe them tomorrow."

"I don't even have enough for the train, Emilie."

Sighing with exasperation, she went to her purse, pulled out a few crumpled bills and stuffed them in his pocket. "Now go!"

"What about the rest of you?"

"Don't worry about us. You never did before, and now isn't the time to start. Get going, Ovila, and don't stop. Don't speak to anyone if you care about your teeth and your nose."

"Emilie, I — "

"There's no time to talk. Go!"

Ovila went down the stairs, and Emilie heard the door shut softly behind him. She tiptoed into the boys' room and woke them up.

"After all," she said, to quiet their protests, "it's only an hour earlier than you used to get up in the country to milk the cows. Now, get dressed quickly and pack your bags. And when you're finished, take all the pillowcases you can find and fill them with everything from the kitchen, except what's breakable."

She woke the older girls and gave them the same instructions. She let Jeanne, Alice and Rolande sleep.

At seven o'clock, she told the older children to strip the beds. "What I want you to do is take them apart."

The children sensed her urgency, but they didn't dare ask any questions. By eight o'clock she had fed them, dressed the three little ones and, with Rolande in her arms, was on her way to the bank, thanking God that bankers were behind their wickets so early in the morning. She withdrew all the money left in her account: twelve hundred dollars. She kept fifty in her purse and stuffed the rest into her boots.

As she was leaving the bank, she ran straight into Alma.

"Emilie! What a surprise. I haven't heard from you since last summer. How's the little one? Oh, she's beautiful!"

"This is Rolande. What about you? Still in Saint-Tite?"

"No, my dear. We just arrived in Shawinigan yesterday."

"For a visit?"

"No. To stay. The country's not my cup of tea, and my husband's found himself a good job at Belgo."

"Belgo?"

"In the accounting department. But he's not much of an accountant. He couldn't even rent our house in Saint-Tite." Alma burst out laughing.

Emilie had no choice. Her heart began pounding as though it were going to explode. "Not your house near the railroad line?"

"Yes. We're hoping to rent it in September. We're going to advertise it, here in Shawinigan. You never know."

"We're leaving today for Saint-Tite!"

"Your husband wants to go back?"

"Not exactly. Our plan is to stay at Saint-Tite for about . . . a year, then probably just take off . . . to Abitibi or somewhere else. It's now or never, with the family almost grown up."

"Well, I'll be! Emilie, you'll never change. Remember how you told me about leaving your father's house when you were just sixteen?"

"I remember it like it was yesterday. And you, do you remember when you burned the porridge?"

"Me? Burn the porridge? Wasn't that Antoinette?"

"Now, now, Alma, you know it was you."

"Good Lord, I sure must have changed, 'cause I don't burn the porridge any more. I don't eat it, either. That's why I don't burn it."

Emilie laughed, wondering how she could disengage herself from Alma politely — and with the keys to the house in Saint-Tite in her hand. She had no choice.

"Alma, it's too bad you're arriving just when we're leaving. We could have visited and talked about the good old days, or gone shopping together. But I have to get going now, they're waiting for me at home. The movers will be arriving any minute." She leaned over and brushed Alma's cheek with her dry lips. "Say hello to your husband for me, Alma."

"You too, Emilie."

Emilie turned on her heel, Rolande's cheek tucked in the crook of her neck. She walked slowly, praying to her father and to all those who had passed away to intercede with Alma on her behalf. She kept on going, refusing to turn around and express a sudden interest in the house near the railway line. She looked left and right, knowing that as soon as she stepped into the street, she would be homeless. She kissed the top of her baby's head, as though she were begging her pardon for having to cross the road.

"Emilie! Emilie!"

She stopped, shut her eyes, opened them and looked heavenward to give thanks to her father. She turned around. "Yes, Alma? Do you have a message for someone?"

Alma hurried after her, her tongue jutting into her right cheek as though she'd forgotten a mouthful of her breakfast there. "Listen, Emilie, where are you going to stay in Saint-Tite?"

"At my mother-in-law's, Alma. It's all arranged. She's expecting us."

"It's just that . . . Oh, no, it'll never work."

"What, Alma?"

"Well, our house is empty, and I thought you could maybe stay there for a while. It's better for a house to be lived in . . ."

"Oh, I don't know, Alma. My mother-in-law would be disappointed if we made other plans."

"That's what I thought." Alma pursed her lips and furrowed her brow. Emilie didn't move. She waited, hoping Alma would fall into her trap.

"Listen, Emilie, do you think you could talk it over with your husband? Maybe you could help us out. Your mother-in-law would still have you nearby, and she's probably forgotten what it's like to have a house full of children. If you stay in the house until September and you like it, maybe you'll want to stay for a year. If you don't like it, in September we'll try to find another tenant, or maybe sell it."

"You're asking us to change our plans, Alma."

"If you didn't have to pay any rent until September?"

"Alma, really! You don't mean that!"

"My husband says a house that's lived in lasts longer."

Emilie felt Rolande growing restless. She had to end the discussion as quickly as possible.

"Emilie, do it for us. You helped me out once before. Maybe you can do it again . . ."

"Well, all right! If that's the way you want it, give me the key. I'll take care of your house. Don't worry, I'll keep it as clean as if it were my own. And in September, if you want to sell it, it'll be neat as a pin."

Alma jumped for joy. She rummaged in her purse, brought out the key and handed it to Emilie, thanking her over and over and assuring her that her husband would be eternally grateful. When they parted, both of them were happy with the arrangement they'd made. Emilie, however, didn't let it show. She had other things on her mind.

She hurried on. One of their neighbours was a mover. She knocked on his door, waking him up, and explained that, due to an emergency and a sudden job offer, they had to leave Shawinigan that very day.

The neighbour rubbed his eyes as she listed her instructions: "Be at my place at eleven o'clock sharp, load all the furniture into your truck and go to Saint-Tite. When you get there, ask for Mrs. Alma Bonenfant's house, and wait for me there. My husband will be delayed, but I'll be there tomorrow morning — I'd rather travel at night with all the children."

Very much her father's daughter, she extracted thirty dollars from her purse to back up her request, knowing that this price was more than fair. The neighbour pocketed half the money, and she promised to give him the rest at Saint-Tite. Next, she went to her landlord, told him the same story and gave him the equivalent of a month's rent to excuse her hasty departure.

Back home by nine-fifteen, she asked the children if there had been any visitors during her absence, and they told her there hadn't. She praised them for what they'd managed to accomplish, especially going on their own to the grocer to get boxes. She urged them to hurry — everything had to be packed for eleven o'clock — and thanked them silently for not questioning her about the move, or about their father's absence.

Everything worked out as she'd planned. The neighbour and his helper arrived at eleven o'clock. At noon, Emilie left the almost-empty apartment to take the children to a restaurant near the station. She sat and ate with them as she fed the baby, and told them that they were to wait for her at the station. She would join them by three o'clock at the latest. She entrusted Rolande to Marie-Ange, Jeanne to Rose, Alice to Blanche, Clément and Paul to Emilien. She paid for the meals and — the height of extravagance — took a taxi home.

She helped the movers gather up the last of their possessions, those that would never fit into boxes, and thanked them. She saw them off and gave them a map of Saint-Tite showing them where to wait. The truck left at one-forty.

She went into the kitchen, took a handkerchief from her bag and wiped her face. Looking at the time, she began to tremble. Then she sat on the edge of the counter and waited. At five to two, she took out two hundred-dollar bills. She looked at them for a moment, then she kept one out and slipped the second into her shoe. She had no choice. She had nothing left to lose.

At two o'clock sharp, she heard the men climbing the stairs. She leapt to her feet, arranged her hair and her hat and went to the door. She got there at the same time as they did, and she didn't give them a chance to knock. She stepped out onto the landing, closing the door behind her.

"I've been expecting you, gentlemen." She was relieved to see that only Bob and Ben had bothered to come. She opened her hand and held out the hundred-dollar bill.

"Just a minute, little lady," Bob growled. "We said two hundred."

"I thought it over, and I decided that one hundred's enough."

"Just who do you take us for, anyway?"

"Where's the big fellow?" Ben added.

"My husband is sleeping. I'd be grateful if you'd let him sleep.

See here, gentlemen, if you're not satisfied, take anything you want from the house. We can't pay you a penny more." She opened the door and invited Bob and Ben inside. They rushed past, jostling her on the way. Emilie closed her eyes.

"Goddamn!"

"Jesus Christ! We've been had, Ben!"

They retraced their steps and looked at Emilie, who hadn't budged. "The big fellow better not show his face in Shawinigan ever again."

"The big fellow is already very far away, gentlemen."

The two men looked at each other, uncertain what to do.

Finally, Ben spoke up. "Come on, Bob. A hundred bucks is better than a kick in the ass."

They left. Emilie waited five minutes, walked through the apartment three times, trying hard not to think about the happy moments she'd had there, locked the front door and went out by the back, leaving the key, as she had promised, under an old, sandy, faded rug.

Thirty-eight

THE TRAIN ROLLED SLOWLY through the night. Emilie was exhausted. Once she'd rejoined the children, they'd had to wait hours and hours before they could board. While they waited, she told them at last, using the tone she reserved for the most wonderful of surprises, that they were going to Saint-Tite to live. When the locomotive finally dragged its iron carcass into the station, she shook awake the younger children, who'd succumbed to their fatigue. The older ones sat up with her.

There were so few passengers that they were able to spread out over ten double seats. She lay the children down, promising to wake them before they arrived in Saint-Tite, at dawn. Sorry that she hadn't brought the Belgo covers, she covered them with their coats.

She placed Rolande on the seat across from her. To make sure the baby wouldn't get hurt if the train braked suddenly, she took off her shoes and braced her with her feet. The children blinked their eyes, uneasy, so she took out her accordion and played some lullabies. Twenty minutes after they left the station, all nine children were sleeping a well-earned sleep.

Emilie let herself be rocked by the rhythm of the train, alone with her thoughts in the dark night. She stared out the window. Where was Ovila? Had he managed to get his train? She took a handkerchief from her bag and blew her nose. Now that the children were asleep, now that they were safe, she could cry. She shut her eyes for a few moments, seeing herself in another train, the one that had carried her and Ovila to Montreal seventeen years earlier for their first wedding anniversary. Their paper anniversary. *Damn Belgo and all its paper!* She turned her head, opened her eyes and looked at Rose. Her poor head, full of woes and worries, rocked to the same rhythm as one of her hands.

A dangling hand. *Louisa!* How long was it since Louisa had left them? *Almost thirteen years, Louisa. And your father was the first to rock you in your final sleep. It was then, Louisa, that your father and I clashed for the first time. Do you remember, Louisa? Was it him or me who slept while you were choking on the milk that was supposed to nourish you, but that killed you instead? Forgive us, Louisa.*

Emilie swayed as the train went round a curve. She watched Marie-Ange, who was fighting against gravity, clutching at the edge of her seat. *Marie-Ange . . . even asleep, my big mule, you're struggling with something. Let yourself go, my Marie-Ange. Let yourself smile. Swallow a bit of your pride. You'll see, it's no harder to swallow than a gulp of medicine. My big mule . . . Papa, can you see me tonight,* your *big mule? All by herself, your big mule has stopped a train that was running on a track with no station. Your big mule, Papa, is rolling through the night, with tears in her eyes and fear in her soul. Your big mule is rolling through a dark night with no end. Your big mule is rolling with nine little ones that are just beginning to grow. Papa, give your big mule a little more courage. Goodnight, Papa. I hope you were happy to find Elzéar Veillette. I'm sure you must still be tearing at each other's hair. Only now you must have angels' hair . . . and not a lock out of place.*

The train whistled three times. Emilie frowned. *The cock, Berthe. Remember the cock that crowed three times? I was afraid, Berthe, because I thought that when a cock crows three times, there'll be bad news. The cock didn't lie, Berthe. The news came yesterday, at about this time. Berthe, I had to send Ovila away to protect him.*

Berthe, was it to protect yourself that you decided not to write me any more? Are you happy in your silent world, Berthe? It seems to me your world must be like this night that's drawing all ten of us toward something I fear. Think of me, Berthe . . .

The train slowed gradually, then stopped in the middle of nowhere. Emilie picked up Rolande and looked out the window. There was not a single light. She shivered, suddenly apprehensive. Taking advantage of the stillness, she got up to check on the children she couldn't see from her seat. She pulled their coats over them and paused at each of the faces that she never took the time to look at closely, so familiar had they become.

Good night, my big Emilien. Soon I'm going to have a talk with you. I'll tell you your father's gone to find us a new house. I'll tell you how he's always been so proud of you. I'll lie a little and tell you that he'll be back. I don't know anything, Emilien. Your father will come back when he's learned to be proud of you. Your father will come back when he's learned to forgive the harm he's done himself. It's true, Emilien, that your father has hurt us too. But our pain, Emilien, is nothing compared to his own. When you're grown up, Emilien, you won't be satisfied with my answers, you'll go see him and you'll ask him yourself.

The train still wasn't moving. A feeling of dread came over Emilie. Spotting the conductor, she went to ask the reason for the delay. She realized that she hadn't put on her shoes, but she walked on in her stockinged feet. *No need for big clogs, Emilie, to make your way. Even on tiptoe you can get from one place to another. Even on tiptoe you can walk with a good stride. Even on tiptoe . . .* The conductor told her that they'd stopped to allow a freight train to switch to another track so that they could pass. The other train, from Abitibi, was running late. As soon as possible, they'd be on their way. Emilie thanked him and went back to the children, reassured. She brushed back a lock of hair on Paul's brow. *Paulo, always serious, always thinking. Do you think your father had a chance to see that train, too? Do you think it occurred to your father that all of us might pass the same train? Sleep, Paulo. I'm asking you too many hard questions.*

And my big Clément, with your fists as big as your head. You're like your father, Clément, when he used to solve all his problems with his fists. Some day, I'll tell you how he knocked out one of my old students. I've already said that Marie-Ange has a false name, because she's far from being an angel. You have a false name, too, Clément. Clemency, Clément, is gentleness. Perhaps as you get older, Clément, you'll learn about gentleness, and about peace.

Emilie made sure that Blanche was sleeping peacefully and returned to her seat. Blanche was smiling. *Go ahead and smile, my Blanche. I know you never liked it in Shawinigan. You're smiling because we're going back to Saint-Tite. So you can laugh with your uncles Ovide and Edmond. So you can jump in the lake. So you can be as good as an angel in school and make everyone think you're so meek. But I know you, Blanche. I know that behind those big blue eyes, there's a will of iron. Your meekness is almost frightening, Blanche, when one knows all the strength that it hides. Sleep well, my beautiful little Blanche. You've got quite a life to look forward to, and you need your sleep.*

Emilie saw Jeanne and Alice reflected in the window. She smiled softly. *If I made up a trio of frowners, Jeanne, I'd have to include you, with Marie-Ange and Clément. But that's no surprise. You spend hours and hours following Clément around. You even breathed down his neck in my belly, you followed him so closely. We'll see, Jeanne, we'll see. It's true that life makes us knit our brows. But life makes us smile, too. You've got eyes for smiling, Jeanne. And for laughter.*

And Alice, with your eyes the same colour as my wedding dress, the colour of the Batiscan when it's touched by the sun. You have the river's clarity in your eyes, Alice. And its murmur in your voice. Remind me, Alice, to tell you the story of my wedding dress that your father and I buried together.

The train gave a jolt. Emilie saw Rose pull in her hand and slip it under her thigh. *Rose, my flower. Little heart in a big body. It's hard, I know, to be between two worlds, that of innocence and that of fear. But I'm here, Rose. I'll always hold your hand. Together, you and I, we'll discover that the world's not just full of scholars and books. There are people in the world with heart, Rose, people like you.*

The train jolted a second time. It began to move, at first slowly, then more and more rapidly. Emilie looked in vain for the train that had come from Abitibi. All she saw was a shadow huddled along the track.

She shut her eyes again and sang to herself, in time to the rhythm of the axles and the rail ties. *Come, holy Saviour* . . . Then her thoughts were caught up in the rhythm. *Tomorrow the sun will rise. Tomorrow the sun will shine. Tomorrow . . . I had no choice, no choice. Papa, it's not fair . . . A devil! A devil! . . . Lazare is a devil! . . . Charles? Your name is Charles? . . . The Windsor . . . Emilie, there's no one like you . . . I've always been envious of you, Emilie . . . and me of you, Antoinette . . . Do you think, my love, that Télesphore will like his cabinet? I've had enough of this damned village! . . . You can be sure, Ovila, that I won't shed a single tear when I leave Shawinigan . . . Good night, my love . . . my love . . . my love . . . my . . . love . . . love . . . love . . . love . . . love . . . love . . .*

The train whistled three times and the accordion fell to the floor. Emilie didn't hear a thing. Through the fog of her thoughts, she had finally found sleep.